New York Smexy – The Gut & The Kiss, Tapio Tiihonen

GW00707261

Love and Luxury, Money and Culture always try to find their way to You. Please, be patient and give them a Chance. I could smooth that rough touch of my words, my Chance, with great actress Victoria June's loving and caring tender kiss. A Thousand Thanx.

Tapio Tiihonen

New York Smexy –
The Gut & The Kiss

FSC
www.fsc.org
MIX
Paperi vastuul –
lisista lähteistä
Paper from
responsible sources
FSC® C105338

© 2020 Tapio Tiihonen

Cover Design: Tapio Tiihonen
Interior Design: Tapio Tiihonen & Book Towns Group

Publisher: BoD – Books on Demand, Helsinki, Finland
Manufacturer: BoD – Books on Demand, Norderstedt, Germany

ISBN: 978-952-80-3499-5

Contents

The First Day

Backward Puetarican Goddess push'd Viking King, as she would be thrust, and govern'd him in wealth, though not in lust.

tapio tiihonen

New York

Smexy

The Cut

The Liss

From the Airport to the Smash

8 PM weather broadcast tells "35 fair, feels like 31, wind NNW 4 mph, pressure 30,70 in". News Anchor Zain Ejiofor Asher smiles her beautiful smile, as she always does, and everybody loves her. But I do not. I look at the screen at John F. Kennedy´s airport in the Queen of Queens and say to a nearby newspaper chub: "Thanks, and more sunshine to your life tomorrow."

It is always lovely to be in the Jamaica neighborhood of Queens. I hum a little bit: "This cherry blossom, greatest of all, eating falafel ..." I´m head taller than the rest, so one little fella sees me, and hangs around. We give each other Bad Bunny smiles and Daddy Yankee salute. And High Five, Elbows and Haven´t You Seen the Rain. He says: "Nastiest over-limit went men, I came through with diseased semen of my pen." I forget him and almost run to catch a Taxi.

It has been two years and I do not even know where the station is. So, I ask a bunch of fellas: "Hey men, where I can call up my taxi, running for a meeting." One beauty with black eyes points her finger and declares an old yoke: "Yeah, just make sure you sweet talk him, so he thinks that he´s gonna get something out of it haha." I look at my watch. Really, now it is 21 pm, and my council shall start at 21:30. Yellow Cab station is as full as empty, cos the last car abandons me to despair just 5 meters away. I take my phone and call +1 646-248-5860. It begins to rain, and I feel times bids be gone.

At the same time in Brooklyn, a goddess figured Puetarican beauty waits for her morning coffee. Her hair is like August crops, wild and air-filled, pliable and elegant; skin flawless, and her eyes, well, this doctrine we shall derive; they are the ground, the books, the academes, whence spring doth, yes, the Promethean fire. They have been the ruin of many decent and well-behaving men. These fires are black like carbon in a mine and brows something more and much more than Madison Andersson's products. Her nose is finely chiseled, lips big, smooth and soft, fingers long and spirited with goodwill and happiness. And her eyes smile and shine like little stars, and this black-eyed beauty is so heavenly fine that all the world will be in love with night, paying no worship to the well-forgotten sun. I later, hm, noticed that my own black brows, straight nose, smooth lips, and manly chin dimple made a perfect match with this female majesty.

Her body is stunning, although she stands at normal Puetarican height. Butts are trained, tight but so womanly that you cannot miss them among the human mass. She is blessed with big and divine breasts. Well, Almighty knows things better than a sinful man, cos her figure has been made for the nurse of love, the dwelling place of exoticness. And she has been a dancer and has dancer's moves and ideas.

Her doorbell rings. Her coffee is coming. There stands a fat, big baldhead, lust on his sweaty face. Soon there becomes to hear her commands "little boy, bitch, you *Papi-Baba, a los tontos no les dura el dinero*".

Some miles away go 17 associates of Queens-based Makk Balla Brims Set of the Bloods fellas. They have some time ago got charges for Racketeering, including predicate acts of robbery and firearms offenses. They walk lazily ahead. They are still fuckangry to the United States Magistrate Judge Steven M. Gold, William F. Sweeney, Assistant Director-in-Charge, New York Field Office (FBI), and James P. O'Neil, Commissioner, NYPD. One member keeps on saying: "*Quien en ano quiere ser rico, al medio le ahorcan.*"

My Guiding Angel

Time is 9.45 pm, and I am running in the rain towards that bunch of members. I see them but I do not have time to bend & twist. They see me, and they salute me, and I salute them. You know, a common language, joint happiness.

One Fatty hits me to my handsome face, and I begin to hear Ronnie and the Relatives - great and beautiful song: My Guiding Angel. What a superb and wonderful song! So, I hit back with all my heart. And I am a joyful and happy fella but sometimes you must pray on behalf of other people, too, cos pain doesn't go away with a bunch of money. It goes away while helping fellow men.

So, I pray from all my heart and soul and fists: Dear Truth, designed to become a partaker of our lowliness, and willed to be one of us corruptible, of us mortal ones, You are so sacred and wonderful, that the reason of the divine counsel cannot be seen by the wise of this world unless the true light has scattered the darkness of human ignorance. For only in the work of the virtues, or in the observance of the commandments, but also at the course of faith hard and narrow is the way, dear brothers, that leads to caring and life.

Four members go to the dreamland's western meadows. And they broke my sunglasses, but my shoot boxing's Kun Khmer, Lethwei and Sanda bulldoze find the way. We do not have vain rules. So, among my kicks come elbows and knees and use of the shins, spinning back fists, clinch fighting, throws and sweeps, come ax kicks, too.

They attack all-around me. Then comes a hit and I fell on my knees. I wait for the final blow, full of never giving up a breath of life. I wait and wait but nothing comes. I hear a voice: "Who the fuck are Y, son of the bitch? You love to fight. It is in your blood." The sight is a little bit foggy, but I try to sing while blood comes out of my mouth: "We few, we happy few, we band of brothers; For he today sheds his blood with me shall be my brother; Be he ne'er so vile, This day shall gentle his condition: and gentleman now a-bed shall think themselves accursed they were not here, and hold their manhood cheap whiles any speaks that fought with us upon this our Saint Lucia's Day."

Total silence. I wait for the shoot. But there becomes a Joy and Mirth - gentle friends and accompanies of these criminals and now my friends. Yes, one fella takes my body and head up. I put my hand on his shoulder and shake his hand. I say: "This has happened once before when I was in France. It was a sign. I found my first teenager's love."

They laugh and murmur that they are going to shoot the fucker, who shot Shaaliver Douse. These drug dealers and gunrunners explain: "Shaav didn't even have a good gun, just blood-spattered one." I look at the watch, at 10 pm, take my smartphone and begin to key in the numbers.

We are at Linden Blvd, and I must go to 73rd Ave, as soon as possible to a building that is the opposite side of Parsons Blvd Chase Bank. That low brick house is the center of the International Book House Organization here, and they are waiting for me. I say: "Hey, fellas I know that Y have quite a different business than me, but this is your hometown, and Y know the quick ways. So why don't Y tell me how I get there under ten minutes?" They seem a little bit surprised, but one acute 15-years-old gunrunner called Cliver smiles, says something in Patois but I understand one word: baik. He looks at me and points himself: "Mi a go jon."

12

At the same time in Brooklyn that Pueta-goddess gets rid of that fatty saying the next client comes after 10 minutes. She taps the man on his crown. They take a selfie and Sam galaxy 10e goes away. It´s time for goodbye, and then she goes to shower. A New Yorker´s life is busy, and her/his working week goes easily up to 90 hours. A New Yorker thinks foreigners as a different race, cos deep Brooklyners do not move all the time, they move as slowly and New Yorker´s legs, when he/she is sitting. Anyway, soon there stands on the floor a smug-mang with a black card. He tells that he is very special and rich and famous and whatever. Queen of the house makes quickly a conclusion: the mang is a fraudulent adulterer. Dvd-plays Lizzo´s Good As Hell.

Mang the Smug finds his way out. Semen is good for skin, although one swallow doesn´t make a summer. Overview, causes, symptoms, and treatments are few if STD is new. She stands up. The next fan shall spoil her in Bayside, Queens, where Marie eighth-grader classmates know how to ask about girls´ bra sizes, or so tells regent Marie Curie Middle School´s news. It has become an expensive region, even at Journal Square 1200 sg.ft. should cost 600 000 ends.

She makes some training motions and then changes her clothes, and now nobody for sure underrates her; she is damn pretty. The skirt is tight, short, breast awesome well, and fine. She is ready to go to the area where NYCHA takes 30 % of the tenant's salary giving a damn if the tenant's income changes or not. A yellow Toyota Sienna Accessible arrives and goes.

My watch says 10:10 pm when Cliver stops VRF800F and points his homemade Glock to the driver´s head. The fella goes and I say: "We have 5 minutes left, I send a text: I shall ring the bell at 10:15, ok. I hope next time, when we meet, no need to think about violent home invasions and armed robberies, including one in a barbershop. By the way, I recommend S & S Firearms for you. The new ammo & weapon cargo just arrived from Afghanistan, unfortunately, it shall open on Monday at 10 pm. So, boys, April showers bring May flowers. And have You heard? One Albany-Drizzy gangbanger took two days before new tattoos and woke up yesterday mickey mouse on his head." Huh, huh, it was this and that.

But now our bike flies. I look, at 10:14. Just one minute later, we are in front of the International Book Town´s office. I know that I own now for Cliver. I say: "I see, Y have that mark in your left eyes left corner and on your ring finger. I have something for Y, which no army or gang member in SEALs or on NYC own. How about." Cliver takes his hand from the trigger, and asks stupidly: "Whut?" I smile: "You saved me. So. Here it is." I tear from my neck chains. There is little coin. And it has an eagle, and it doesn´t hold in nails a marmot but a swastika. I say: "Citadelle, Prohorovka, the world´s biggest tank battle, from one *Leibstandarte-kamerad*. My grandpa gave it to me. It brings luck." He looks at my eyes to eyes: "Mi deh yah, zeen." Then I turn and ran, and ring the bell. Very nearby goes a yellow cap which stops near a rustic plate, where reads: what you long for will be given to you, what you love will be yours forever. And in front of it is an old bum who begins to walk away.

Don´t call us, we call You

The door opens in front of me. A polite butler Mr. George salutes me: "Master Tapio, should it be better that we go first behind to do some repairs. I had said it before, and I say it again. Master Tapio, I am not going to bury You." He puts a shoe brush in my hand and before the door closes itself give Cliver sign of four full hands. I know he didn´t want to be in Queens, in the enemy territory.

Mr. George and I go to a backroom. He takes a hot iron and irons my Versace suit which has wrinkles in its eyelid. I see my face, and smile: oh, yeah, now I have some manly remembrances more in my beardless face. My sporty cut blond hair needs just comb and gel, to put it back behind. Eyebrows are alright, just hid some scratches with Agualan, split blood out of my mouth, brush my white teeth even whiter, and that´s it. Then we go.

At 10:17 the president of International Book Towns, madame Gunnel Ottersten and her treasurer Johan Deflander see a trained man, well-suited, smiling in front of them. Well, the other eye of that fella is how Y say it, masonry overgrown? Anyway, Gunnel comes and hugs me, and I shake their hands and say: "How are Y, everything alright? Chestnuts roasting on an open fire, Jack Frost nipping at your nose, yuletide carols being sung by a choir."

Gunnel goes quite a serious: "What has happened to You? I call a doctor." I say: "No need for a medicine man. My girlfriend doesn´t love me anymore." Gunnel says: "I do not have time for this. Have a meeting in YK, at midnight." I know that my timing has gone to the south and my guardian angel has left me a long time ago, when I did my first kill on the battlefield, and so to say cut my long hair short.

Then the shit comes straight to my face. Gunnels says: "I'm not sure I can answer all of your questions, but let me try to start: As to my knowledge, the IOB is not much aware of the different initiatives of ... The concept of book towns is always closely linked to economic revival and cultural/economic development of rural and potential touristic zones ... For me, it would be good if the IOB could develop a sort of informal think thank of members that are willing to work on this, and especially on sharing experiences ..." She talks and talks, and her pointing finger comes closer and closer to me: "I would like to bring you in contact with Alberto Azuaea Grande, who has developed a Ph.D. on the future of book towns in Spain and Ana Maria Urbania-Breide ... Your request on the IOB strategy plan: there's not a plan as such ... As for the question of EU projects ... Let me know if this helps you. Best wishes and I hope to hear from you soon."

Shit, they haven't done anything. I flew to NYC for nothing. My part of the deal goes on, but their part sits steadily and takes a nap. They want me to give them as soon as possible 35 million dollars, before 13.1., and then they shall give me my share 40 million. But how the hell I get that money? Perhaps that gunrunner Cliver has an answer to that? I stand up, shake hands, and walk back to Mr. George and put my hand in my pocket and take there a little gift-card. I say: "Dear fella, this is for your son Charles, the ticket to Brooklyn NBA-teams matches, for springtime. Take care." I tap his shoulders and when I go away, he says: "Master Tapio, I hope somebody up there hears my pray and should give just once a blessing for Y. So, some sunny day Y might live an abundant life and be a blessing to others."

I Found My Million Dollar Bab in B.G.E

I walk hands in my pockets to Cliver and say: "Let's go. I do not have muscles for Y, but I can use Y, robbing a Queen´s Municipal Credit Union, if it is ok with Y, my friend. They have cheap Rates and true loans start at 6.9 % compared to other banks they start at 9 %. The union is chartered in response to the concern of New York City Mayor, John Purroy Mitchel, and 19 charter account holders have combined deposits of 570 dollars, brother, they have 19 branches, half a million members and so." I keep on talking, and he understands and says: "Where I take Y?" I say: "Take to B.Q.E. I go on from there." At 10:55 pm we are there. I take up my wrist, there is a number. His phone clicks a picture and goes. And I do not know that June and January are very close to each other.

11 pm in B.Q.E., "most challenging project in New York City and arguably in the United States", or near 6907 Northern Blvd, Woodside, I take a cap. And say: "Go far away from Sunnyside to Bedford-Stuyvesant." I say the address, and just think that Bradford and Romana are just so kind. I just love the hosts and their friendliness. The cap goes.

Nearby another taxi finds its way to B.Q.E. Puetarican lady, before said June, and one fella, they sit backside. The fella´s hand finds its way under the skirt of the lady. The fella hugs her tight. Her nipples are big and up. Those two caps drive in a row, and there is 307 Meeker Ave. Jane´s cap goes first, then comes mine.

Everything goes sweet and fine but then comes the hand of Almighty Smiling Friend. Mademoiselle-June´s driver looks full of enchantment to backside, and sweet finds its way to his eyes. "If only my dear wife had just amazing breasts, they are too big melons", his thoughts guide him from the BQE's hell and misery. There is no use of the Department of Transportation's plans for BQE's triple-cantilever section when the first cap's driver's hand has found its handjob way and eyes go back-not forward. Everything happens in the second and a half: NYC time says 11:05:31 when the schnozzle takes a kiss from the front left.

The Peterbilt 379 hits the front and it goes right and back comes left. Our cap behind is in the collision course to mademoiselle-Jane's cap. My driver is hypnotized. He is frozen. Fear hits like thunder the brains. I sit right side, and these words, which I cannot forget, come to me: Saint Lucia, defend us in battle, be our protection against the wickedness and snares of the devil, may Smiling Friend rebuke him. We humbly pray, and do thou, o lady of the heavenly host, by the power of Our Friend, thrust into hell all spirits who wander through the world for the ruin of our great and beautiful souls. Amen.

At the same time, my hands take the wheel, and my legs go to pedal, cars go left and right, and now everything is like in slow motion – like in the battlefield when fear attacks on your brains and says to turn it off, let it go. While the first cab is turning, I push the pedal and our cap goes behind the left side, following the first cap's butts. The first cap is going forwards although turning, so its rear goes off our car's way, and our cap pasts the first cap, which is still turning - it goes forward while turning 360 degrees. I press the cap's break and miracle! our cap gives a little kiss to Jane's cap and it stops fishtailing, and goes steadily, even though the driver's brains do not give orders yet. But his eyes see, like in the battlefield terrified soldier's, when the alarm button is off. The command goes and the first cap's driver wakes and so do my cap's fella. Wakeups drive near the right-side railing and continue to drive together towards Commodore Barry Parks. I try to be funny: "My

18

grandfather has the heart of a lion and a lifetime ban from the Zoo."
The driver looks at me: "Nincompoop and so swagga."

At Gold St, our caps stop. The drivers go to look at their cars.
Meanwhile, the City isn't flush and in bloom, but if we think it so, then
Pueta-goddess June is even more radiant. Unfortunately, the rosy
thing doesn't always lead the way. The fella, the paying client, shows
his disapproval of the situation: "Hey, why we are here at Sugaring
Paste." He begins to kiss Puetarican lady. Although the product isn't
just good but best and the customer is always more than right, there
is one party pooper - me.

11:20 pm not from the stars my judgment pluck, nor I can fortune to
brief minutes tell or say with princes if it shall go well, but St. Lucia
knows better. The fella takes the goddess from her hair and
commands: "You promised to do the blowjob for 100 dollars. Let's
finished the job." He takes for granted the candy is his. He begins to
hear singing behind his broad shoulders: "Doubt thou the stars are fire;
Doubt that the sun doth move; doubt truth to be a liar, but never
doubt I love Y so." Interrupted mid the session high and mighty fella
begins to understand high and dry. He roars: "Who the hell Y think Y
are, man. Not your business!!"¨

I laugh. I really have a nice time. All evening has been a joke, but this
is the best of it. I say one more thing: "Y talk about 100 dollars like it is
a star in heaven. I'm talking about things that Y aren't worthy of." The
fella thinks too big of himself and becomes to come. I have my limits,
too. I hit once and then comes the silence. One in fear to lose what he
enjoys, the other to enjoy by rage and war. These signs forerun the
death of something and rise of something, too. I look at the woman
left alone and say: "My name is Tapio." She looks at the fella, who has
a nice suit and a black eye, and says: "My name is Victoria."

The Second Day

I Missed You

El Domingos – Luck Me I`m in Love -Killer NYC
Uptempo Doo Wop (yeah, Brooklyn style,
sorry, no lyrics available)

The Momentum, once in the Lifetime

It is 11.35 pm, and the next day is knocking on the door. Victoria asks, looking on the ground: "Is he dead?" I say: "Yes, as a doornail." She begins to think: "Shall we land him like Sally." I think back: "He is kipping, without morning glory. Early in the morning, Sugaring Paste shall give him face treatment, 80 bucks, blackhead buster 10 d, and sugaring, the most gentle, natural, long-lasting treatment." She looks at my eye: "Perhaps Y need more it than he does."

Her finger with blue nail touches my blacked eye: "I have worked with old people, and Y may have sepsis blood poisoning. Poisoning progress to sepsis rapidly. Your causes are an abdominal infection, exposure to open wounds, and skin infection. Recognizing chills, rapid breathing, palpitations, and paleness of the skin."

Her shining eyes drill into my mind and begin to build a crown in my heart. There are many helping places: St. Johns Recreation Center in BK, BronxWorks Senior Centers, Ninth Street Espresso Brooklyn at Threes Brewing, Birch Coffee. Is Victoria one of those who have answered "yes" to a question: need someone to accompany your aging loved one?

I look at her: "Can Y trip the light fantastic, EDM?" She begins to laugh: "Hell yea, u know I can. Desperate fuk***rs try to find a chick to bang, so, rap solid, about to eight ..." I understand that soon Rusko & 6blocc and Mala & Kode 9 shall be seen with ID & T.

Cap-fellas have found nothing bad. Their cars are in order. They say with one mouth: "Where do Y want to go? I say: "That silent partner there, wants to go home. Y shall find it in his pocket." Other of them says: "What?" I say: "Wallet, Y crazy." And then I turn to that other fella: "We want to go to, hm. Friends and Lovers, House of Yes, Xstasy, hm ..." Victoria, or may I say, Y, give five to Williamsburg, daytime, but not nighttime: "Xstasy, is the right place. If Y are dang, they overcharge your credit card and do not care what Y shall say to your credit card company the next morning. I've always had a great time there, no matter the day of the week. Drinks are awesome, and stoopid fellas cannot leave out the dancers, cos of their bodies and cool talks." So. Our Smiling Friend does not give us not only our possessions but his god services, too.

Towards Manhattan we go. Victoria laughs: "I'll daym you." I say: "No Y don't, m braven Y." I knock my forehead, but unfortunately, my hand touches a little bit too hard to my black eye, and its corner begins to bleed. It is 0:15 am when we arrive at the doorbells. There is a queue, but I take you and lead Y to the entrance. Everything seems to be sweet and sound. Inside the fast house, but in my brains goes Five Pastels - You're Just an Angel, and I smile.

Unfortunately, the world isn't a safe place for great fellas like me. Gays and loudly losers have conquered the world. Men like me must be stopped. A moody bouncer looks at my blooding eye, and does not understand: "Get lost, this for descent folks, no place for Y." I say: "What do Y mean?" There is a group of beautiful women, and he wants to get attention. Bouncer gets on with me. His big hollow of the hand finds its way to my neck. I go very fast behind him and press a normal halterneck. The bouncer goes to the midwinter night's dream. I take care of his head so it doesn't bang to the ground.

Then I suddenly remember, with whom I'm there. Great and beautiful Angel is with me. Do I fuck this now up once and for all? I press the sleeping bouncer's neck from the left side. He stirs a little bit and opens his eyes. I put to his hand 150 dollars: "Nice to meet Y, I get a ticket for the Brooklyn match, but I missed it. Is it ok?" I put 150 dollars more to his pocket. He understands: "What about your eye?" I say: "Do Y have Marker's Mark 46 or Garrison Brothers, TX, then everything is alright. It really burns." He nods his head, and here we go. And then happens something which changes everything. Victoria isn't happy.

We are in. Good music, lovely bartenders. Some instinct gets me to say to Victoria: "Do they lose here their security videotapes?" Then I begin to understand where we are. This is a gay bar. At once I turn and take Victoria from her hands and try to lead her out. But she isn't ready for that at all. She says: "We are going nowhere. This is the only place in this whole world where men leave me alone. And here we can talk." I accept that: "Well, here are ladies also, hm, and Spanish dancers, music, and performers speaking Spanish. Hm, ifit suits Y, can we go far away from candymen and so. Perhaps we shall go there, those people look like gays, straight and curious folks.

We go to a trap, where sit three black Spanish women and a guy. They listen to iPod nana and their favorite Nicki Minaj, and Victoria likes Anaconda and so, too. And I say: "Do You know why they have dogs around their swimming pools in Brasilia?" What a stoopid thing, but Victoria saves the situation: "No, why? I dexify: "Anacondas cannot go swimming there." Huh, huh, but I buy a drink from their limited stocked bar. I begin to understand bit by bit that gays aren't the only visitors and notice a Latin vibe. I want to go dancing floor with Victoria, and at last, have with her in a private magiclike.

So, we dance, and your figure throws shiny good deeds to my illies and kick them down from the bluff and cliff and then no shape so true, no truth of such an account. And for myself, my own worth does define.

As I all other in all worth surmount. I begin to move like a domestic cat, and hot waves of love attacked my mighty heart. Y whisper to my ear: "*Dame esa vaina.*" So I do some "CCS" and moves such as 6-steps, but not pretzel or under sweeps, but all doomed, cos to dance with Y, who knows how to win a man over, your dry hands and it makes me loose, and my shum liam ... I just take y near me and say: "With a girl like You I don´t give a fuck about the *chios* and ..."

Suddenly when the set is pretty illy, a drunk guy says to me: "Hey man, do you know where I can get a couple of illies?" I say: "Do not know what Y mean. Bog off. I don´t know any cocaine-Jesus. Do not bike past this way in your way home." He says: "You are lying." He wanders away, and the sound of the music (Nelly) is muffled and it is rather drafty. And then Vitoria & I begin to laugh. I say: "I want to show Y something." I crowd out some kissing Latinos, and I ask a bartender to come to me. It is time to show how things can grow and save the world.

I ask the bartender to give me two double Carrison Brother, TX, four plasters, and some ice. Then I take Y to the DJ and put two chairs near the new Tiesto. The bartender came back, and I turn those whiskeys to my wound, and it canes a little bit. He puts the ice and plasters and says: "It should be a shame if I bleed to death, after so many hard years. Victoria, you want to hear this." New Tiesto and I blather something, and then I turn the bass-heavy, and there comes a Legion Etrangere rhythm from the drums.

I say to Tiesto: "Now mix it with Chaabi." He asks: "Why?" I: "Foreign legion drummed in the marketplaces and Bedouins answered it with their own drums. Hundred years practice and they sound great together. That ´drink´ I call Morocco´s Spanish sound, ok. It fits with your EDM. Please do it." So he does. And the weaving mass of dancers and others, prick up its ears. But it sounds fast and slow at the same time, the Bedouin's rhythm runs, and draw the tale, Legion rhythm.

Then I put there the Melody; when there is a manly rhythm you must have the female Melody. So says Claudius Martella, who lived last Roman days in Carthago, so near the Moars' place, so he knew. I look at Victoria with a burning, sheepy gaze: "*Adiós Gloria* and welcome Victoria."

Tiesto puts there Manhattan Transfer's Gloria, but take the voice off, and let the instrumental thing come smoothly as the hand feels the woman's knee. I take the microphone: "I dedicate this to you all, and of course to MyLady, I hope you like it, thank you very much."

"Victoria!" the bass and the drums put the Melody to its place, and Tiesto helps with the choir-things. And Icontinue: "Victoria, Victoria it's not Marie, Victooria (like Toscaaana), it's not Sherieee, Victoria, but she's not in love with me". The choir does it 3/4, and I sing: "Can't you see, it's not Marie? Victoria, it's not Sherie, Victoria, but she's not in love with me. And, maybe (choir: maybe) she wants me, but who am I to love, and maybe she'll want me, but who am I to love, Victoriaa-aa!" I repeat that again, and I show with my body and hands, well whatever, and wait that they take the power line off. But nothing happens, they look at me still. So, I continue: "She is not in love with miiiiiilll. But I love You Victoria, and want Y to be my Bab. Another night, when I went bed alone (I brief deeply and take all that comes from there) when I was dreaming Y, now the dream the real, I don't dream of Sherie, Adele, I dream of VICTOOORIaaAAA." Now comes the real test, which tells why so many New Yorkers have failed with this melody. My voice goes up, but Miracle! it breaks not or goes to nasal. I give the microphone away. I think: "That's it. Oh, now I screw the pooch." I look at Victoria. Her beautiful eyes smile, she looks like a goddess, I had never seen so ...ooh ... this is the momentum.

I do not move. The very simple Melody, very beautiful, from Brooklyn's up-tempo doo-wop times, and, and ... then it breaks. Huge, almost spanking the ham applauses. There aren't any more gays, Latinos, black Spanish, whites, angry this and stupid head that. There is just joy, a double rainbow all the way across the sky. Whoa, Uu, Whoa, whoa Oh OH, tell me, too much. Victoria is there, and I take her hand. Music starts again, like gabber.

Cos Tiesto took Melody from DMCA YouT, that tech-system didn't accept that "but she doesn't love me" and take for granted that those words much be replaced with other words. And before I could brief or even try to kiss Victoria, I do not actually know how it happened, that so seems to be in every page of youtube, or didVictoria say it to new Tiesto, I do not know, but anyway, there comes a Melody, Vince Vance & The Valiants, All I Want For Christmas Is You, and that's sure, that beat wasn't chosen by some bitch from Missouri: yeah, on the top of the Christmas tree, something is true. Those two, Victoria and this ... shit ...

We, Victoria and I, are celebrated. It's a great night out. Arturo the owner is at a location to help, serve, and ready to troubleshoot any situation at hand. He shakes my hand and hugs Victoria, and his words haven't mean stare-downs: "Come back soon."

Somebody may say Jesus welcomed us, and I do not mean the drug dealer - but I do not say that. The outside bar I put my hand to the doorman's shoulder, look at his eyes, and shake his grab. And he doesn't talk about keeker. Word 'brody' was mentioned, once, twice, or thrice. Then, then it is time to hope Victoria doesn't pull an Angelita move on me.

I take her in my arms, and She/You say: "Where are U from, and why are U here?" I look at that beautiful thing and say: "I thought that a good deal shall be made with the IOB-towns and my company. But instead of a proposal, I hear phrases and get pressure. I think this visit has a quite different meaning. Wherefrom am I? From the deep north, not far away from my place blaze northern lights, and they can be seen sometimes from my villa, too. My name is Tapio, and it means ´forest god and king´, and my court is called Tapiola. There are many nice poems praising YourTapio. For instance, when hunters want me to give them kill, their prayer goes: ´Mighty Tapio, King of the Forest, accept these offerings set on your Table, take this bread, made from the three ears of rye, take this holy ale brewed from the water of your spring, made from the three ears of rye, now bless these weapons of mine as I lay them before Y on your Sacred Table, Y Mighty Hero.´ So animals are always my friends, and no god or cat be afraid of Mighty Tapio, and there is no dog who doesn´t think me as his/her true friend. What about Y Victoria. Are Y the personified goddess of the victory. Angels are said to company Y, all around. What Victoria says to a man shall always be written on-air and the swift water."

Victoria stops me: "O angel dear, wherever I go, save, defend, and govern also, though I may not thee see or hear, yet devoutly with the trust, I pray to thee. My body & soul keep thou in fere, o blessed angel, to me so fear, govern my deed and thoughts in fere." I look again to Victoria, its 2:15 am, and we pass Saint Vitus, Lobster Joint, and East River Tattoo. We talk much, but we do not listen. No particular words needed.

 Near Milton St, we kiss. The temperature is -4. And I say: "Here, I´ll give Y my jacket." One more hug for your lips. You axe: "Why are Y kissing me?" The meeting of two pairs of lips. We are at your door. It has begun to rain heavily. Y say: "Great time, nearly loved it. Bye." What can I say, so I say: "YLISHAH." Y look at me: " Y say very quickly: ´Ameme cando menos lo mereszca, dear not Babi, por que sera cuando mas la necesite, siempre habra un mismo cielo que nos una ...´" I do not understand a word, but do not stay helpless: "There is nearby a training center, how about tomorrow:" Y tell: "I cannot tomorrow, work to do." I say: "No need to think of time, we can go there in the night also." Y ask: "Really?" I explain: "Yes, we have a Guardian Angel, and he is called Cliver." She looks at me and I look at her, and the joy of love is so long, and the happiness thereof, and what cometh thereof, dureth over so short that it vanishes. Nothing can stop the clattering of bells.

We go in. A little dog looks so nicely to Y - and me.

I take the little thing in my arms and kiss it to its mouth. The little fella´s ears go up, and he seems to be quite happy. I turn to Y: "Gnite, Victoria." I look at that little thing in my arms: "See Y too tomorrow." Then I run in the rain.

Spending Quality Time

I run, am 3:25. Somebody says it is cold, -5, but that´s not true. Somebody says it is raining, but that´s nothing. At Pulaski Street near my bed Bedford, there comes shooting from Crown Heights. Hm, there comes running polices, one of them seems to be well-known James P. O´Neil. I say: "Watch´s up?" He runs away, then there come three cops more. One of them, young fella says: "Just a pair of shooters in a group fired 18 bullets at another group of individuals, striking one of their intended targets and injuring three other uninvolved bystanders." They ask me to leave.

I go on and think something: Mr. Mayor says that numbers are very small. Just 29 murders in October, an increase of just over 61 % from 18, during the same month in 2018. But who is perfect here? The only thing is sure: my life has changed tonight. I'm totally in love. That isn´t a punishment.

In my black eye and another, I see the gates of gold and raindrops begin to give the rhythm of the melody, which sounds - yeah, jewiger BQE: a mixed Shells Angel Eyes and Daddy Yankee - Mtv Live in New York (Part 1). I open my door and go to bed. And find strange land, Y know, *si esa mujer fuera para mi, perdoname, te lo teniaque decir.* There is something about Y, I cannot forget. Let´s call that Angel Eyes.

And I know, somewhere in Brooklyn is a dog and, and I sleep long – almost to 8 am. My business-trip to NYC has gone to the south, and I had got some thresholds to stumble. But those were ridiculous things compared to what else I had got. I understand that I may win the game. But the risk is that I surely lose the lazy days for the rest of my life. For whether ill-stored or unwisely spent it is equally lost.

Victoria has already eaten and fed her doggy. She has been training and is ready to go to some meeting considering her star profile in some and so. She must look fresh, not a draw away from the image. And she is very, very, and very gorgeous. And even she is in a hurry. She thinks: "Ma man loves me takes me everywhere?" She thought more: "But what if he flies to that northern hole of his, and never come back? He was so, okay, amazing type, not sitting in every branch here."

I go downstairs and the landlady doesn´t look happy: "Ahah, you have finally wakened up. Shame on you. Every time you come to visit you oversleep." I say: "Give me bacon and eggs, and one Texas-steak, and, as you know, a big glass of banana split." She looks at me: "If you put that steak on your eye, it shall be fresh in no time." But I don´t listen to her. I think about Y, Victoriaaaa. I have fallen in L. And what happens if I do not reach Y soon? Check it out. I do a brainer and find out the phone no. I say to the landlady: "Please, shut up. This is very important." The phone doesn't answer.

I leave a text: I want to meet Y soooon. There comes back text: "Habana Outpost. 4 pm. I have a moment for Y. Best Cuban sandwiches in the entire world." I text: "Why don´t Y answer?" Y: "No time to hash-hash." I: "Rlly?" Y: "Really." I: "By the way, chicken plate and burrito have a large serving of rice and beans, but the burrito is small and nowhere near the same portions of the bowl. The frozen drinks are small and are 11 bucks, and they´re cash only." Y: "Yer Maw." I: "See Y, L Y S."

I take the steak off my eye and drink the banana split. I kiss the air on the landlady Margaret´s hand: "I love Y." I ask the iron and iron my clothes. Then I call to the IOB-office. The lady of the office says: "Good Morning, we shall be open at 9 am, have a nice day." I text to the president of the IOB: "I do nothing if Y do not do your part of the deal. Y can terminate the contract, but then I make the whole media known about that. If I make a deal, as we make up, then Y shall give also 5 million. OK?" I go to my baggage and put my training clothes on and run out of the house. Time to have some sweets of mercy & fun.

I'm in Prospect Park. This is great; here beats the heart of Brooklyn. The Place is really a paradise, Its interrupts my regular device-filled schedule for some hands-on things. Yeah, getting outside during these cold weather days is a great mood booster and a real welcome break from the winter grind. I do not want to think about the IOB-office people, I think about MyVictoria. I do not imagine real her, but an image of her flies in my mind, like a storm bird. I smile. Here I'm, running, spending quality time, getting some nice memories during the most wonderful time of the year

The Break

It is just 10:30 am. Almost six hours to meet the lady of my dreams. I shall spend this time for a good purpose. Hey, there is Gilded Frame Making. I'm not going for holding photos and pics of other special memos, but, hey, here are a lot of youngsters, about 13-14 years old pas! Hm, every park those fellas look the same, in Prospect, or Claremont of where-ever. I salute them.

They shout at me and want me to give them some cash or so. I yell back: "Boys, sorry I have spent all my money last night. I got lucky." They show me a box cutter, and I salute them as we do in the army, with my dirty palm. I continue to run. And after a while, I have come back to that part of the park where the Sports are.

I go to them: "Hey, I have heard that this isn´t any more a very safe place to be." They lolz and curse me. I say: "You talk ten-dollar words. You, there, a weighting barely 110 pounds isn´t much. It isn´t good for your mental and physical body to travel in packs, hang around making a lot of noise." He spills it: "F-k you, suck me d-k." I say: "Boys, it is a long way for you to do what you want to do, cos you do not have the money. The neighborhood may need more policing and the park more lighting, but you need more muscles and brains, fellas. I have an idea. Wanna hear." They keep their ears to the ground: "Common, before we beat Y, the big fella." I laugh and show my wealthy teeth: "Make muscles. Go to free training clubs and places, or go there for free, fix your know-how. There are four training places nearby, where Y get also food. I think Y need discipline, so in harbor, as Y know, is the army place. Harbor Fitness Park Slope, Bay Ridge, and Mill Basin, yes, they are expensive, although round the clock. But there is also in Gowanus Bay near Sims Municipal a group called TangouYF, a band of Afghan-veterans training place.

They are big, and they are tough, but they are straight, and the best you can get. They are my friends and believe or not they are friends forever. They do not need your money, they do not need your sweet words, and they do not need your courses, and cheating things, but there is one that they need: they want to help Y if Y are worth of true ergometer. After their session, Y can shoot, run, fight, and that I promised Y, Y begin to respect weak people, and do everything for them."

The fellas look at me: "Y think we´re going that kind of bungee jumping. You´ve lost your marbles." I say: "I think Y do, there some Legion Etrangere and some SEALs also, Y shall love it, you Jabob Reeds. I can show Y something." They murmur but then they say: "Ok."

I show the kids first some old school: BBoy Battle things. It put the simple on their face. The smallest one shouted: "Totem, yeoww!" Another kid: "Wow!" Third: "Y Kalene, Y yay!" Others: "Onfg liek, so kOOl!!!" I say: "How about? First jump and then ..." They come to battle clumsily, but they come. Toprock goes quite easily, but not down rock or freezes. I don´t panic: "Do the real shit, never copy or do the same as before. This is called warming up, broods." I look at my watch at almost 0:30 pm. Ooh, I say: "I show Y some more. Y can run, Y know the police thing, but after warming comes always deadlifting, before Y go to train speed." I take that box cutter and cut one branch nearby. People far away are looking at us. Somebody talks to his phone. Well, no time to lose.

My hands are about 150 cm separated. I take the branch from the ground to the straight hands: "Do not rest. Do the first ones slowly, then quicker, and slowly. Always surprise yourselves. Never do the same way, but always one more than before." I did just with that 40 kg branch 300 repeats and brief: "Start with the stick that Y can put up 50 times and there it goes. Now I must go, here is my number, call, Y beyotch. I tell the boys that some new fellas wanna come. Perhaps some sunny day, if Y are good, I can call Y, amber roses." I go on running. They shout: "Where are going?" I smile: "I´m going home." And point my heart. And they understand. And I'm in a hurry, cos love doesn´t wait. I run to catch Y, MyVictoria.

Habana with a Kiss

I change a light suit on and ring to +1 718 858 9550: "*Como esta usted?* The table on the middle of the rainbow, name Tiihonen. We are coming in half an hour. I take fresh corn dosed with mayo, what Mexican cuisines. Really? That´s great. No, no, not a Private enquire. Senora mia makes her choice. What do You mean, many people at the same table? Of course, it suits us. My *querida* is a social type, and I a humble servant. Thanks, buy." Well, that´s it. I go.

Comes a phone call. "The IOB´s president here, Y made quite an impolite text. Do Y have anything more to say?" I say: "If I begin to make festival-arrangements, I do not take it from my pocket, half and half, okay. By the way, I have some expenses here in NYC, shall Y pay right now. M not going back to F in a cattle class. Send me a diamond card. Yes, thank Y, Merry Christmas, I shall be in London at New Year. Buy, buy."

There is not raining and no car doesn´t throw anything, so I stand at the door of Habana. Full of people. There they sit and eat and sit like a flock of sheep. And soon I must go there with MyVictoria. Well, it is just love that outweighs all other virtues.

You have a Y-cap with your stiletto heels, normal awesome makeup, and tight dress on. Y say to a client: "Sorry, I do not hear, my computer and phone have broken up. I cannot hear a word. Did Y say the best smiley dan ever, sorry, wrong number, Mr. Houston High-five?" MyVictoria has washed her doggy with a very good hair care product, Moroccan oil, dried the squeaking thing with a hairdryer, walked it a fresh mail. So, Mr. Doggy was left very happy on the balcony to bark every bird which dares to come near.

MyVicoria is a little bit nervous: "What about if some jealous crush of fan or black card fella comes and beats MyPoorTapio? It may happen, cos MyTapio is a little bit temperamentand doesn't go by the book. Well, what can I do? Paint my nails blue? Ohh oh, that fella doesn't get a glue where he is mixed with."

The cap stops. From the cap comes awesome Y. I do not notice everything, cos I am nearly falling asleep again. What a boring place. There are many eyeglass-fellas telling to their ladies that Che Guevara and Fidel Castro have been here. I think: "Oh, those big mouth fuckers who ruined Cuba and killed thousands of wealthy people. Veterans tell stories about how they have a fight with those back-shooting Castro's Cuban-shits around the world. But there is one thing which YourTapio doesn't know: this place is a story about LOVE. Love for bringing people and V & T together. Love for feeding Y & me authentic Latin food and more love. Love for having fun and great kisses and hugs.

You come to me. And before Y say a word, we kiss, not xx but s.w.a.k. Muah love ya lot: "MyVictoria, when proud-pied love dress'd in all its trim hath put a spirit of love in everything. My eyes hath play'd the painter and hath stell'd the beauty's form in table of my heart." All these words do not go to the wolves, cos an old lady says: "We must come here again."

We go to sit at our table. MyQueen gets her *Daiquiri, frappeado,* lemon juice, and sugar. I do not drink *cubanito* or *saoco* but mineral water, with a lot of ice. It tastes much better than *Havan Loco* or even *Crema de Vie.* Then I take your hand: "I'm not going to say another poem, I just ..."

Blessed are the Merciful

At this happy hour, one drunken fella stands up, and Y see behind me a big tattooed stand-up guy. When we are kissing, you think: "Now it ends. That blaze sticks and Stones." The black card fella stands behind me and murmur: "HoLLLLLY crap." I turn and say: "Ah, we have waited for Y. Can Y sing *Tan Buena or Asi Mismo,* Actually the last one is better, or what Y think, Bab."

You say: "Tapio, it is better you go now: ´*Mi lindo barrio donde la sangre salpica.´* Not nice." I am surprised: "Well, the first ones *yo era tan feliz con un solo amor, y ahora tengo diez y me va peor, y hoy te hago fufrir.* I like better *mi fortuna est mi vida* -thing. And what do Y mean, going away? I just came." Y point: "Rodriguez here ..." I look at Mr. R: "Ah, You mean this fat friend. Now I understand. Y want him to leave, *comprende?"*

Hm, much 130 kg or even more. I cannot deadlift that steak. And here are a lot of hilarious people. No need to demonstrate anything. So, I say to the fella: "Y want me to fuck off? Do You? And Y want to stay?" He yells: "Yesss!" I say: "Well, so be it. But there is one change in the

35

plan. I do not want to go." Rodriguez has a big hand. I take it and put it on the table and take a fork and hit it through the huge hand. Now the table and the man are united, and one does not leave without another.

I think: "Hey, there is a guitar man. Let's call him here." I whistle and while people are terrified and going away, and MyVictoria thinks me as a troublemaker, and a hero, the trembling fella comes to us. Rodriguez is crying.

I say: "Please, sing a nice Mexican ballad, here is a broken blood man. Let's give him some light to his life. Do Y know the song *De los Besos Que Te Di*? Please play it." He starts a very nice song. I take the fork off the hand and the table and put some Mojito instead. Mr. R yells. I put a bottle in front of him: "I never leave a friend. So please tell me how good a friend you are. Let's drink a snap to every letter of your name." I smile at MyVictoria, and then I take a snap with my new friend, (^-^)7." After seven snaps Rodriguez begins to laugh and people do not care about him anymore. And the bartender says to me: "Thanks." I say: "Just wonderful are the ways of the L."

It's time to break down the wall which has arrived between me and Victoria. I say: "Do Y love me?" Y ask: "Shall we call an ambulance?" I marvel: "Why? Everybody dies someday. And this fella does not die. No need even to sew. So do Y want to know how much I love Y?"

I say to Y: "Think Scot Salvatore charges a mere 50 000 d to spruce our place up. Surrey's gives a smashing Deck the Halls package that includes a festively decorated room, four ice skating passes, and a gingerbread making set. The deal is a three-night -stay, and we simply must use the Presidential Penthouse Suite, which costs only, think MyVictoria, 15 000 d a night. 51 000 d with mean little taxes. Exhausted, Bab? Do not be. I shall recover Y with a quick 10 000 d martini. But if the duchess, Y, fly with her relatives to Finland, Y can serve turkey, carved table-side, like in agent courts and feel at the same time cozy."

You wonder: "I do not understand?" I continue: "Yes, Y do. We shall have here a great time, better than Ted Leo and the Pharmacists go imagine, and then even better things in my homeland". You say: "And that is how Y comfort me after having shameful acts here and there? Asking me to come to wolf-zone and poverty and dark and nothingness?" I say: "Yes. But we can have here at Plaza Hotel for Eloise's Rawther Fancy Tea which is almost free, just 100 d per child and 50 d per us, and there Santa has promised to read us a story. We can reserve the 2500 table 55 at the King Cole Bar, if Y, MyDear, are feeling a bit frugal. I lov Y so. And what could be more fun that a caviar splurge at Cafe Boulud? The Christmas pre-fixe in only 175 d a person and for a trigling 275 d Y can enjoy 30 grams of Kavari Ostra caviar, think Bab.

And if Y come to F, there is a luxury, and no need to look at Merrie Cherry performing in music veds, at international drag festivals and see how he and drag mother RuPaul kiss each other. In F no need for Drag Renaissance and think who is now credited as the pioneer of a quirky, rag-tag type of drag. No need to rush for bk Nightlife Awards, competition DRAGnet, and rush to Metropolitan. Hm. If Y think this differently we shall, MyVictoria, describe always Williamsburg chill, adventurous, and home. And in bk, we don't haveas many tourists in the way when we are trying to get around." Y stop me: "Wburg is an Italian neighborhood, and, DearTapio, there is the best pizza Sal's Pizza. And Cherry is a nice, big man in a dress and a crazy wig. Think about the kid sitting there, near that Queen, the child feels a little different, she sees that Queen and gets more of an idea of what else is out there in the world – not just the small world their parents have created for them, think Tapio."

I say: "I see, perhaps, krhm." Y continue: "And if we get Bloody Marys at Zona Rosa, there is a fella on Bedford, and North Eight Street who just have a ton of books. And Martha´s Bakery is the fine Place. And whatever Y do, there are just two minutes of merriment." Well, Y are right and I'm wrong as always. And I do not think about preludes and Heavenly Rest.

We kiss. I say: "MyVictoria, do Y want to m..." And Y continue: "And there is Broadway and Bubbly." I say: "What about missing persons out there in the jungle? What about houses with two bedrooms, 500 000 d. They are like dirty boxes. I think gift boxes in South America, where the drug-barons put heads of their enemies and send them with the bible and words of Jesus to an unfortunate relative, Uncle Dave. And people ask, who has bought that box/house, and the answer is the coolest man in the family, and if Y have some issues, just Y got to go take on Uncle Dave, the master of the box."

Before you say anything, we go. I take your hand. I say: "Clerks and priests are sleeping already, it is 6 pm, so do not need to disturb them, but ..." You say: "What about Rodriguez, he is so ... tired." I say: "Rest in Peace. Let´s have some feliz ano neuvo before it begins ..."

"Where we are going?" you ask. I say: "Well, I like more the west." You: "Why?"

By the Light of the Silvery Moon

I tell: "We go to the Army Transformal Center. Y know global solution & scale. Boys have big lights for big guns. Y should know. Sorry, lost wit my mind." You ask: "Is that legal?" I explain: "There are lights for EDM-trap house -thing. We have a party. Not a field court & Marshall." Y: "What happens when the police shall come?"

I laugh: "They shall have a good party." You are not happy: "Do Y really think so?" I say: "My GreatAndMoreThanBeautifulVictoria, I do not think. I just follow the order which says that patience is a 21-year-old male, who has now bdp." We take a y-cap and the lights of the party come nearer.

And I explain facts and funs to the nervous driver: "We throw fete on the whole street." He is afraid: "O holy shit, there, there are popos, and they are after something." I put my hand on his shoulder: "Let´s go and have some fun. Fuck with the police."

But the driver isn't over the moon. And the boys on the blue do not relax but try to shut the rainbow-lights. MyVictoria looks at me.

I go to the nearest squaliee: "Please stop beating in the bush and cut to the chase. What the fuck, do y want?" My army's great mentor Napoleon has said: "The winner is the man who first controls his enemy's chaos." So, the situation cannot be in the hands of boys in blue. I say to Victoria: "Relax."

I tell the fella that it is Estate & Grounds Management HSL, a commitment service for the peace on mind. I take from my pocket, while their gats are on me, a number: "Please, call here, and live. No hard feelings." The police officer looks at the number, takes his phone, and makes some calls. Then he says: "We are very sorry. HSL is always more than welcomed to have some public activities."

Y ask: "What was that number?"

I answer: "I got the number from my book town's president. We have made deal with CEO-project and I'm as Y know festival-CEO of book towns IOB. If they called the CEO, that's true that there is a festival. It's like Habana outpost, it has so many restaurants. So, the police officer didn't ask details. Why? Cos then he should have had to tell his name."

Mayor gets every Tuesday official records, and if there some department's police officers asks his doings it doesn't look nice. Just take care of po-po's chaos and the party is free. Y look at me: "I think Y were lucky." I kiss MyQueen.

So, Y & I are tripping the light and get down a groove. And what a dancer you are. My ex-army fellas ask: "They left?" I say: "And for good."

Christmas eve EDM-sounds like real crimbo. Or may we say Christmas adam, cos eve comes then.

And MyQueen dances sweetly and fast. She laughs: "Why don't Y get tired? I say: "Y shall see why." Y: "Tell why beforehand." I: "How can we sleep when this is better than a dream." You smile: "And we shall feel quite queasy and say: it was New Year Eve last night." "And between those goes Twixmas", I say.

It is 22 pm. And there is a lot of folks. Not an old-fashioned Christmas party but a new one. Well, most common house, trance, and trap, but also some old school fast rap. We do not like it too slow. Here shall not be drug-related deaths, cos addicts we kick ass.

Do not need Tattoos to know, who stays and who runs.

Y begin to be curious: "Who are these guys which Y know? Mercenaries?" I: "No, no, real stuff. Bredrens & dawgs or what's up dwags, heh, heh. They are men of honor. That Frankie was in Chad, seen once, twice. Most of them are Afghan-vets. Some have university degrees, most come from the shadow side of the street, but they are not crims, friends of late-night Saturday party. They are not Pachuto boys, who beat people up and steal their wallets. They are not kenlays, who steal people's retirement savings and their security. They are, hm, today's, do not laugh, knights and hoods, they take from the fu***ers and give to great poor people, and, heh, heh."

Y: "Are they killers and soldiers of fortune?" I am surprised: "What a stupid question, MyVictoria. They all serve as they wish and with honor and fidelity. If Y are among them, like YourTapio, each of them is my Bro, hm, in arms, and Y show them the same close solidarity that links the members of the family. Nothing strange about that, MyVictoria. Respect, devotion, discipline, and comradeship are our strengths, courage, and loyalty to our virtues. So, no use to mess with us, we kick your ass. We are, hmkrm, proud, we appreciate dignified but modest behavior. Bab, as an elite soldier, you train rigorously, you maintain your weapon, we fight against pretzels, with weapons aren't for us, bloodegics. We take constant care of our physical form. Y know, we risk our lives on the field. It is easy: try to act without passion and hate, respect defeated f**ers, and do not abandon your friends or arms."

Y think: "Sounds terrible. Y should try to act inside the law." I: "These fellas are the law. In no-mans-land where they live, and where normal people do not dare to go, they make laws great & beautiful. Most of us are retired. The hard stuff belonged to our younger days. Do not need tattoos to know, who stays, and who runs."

We continue to dance. I must somehow show to you that I'm not a cockfighter but just a descend man, who does not cheat but lows just my wife's pasta. I have an idea. I take MyVictoria's hand and then we go. I shake hands with Frankie: "See Y, take care. I send some tinny park boys to your training place. Make those giggling odd-and-ends real and true."

I take my phone: "Hey, man, do Y still have that bike. Two passengers." We begin to walk away from warehouse A (that 200 by 980 feet). I take Victoria to my arms cos three railroad tracks ran through the space between the warehouses. We say so long to NYC Ferry and are on 60th Street.

Cliver arrives. I say: "Here are 100 bucks. Bedford Av. and Library Café. No time to lose. How are Y?" Cliver: "Like your care. Who is Macy? So are yall talking or is she free?" I know that there must be some action, or MyVictoria begins to count how much she is losing per hour. I must keep her happy as the Happy can be. I do not have a diamond ring, but I have my head, and it is working with her - a lot.

We go to Library Coffee's cafeteria, but nobody needs anything. We enter the computer room. I do not need the Whitehead underpass, Campus rRd, cos my university oyster card is a presgo. I just present it and in we go. Cliver: "How's that possible?" I say: "Very easy. Work some years as a scientist in the University, write ten books, and put them to academia.edu. A good life, the happy memories."

 Now it is time to say g-bye to Cliver: "Hey, how much bench? So little. Come tomorrow, to B-gym and I show Y how to put butts up, and cheat 100 kg, ok." He goes.

It is time to convince MyVictoria, or she begins to think of me as a fan, or a director. You say: "I must go to work soon, or my manager shall call to the bank and they sustain my account." I wonder: "But she is your employee. Your deal says safely and soundly, what is her duties. And among them isn´t breeder´s privileges."

The fast day ends, and a faster day begins. And there shall always come the final day when someone shall be sent into Eternal Fire.

The Third Day

Management is a practice where art, science, and craft do not meet. It is one of the simplest ways to cheat, which means that you lost the cheating time of your life. That unbelievably sux - and there is another of woe you get my drift.

Gift Boxes Freestyle

While we are sitting there, and I open the golden Panthoras´ or so, Cliver goes to his home with a huge gift box. His mom and pap are surprised. Cliver says: "Take or leave it. For you." Mother looks at his son, who has a swastika-medal on his neck, with the strange year 1943 and text "*meine ehre heisst treue*". Mother touches the medal and asks quietly: "What does this mean?" Cliver says: "My Honor is Loyalty." His father asks: "Where do Y get that?" Cliver: "From a compare full of honor and bravery."

Nearby last-minute shoppers, who had found themselves from the bar, are going home. They have the final items with them. Luckily for all the procrastinators out there, some stores stayed open late and gave everyone a chance. Those last shoppers were out in force across New York. Times was running short but not too short. One fella in the bar says: "I just had like a shortlist, what I forgot to get, pop into e few stores and that´s it." Many drank buyers thank God that Target and Kmart were open. So, they are going home and at the same time 7 gunrunners from the garden come from the harbor, and so tired, and proud that they cannot even think about stealing these drank f***ers.

At the same time, nothing important happens in lower east side restaurants. Cliver´s gunrunner friend drinks too much and police officers are looking early Morning Grinch who broke into three restaurants on the same block on Manhattan´s Upper West Side. CarlG goes away with thousands of dollars. He enters to Bistro Cassis and ransacks the place. Mr. Colon, the owner, says: "It´s kinda like worrisome."

CarlG takes care of three restaurants on Columbus Avenue between 70th and 71st. He breaks through their back doors overnight and grabs all the cash he could find. CarlG has in his hands the total haul more than 5 000 d. Colon looks to the dark night: "A loss I a loss. It´s just, it´s a loss." The police officers in the 20th Precinct are looking at these cases as part of a pattern. Well, the camera took a picture of a man who threatens people with a knife on the Upper East Side. And another camera takes a picture of a knife-wielding man creeping around the sleeping man´s BR-home. Well, a man and a woman caught on camera punching victim in Bushwick. So, nothing much, oh, one garden youngster´s shots fires on a police station. No one is injured.

The Philosophy of the Kiss

We look at the computer view. There is a scene in Northern France. Then there comes a castle, 25 meters high and 150 meters weight. I say: "I think this shall be a much better dancing place compared to that army-thing. And surprise, surprise, guess what its price may be?!"

Yes, I have kissed Y, and Y have smooched back, and we have hugged, cuddled and I have squeezed, and colled, and embraced once, and held twice, but we haven´t really kissed.

There is St. Michael´s arrows everywhere. A vigorous exercise of my emotions says that there´s no more Nutella in the kitchen. It is momentum. La Lliona does not cry on the river. Our lips come together. Dreama is such a Crys, makes a quiver.

Vibration travels lip to lip, the chance, the dance, the show, blender bliss, burning flame with the kiss. It isattacking bolt from the blue. The fire attacks like the dogs of limbo. And love over lol is how we love to kiss. Kissing goes day to day, month to month, year to year, ages to ages.

MySoul: "MyVictoria, I love Y with all my heart and End of Time, no, not a 5-piece band full of wannabes from Delaware." *Oh malamente, báilame como si fuera la 'ltima vez.* I shall bring ten roses, nine real and one fake. And I will love Y till the last one dies.

A bum goes by, and he sees our kiss. He hurries away; he has wasted time, and he shall put on a real spurt. No need catchy indie pop, no need to check out stars, Broken Social Scene, and Metric. And no ayyy wagwam fam. Sweet with sweet delights in joy, so sadly it means gladly. We feel the shaking, trembling, and a githgake, aftershocks but not Hackensack thing. *Cara essa KISss e tao minha.*

L´Éternite, C´est la mer allée avec le soleil

It´s 2 pm. We listen to music and look at the same time local tv-channel. The news shows big lights from the army terminal. There are camera shots from dancers, Y and M, and a reporter talks something about a star and a tall fella, who isn´t a US-actor or -star. And a 13-year-old-cute-girl tells why she and her friends hang out tonight. A police officer says that classy and fabulous female persons had been lured there by the bunch of mercenaries. And the police officer shows me on the vid and says: "Do You know this soldier of fortune, if you do, please, give us the information needed - now."

The police officer promises to his fella-officers that he catches this baby boomer Merced border brother, who probably spends his day

spun ducky woo woo. Officer J. Douglas Scott warns good citizens of NYC: "These closed-minded, closet-cases, hicks have come to town." I laugh: "Awww man, you just got merced."

Red cravat gov. Cuomo comes to the picture. He agrees with Mr. Scott: "This is not an acceptable attitude for New York." And he begins to talk quickly about NYC must avoid the L train shutdown and every transit dream is still possible.

You say: "There goes your green card and bye-bye Y." I: "What green card? I have always come here through the consulate. And by the way, I know those engineers who review past plans for high-speed rails along the Empire Corridor. They are with CEO-project and mister Cuomo does everything he can to get that cost up to 14 billion d. 2/3 of those engineers come from Europe. I can assure Y, that we can put there more experts who shall say no to London speedway and to this one. So, no fixing for the subway. Cuomo understands money talks. He shall tap my shoulders and give a green card to me and I to him."

Y:"But think what Y did there." I: "I didn´t say anything wrong. I said that the mayor comes to our party. Hasn´t he." Y: "Y are a man of explanations, are Y?" I say: "No, I´m the man of great love. *L´Éternite. C´est la mer allée avec le soleil.*" Y: What does it mean, Y soldier of fortune?" I: "It means *la tu te degages. Et voles selon*: With Y, I fly." And a man of great love can easily explain to the not-stoopid New Yorkers this: 'It is against the law to ruin the party, which a block council has designed with the help of some pros, who did it as a voluntary job. And it is more criminal to charge poor me, member of the IOB and that project, who, in the bottom of my heart, invited the great mayor also there to enjoy the goodwill of the citizens of his town.' If Y do not believe me, don´t. But I talk with that Mr. Scott right now."

The Call

I say more: "And what are those little lights compared with the ball. Waterford Crystal sphere. The 12- foot - wide ball weighs are covered with 2,668 crystals illuminated by 32,256 LED lights and is stopped by seven-foot-tall "2020". That whole thing weighs in at 11.875 pounds, weight of an African elephant. And there is just LL Cool J, The Village People, and Alanis Morrisette, and police doancare a damn if the lighted ball drops 70 feet in a minute. And what about Dick Clark´s Rockin´ Eve. I love NYC and am sure NYC loves me. I call now Mr. Wonderful Scott. He is a good god Cameron and has a heart of gold in the end - and I donmean the song of Hybrid Theory and its Linkin Park words."

I say to Y: "I love Y so, and there are many events more now, like Broadway Hadestown, Carnesecca Arena St. Johns Red Storm vs. Butler Bulldogs, Yuja Wang, Carnegie Hall, The Stadium Tous: Motley Crue, Def Leppard, Poison & Joan Jett, and the Blackhearts, Broadway Hamilton, MetLife Stadium Kenny Chesney, Florida Georgia Line & Old Dominion, Westchester County Center The Harlem Globetrotters, J.B. Theater Alanis Morissette, Radio City Christmas Spectacular at Radio City Music Hall, at New World Stages The Gazillion Bubble Show, Big Apple Circus, Circus du Soleil, Yo Lang Tengo, Mean Girls from Virginia, Judgement Day - and no fucker cares if poor children fall through ice on a pond in for instance Queens park. Bab do Y know that Times Square is to be flooded with thousands of cops in a few days. How about helping poor people? Virtue makes virtues profitable.

NYPD will deploy those lazy uniformed police officers and counter-terrorism teams to keep millions N.Y. revelers safe, that commissioner Dermont Shea announced. How about putting our fine veterans there? No terrorist shall come then there, cos they should know, that there are not some puppets against them but fellas, whom you can play no games. Those fellas shoot you. And despite a threat, this advice New Yorkers and deep Brooklyn fellas surely like.

There are millions of eyes and ears out there that aid the police, so if anyone sees something, something that doesn´t feel right makes you uncomfortable. Those shutdown areas between 38th and 56th as revelers begin to take their spots in 65 views, ´pens´. NYPD shall take a heavy presence in the air about Times Square. Aviation units survey rooftops, and NYPD deploys its fleet of drones, Plainclothes officers shall appear, weapon teams from Emergency Service Units, explosive canine detection teams, radiation teams, and NYPD bomb squad. Think about all those units just in one place. Visitors to Times Square shall pass through multiple levels of security, access points located in 5 streets. There shall be police dogs, heavy weapon teams. Bab, politics gather medals and people of NYC shall be left without protection. And, and these b***stard accuse true veterans of criminal activities and so. Now I call Scott."

So + 1 718 258 4411 (no 212-like in tattoos) and there comes a voice: "63rd Precinct, how we can help You?" I: "Connect to Assistant chief R. Scott. Here is the man who he is looking for?" Silence, then there comes a river of words. I stop the flow: "Tell the fella, I come to meet him right now. I do not have time for your vain words. I shall be there in half an hour." Not far away is 1844 Br Ave. I send a message to officer David Balkin, cos I have heard he knows the neighborhood, its people, and its problems so well as only a policeman can. Time is 3:15 am, so no meeting hour, which begins at 7:30 am.

I look at Y: "Do Y want to join the party, MyVictoria? I´m going to meet some officers and do not forget to say hello when I see them. I reach one of them in his bio. So, I shall say to Davis - Hello! He does not complain about going the extra mile to complete his job."

The Morning Glory

It´s 4 am. We are in your apartment. We are in the kitchen. The great tune of punk against me vanished and there were red bra and thong, and Y undo your bra and laugh: "*Cuando era nino con conquistar el mundo, ahora me doy cuenta que tú eres mí mundo y me has conquistado.*" Y rock the boat, and the angels sing: "*Esta vida es mia, pero esta corazon es suyo. Te arresto en mi cama y te pongo las esposas. En esa curva le doy pam pam.*"

The opposite to love is more love, the opposite of faith is much more love, the opposite of life isn´t death but the resurrection of love. It isn´t a lack of love, but a lack of more love that makes boats sink. Love does not die of blindness and errors and betrayals, illness and wounds, weariness. It doesn´t die. So, millions of people must dream of eternity at least an hour per day.

We sleep and outside the flu widespread in NYC. More than 3 K cases this week. And above us comes the heavenly mark. The 2020 Waterford crystal ball arrives in Times Square, being roughly the same weight as a healthy killer whale. And there shall be Livestream Moby Dick Clark´s Rocking´ Eve.

I wake up after three hours of sleep. I had a dream where I shot the Waterworld Crystal down. And in that dream, I met Grant Rant. He was praising his exotic cars: "Stop wasting money on junk." I kick ass the hustle moth***cer muscle.

I go to the kitchen and kiss the doggy on the mouth and give him some good food, like steak and eggs. I also take 6 raw eggs and a banana shaken-shake. I begin to sing loud: "Each time we have a quarrel, it almost breaks my heart ... each night I ask the stars up above, why I have to be so much in love. I cried a tear for nobody but Y!" Somebody upstairs yells: "Shut up! A noice voice, but I must sleep, night turn!" I: "Ok, and thnx!"

The phone rings. I: "Yes, what can I do for Y?" The Voice: "Nothing, fuck off, I give the phone to her. I shall be there soon." I: "Excuse bro, isn´t that a little bit hasty of Y? Who Y are and what do Y want?" The Voice: "Birchy, one more time: take a hike, and stay out of my way. *Capiche*?" Soon the bell rings. I open the door. A fella about some centimeters lower than me looks at me: "Still here? Where is she? My cards she needs. Shut the door when Y go." I stand in front of Mr. Peng: "By the way, my name is Tapio. What´s yours?" A chapped moob looks at me: "No names, Y must be broke, a mot**ucker." I smile: "Still in business. And I do not mean birds or a brick. Are Y flipping birds my friend?" His lazy hand attacks me. I laugh. What a bad exercise for how-they-call-it "wake and break"?

I put my other feet on his other feet and turn left and my elbow and gravitation take care of rest. The well-eaten fella fells down like an American oak. I put my feet on him: "Now, tell me, are Y going to Time Square in the New Year Eve Celebration. Shall Y throw introverts? Eat a 1 200 d Times Square dinner? Do not panic. There is always something to do. Extrovert? Hm, perhaps introvert. Dare to go to bed early? Well, if Y are E-wert go to Felidia, or Heaven, Fleming´s Steakhouse, The Mermaid Inn, Serafina 105, Bustan. Early birds can go there at 5-7:30 pm. Well, Crave Fishbar always makes an oyster gray happy hour, Red Rooster, awesome Pappardelle, RDV, Daniel, Mexican Festival ... well, they all have 4 ½ stars. GrubStreet's round-up Prix Fixes has definite splurges, incl. a 1 200 d pers person six-course - dinner with a courtside view of the ball dropping, too. If Y are an introvert please order in a 200d lasagna from Union Square Cafe, cos Y deserve to celebrate Y. An extrovert: go to Concert for Peace, introvert: NY Philharmonic's tribute, culture vulture: e: poetry reading marathon. I: The Film Forum; if Y go out with a bang E: free fireworks with a hoard of fellow Brooklynites; I: "Flee, Forbes has rounded up a slew of very quiet places. I do speak no more. Go. Y have much to do." The fella runs out of the door and does not watch the steps.

Madame Manager and the Intangible Cultural Heritage

I take my phone and begin to calculate how much I have lost money, cos of coming to NYC. Just 5 200 dollars. That's nothing. Hm, how about putting more money into marketing.

The phone rings on the table: "Victoria's residence. How are you, I hope everything is foin? If you are looking for ... What? You're a manager. Really? Let us not be weary in doing good. Does your star play ice hockey, tree hockey, gridiron? Aha ... sorry, I go and tell her. Y want to tell yourself. Well, please come. I go to the shop and buy something. Perhaps fish, Italian salad, and ice-cream??? Fifteen minutes. Lady, for you, I'm really ripping & running. Always nice to meet Y. See Y soon. Yes, I can then introduce myself."

The manager is coming, and MyVictoria sleeps like a baby. I do not disturb her. And Doggy sleeps, too. So, I go to Fulton Mall, Empire

Stores. Nice coffee warehouse, I want gastronomical delights, goods like animal hides, and coffee from all over the world. Cecconisdumbo pizza, some whipped ricotta + truffle honey, I run back. Oh, there is Fellow Barber for dogs. Now I understand better Victoria. I run, 5 minutes to 8:50 am ... five minutes to make something to that manager.

I wash my teeth, comb my hair, wash my face, hone my nose and forehead so they do not shine, someone hand pressings from the ground. That´s it. Pizza smells great and ricotta-thing and ice-cream are ready. Bell rings. I open the door.

Ah, lovely lady. "What a great pleasure, Madame, I have waited for this for a long, long time ..." The lady off-the house: "Nice to meet Y, who was it." I: "Pardon Maaamm, it went over, may I introduce myself: Tapio Tiihonen, king of the forest, under the Stella Polaris. I have got acquainted with Mademoiselle, and very elegant June at Christmas."

She: "Very interesting, you´re are a client, who has traveled a long trip for short vi ..." I: "No, no, and many more nos, of course not. If I may call Y by the first name, or just You. I´m not prayer or paying for anything ..." She: "I see, do Y know, if this happens often ..." I: "Madame, this started all so wrong, perhaps we eat something. Please, come." I take her hand and so we go to the kitchen. I: "Look what I have for our great breakfast. Sorry, no herring and tobacco and so, but please, sit. I bring Y Italian Lungo. It wakes your brains up. In *Legion Etrangere* we called it *café allongé*. Heh, I put there on that thing some creamy hazelnut gelato, si, and frozen yogurt, and it really melts with steam – I call it the delight of the day."

Madame Manager sits and drinks the coffee: "Tapio T, this is marvelous! This really wakes me up, ups." I: "I did not put there any freshments, so no need to be afraid of police while you are driving your car in the busy streets of Br. Hm, and Y are Ms. Junes Manager, I assume. About two years, yes, oh take this pizza, I have put there some Cinnamon from India. Ahhh, Y love it, great ..."

She speaks straight: "Thanks for your conviviality, but if you aren´t a client, so are Y a neighbor or a lucky tourist or a nightstand ... So, I cannot talk wit..." I: "Please take this squid wafer and this Sardinian great delicacy. In this time of the year, they put in Sardinia and Corsica honey to the chocolate, not just in a certain day, or hour but certain second, hundred years traditions make miracles. Do Y like it?" She: "This is (a teardrop comes from her eye) this is so lovely." I make a bow, French way: "In army my name was de Hauteville, and I had many noble friends there, who look some adventure to their life. So. The Italian kitchen and French cuisine were there happily ever after married. So lovely marriage, no quarrels at all.

Y know, Francois Pierre La Varenne and Marie-Antoine Careme and appellation *d´origine controlée*, and Auguste Escoffier and *haute cuisine, cuisine bourgeoise* ... Yes, please, eat that intangible cultural heritage. Think Y Madame, pastry cooks, *charcutiers, patisserie*, terrine, bisque, foie grass, but not *Croque monsieur*." I look at her eyes: "Their hardness are melting, and some romantic thing gives its birth and begins to rise and shine. So, I: "I am not a night or an hour stand, who band a chick with the intention of never seeing or talking to June ever again."

She: "So how a clepe Y, Mr. de Hauteville?" I: "Y can call as it pleases Y. It isn´t important. More important is that we here have fallen in love. Y know romantic kiss and apocalyptic night. So, the fault, dear Madame, isn´t in the stars, but in her- and myself. I promised to show her some European hinterland and blackwater. We made a golden deal." She: "A Golden Deal? Signed and so?" I: "Not yet, but as Y are here, Y can conform it, on your behalf, ok?"

She shows her temperament: "What is this, a Happy New Year joke!?" I: "Oh, no, no, and no, take a shot of this." I give her, not a love potion but, as we call it in the army, burning star. There goes my concentrated dose for a bad day. She smiles: "Yes, Victoria has found somewhere a true Travis Pastrana. Do Y mean that my business is over with Victoria and Y just come here and win a prize for a song? Y are out of your mind, Mr. Tapio, hahaha."

Same language, same happy joy: "Do y mean that I´m the team acquired player, client, who was like a 4th or 5th draft pick, for a song, but I prove myself now couple troublemaker who eventually not help Y win the championship? On the contrary, I help Y make money and give it to us, too. To this very day, Y have put it in your pocket, why not put it in ours, too. Let´s make this a great adventure, film it, and give it for the common good and teaching. Somebody clever enough shall find a classical happy end. I give you a proposal some sunny d."

She: "Hm, Y really think Y are smart enough to use that bad and stupid word ´film´. I prefer to watch films made by underground directors at my local bijou. In those pictures, men are corrupted with lust and more lust and money. And now Y suggest that we shall do an opposite movement and claim that it stands for the Internet Movie Database or what?" I: "I do not claim anything, no Snapchat claims thanks things, I just say that we are in love and there is nothing even Our Smiling Friend can do about it. It just happens, Y know. Death may cure for life, but life can also cure of death, which is just a part, like testicles of life, great, cute, funny. And how can I deny everything and just be a little bitch like gang shitter tv-millionaire? Two days, and a proposal, ok. Well, that fine. Hm, now Y may tell perhaps something about what goes in your mind?"

She: "V has broken our deal, in every possible way. She doesn´t respect our contract, comes her own ways. Do not want to do as she is clearly asked to do. If somebody makes a deal with me, then that somebody is under that deal. I ordered the bank to suspend her account. And now Y say this. You are ridiculous." I: "Well, do as Y wish, but I hope Y wait those two days. Then I promise Y think twice before Y shall send New Year Promises to your employer, Madame Employee."

She says: "V instructs her bank to make a payment. The bank refuses now to follow her instructions, and Y can call it suspending, freezing or whatever Y want. I explain to the bank that there is a dispute over who owns the money in the account and who has use of the account. I´m the third party with a reasonable claim to an interest in the account. I design operations and cash flows go as I wish, and if not, our deal has been broken, and I have the right claim for suspension. Do Y understand?"

I say: "No and yes. If it shall be made simple: there are more vids and pics and even those which Y see, and Y cannot see the cash flow as Y are ordered in the deal to see it. So, you do not get your profit, %. There is smoke on tax residency and related information, the nature of that entity and the tax residency and related information of the individual, Y, she holds that account for or so. Y say, Y made the budget and found out that Y pay taxes from the money that Y do not get? These little problems?"

She: "Yes, I did my budget and find out." I: "So you plan, direct, oversee fiscal health of a business unit, division, department, or an operating unit within an organization. And you make at the same time her budget, too. Y control her in a fiscal way." She: "Of course, and we have a deal, and at the same time with LA studios, so they are bonded together. And all the four parties´ budget must follow that deal. And there are more, there are other studios, too. So, I'm a manager here in LA, but what about those other, and what about she says she goes away to the east, to, hm, Miami, and so I stay on the lead, on the

California beach playing. I´m part of that deal here, not everywhere and cannot be."

I: "Please, stop now. Y take care of all her fiscal things but do not take care of it. But Y deal says so, why do not Y do as your employer sees it so. Why Y think like an employer that that is only true what Y see.

Perhaps Y must do not talk. Draw a picture of Victoria´s whole net and structure, and then put cash flow, and its time and place. One big picture, no tens of thousands of loose words. In the army, in the heart of logistics, there is a room. Every day the main officers go there, and there is a so-called interactive board, they put their HoloLenses on and see at the same time all details and stuff with their calculations, and they see that interactive board. There comes every minute, every second, more information that board lives on life. Please go to Micro Center in 850 3rd Ave and buy from there what I order now."

Go and Buy

I take a phone and put the no. +1 347 563 9880: "Good Morning, so Y are open at 1800. Here is Tapio Tiihonen, I book there The Elite Screens WB60V that with a 120-degree viewing angle suitable for a large room. It sends everything y to write to mobile device. Ok, there comes a lady, to buy it soon. An hour. And then serve her HoloLens 2 with Dynamics 365 Remote Assist. Hololens 2 and Hololens 2 Development Edition. And if there is a better board, and quicker and bigger, show it to her too." I continue: "Make those Holens 2 system two, thank you very much. I appreciate Y."

I look at Madame You: "Two holo lenses and one interactive board. They normally give Y with those some normal computers and tablets. And come to install them. Y must think of the room where to put the board. The board is Victoria´s business heart, there Y and she can read all, 24/7/365. It shall coast about 4 500 dollars. But no need to calls, meetings, long quarrels. In one big picture, Y see it all. Put the HoloLens on and Y can talk with Victoria, and she to Y, even if Y are in the north pole, and she in the south pole. And from those holo lenses, Y and she see that board all the time. That thing updates itself all the time. So nowadays schools, good once have it, and children love it. So have some fun and learn the board and holo lenses. Every schoolgirl and - boy learn them someday. Okay. Shall Y go to buy them?"

She looks at me: "I, I appreciate a lot what Y just said." I: "They pay that 4 500 dollars back in time and space. You have no problem anymore with time and space. You are present just now, not yesterday or tomorrow. There is your living business in front of Y. And what is there isn´t for anybody else. Well, perhaps we let MyVictoria sleep a little more. Y know, when Y sleep your brains do the most of their work, they update Y. Have a nice day. I appreciate Y liked my cakes and so."

When her high heels´ clatter stop being covered, MyVictoria comes to the kitchen: "Oh, MyTapio, we had a wonderful time. But I´m sorry, my clients shall need their services soon. Do you understand? I have some issues with my manager. All this takes very much of my time. I can make some coffee for us. If it is alright with Y." I kiss Y, and say: "What more do I want?"

Well, we sit, and I tell you about one client and one manager, the first one shall not see Y later, but the later does, B.E.Z.

"MyVictoria, guess where Madame Manager is?" I ask U. Y look not much surprised: "Drinking more her morning Coffee?" I: "She flew to

Micro Center at 850 3rd Ave." Y: "Why? What did Y say to her?" I: "I just said that your quarrels end there. And she believed me." Cos little sums from little means shall produce as much as great sums from great means. And that's why I'm always at your service and ready for every good work.

Y: "How can it be?" I: "she had 4 500 d." Y: "Y gave the bitch 4,5 d. Are Y out of your mind?" I: "She was outto dosh."

I: "Everything is good all gold. With her went there the reason why. Her home-made math changes on interactive board to open knowledge-profit. She runs for chilly dosh."

Y: "Now I missed my bus. Gotta run." I: "No need to go. 'The bitch' rings the bell soon. One picture on the living board gives a vision." Y: "Vision for what?" I: "it calculates your every movement's value. Y see what motion is worth of money and worth of growing money."

The bell rings. There she comes. Y: "What now? Are Y going to charge me face to face?" She says: "Here are the machines that finally shall prove I'm right. Let these fellas put the interactive board here and I I put there my budget-calculations, and this Mr. Hauteville here is our witness. We can check your criminal acts from the interactive board's big picture. That also is a prove to the bank."

The Big Picture

The fellas put the big picture up. I help the Manager to find a way to summon the data. I ask her to push the update button.

That digital whiteboard makes graphics and statistics and summons the whole budget with cash flows and forecasts. The manager looks shocked. The board shows that many cash flows Y do in your porn star carrier. It shows spontaneous ways and elegance, a new way, but Manager's dealings show easy solutions with no cash flow profit forecasts. Her acts are common and used by many.

She becomes a little bit restless. I try to calm her down: "More of Corsica's chocolate cake, it helps You also swallow this." She takes a piece and you take another - piece. Y say: "Tapio, this is delicious." I smile:" It is from a beautiful island Corsica. There the man who found America and great Napoleon were both born. On that island is amazing weather-change; in the mountains, You can ski, and on the beach let the sunshine in. It is a perfect place for producing excellent honey." The Manager: "So, this board is bad, it doesn't give the right results." I: "It isn't a Middle Ages court of heavenly law. The board just shows how earthly things are and five an earnest testimony to us in this present life."

Y say: "So what can we do with that board? Throw it out of the window?" I say: "If Y want. Those numbers tell something else, too. They go with the porn business, not with the normal business- like cash flows. What to do so business shall go hand in hand? The marketing must consider things that are related to normal advertising. That is possible in literature, festivals, theatre, sports but cos of fake IDs, fake business cards, and divorce papers, there are certain rules, which separate blowjobs, dog style and so from another artistic life. It is anytime, anywhere, but it is under assault: the business of pleasure is a risk to the young, cos of those running studios, directing firms, and the next generation of adult companies. DVD sales are down 50 % from last year, piracy takes care of that. Sex-related sites make 60 % of daily web traffic, so this board is for Y. It calculates what you calculate in 10 000 years. And one picture tells where your business goes. Tech has attacked porn, so use the tech. The board is the answer, not a big enigma."

I continue: "And Mrs. Madame, what about me? Another threat here? What can Devil or porn-mafia do against true Love? Perhaps they can declare 13 billion dollars war and charge Love to court. What they can say: hey, I looked out my window the other day and saw this Love trying to boast my ride, so I made a killing shoot. This porn star got in love, and BOOST. Tapio boosted our star. Ayee must kill the Nab."

Mrs. Manager wonders: "If these numbers are right, what is my job?" I: "Y keep the news on the sunny side of the street. Y and Manager have a lot to talk about. Hm."

Meanwhile, 3 pm, 2 million people are in Times Square, broadcasts, Clark, and Harvey give their voices to the spectacle. Some track fire in the tunnel between Queens and Br alarm firefighters make their day. If you go to World Trade Center take A, C, E 2, and 3 lines.

Madame & You have a conversation: Y: "Tapio & I are going to Provence. I shall take the HoloLens with me, so no hidden agenda. It is a place where I have always wanted to go - with the right person. There it shall happen." Madame is curious: "What? Death end, reason and reality, separate interests, wasted time, and money?" You do not care:

"Food and wine shall give better inspiration than in complexity. Just simplicity." Madame´s reason finds its silence.

I serve ladies more fruits and juice and coffee and biscuits. I try to give something interesting: "Madame nobly loving has born in court. There is VictoriaCourt, and there were courts in Aquitania, Champagne, Normandy, Norman kingdom of Sicily (Roger de Hauteville), and the heart of those courts was Provence. There born courtly love, amor courteous: love with erotic desire and morally attainment, passionate and disciplined, humiliating and exalting, human and transcendent, fire with chivalry amusement. In Provence, stormy and fruition attacked and mixed lust and eagles mind infirm desire, which cannot be taken by beak or nail, body trembles. Madame, that love has now come back in the higher will, expressing its spirit in courtly, woovly nightly kissing way."

And balls drop at Times Square, and millions and millions of people cheer. And Madame sees the kiss of the year and her resistant melts and blows up and burns away. She says: "Just a kiss?" I laugh: "Hey, a glooming peace this morning with it brings, go hence, to have more talk of these glorious things." Madame leaves from our lover's net.

Streetlife

You tap the board: "It says that net must be updated." I laugh: "Real guardian of the courtly kiss. Y & I must go and see the IOB-president and her bogue. A preliminary contract must be done as soon as possible. No windy air between them & me and thee."

Meanwhile, a fella, wearing black and white, attacks a 71-year-old woman. LvBrat-brother, other warriors call him SlimBFat, punch the woman in the side of the head, breaking her jaw, on a pavement in the Prospect-Lefferts Gardens. It happened not far from an empty police station. The police force is in the Times Square, so streets are left for the gang-, block- and building-warriors. SlimBFat calmly walks away hiding in a grey sweatshirt and tracksuit bottoms.

Some brothers of Nine Trey make a social club visit and left four men died at the scene. This happens in the Crown Heights two blocks away from the empty police station. The Police at the Times Square does not have time to think vain motives. It is forbidden to go to Times Square with baggage and alcohol, but there is Mr. Smith with 100 000 d worth of birds and he does well in his daily business.

Good Singer Tekashi, who has Fefe and Stoopid, is in an almost empty police station. T/Hernandez says angrily: "You call these nine things crimes, but I did this to increase my standing in Nine Trey, and of course NT-brothers have guns. You discharged those guns, are Y stoopid.

I helped brothers rob people at gunpoint as part of a pledge, no big deal. And yes, I paid a Riley to shoot at a rival member just to scare him in Manhattan. Yeah, I participate in the sale of a kilogram of booger sugar."

He smiles: "Can I go now. Yeah, yep, I apologize to the court, to anyone who was hurt, to my family, friends, and fans for what I have done and who I have let down, but can I go now." The police understand T, who has 15,5 million followers on Instagram, and Day69 among the top-sellers on iTunes. The fella likes to make the sex-vids also, the age of those involved isn't an issue at all. No need to block a good cause. T goes.

These things do not shadow Br College's Policing and Social Justice Project claims that the presence of gangs is overstated and demonized by the police and media. Supporting activists are winning the fight for the rights of those who may be legitimately connected to gangs and crews, the authors call for abolishing the NYPD's gang unit, ending gang takedowns, discontinuing precision policing, and eliminating police gang databases.

The Knight's Proposal

No need to talk about Pride parade, or Ljina and Nick Wallenda's 25-here wire walk or body positive catwalk in Times Square, I call to the IOB's Madame Ottersten: "Hello, Mrs. President, yes, here is Tapio. Yes again. I do not give up easily, do I? I have a proposal for you. I have studied one board and another and found a melody between them. Yes, that's right like shoes tapping in airports, nice melodies. Frankfurt good, but Heathrow very bad. Yes, you are the boss; yes, I must be on the line; yes, you are busy, but can I continue.

I have found a Charmante Star, yes, mad hot, and I have fallen in love with her. No, she isn't milking my money. And I'm not pushing anything. No m8, really, no charity love, but love and chivalry courtly love. Cannot you see it? I'm in love and, and she is, too. What, Y imbecile, stupid cow shazoo. I'm not a teenager in love. Madame, in this angry sea, grows the most sensitive pearl, the precious outstanding white pearl. I rode between the barley sheaves. The sun and love came dazzling thro´ the leave and flamed upon the brazen greaves of me."

Mrs. Pressident: "Proposal? Mr. Knight."

I: "Well, information channels give us the opportunity to multiply the possibilities among the rural and national identities. We shall advise people to put the right words here and there. MyLove, the StarActor, connects east and west, south and north, and all the rest. There are many kinds of stories about Fonenoy-La-Joute, Ascona, Hay-on-Wye, The King, Obidos, The King & The Queen, La Fournier, Alcaravan, Cuisery castle, La Charite-sur-Loire, Monmorillion, Ascona-Locarno-festival, Bredevoort-festival, Clunes.

There are many kinds of groups which MyVictoria can also market, in her own pages. She is a pro and she has also other pros marketing herself in that sexy way. There must be time and space marketing together and separately. The international business has secret, invisible, known fronts, but that´s not ab issues, cos the cash flows show them. The problem is the hidden agenda. Book towns work in an old-fashioned way. They do not show themselves much in the net, Twitter, Instagram, Facebook, Linkedin, but there is not open knowledge = open marketing. Open marketing is the concept and strategic marketing. My proposal´s preliminary contract is this:

V & T love adventure shall be put together like Light novels, Erotic Romance, Picaresque novel, Hollywood novel, and Confession. The cash flows and shows hidden borders and scales and duplications, multi cations, timelines, timewaves, focus-points, season bests, year and even century best, cash flows go those streams. There is your business brain-system. Cash flow goes with cultural data activating groups of business bodies, processing, integrating, and coordinating. There are cultural data centers where cash flow enters. What happens when the cultural data, cash flow "the wave" reaches a cultural group of actions "the synapse"? Heh, heh, it provokes a small abound of neurotransmitter molecules, so there comes something totally new information with totally new connections and groups. That new information is prior information to the other people brains and they copy it.

Mrs. President becomes angry: "You be trippin´!?"

I kiss MyVictoria: "No, but I am in love. A love story has many kinds of nappy roots: Nordic countries love, southern Sweden love, Southern Norwegian love, Northern Germany love, middle Germany, border French-German love, Belgium-Holland, Southern England, Wales, Scotland, France has five different love zones, Spain four, Italia three. Around Barcelona, there are three love centers. Courtly love is for them, the USA, and the world. If this sounds cow mild, there is more smash the pasty, ´laying the pipe´ - and ´crush it out´ -thing. And if it is too much, put there narb and nrb and the god. Our board measures the feelings."

Mrs. President: "You talked about those Book Towns groups and their nets and zones and you argued that they are there but we don´t see them, and you argue that cash flows and cultural data can be the best find were the biggest feelings are. I know that in France they have made holograms about loving text messages of people in Nancy. But it doesn't prove anything."

I: "Connect marketing with those, there begins a big Fuego. I success that this actor's manager and You shall meet. I tell You later, now I must go, catch the fat and loud, black and proud day."

Robbing the Bank

Y: "Can my manager and your president meet?" I: "I do not mean they evermore peep through their eyes, and laugh like parrots at a bag-piper, and they'll not show their teeth in way of smile, though some wise menswear the jest be laughable. I mean they are but loveable human beings. They are both sellers, so profit lives, and everywhere else value dies. If they meet, they cannot cheat each other. It shall be an honest conversation."

I take an apple and am ready to go when the phone rings. I say: "Hello, please come upstairs. Everything is ready for Y." Y: "Who was it? I shall have bags." I: "The first one is coming up. Seems to be a blackfella. Well." I open the door. He looks at me: "Rocketman. Hey, fuck you." My fist goes straight to the nose. He attacks. I kick to his stomach. He takes a second hit, and he goes to Wonderland. I take him to my shoulders. And carry him to the parkand throw there. People walk very fast. I do not. No need to fear the police. They are in the T S. I run to MyVictoria: "I must go now. See Y later. What about those clients? I'm not going to be in bed with Y and an unlucky guy." She: "I tell Y. I tell Y when 7 digits or FML."

Well, I must make a very fast green. Talking and the board just marks the achievements. So, achievement must change their course right now. I open my phone: "Cliver? Do Y want to rob the bank? It´s very easy to be a millionaire but much harder to earn in ten minutes 5 million dollars and say: ´Hey I borrowed this. I'm both the employer and the employee.´"

Y look at your window and wonder where MyTapio is now putting his head. The doggy jumps to the window frame, too. He liked very much that Spanish steak I gave him. Yeah, brush four 12-ounce boneless rib-eyes or strip steaks with olive oil, season with salt and pepper, and rub the f***cking thing with Spanish Spice Rub on, hm, on the side, yes. Then, how it went, grill rub-side down over high heat, 3 to 4 minutes, then flip and grill 5 to 6 more minutes (for medium-rare). I hope it went right! Serve it to Doggy with Sherry Vinegar Steak Sauce - and I get a friend for my lifetime.

Had Y a clue what I´m app to, Y should abandon me to despair. Well, Time is 15:00. So, we have three bank hours to accomplish this devilish act. One of my army friends did this in French and get caught. And his noble father made long discussion with a police chief before they turn him loose. Had he been a poor fella, he should have been in jail for a long, long time. I pray MyMightySmilingFriend for forgiveness but feel that right now I do not have any friends - well, except Cliver. He says: "At last, I almost thought that your street-cred has been gone. Man, this is so bread in the face." I: "To 13th Ave, 11219, time goes fly ..."

I think: "A man must do what a man must do. No more clients. What if she wants them, anyhow? Then Doggy must go, and I shall buy to her a Baskerville hound."

Banks Bancorp. inc. are 11,71 d, going down 0,32. The bank director talks on the phone: "Quarterly dividends are expected to be maintained at 0,17 per share implying a high dividend yield of 5,7 %. Oh, yes, liability sensitive balance sheet is expected to drive earnings growth next year. Loan growth offers support to the bottom line." Then he sees a tall white man with a brandy suit and a suspicious mixed-blooded fella with a tough smile.

We walk quickly to AmTrust Bank. Nobody remembers anymore how the bank was shut down by the Office of Thrift Supervision and was placed into receivership. This nobody may say that today is the revenge day. I go to the bank director: "Hello my friend, I want a personal loan. You said that when we´re financially stuck, these loans can help you in a pinch. We do not need lenders or loan connectors but that loan right now. So, you promised the best terms and lowest interest rates and best personal loan available. Let´s go to your room. This fella is a gunrunner and you are a chief, so we are even. Let´s go. Or he shoots your balls out. Keep on smiling." We go upstairs. I mentor in my head: "How strange are the ways of the man in love; its good deed shall be my joy and my crown."

We are in the director´s room. And there two symbols: a gun and a signed loan paper.

I say: "Fast now. Go. I change some words with this fella." Cliver runs downstairs and takes the loan and buzz off with his stolen bike. Now there are me and the director. Heat is on, as the angle of the dangle. Yes, h is o. I look at Mr. D. Yes, he´s big in banking. About as big as they get. So, all the way to the top of the pyramid, and I do not mean girls arrange themselves perpendicularly. And this D is not a Mack Daddy, not at all Glen Frey. Sweet drops from my forehead to the eyes."

He says: "This is your judgment day. Death ride." I'm easy on the eyes: "Well, in my tombstone shall read: this man gotta violence as the birth present, and still, the purpose of this fucker was to be useful, honorable, compassionate, to have it make some difference that you have lived and lived well. And you fucked my worries and pains away." I look at my watch: 17:05.

At the same monkey's birthday, Cliver finds friends, who give him something. The upper: "You got a Bryana." Cliver gives them 5 million d. Now he has something very hot if he shows it in court. Oh, Moses, smell the roses, they give him the key. Cliver's hands tremble. In front of BCGA Concept Corp, he takes the burning key off his pocket and gives it to Weez-very Crispy Gangsta -fella. And behind him smiles 'Murder', 'Flash' and 'Smokey'.

It is very easy to murmur: why do we care about these warriors' lives? They destroy other people's lives and social structures. They're just a bunch of messed up children, turned criminals. So, lock'em all up and toss the key. Well, this key has a different story. Somebody may say more grist to the mill. Cliver looks and sideway gunrunner, he has finger loose on the trigger. Damn.

There is a table, and there is a gun laying on top of a Bible, several bullets, a scale of drugs, and a book of the law of attraction. Some Weez-very smoke Mari and drink beer. One fella is bleeding, cos he has been shot in the leg. He has a bloody knife in his hand. He puts the knife in his leg and searches the bullet. Two fellas have taken their shirts off. The other fella is from the Trinitarios. If he wins, he can go. If not, the river swallows the body.

Three fellas lie on the street, after hanging googly out and do smoke. But Cliver has been at memorial ceremonies were these members mourn the death of Simbaa. He had died after being stabbed 20 times inthe chest in Williamsburg-Brooklyn. Flash comes to Cliver, gives him a bag: "g2g."

Murder holds a gun that is bought for 250 USD in the street after guys from another gang stabbed one of his friends in the neck. Smokey looks after Cliver: "Sooth the mother***cer." Murder says: "No." Smokey: "Whyn´t?" Cliver jumps on the bike. And at 17:45 Cliver goes with the baggage to the reception desk. He opens the baggage.

Ohjhuu, cabbage. There comes a guard: "Can I help you? We shall close in ten minutes?"

"Yeah, where is the wastepaper basket? I have bagged, not that, but my dwell." The guard goes away. Cliver finds from the bag oxytocin love, c11h15no2, A5 hour orgasm, weed, Coca-Cola, XTC, MDMA carbide. They go. 17:55 he goes to the table. He takes 100 d, thousand, a hundred thousand.

The guard comes. The lady of the table says: "You are giving back the money, which You just loaned?" Cliver gives the bank director´s signed approval and hopes the best: "Yes." 4 million, five, six, seven, eight, nine. Ten million and 2 hundred thousand. Cliver: "Put to this account of Tapio Tiihonen 6 million, leave 4 million. Give me 200 000 d." Cliver takes the cards. Then he comes to us with the guard.

The director chief says to the guard: "We handle this personal loan, please Carl, you can go to look Islanders vs. Buffalo. Hope the Islanders win." The flabbergasted guard goes away. The bank director called Bop says: "Here is your money back check. And here is 200 000 d more. I take care of running money things. You have gone too deep. I charge you about money launderin´. You have now accounts. So, nothing can help you."

He gives 200 000 d to me and Cliver takes a picture. I say: Well when you charge us cayman island fellas you must explain also why you gave me 200 000 dollars. Bro, we are partners. Your bank got over double what you loaned. This is now our common bank, not those 71 others in NYC."

Cliver and I bog off. I say: "What did Y change to that 5 million d?" Cliver: "A key." I: "How can you be alive?" Cliver: "Murder, Flash, and Smokey are my friends."

Damn Skippy

Cliver drives Caddy ct6 Hardtop Comfortable. And he says: "Do you know where the key was?" I think: "To some drugstore?" Cliver shakes his head: "It isn't for a street pharmacist. It was for the mainstream that has taken 12% of YouTube. It is the Key for the Meet-Eegan piracy laboratory. They steal porn, but nobody says it loud and goes to the blacklist."

I ask Cliver: "You got the Key. From whom?" Cliver: "Well, Meet-Eegan didn't have a deal with YB (Terror Gang Villans), who are neighbors of Weez-very Crispy Gangstas, but believe or not they were GSC – G Stone Crip's warriors. Think behind the Get Guap Family. And they made a deal also over Rock Starz Forever Chasing Money. This is a ... how Y deep Brkners say it ... a sacrilege." I smile: "Two questions more: why you were there and how can y pay 5 MD and get 10,2 MD?" Cliver: "Smokey's idea. If there had been a member of Weez-Very Crispy Gangstas they should have killed him as gladly as 816 Crew or YG (YGZ-Young Goonnz's warrior. But I'm from the gang, much worse than BDS (Broad Day Shooters). They tango down twice, even thrice before they pop a cap."

Well, they had those Mari-ideas, and the Porn-geek has cash, cos he can do what he wants. Caddy stops again near your door. High-five and Clever go - with the 4-million-dollar -smile on his face. The medallion around his neck is a real lucky thing.

The Million Dollar Kiss

I run the floors. And Doggy's tale swings. We kiss, and kiss more." Y: "Where have Y been?" I: "We went to 13 Ave and get lucky. Director welcomed us. Then we made a deal, and Cliv went to the front of the money, and then we got luckier and doubled up the loan and gave theloan back. Look, here in this picture, the director tries to bribe me, with 200 000 d. Isn't it marvelous? And I got a card. Really good customer service, an hour deal, account, and ATM & Visa Debit Card, not with CREDIT, unfortunately."

You aren't convinced: "How a deep Brkner can get so lucky and do that?" I: "Cliver had a cueta, and he didn't need to drop his cueta after having shot the fool, cos the director was a Wiseman and viewed the thing in a practical light. And he also mercilessly diss the things which deserve it. No loopholes, non-core jobs, and it got approved by someone higher in the chain of command, and he opened to new information and data and weight it impartially. There was an objective evaluation of risks, and we avoid getting bogged down in a discussion of minor issues, and the deal didn't die, cos of a lack of momentum. Bab, there was a real Key takeaway. No M&A considerations and Implications, just an agreement."

Y: "So. Y made a money laundering. But how he allowed that and how Y and Cliver got an Argo's cash? Drugs?" I: "No, no, no, 3Ni Trinitarios

Latin king Niiio´s Malos, just one who fights with one Weez-Very Crispy Gangastas, or they are fighting right now. Question of porn-piracy. One fella took Weez-Very under his wings." Y: "How can a porn-baron make a deal with those?" I: "How not? Mr. Meet-Eegan can, or he thinks that. That happens. And Cliver´s brothers-in-arms, Looney, Chucho, Smokey, and Buckets had a long day at meetings and rest in their apartments. I'm sure East-Side-tribe-leader Smokey sits at the Bushwick Housing Projects and keeps his warriors from smoking anything else that is not Mari. He wants them to be able to protect the hood and defend the Key at any time. So. The porn-piracy shall grow fast and that´s the story of the lab-K."

Y: "So just Mari deals in a housing building and my profession´s dark side piracy deals, too. You are going to smoke my business?" I: "Yes dear, I love Y so."

It is 22:00, and the third day is breathing its last hibiscus. Y find the boto-sword, and I have my no-stink wrinkle, and we get winded, wet bodies buffet each other, my finger touches your lips, and Y say: "No clients?" Well, if it is true, that to be the President of the United States, is to act as an advocate for a blind, venomous, and ungrateful client. Then why not?

The Fourth Day

The Sun rises late and sets early

Putting together Sex and NonSex

It is at 8 am. Y wake me up: "I must go. I have an appointment with some sponsors. I must represent our latest movies, give autographs and some speeches. I must be behind a desk and look - attractive. I shall sell the product and be a good associate and a member of the group." I: "That's your natural gift, you warm Miyu, kinda space. You are boob-bombastic in your attire, and flamboyant. Oh, if I compare my byah with that Im a flunet ring ie, bullshiter, crap talker, ringo Linquist, bullshit fantasist, real poobleater ... Babies begin to cry, mamas get nervous and men look at their phone to ring the powers-that-be." Y ask: "Y do not wanna come and market with me, so I can see your real skills? Are Y hidden your head in the ground like an ostrich?"

I: "If I tell these WISE and lusty and horny people that actually my heart look more to the Academy, Defion International, Aegis Defense Services, Triple Canopy, G4S Security Solutions and even to the army last night party areas (72nd Precinct) 3NI, KCF (67th Precinct), Boss City Bomb Gand (90th Predict), Get Touch Boyz (113rd Precinct), M-18 (115th Precinct), Shiesty Ave/Shiesty Over Everything (44th Precinct) and even those mild Columbus Ave Gang -members (24th Precinct) and say that lusty fat fu'**ers aren't my type of friends at all, that should be a funeral for me and – over great and beautiful looooV MyVictoria."

Y: "You're hiding something." I: "I hang around and think something about business. By the way, Y can good Spanish, and one fella from the Uruena Book Town had just sent me his Doctoral thesis in Spanish. Y can enlighten me on a bid. I have thought about our connection to book towns. One great way is via festivals, of course, and even more relevant is sports & dancing. I have begun to make links to schools and sporting clubs and teams. By the way, do Y dance in night clubs still? Like Sugardaddy's Gentleman Club, Rick's Cabaret, Sapphire, Pumps Bar, The Slipper Room, Hunk-O-Mania, FlashDancers. Show Place, FlasDancers, Foxy, Le Rouge, Headquarters."

You push me out of the door. I go with my modern suit on and hands in the pockets, like a Great Depression fella, thinking more and less vain things. Well, it is very hard to try to put book town schools together with 3-star strip clubs. It may be must easier to link them with athlete-teams and -clubs.

I must meet at Suggardaddy's fake-butts-and-tits. And there are those Dr. Miamis and Dr. Dykmans, and services specials. That hookah must be ok, although the club is clean or not, the ambiance of a Motel 6 lobby and needs a serious cleaning. How book towns NYC-visitors should like about wet and filthy bathrooms without paper towels? The sound system is so muffled. Do they like food frozen and then fried fare? What do chairmen of the boards think of hotter girls kissing each other? Of course, women, Latinas & Black, are good and have fake asses. Do Book Towns' management like to get to secure the bag? What is the situation while provoking the rain, a pep rally? Do those Europeans like real big asses? But the truth is these Latinas have fishnets, so strong dancers make weak fellas drink Jack Daniels on the rocks and Tito's vodka sodas. Do these book town dilettantes like to throw money and make it rain? Shall they be afraid of the hookah fella who is dope and the cameraman who is cool as hell? Shall a London-businessman say: "Not trashy and ratched at all."

I continue thinking: "These girls do not wait too long for the money. They move on to another client and potential thing. These eye candies give pleasure to these sport - and business fellas in this bizarro world. Lap dances, awesome energy, that´s it. I do not want to think about trashy, kinda classy. If I take MyVictoria to the festivals, she doesn´t become to dance alone there. And how about putting dancing and sporting together, not last paying for the first, but sporting & dancing being the selling thing – together? Who wants to leave a festival which is a training and strip club at the same time?

If you put together a game & strip, isn´t that the best cultural adventure that you have? The atmosphere, serving, touching, feeling, making love say bye to good people. Well, there must be more disciplined and reason, and that gives timeline, beauty, and experience.

I sing: "M honey takes my money, but I think it´s ala fair when there´s a pretty face in lace I´ve got some twenty´s to share. I´ve got ants in my pants when you pranced, I glanced, then tell in France, so when fancy pants get a chance can this man have another lap dance." The phone rings: "You talk with the fans and have fun. I shall show myself after a hour." if I throw my love to lust, it goes down the drain.

Trying to listen

I must cheer up. I go to 8 Berry Street. Nice Gym. Coaches Paul and Tasha hang around, but when I put up 60 kg biceps, they go away. I look at the fellas, a lot of tattoos, and black training shirts. There is a bromance. A fella, and the dog in his arms. People are jumping with balls.

I begin to do biceps training, no rest, just putting it up. Around me people do five minutes training sessions, then they change the movement. Their muscles do not get surprised that way. They are in their comfort zone. I went away a long time ago to pain & misery training. After an hour, I wash and come towards the center where you give your performance.

I call Cliver: "Hey man, any 2-11? Cliver answers: "Yeahh, nice to hear Y too. Dat bStch ridin´ clean on´nem sperwells. Look like we, deepbrer, do not gonna have to make a stang." I say: "Yes, I shall go to listen to MyLady´s speech to her fans." He wonders: "Really? Some fandom hustlers, Y do not mean dope fresh nation?" I: "Do Y have that Caddy, right now?" C says: "I sit on it. And it blows and goes, real rice burner. So what?" I: "Come 8 Berry, and give the lift to that center, ok. I must look good, when I arrive, that employs a bit of nerd-herding." C: "Well, tell me what is in your mind, okay?" I: "So when we go there, Y go to invest 3 million to that porn-piracy fella Mind-Eegan or something - if Y know where our Key belongs to. Do Y?" Cliver: "Yeahd, perhaps I know where the lab is. But m not a hundred sure." I: "Don´t fuck up. Go to check, k?" C: "Well):(, cos there are wymen, 24/7." I: "I can come with Y if Y are afraid. And call MyLady and say that I do not have time to listen to her speech, cos I have better things to do." C: "I go, but it´s a tough call. Bai bai."

After 15 minutes at 12:00 I sit with Cliver in Caddy. I: "Y do not need to go near the thing." Cliver: "Of course, I must, cos fake things are there also. And they recognize, that´s it." I feel bad. Bad but not so bad that we do not look at each other face to face and smile. He says: "I message, and then Y come, to that address with this and then we fuck off. Ok."

Inspector J. Mastronandi's 75th precinct takes care of Eastside Brooklyn and Cypress Hills. And New Year is justover. And the station begins to find its normal steps. Meanwhile, Weez-Veries put the Guns around piracy-lab. There goes first wave: 25 fellas, and no Mari.

The Lab has 18 nerds who are more educated than those pirates that used BitTorrent and VPN 7 years ago against ISP and four other security-system. Streaming media cannot defend against their all the time changing IPs.

This lab is making also legal porn, and by its actions, many people have fired, sued, exposed, and blackmailed. Mr. porn-Mind has good business, and nobody sues it, cos it has money, lawyers, and guns. Well, so they assume. I and my friend have no time to think about saving our lives. Well, if your days have gone just fighting for your life, a cocaine cowboy's threat means a shit.

We do not open caddy's doors. We jump over aboard. Fist to fist. I say: "God speed." Cliver goes.

Yesterday it was close. I try to cover with my hand my laugh. Today it's time to show Cliver some true friendship. I know from the battlefield that people can come friends forever in a few seconds. And civilians have known each other for 20 years but do not have any trust in each other, cos they haven't met hand- in-hand up the ante.

I go to the center. I see a big screen and below it a lot of people. There are fake-made gorgeous ladies, some fellas in front making the show. There are a blackfella and a black-hair-lady and, yeah, you. Blackfella congratulates you and that other lady and nods to those other women on stage - and you get the microphone.

At the same time, there comes a text: "Block and building mobs here too, FK." Text goes on: "Some warriors from Rock Starz Forever Chasing money, Terror Villains and Hood Freshes. They smoke Mari but try to keep an eye on a bigger circle. Shit."

I know that LA Direct Models have canceled many contracts. An Asian girl who got price Best Year Actress of Adult News Awards died just some time ago as 7 other young actresses whose contracts had closed. An official explanation is the overdose of drugs or alcohol. Those girls got max 500 d having sex with a woman, with man thousand, more when there were four women one man. The girls had to take fans and fuck with them. And that leading Asian said in her last text: "I do not care."

I look at you and others and think: "Here it is safer. And they know their neighborhood. But on the west coast, it is something else."

You speak: "Thank Y very much. Your support made this possible. Our movie is now the most ..." You see me. I smile.

I get another message: "I go right now along Myrna St, and I go to that Lab-building, which is 20 meters from Liberty Ave. Y go to the cross of those streets. 15 min."

At this momentum, Cliver sees inside the underground lab, which has thick walls. But Weez-Very -fella Cande sees him. He shoots his gun.

In Cliver's head, something explodes but does not turn off. Cliver attacks and hits with a wood stick Cande to the forehead. He goes to sleep. Cliver tears part off his shirt around his head. Blood doesn't drop to the ground. The Dunde's forearm is full of needle marks.

With trembling hands, Cliver takes a needle from a pocket of Cande. Now my friend is in a hurry. He sees a micro nearby and some "aspirin"-smack and puts needle and asp to the micro. After some minutes he takes the needle and asp out and put asp to the needle and give Cande a good shot in a forearm. Cande shakes a little bit. Three Weez-Veries come: "What afk. He is out. Smokey shall kill him."

You and the other ladies get huge applause. Fellas whistle and shout naughty-dirty things. But you are so elegant and your eyes so beautiful. I come to Y. One guard tries to stop me. I kick in his balls and say to Y: "See Y on the flip side. Sus." I run out of the door. Jump to the Caddy. And drive thought red lights. 10 minutes to the meeting.

The Trigger Finger

Sewer rat Cliver comes up from the Huffington Post. He is all dirty, blood has come through the skirt, and begins to flow and drop to his face. It comes to his mouth and he feels the warm, sweet taste. He is almost going to his knees when I catch him to the Caddy.

Before he faints, he hears me saying: "Now we put the motherf**er porn-baron to his knees, not you. The Fuc**er is poisoning girls in LA."

Well, I step on the gas. Cliver has founded peace - for a while. And somebody dwitz shoots me. I take from Cliver´s belt a gun, and clap back - one fella fells down. People run, and we pass by Love Fellowship Tabernacle. Nice True Cine Tabernacle Church Hall goes by, and Caddy goes 120 km/h near the 75th Police Precinct Station House. Yes, behind us comes a convertible. Shooting goes on.

As everybody well knows 75th Police Precinct is a historic police station, New York, New York. I smile: so near the porn-lab and the police station. SGT J. L., Po M. S., Po A. B., P. N. A., and P. A.C. do not believe their eyes. These good people spend all their working hours within the confines of their assigned sectors, actively engaging with local community members and residents. They know their neighborhood extremely well - they think so.

I say: "Shit, I must take the whip quickly out of here and do not show it to those f**cking cameras." Then no newsroom, publications get busy. Department shall not explain how it protects real Brkners against my kind of deep Brkners with a means of hearing, watching, and stories of hardworking officers.

Tom B. looks at my firebird and shakes his head: "Cops don't even go to give that fella a ticket or arrest him. As they say 'we are too busy and don't have the manpower'." Tom throws himself to the ground when shooting continues. Angelo C. shows his middle finger and shouts: "We don't leave until we get justice!" Andrew M. says: "And they wonder why they have a negative public image." Shooting goes on. Robert D-son is angry: "So marijuana dealers are not heroes?" Cliver wakes up. His face is full of blood. I shoot and the Chevelle behind gets a bullet to the left tire. The car stops right away. Police cars are off long away. I have a chance. And I try it.

I curve the Caddy. I must go quickly to the nearest hospital. A Blood-faced friend isn't a very nice sight. I go to Logan St, New Lots Ave, then Lenox St and Downstate Student and employee Health Service. I call 270-4577: "Yes, my friend has a scratch on his temple. Yes, we come right now." Cliver keeps repeating: "Weez-Veries didn't saw me, but they saw Y. You are a dead fish." I: "M I? Take it easy. They are just kids."

When students clean Cliver's left temple and I look if the police are coming. Nothing. Meanwhile, B-Rad, Looney, Chucho, and Buckets come out of the car, which tire broke down. And a piggy whip stops near them. Wheez-fellas put their hands over their heads.

At the same time, Smokey isn't happy. He talks at the meeting. It is at the Liberty Ave Park: "Just on daylight, a *gabacho*, who doesn't want to give driver's license to immigrants, shoots our car, visits our friend's lab, and goes away. He pulled first!" Gang members yell: "*Amor de Rey!*" Or something like that.

Meanwhile, Cliver's temple has been cleaned and dollars put to the table, no names mentioned. We go to Caddy. I: "Ok?" Cliver: "Im." Lies that people tell so often to other people are mostly happy lies.

I: "I must go back to the festival center. Can Y drive?" Cliver nods, likewise they make a nod to the strong influential role, you know, boogie down Bronx.

Meet-Eegan

I say: "So now we have checked the place. Then we must take care of Mr. Meet-Eegan. There are a lot of Brazzers, Pornhub and so. Let's cut those connections for a while to Miami and LA, ok. Ferry A. and the boys shall get a surprise. It has those free and paid sites. Let's put everything in that piracy free field and give fake Verge cryptos to them. Let's put the virus to their nets in Virgin Islands, Curacao, and here. Let's change a glamcore to a shitcore. After this, the content stolen from performers and sex workers and uploaded for free shall have other uploaded for free versions, too.

Somebody spends on travel, renting the location, hiring film cameras, photographers, lingerie, hair, nails, and 400d STI tests. While another pays 15,99 d for a month's subscription to OnlyFans account, and in ten minutes the fu*er has downloaded it all, uploaded it - done. And when these sex workers begin to study what really happens, they shall be found drug overdosed. Let's fuck with the bastards.

These nerds take easily IDs and take these things to their master's sites for free. And if you do not accept it, you die. If you think about drug- or porn-barons, y must think also nerds, who make those paths, which gangs protect. Let's have a chat with one

Meet-Eegan-begfriend. He shall put his homemade Meet-Eegan account and download it all, uploaded it - done. And send it to, for instance, Open Knowledge pages and wherever. He and his lusty nerd-friend shall download and upload their boss-material. And then a little bit action also, so that those porn-fellas do not mess with the real gang."

Cliver: "If we do that. They shall chase us forever." I: "Well, our Truth is like a lingering fart: everyone can smell it, knows it is there, but no one wants to admit it. Nerds shall do the ass puzzle, calling the last fart before they shit themselves. That's it. And 75th doesn't begin to shoot millionaires, who give a dirty job to streetwise, who do know how to react to situations such as being threatened and bullied. My friend, y and your friends - a tap to his shoulder- give to those millionaires a response such as killed it."

Cliver: "Let's go to eat. Im hungry. And not after drinking." We go, cos hungry is the worst possible torture someone could go through. It means that one is not getting the nutrition one needs in order to survive. And the sinner cannot stand before the judgment, for the measure of gifts does not rest upon the quality of our deeds until each one is rewarded according to his deserving. After that, the downcast can be lifted.

While thinking these strange things, in my head goes more strangely Killer NYC: Vocaleer, The Night is Quiet. I put Cliver's gun backside on my belt and go to the center.

The Night is Quiet

What shall I say to Y? "Do not even think about I shall take Y to Amour V`Cabaret on PUMPs. Do not want to go to the crude and rude place. And do not want to go chat with each of the performers up close and personal. Well, a bit expensive for E. Williamsburg. And they do not allow me to bring my Burger King inside. No need to try their flame-grilled chicken fries. Just to Y, crispy, tender, all around pleasure to the buds. And just wanna talk with you, not with some drunken old-timer, who has a girl on his lap, and how he tells the drinks were once cheaper and they had beautiful Brazilian,

Puetarican women that were so sweet, now they get some ghetto hood rats that are not sweet at all, they will get mad at y if y don´t tip them y have to tip them every time they´re next to y. And I do not wanna strong drinks which shall make me a little looser with my singles lol. Not wanna tip every girl that walks past the bar and put their boobs in your face, it´s kind of wack. I tip my money to MyVictoria, please don´t make it a chore. And if somebody should say to me, something like, ´It Y ain´t got no money, take your broke ass home´, I shall kick him to his ass. I do not wanna bring enough dd to spread the love this Brooklyn way."

I wake up from my daydream when you stand in front of me. You say: "Hello." I say: "Hello." The only word that has nothing to do with sex and drugs. You give some data: "Have you heard NYC broke five Guinness World Records in 2019? The world´s longest feather boa has its own NYC *boulevard*. TheGreatAndMarvelousBoa was stretched out along West 42nd Street between Seventh and Eighth avenues. The

Pride Run shattered the world record for the number of people to complete a Pride charity event, with more than 10 000 runners crossing the line. Do not have anything to say?"

I: "Thursday high 48, low 30, 7 mph winds, with gusts up to 18 mph, January, light raining until morning, starting again in the evening, Saturday light raining throughout the day, high 48, low 42, Sunday, possible drizzle in the morning, high 43, low 34. Parking meters stop taking credit cards after 2 am. You know, new parking headaches for drivers - related software glitch meant they stopped accepting c-cards. The Department of Finance says: 'There are other ways to pay parking meters and ensure drivers do not receive a ticket. NYC parking meters also accept coins, and drivers can also pay using the Park NYC app.'"

Y look at me: "What Y have done with that Cliver?" I: "Well, no need to begin to talk about the city's plan to convert a vacant warehouse in Glendale into a shelter, and the shelter's opponents calling homeless people drug addicts and sexual offenders who should be locked away forever, and low life pieces of crap."

MyVictoria's day has been perfect, and I'm sure she has some wise words about that Meet-Eagan thing. But now I take her hand and we go to Br Cupcake, where I shall give her the heritage of Puerto Ricans, Italians, Polish, Dominicans, Russian, Haitians, and Chinese. Just some Dulche Leche and one Vanilla Rasberry and - she insists - Cookies & Cream. And Carmen Rodriguez and Gina Madera have a menu of very awesome Puerto Rican inspired cupcakes.

We go with the Caddy to MyVictoria's place, and nobody pops a cap or try to collar us. And it reminds me of the time that day brings another moon. Your taste is like the merriments, nimble spirit of mirth. We question our desires, examine well, the blood of the horse and the rider. So rise, lives, and goes one peak in single courtly blessedness.

I look at the computer Meet-Eegan data. If I try to find something exact about the budget, the server put me to Luxemburg or Montreal. Well, porn money goes to cultural business via South America vending machine, paly on the playa, to the Catholic Church, in Spain, Turkey ... but there is one problem, if you miss the point, they crush you like a cockroach.

Breaking in

I wake up in the middle of the night. My phone surs: "Yeah, what´s up? How many? I come straight away." I run to my clothes. I jump those floors and to the Caddy and go.

Flatlands Ave, then Jefferson Field no baseball players, and at last Egan. We are so near that very bad Vandalia Ave, where one of my friends went straight to Walhalla. Cliver comes over the fence, and jumps to the car, in front of us are a bunch of brothers of Straight Cashs/Get Gwops. Gunrunners point tech-nines, but we go faster. One fella gotta a hit and flies over the Caddy.

This is fine. I came to NYC to make a deal but found myself in no-mans-land falling in love with a hooker. And I always have tried to be cool. Cliver: "These dizzels know that porn-baron and Weezs have whuz tha dizzel, muh nizzel." I: "Remember we have the credit cards, which play the song, they do not have them." Cliver´s humor does not dig my humor: "But someone is taken away gun control black card." Bullets whistle all over. And although they praise Wentz´s new band, Black Card, FOB is waaay better. Our car takes us to Linden blvd and Brownsville. I: "Why are Y here?" Cliver: "I hang around." I: "I have also

a mystical creature, has clairvoyance, and it doesn't matter if she rips out my heart."

Elbow to elbow. Then I have an idea: "Now when we are here. Why don't we take the next step? Some miles away are Meet-Eegan nerds, who, if a brawl breaks out, won't fight for you. Let's go to say hello to these good people." Cliver: "We cannot go there. Weezs don'tsleep." I: "Yes we can."

I say: "Y know the doors. So. No problem." Cliver: "What do Y mean 'ok fine porcupine'." I: "Looping plopper, and fellas come and go." Cliver: "Y mean one door, one nerd, before or later." I: "Yes, they look quite different compared to these Weezs. And police station is as near as Y can throw a stone." Cliver: "But they look at that direction." I: "No they do not, cos they have no problem with that direction. Nerds go that way. The 75th Precinct station is on the other side and on the other side nerds may get to meet nearby Front Side Bloods/Hoe-Hansum gang, Back Side Crips/Eastside bangers, Rock Starz, Miller Made Crew, Straight Cash, Loopy Gang, Paper Chasers, Pink Houses 1 & 2, 7 & 8/Caveman/Holywood, Pink Houses Center side 5 & 6 areas. They want to feel safe."

Cliver: "We stand nearby the station and kidnap there a nerd." I: "No, no, we follow the fella, and look where he leaves and then we enter his apartment when he isn't there. We just steal from a thief." Cliver: "If my bros here about this, they kill me." I: "Did they kill Y, when I gave Y that medallion? Trust me." Cliver: "Trust a deep-br? Mofo, mad dogging me?"

We stand at the corner nearby the porn-lab and police station. Very quiet, time is 3 am. Then it is 3:20, 3:25. Some Weezs go with one silent fella out of a door. Weezs smoke their Maris and the silent fella has his

RIP-style. The fella gets in his car, and we begin to follow him. Cliver looks like L.O.L Spring Roll, and splings a lot.

We roll on the Brooklyn-Queens Expressway, where the Democratic gov. Cuomo pulled yesterday the stunned man outto a white van that slammed into a BQE divider. Governor cut the man out of his seatbelt and helped his safety.

We follow to Jackson Heights and the fella stops at 34th Ave near El Gallito Deli Grocery. He goes to the 6-floor house and locks the door.

Well, we avoid high fees from a locksmith and bad questions. To pick a lock on the door, we need 2 bobby pins and patience. One pin serves as the pick and the other as a lever. I open a pin and bend it at a 90-degree angle. Spread the wavy and straight ends of the pin apart. Remove the rubber tip on the straight of the pin. Stick the flat end of the pin into the top of the lock and bend it. I bend the wavy end of the pin into a handle for more control. I bend the tip of another pin to make the tension lever.

Stick the tension lever into the bottom of the lock, push the lever counterclockwise to apply tension, stick the pick into the lock and feel for the pins, push down on my lever until I hear a click, lift the rest of the pins in the door lock, turn the tension lever counterclockwise to open the door and the tension lever rotates fully.

We go in. Clever: "Hey man, here are deadbolts." I: "Yep, they have pins and tumblers, nothing new under the sunshine. Some tips, if your girlfriend is in a bathroom: insert the pin into the small hole on the doorknob until you reach the internal locking mechanism, then turn it to unlock the door. And a tinny flathead screwdriver also works."

Cliver: "He is on the fifth floor, second door left." I: "How do y know?" Cliver: "This is not the first time I listen to things. He has thin-soled shoes." We go out. I say: "I take a car and Y can stay. And do not fell asleep."

Cliver isn't happy, but I can't wait to see you. The car goes and I fly back to bed. You sleep like a baby.

It is 7:30 and I get the text: "The fella left with r31, come." The 34th street looks nice daytime. Ladies with their kids, big trees. Cliver opens out-door. We go to the 5th. The lock says 'click'. And inside is a spring lock, but a credit card opens every door. There is a combination lock. I pull up gentle on the shackle. I hold it in place. I turn the dial clockwise listening carefully until I hear the clock says 'click'. I set the first number my starting point, turn counterclockwise to find the second no., I test the catch, these numbers fit a pattern 4 (ending).

We go in. A huge room is full of computers. It is easy to find where the fella works most of the time, nearby full of software and so. The computer isn't closed. It is sleeping. Now we must be careful, not to wake it up wrongly. The fella must have here a fingerprint touch. Where we get a fingerprint? Normally the kitchen is the fingerprint place. He eats, puts hands on the table, but mostly he goes to the fridge. Yes, there are good stains. I take a knife on the table and take off a piece of the surface. Now we shall see is it a touching screen or marking screen. If it is the first, then we must take the hard disk with us.

I put the piece of the surface to it. The computer opens and there comes: "Singing my space songs on a spiderweb star 'Life is around you and in you'." I go in. Well, and what amount of home porn and office. This fella must have a legion of bang Manti Teo's girlfriends.

I call MyVictoria: "Hello, yes, I luv Y. Yes, sorry, making a deal, hm, well, later ..." I go back: "What BDSM, Casting, MassageRooms, Brazzers, Spankwire, Trumbzilla, all Pornhub thing, mobile adult services, yeah,

Twistys, over 200 hundred pages, Mofos, all webcams, yes, all Alexa rank things and more and downloads.

Cliver: "What shall we do now? Choke the Chicken, jerk off, wack the Weisel, beat the meat, free the whales, or Jack the Johnson and our brains out." He laughs and I laugh. Crazy, crazy, Jackporn. Let's shoot them for good.

The download things. Let's show these ID-footprints. Straight to these nerds. And to the house of Mr. Meet-Eegan. Or perhaps first their own new private movies and webcam and so for free public distribution. How this fella can have these all? There are nerds' codes, and ID-masks and secret paths. Enough to show the way who is the father of porn-piracy. Mr. Meet-Eegan cannot overdose police and law and great people of the USA. I put those nerds' codes to Pentagon and White House.

Nosotras temenos prise, cos nerds are quick to notice data flows. I close the computer, give that plastic fingerprint to the screen and it falls asleep. Now we have true friends, they walk in when the rest of the world walks out.

At the same time, on the internet goes an article: "If you are connected to the internet, this may be the most important article you'll read. Your computer is a personal storage facility, and it contains your most important, precious, and private files. The problem is, your home computer is much easier to access than government or corporate computer systems, making you a prime target for cyber-criminals.

Here's the deal: TotalAV are giving away instant virus and malware security scans to all computer owners for free. T-AV have a cutting-edge algorithm that can be detected and remove any viruses, adware, malware, and spyware that may be lying undetected within your computer. This software is complete automating the process. It is super quick, and you do not need to be technical to get started. TotalAV just 19.9 d. Make your happy day."

And the Value goes down

At liberty Ave fortress the nerds burst to laugh, and chuckle so, lol but with a twist. Great article, and so false. Suddenly Meet-Eegan-fortress goes to chaos. Yes, they cannot steal their own public stuff, and they cannot know how to hide when the news shows their secret codes. Their value goes down.

Mr. Meet-Eegan CEO Ferry A., once an engineering graduate of Concordia University, arrives with a huge convoy of cars. He jumps outto a Pagani Huayra. He hasn´t his usual Lamborghini Aventador SVJ. He has come to make business. And he does not need to care about the mayor, the governor, or the police. He can handle those little things with the rain of papes. Mr. HighMighty looks very pissed off. He was pissed off when he read Mr. Byrnes's driddy statement from The Guardian: "Inequality is not a tipping point." He had cried: "Josh, take care of that fu**er!" The King of Online Gambling just loves to do business with Mr. F. Mr. Josh had served 90 days in prison for counts of cocaine possession in his younger life. And he had criminal things for telemarketing fraud, and he owns most part of his brother D´s firm. The great brother laughed to any claims, and a spokesman said: "Through prejudicial leaks, false declarations, and persistent insinuations, this affair is transformed into interminable fishing."

Mr. Josh jumps outto the car, too. Securities watchdog sayings that brothers and Mr. F are beards for many owners share doesn´t mean a damn. Mr. F yells in front of the lab-fortress: "Where the fuck is Bob, and the security chief here right away!?" Soon Smokey comes to meet Mr. F and Mr. Josh. Mr. F: "Any clues?" Smokey looks at the modern suit fella: "We went after a fella, who hang around in the morning so gn. That badass had a Caddy, he fucked away." He snaps his fingers. Mr. Josh; "What do Y mean fucked off?" Smokey: "Yeah, he has disappeared like a rich man´s wallet." Mr. F comes to the limelight: "How he looked." Smokey: "He looked like a WW2 German soldier. Blond hair, combed behind, straight nose, black eyebrows, and the pit in the jaw. He looked like an aristocrat wagas, He didn´t give a damn about slugs around him. Quite a colin goss."

Mr. F shouts: "The draftsman here, now!" A timid looking servant runs to his boss and tries to say something. Mr. F looks at Smokey: "You and your man describe that fella to this chub here." Soon the picture is ready. And Weezs-Veries nod their head: "Yeah, that´s him." The nerd call Dry-John put the picture to the files and the portraits begin to run. Then suddenly they stopped. And D-John takes a copy and run with it to Mr. F and Mr. J. Mr. F loses his nerves: "Why the hell Y bring to me a Nazi-butcher´s picture?" D-John: "Sir, this matches the best way to that picture. And this is not a Nazi but a Waffen-SS officer, one of the bests. And Americans or Russians never got him. He went to the Foreign Legion, and the story tells that he had a dog."

Mr. F: "How dare Y talk to me like that? Quickly a new search, and a modern suit on and updated today, quick, no time to lose." He tears the picture and throws it to the cold and rain.

Two minutes later there comes a new picture. Mr. F looks at it: "Hm, nice suit and the fella seems to be even more trained than that Nazi-fu**er, manly face, I must say." Josh begins a little bit pushy: "So, where this fella lives? He doesn´t look like a Sudanese water carrier. Find him, bring him to me, and I cut his balls, and make him eat them." Smokey looks at the bros: "That n00b is behaving like a bloody git."

Then at last there comes an answer. D-John: "He is from Foreign Legion and Academy, and has something to do with SEALs, has been called Tapio de Hauteville, no names in other registers. Nothing after 2011. He has vanished." Mr. F: "Well, now he is in downtown, New York, New York. I wanna him alive, no drug-things to him. He shall have the end in the long run." Smokey says: "Krah, but we do not know if it is him." Mr. F: "I do not care what you think, bring him to me. We have lost a lot of money." Mr. F thinks: "How can a man of the dead past and today's fella have the same style. The faces aren't the same, this older fella has charm but this new fella more."

The Dinner

We have dinner at The River Cafe. We look at skyline views, feel the gorgeous atmosphere. Cliver says: "Here is very good wine, I've heard." I look at flower arrangements, listen to piano music, and seamless service. I take my phone: "Hello, MyVictoria, have Y any spare time?" Y answer: "Yes, it's 8 am. Where are you?" I: "At one of the most romantic and noteworthy settings. This plays cries for romance, The River Cafe. Do Y like it? This elegant dining room has an awesome menu of elegance and refinement, Bab. Here is a suit jacket required for gentlemen at dinner, but Cliver doesn't have it."

The butler respects us with his presence: "I am very sorry to tell you sir, but haven't you seen the important dress code information." I give him five hundred bucks: "So go." The butler: "Pardon Sir, go where?" I: "To buy to my merry colleague the suit." The Butler: "I am not ..." I put to his hand more dimes: "Yes, you are." After a while, he comes back with a great modern blue suit, and Cliver goes to Winston and comes back as a new man. Behind us the Lounge Pianist who invented Samba Funk begins to play: "*Je suis nee ce matin, au milieu de la Mer, entre Deux de la mer*."

After fifteen minutes you come, an amazing dress on, where is gold hidden under the cinnamon gold elegancy. It suits perfectly to your blond hair. One of the most beautiful restaurants in NYC has got a bright shining star.

We, Cliver and I, both gentlemen, rise and shine, Cliver nod French way and I kiss the air on your silk-pretty hand.

At the same time, Mr. F and Mr. Josh head for Brooklyn. After a while, they decide to go to eat a good dinner. And we are having fresh abalone, citrus, soy, lime, Kusshi oysters, cucumber Champagne mignonette, Nantucket Bay scallop ceviche, sea bean, tomato, coriander. I tell a story, how in Italy the oyster must be cheated out of the shell. Mr. F and Mr. Josh march in like victorious generals.

We are cheering loudly but not anti-elegantly. Mr. F and Mr. J give no glance at our table. The owner Michael O'Keeffe in his great person comes to meet these remarkable billionaires. A table near us is forTheir Highnesses.

We attack sea bass fillet, wild shrimp crust, lemon, olive oil and saffron nage, classic Romesco sauce, zucchini. Cliver gives his best joke, a sneaky aspect, not lol way, which is full of belly laugh: "Jack: 'Hey I want to make to sweet love to your sister.' Jill: 'What??!!!' Jack: 'IJK!!' Jill:' O! Ha Ha!!'" The masters of porn sit in their table like marble statues.

And I stand up, to ask: "Special favor to MyLady, please, butter-poached Nova Scotia lobster, and of course, heirloom apple *beurre blanc cauliflower purée*". At the same time, Mr. Josh stands up and is ready to go to send a message to his hitmen concerning some secret mission. We stand up at the same time and so he is on my way and I on his. We look at each other. I smile and salute the fella and he is ready to go forward when the hint hits his brains like a bolt. "WTF? WhoTH? WhenTF? WTS? Tm!"

The modesty man pines beseech and languishes, but Mr. Josh murmurs, pouts and rage gets the control over him. He attacks and gets his face on the ground and my shoe over it.

I laugh: "Yeah, Mr. Gambling King, today is not the lucky day. But do not worry, have a little patience and Y can feel joy while having a bad day, a bad week, or even a bad year. Lace-up." He: "Y, POS, I kill Y!" I: "Chill out. Please." He: "Fer, he is it. He is the bloke!" The bell rings in my head. Now they see MyVictoria also. What shall I do? There is only one way.

I say to you: "An unfortunate misunderstanding. Perhaps Y shall find something interesting from the dessert menu?" Y smile very beautiful smile: "Just Chocolate Brooklyn Bridge: milk chocolate *Marquise*, coconut sorbet, coffee Chantilly, *espresso caramel*, or no, I take Hot *Soufflé*: Dulcey, *soufflé*, roasted pineapple ice scream spiced." I: "What an elegant taste." Then I say quickly to Cliver: "The gun, here."

Cliver throws the *cueta*, and I'm not going to drop it or shoot the fool. I shoot the security camera down. Then I say to the owner of the cafe Mr. O´Keeffe: "Thank Y very much of your special services. Now those security camera tapes." I nod to Cliver. Then he and the butler go. Mr. O´Keeffe stays on the target. I say to Mr. F: "I'm very disappointed with this fella´s behavior. Perhaps he goes to yoga-tutorial and tries to eat some vegetables. It is good for your brain- and the nerve system. I suggest he goes to Yoga Tribe Brooklyn, just 40 d/a month, and he shall feel and look great, brand new. That´s a promise. He gets a creative state of mind. 1120 Washington Ave. Y know, shapeshifting, strength, flexibility, and he can focus, how his life rockanrolls. He can train in the middle of the street with Mary Jarvis, and the mind and body shall transform itself, gaining also stamina."

Mr. F does not show any innovative ideas: "Y shall be for this. You shall be." I: "Well, perhaps Mr. F, you shall go too with Mary Jarvis. Nothing to lose. Meeting the team shall be the best day of your life. And Y & Josh shall feel open and clean. Go to Bikram Park Slope, please, think about it. Y get to your sore points bot Y TB and Minka & year-round acupuncture 2-6 pm and 10 am – 2 pm. Boys (my shoe is still on Mr. Josh's face), a gentle lift-touch therapy provides improvements in your wellbeing. Bach Flowers are safe preparations where only the energetic vibrations of flowers are sourced to provide a healing tincture tailored for y, boys. Supports inner harmony and emotional balance in its all branches. By the way, Mr. F, do not try those hand marks or I shoot to your leg right now."

MyLady eats with good appetite fresh pineapple ice-cream. And via my gun commands, piano-fella continues his slow and warm beat. Cliver comes with the tape. Steak is burning in a nearby grill, so I throw the tape there. You are ready and stand up. I ask the butler near to me: "Here is for the bill and some tips. Thank Y very much." And to the boys I say: "If Y come after me, remember, if Y really wanna the rainbow, Y gotta put up with the rain."

Cliver says to me: "Perhaps we shall buy a new El Camino?" I: "A good idea. Do y like Buick or real classy Karman Chia? Cliver: "Ford Mustang Shelby Gt500 shall be fine." I: "Okay."

All's Well that ends Well

We walk outto the cafe. And then I take you in my arms and we run to the Caddy. It is 10 AM, and there we go to 50 Old Fulton St, and to Sam's. It has been closed now for four hours, but I know Sam and Jimmy do a good job, no matter what the time is. Soon the Caddy is theirs and we get a Mustang: 2007-2009 Shelby GT500, quarter-mile record at 12,4 s with a speed trap of 115,8 mph. This trimmed thing goes closer to the 11-second run. And money changes the owner and owners are most pleased, everybody wins.

We go to that 34th St in Queens and check the nerd's latest updates. The fella hasn't noticed our visit. Now I take it out again, and the computer wakes up ... This nerd updates all his computers at the same time. Nothing about Y. Your long hair was up, and your lips hadn't more that stuff, and Y had sunglasses and your tattoo was covered. No birthmarks, your left cheek didn't show anything, cos of your make up and so. And no voice-things. You are in clear waters. Nobody connects Y to porn and client-affairs and having fun with vids.

But Cliver isn't a mystery man anymore. And Makk Balla Brims are no longer Bloods. NYBBA has officially kicked them out. Cliver, chatty bytch, has been recognized by Weezs also. A young Nikka writes: "Fukk this Blood shyt too much politics." But the gang doesn't sign the outkick, and it sounds to them suspect and chatty, af. foh, FED. "No is publicly speaking about it and I'm still waiting for you to reveal your source of information, and I don't give a fuck what you are, the fact is you're not and you shouldn't be talking." That kind of thing appears. There comes a text: "Only thing that matters to me is if they wooK."

Nikka says: "If Y even remotely follow other Bloods, you would have seen this a million times over. And if they are posting it public, then they don´t believe it´s private. They made it publicly known Makks are no longer valid. Take that up with them. If I pulled a private transcript and made a gossip rag, and you are not even Blood, so why you need to know my source of info? If you are, you should know this is public information."

Somebody out of gangs tries to do harm, which he cannot do. The Bloods have but virus all over the net concerning them.

FBI put charges against Makks. The long list of other prisoners comes now. Many Cliver´s brothers, as the words go "armed gang membors": M-13 fellas, Chief of Security of Gangsters, Wilmington Gang members, founder of the Blood Haunt, 18th St Gang leader, Grape Street Grips members, leaders of Latin Kings, SCO, Latin Counts Gang members, and many others. Porn money talks. Us Attorney R.P. Donoghue says: "We are working tirelessly without law enforcement partners to ensure that our community is protected from the threat posed by violent street gangs."

It is true that while wearing masks, Darby and Raymond, went in one home with guns and tied up the victim with an extension cord and demanded the marijuana and cash. When the victim stated that he did not have Mari R. and D heated up a knife and repeatedly burned the victim´s legs. And it is true Robertson restrained other victim´s families with zip ties and he shot the victim in the stomach before fleeing with jewelry and electronics. But the main point is that porn-billionaires now desperately try to find Cliver and me. And let us out of our days. Josh & F calls privately us the public enemies.

Cliver calls Makk-brothers: "Yeah, porn-fucks start throwing cookies. This is not a pump-action shotgun, I ask Y choine the ribbin Tickets to

Hell. Fuck with the armed truce, can Y come to Liberty Ave near the police station? Yes, that pig pad. Yes, a minimum of 15 brodies and weegees. Of course, TEC-9 semiauto-pistols and Ganzo´s a lot of match uzz18/7,62´s, and I aoncare if Y bring bigger guns, younger shooters. Take from RT Smoke N Gun Shop, Olinville Arms, and Parchester Rifle & Revolver. Damn cqb go off at 2 am."

I write on paper our breakthrough and Cliver clicks it and sends it to the brothers. No questions asked. It´s like in good old times: go, kill those and those. It is 23:33 when Cliver leaves us.

The Fifth Day

The Day shoots down the idea about noice porn-billionaires

Brooklyn freestyl - G´d up

I meet Cliver at Liberty. He has with him gunrunners. When porn-blue hundreds talk to you, you can fight with the fuc**ers rules.

We get lucky, the big boys are in the lab. The car-convey waits for masters. I begin to walk nearer the net. Cliver: "Where´re Y going. They´ll pop Y like a quack." I: "Before the ever-great battle you must fang a challenge, fuc***ing gays call it making the beast with two backs." Cliver looks at brodies: "He´s making a B line." In the middle of the street I shout: "Mr. F, you didn´t care! So, let´s meet now! There is no back door! If Y don´t come out, we are coming in! Your choice!" Silence. Inside the house, Smoky looks at his warriors.

Mr. F comes with Mr. Josh out of the nerd-lab and says: "Shoot that piece of shit right now. On my command, fire." Nothing happens. I stand in the street. Mr. F: "Take the names of all who refuse to shoot. They shall be shot also." I walk nearer: "If anybody wants to shoot me before the fight begins, here I'm." Smokey comes out of the door: "Ello. M Smokey, what are y called?" I: "I'm Tapio, shall be a noice day. I have missed the blue sunshine, let´s make it red." Smokey: "Jeah, let´s do that."

We look at each other ftf. At the same time, Josh has taken his Archon B, tilting barrel, and aim at me and tries to pull the trigger. Coucho comes and hit Josh`s neck hard, Mr. Porn fell like an American oak. Smokey whistles. Now ends, at last, the dry spell of fighting. Murder pushes Mr. Josh out. Bit by bit the streets begin to fill with men. Time shall tell who stands on the sunny side of the street. It is 4:30 am.

The mercenaries, the bodyguards of Mr. F, and Mr. Josh come out of their cars. They have noice sunglasses. There are from old Academi, C4S, FDG, and DynCorp and used to make war for money. They do not back off, and they are good. Cliver gives me a hand grenade. It is homemade. I say to Cliver and Makks: "Look straight forward. When I make my move, fell to the left and aim to the right, so you get straight. Do not shoot up shoot down, bullets make it up. Then, at the same time with the explosion, run towards the house and from the down left to the right. I give us three seconds advance. And after that our surprise falls to pieces, in five seconds, if you miss." I throw the blowing death to the convoy - quickly. At the same time, Weezs and fat ex-mercenaries put their guns up.

Later I heard that one Iraq-veteran BB made that grenade. It really disperses shrapnel on detonation. It is like throwing a baseball. It is very easy to make the M61-model like a little devil. Those poor bastards do not know that it can be catch and thrown back to the thrower. One huge jeep explodes and goes up. 1, 2, 3, 4, I and Makks run and shoot. Bullet whistles around me, and four Makks fell, but we shoot better. Smokey and the Weezs get hurt. Mr. F and Mr. Josh have run behind bodyguards, who cover them and shoot. We enter the building. Bloodthirsty Makks begin to shoot at nerds and their computers. Then they go to the windows and shoot there to that convey and five bodyguards get bullets in their legs. What a mess. The convoy begins to move away. And nerds stand in front of the walls and Cliver and his bros gather loot: money and engines, discs.

There is a great selection of porn for home use. I count: the whole attack had lasted 30 seconds, shooting about two minutes. There are four hurt Makks and seven Weezs, one nerd has a bleeding hand. We must take them outto here, and to the hospital as soon as possible before the police come. I throw Smokey and Flame to my Mustang´s backside and two Makks also. Others shall take care of the rest. We go. The main thing is that now porn-kings know that they aren't kings of the endz. The streets are for them who take the action, not for them who give the money and run.

I ask Cliver: "Do Y have more these grenades?" He: "Yes." I: "Why don't Y take here more of them?" Cliver: "Veteran BB didn't want to give them." When we drive away, the street is empty and the whole thing has lasted 7 minutes.

We take those fellas to that student-hospital. And I talk some words with Smokey: "Stoopid thing to shoot each other. Next time just those porn-fuckers. By the way, I go to meet them one more time. They do not come to mess me again. I know the way." Smokey: "What's that? I: "Just a personal thing, nothing much. The only problem with this thing is that the world is full of weak people, and they are in power now. Porn is their hobby." Smokey: "Y may be what Y are, white deep Br-ner, but one thing is sure, I can, Y POS, always trust Y. Go before the popos arrive. I can handle them. I'm not broke, I have money." We put three fingers up, and I say: "*Sieg Heil*!" I shake their hands and tap all the fellas on their shoulders as we used to do in the army. Cliver and I go away.

Cliver begins to recover from that shocking attack: "Brody, it was betül. I looked when Y run. Your movements were like Moose. So smooth and easy Y moved, what a combination of muscles and running." I: "Well, the speed is the ability to take a decision in view seconds. And when I was there in action, we never walked, in my platoon, we did our jobs always running."

Doggy and I

I come to your place at 8 am. All descend people are at work, and MyVictoria is going to market her specific qualities with her manager, and what shall I do: I´m going to bed, and sleep well. I'm putting curtains in front of the window when MyVictoria asks a difficult question: "Have Y heart what happened in the 75th precinct. There have been nearby the police station heavy clash. Even grenades have been used there by some villains and no goods." I: "Oh, really, I cannot even imagine, where this world is going to. No respect, no understanding of beautiful things, and whenever good people are creating beauty around good people. They are restoring their own souls. Bab, they say that nothing makes a woman more beautiful than the belief that she is beautiful. Y: "What do Y mean? I'm a very self-love type. I love my picture." I nod and say: "Ok, that is true, but after YourTapio kisses MyGreatAndBeautifulVictoria then there look at Y on the mirror - Eternity. Y have sent to me or after my touch has taken two pictures, and in those pictures, MyVictoria´s beauty never dies." Y kiss me. I: "Y really self-love yourself."

So Doggy jumps to my lap and I fondle its neck and back and kiss his mouth. His big beautiful eyes look at me. I: "Ohh oh, do Y mean, steak again. Let me sleep for some hours." You are going away, and I say: "Can Y buy some Spanish steaks to this growing hound?" Then Y go, and Doggy gets some meatloaf. It proudly puts its chest up and marshes away. I draggle to the shower, iron, and brush my suit and teeth. Before I shut my eyes, I see Doggy sneaking to the kitchen to take that substitute of the steak.

The night has been fast and furious. And everybody knows in this weary world that the sight of blood to crowds begets the thirst of more, as the first wine-cup leads to the long revel. Ohhohhoo, I shut my eyes and see a Merryland, where the Butterfly, Happiness, which when persuaded, is always just beyond your grasp, but which after all and more, if you sit down quietly and look at the mirror of blueskies, may alight upon you.

I wake up at 1 pm. I open the TV. Some news about Trump and his democratic molesters. How boring ... how these women can hate so much this old fella, who says what he thinks, straight and honest way. Then ... there is a picture of Liberty Avenue. My grenade had kinked that jeep and melted it like a tin. Mr. F and Mr. Josh aren't happy, in front of the Media. Mr. F: "This is not acceptable. We demand that you listen to the voice of the people of NYC. Too long candlejacks have bieber-rized good people's life and happiness. Look at this macabre sight. Think about it. Never again. And just 500 meters from the police station." Nearby is Mr. F's dream car full of bullet holes.

I look at the fella: "Why this Bucarooni talks so much? Cannot be shut up? He isn't an artsy fartsy, whatever he says comes to sound like a frog's croak." I look at my suit. Hm. It is full of powder burns. MyVictoria doesn't like that. She does not wanna be with a sweats-cheeks-slacks-fella.

It was over 4 000 years ago, when women lost their matrimony, and men took power. And even 600 years before Jesus, in Italy, men make up themselves. They were the beauties to those leading women, but then came great Romans, men with honor and bravery. One young Roman went to gay-town Sybaris in southern Italy and told lizzing make-up-fellas about a deal. Those coquettes and justinbiebers rock their hips and giggled. The Roman said: "If Y do not answer by tomorrow midday, we burn your city to the ground." It was a great amusement to these one-directions. Romans declared war on them. And the gay army (many gays were good soldiers, too, you know, can cavort long times with young boys) met the Romans. The Roman general laughed: "Take the flutes." Romans began to play flutes and justinbiebers' horses begin to dance (they were trained to do tricks in pufta-partizzles).

I go to buy some Spanish steaks to YourDoggy. So now he jumps to my lab. I take it to my shoulder and say: "Let´s go MyFella, let´s go and buy a new suit." So, we go. Doggy is for a while a little bit bemused but comes in order in no time. Hm. We go into the Men´s Warehouse.

Yes, some Eagles blazers, not interested in ties but socks, ok. The seller laughs: "This little fella seems to be here in spirit and real-time." I look at the trimmings: "I wanna Versace-suit, do not have ... hm ... have y change the prices to try to upcharge? I take that sportscoat and tight trousers and brown shoes. Yep, grey, so some blue under. Ok. Thanks." I put them on, and the oldie goes to the garbage. In the hall New England Patriots champ Rob Ninkovich speaks: "It´s a subtle way to show your team pride, and inject fun into your look, while still looking tailored. That´s it with this suit on I can run more freely." Doggy stays on my shoulder.

We go the Atlantic Ave to Prospect Park West. There are ads like Lose Weight at The New Year With WW. Is there good control over the meetings? Silmara Roman is a Coach at 23rd Studio. She says: "Are y eating too much sugar or snacking too much? Add fruits and veggies. Workshops help seven days a week." Then here is more news: one teen falsely arrested, chained to a bench for hours. Well, that kid gets a good lawsuit. Ooh, most cloud today. Visibility 10 miles, 9 mph winds. Tomorrow dangerously windy overnight.

I begin to think about how the IOB's president and MyVictoria's manager shall meet, or shall they meet at all. And ofc, how I shall meet one more time with Mr. Josh. He has been barking here and there and is right now in the World Trade Center keeping his New Year Business Speech. I must take Doggy home and then call the IOB's president and MyVictoria's manager. And then change some words with Mr. Josh before MyVictoria comes.

Mr. Josh's Inspirational Speech

Phone rings. "Police got nothing from the hospital. Just one fella was there, but get outto window, and escaped", Cliver says.

At the same time, Mr. Josh is keeping his inspirational speech. Mr. F tells about parties and free breakfast.

Meet-Eegan workers also get free mech if they're ok with fearing porn shirts in public. Nepotism is real. People are promoted to managers who do not know anything, cos they're related to someone in the building. One manager tells his entire team that copying a photo and pasting it into a word document will show them anything that has been photoshopped. He sends that as a formal procedure to the entire team. Another manager isn't a dumb, but close to it. She plays everyone against each other and tries to get workers to rat out their colleagues while off work time (messages the workers on Facebook messenger to get details about other coworkers and then stores that information for later if she needs to fire someone). A cool HR lady is fired for trying to stop something from being put into place. People are fired with no notice and security comes to their desks to walk them out. People worry about losing their jobs, so they don't ask for proper raises. Guys assault girls in the bathroom at Christmas parties. Managers give lateral promotions with no raise.

Pregnant girls get bad performance reviews and the manager blames it on them begin pregnantly and being hormonal. Workers think the place is garbage. But they cannot stay away.

But Mr. Josh tells a different story: "Ladies and Gentlemen, Meet-Eegan Rocks! We have a very professional work environment with strong leadership. Management is positive and transparent, encouraging employees to come to them with initiatives and strategies. Ladies and Gentlemen, incredible people and a very relaxed atmosphere that is conducive to productivity. This is a really great place to learn cutting-edge digital marketing techniques. The focus and support for employee development are above average with numerous incentives to gain new skills that will help employees move up within the ranks rather than look elsewhere. Fun place to work. A dynamic company where there is lots to learn and there are plenty of resources to guide you and create a lasting career path. Great perks available, like an annual gym allowance, and access to Linkedin learning ..."

He looks to the audience. He smiles self-confident glance and his overview goes left to right, and he sees me. His head comes red. His temple veins hurt, he feels so thirsty, and drops of sweat begin to appear on the forehead. His voice goes down while he continues:

"So, believe me, yes, we create to Youuu a very indeed lasting career ... sorry ... wrong line ... me, I mean we all give just for Y a lifelong balance unlike most of the other places that require, well y know or not, lots of OT or weekend shifts ..." He tries to give hand marks to guards and point them my place.

He cannot stop now: "These all workers, men and, yes, of course, women provide 500 d/year fitness allowance that can be used for a gym membership, yoga classes, or anything else. This is just wonderful. It doesn't all need to be in one place so mix and match what suits them all best, from ..."

More hand marks and he whispered to the nearest guard: "There he is ... take him ...catch the fellow ... now." A guard called Henry understands and goes to tell others. Josh continues: "Fast-paced with solid management and collaborative grounds of people that challenged me and my very great ideas making even me better at my job. You'll never, ever, get bored ... to death ... and always, every single day, look forward to Mondays!" The audience begins to wonder and murmur when guards go to their lines and push people away.

Josh wipes the drops of sweat from his eyes: "Ladies and you Menschs, so Gentleman, think! If you're into interesting projects and flex hours, Meet-Eegan is the gold Star & Standard. A place where you work hard but play hard, too. Always, every day, except Sa and Su, free breakfast every day, monthly companywide free superb lunch, and incredible parties throughout the year: Hallowe'en, Christmas, Summer BBQ, you name it and I tell you..." Two guards come straight to me. I kick one to the stomach the other one gets my fist to his neck and fells and doesn't come up. A lot of shouts. People turn their heads.

Mr. Josh speaks very loudly and quickly: "Meet-Eegan offers a lot of room to learn and grow. We truly care about our employees and offer, fuck take him, amazing benefits. It's quite a large company now, but within each fucking department is the ability to feel you're truly part of a, you know, team. Every fucking day I find an amazing work environment plus the latest tech and so, and so tools to facilitate my tasks and learn. There's constant team contribution and there is nothing true about piracy lab as CNN lies and a very capable management team keeping the company at the forefront of hole digital marketing. Lots of room to grow for ... our culture is outstanding, I look forward to growing with everyone here - take that fucker, take him now!"

I shout at him: "Lol what a joke, bro!" One visitor begins to yell:" Worst environment ever! Good perks, free breakfast, free pizzas on some occasions. Toxic environment, hostile managers leaving themselves the right to scream at people." The other cries: "Stay away at all costs!!! Free Breakfast and that is about it. Overworked and underpaid, toxic environment, owners care about lining their pockets with dirty money, worst HR department ever, VPs all part the ´BRO´ club, what is the ´BRO´ club?, ask the owners, bonus Grid -unfair, and total nonsense, incompetent Managers!"

I look here and there and see hired hand killers, those nerds from porn-lab, now on their chests read: web developers, software developers, product managers, video editors, software engineers, QA analysts, senior software developers, software quality, assurances, analysts, customer service representatives, web analysts, data analysts, engineers, VFX generalists, and managers.

More guards come to me. Josh runs towards me. I'm not going anywhere. Cameras show how I hit the first fat guard. And that is a true cause for me to rejoice to the glory, cos so many saints are gathered, the very angels must be among us, too.

Welcome Fight and Never come back Wishes

At the same time, Cliver & the boys eat at Louie & Ernie's Pizza some pizza, when they see on CNN some more action for today: Inside Western Hemisphere's tallest building and already an iconic landmark, first floor, big hall, happens. Cliver runs out and with him goes 11 other Makks, Bloods' members. One of them yells: "Yeah, look at Birchy, death gorgeous true blue!"

I take a chair and smash it to a living target. Somebody hits behind. Bells ring in my head: "Happiness is the enemy. It weakens you, puts doubt in your mind. Suddenly you have something to lose. Am I happy?"

Near the One, WTC goes Frank and a bunch of his comrades. The mighty has the rumor mill going on. Then they hear a huge din inside. Frank says lazily: "I check." He clumps in and sees what he sees. He codes and rules out: "Grab some real estate! Come!" The mercenaries go in. Frank attack the nearby guard: "This is not fair. Do not attack a ronery guy, just one by one. Beat your face." The guard fells. There are some NAPs, FiSTs, SEALs and so, and they beet feet. They go to action as soldiers always do. They don't get wrapped around the axle. Nobody surprises them behind or front. They steer clear of the little problems and move on to the real issues. They go like a big fist: azimuth check. The nearest guards are light oats.

They use what they use: there is acquired gear. The youngest of these sinful mercenaries do the good idea fairy. They hit hard and they know why the sky is blue: True soldiers are trained to hit that the sky is not blue, cos air particles transmit blue light, it's blue, cos these great infantry soldiers are denoted by blue cords, discs, and badges, and the God loves the infantry. There come everywhere more guards, more and more, but the denser the grain, the easier it is to mow.

Great mercenaries come to join the party and true brothers keep this as a lubrication for the Walhalla. And it means just the fourth point of contact: first, we hit the balls of their feet, then we roll across the ground on their calf muscle, tight, buttocks, and finally the torso.

I kick Josh to his balls and throw him away from my sight. We come upon the net, so our fits communicate with our bunch what is going on with our mission. Two youngsters get hard from guards but joes and private joesnuffies stand up, and jolly go round. There comes PX Ranger-hits, a lot of unnecessary gear, but all of them are CAB Chaser, who try to get into an engagement to earn a combat action badge. Guards try to circle us but beat out boots, we stand with our legs apart, hit enemies´ boots or shoes with our hands. We punish them. Guards are falling, dash ten, eleven ... We really earn sham shields.

My hands fire another volley, and we say again our last. Guards find themselves zipper heads and lost in the valley. Our skiff and stage work well. And we FUBU (fouled up beyond all understanding) them. The guards lay and we err with them. We tap their shoulders and shake their hands and say "well-done" things. Then I go to Mr. Boot, so Mr. Josh. I say: "Now Y cheesedick, we have something to talk about."

Cos the police are almost there, I take Josh to my shoulders and went to my Mustang, throw Mr. Gambler there, and I am just saying last words to Frank and his chem light battery and dark green things when Cliver and his Makks arrived.

He says: "Ohh oh, Y have Devil Dogs." I: "Yep, they made gape duty. But their cover on my grape." Cliver smiles. Frank says: "Who´s this?" I: "Just the flight deck crewman on a carrier tasked with fuel handling."

Cliver says: "And Y doughboy?" Frank: "Frank 15 minutes prior to 15 minutes prior." I: "He is a good piece of gear." Cliver: "Damn, I thought a wyman is a jackass, but he´s a wyman alright." Frank smiles: "And y´re back on the block, with the birth-control glasses." They do not take up fives but do it the right way, shaking hands and tapping shoulders. Frank and blue buddies go, and I go with Cliver to the Mustang, where Josh sits.

We drive away. Time is 4 pm, and our little battle took 10 minutes to take down 15 guards and 10 others almost. I have that drug deal with Josh to make. I must tell him to make a hole. Mr. Josh doesn´t say a word. Well, why should he? He had already made his speech.

Now it is my turn: "If Y come to Brooklyn again, I shoot Y. And if Y send cleaners after me, cleaners come after Y. Y made something first, and I after that. We are even. If you do not accept this, I kill Y. Your bodyguards cannot challenge street and field warriors. Your fellas are high and off to the right. We have pop smokes that You do not have. Do not collect Toys for Tots."

Mr. Josh keeps quiet, but he thinks madly something, and cannot find words. Then he says: "My brother met some years ago Manhattan fellas and Blackstone's credit group threw my brother on the street. We left the building, and my brother´s guys were having heart palpitations. The whole time my brother was still negotiating with the sellers and saying. Hey, I'm money good. So I´m, and that´s your big, big problem." He nods and he leaves. I look his way back to Manhattan. I know that fella has big plans, but not in Brooklyn.

Fin´amor

This has been a busy day and I must go to buy a new suit. We go to 139 Flatbush Ave. Cliver stays out and I go alone look Cole Haan technology, stylish monk straps, traditional Oxfords. I have made enough entrances today, so I do not want a suit to make an entrance, but the sporty thing is a must. I just love those aggressive salespeople who don´t care about y once y buy. I get back what I deserve. Now it is a blue suit and I like it. "Very nice, and thank Y." At last, some light can be seen at the end of the tunnel.

Meanwhile, you have made a great day. And it shall be very soon when your manager and International Book Towns´ president shall meet.

It is 18:10, and nothing ATFU (ate the fuck up) nearby, just love and weed. I shall meet Y and Madame Manager soon in citizenM NY Bowery. There reads in big letters SEPHORA. I think: "If this is not the place, nothing is." The place is just minutes away from the nightlife, within 20 minutes (walking) from SoHo, Lower Manhattan, and Little Italy. I look at the floor and lamps, well, perhaps I shall look for Mademoiselle Victoria and Madame Manager, too. Nice view outto windows. That red & orange is like my mother´s designs in hotels in the 70s. Somewhere there sit two women who agree that the bar is very modern. Really. I think it´s BOB (stands for a big orange ball). They say it is a cozy room with all the essentials. So, it´s so, where are the ladies? Ah, there, MyVictoria keeps her hand up. I come to Y and Manager. I say: "Oh, watta lovely day, everything is so noice."

Nothing that remembers nights and afternoons FODA (fuck off and die asshole) things. So quiet and charming. I nod French way my head and say some vain & slicky words: "NYC never stops giving more surprises, and especially Brooklyn is the place for wonders, night and day after I came back here, deep Brkner, everything has been so amazing, storming lovely, my heart beats hear three times more than every else, just so cool and amazing. Madame, and ofc MyVictoria, it is a great honor to give you, both beautiful women, my proposal."

After a hard day, these words sound to my ears no fucking good aka, busted, nonfunctional, broken, but perhaps too many hours with the tough guys, know it is time for pleasure and relaxed entertainment. Perhaps now after lead to astray, this restores me to the truth.

I continue: "There´s one interesting connection with the IOB and porn-business, and it is the adventure. Don´t travel just to see. MyVictoria, Madame, when in doubts, travel, please. If you still have doubts and need an extra push, then porn and cultural adventure shall tell it all. Let´s put them together from inspirational to cheesy to spiritual even. So, yours is also an adventure, so take it with your tour. See, try, listen, feel, taste, fuck, learn, smile, and even cry for happiness. If you do not take loving risks, you´ll be a wasted soul. Once upon a time, there was a knight ..."

Madame gives a sight: now it begins all over again.

I go on: "The knight, full of true, such love I call virtuous love says: ´To reach your side I would give everything if I could make this come flaming true. I would climb all the mountains between us, sail across the oceans to find y, and once I finally reached your side. This must be done with haste. For night´s swift dragons cut the clouds full fast. And yonder shines evaluating harbinger. Having risked my life, said the knight, to reach Y this night why would Y need more to prove my love is true and for y? What would y sacrifice for me? What worth and honor stand by your side?"

I: "Madame, the story is told everywhere. They have measured and still do the worth of the Knight and his lady. Look at Montolieu, for painters, sculptors, photographers, book craftsmen, working holidays, Librairie du Center. Look at The Cholocate Obidos Medieval courtly love festival. Look at the Obidos Livraria da Adega. Look at Redu's La Reduce art events. Look at the red-winged woman and Vignerons Wine Festival. Look at St-Pierre-de-Clages airy fair. Look at Midsummer Festival in Selfoss, Sidney festival, Tvedestrand's crime festival, great events in Ascona-Locarno, in those mafia places. Look at Becherel's annual festival at Eastern, also traditions from Great Medieval and the Renassaince courtly love times. Look at Bellprat's conferences, round table, musical performances, art exhibitions, Celebration of Catalan culture, Saint Jordi Celebrations. Look at Borrby festival, meetings, Bredevoort's festival of flags and heraldic things, Bredevoort courtly loving kisses, Clunes ladies and knights talks, Cuisery's kissing on-air noble smash, Damme's knightly memories, Featherston's St John's market's and troubadours, Fjaerland Viking king smash-smash, Hay parade of great poems, EDM-everywhere, high tech, and house all over the world and millions and millions of people feasting, loving and singing. It isn't a joke, there must be a measured trust. Great Knights needs that, peasants do not. Knight go, they do not eat a cloud of flying dust, and do not never come back. Others leave with it and surrender to the shame a hundred times a day."

It is obvious what those festivals, cultural & adventure tourism needs. It needs hardcore porn changing to courtly love. That cultural tourism adventures need. If we can do that, nobody beats us. If we put in front of EDM- and literary festival the U.S.-trip-clubs' pole-dancers and money the thing doesn't blow to pieces, cos with the money whores change to cultivated ladies. No empress is a whore.

The Romans know it all: Cultural spirit, gyms, and dancers make it together. Religion called in sin, but one old Roman soldier´s tombstone tells it all: There doesn´t read "peace with bloodshed" and it doesn´t list blessings like *Fortuna Redux* (good fortune), *Spes* (hope), *Bonus Eventus* (success), *Felicitas* (prosperity), *Securitas Populi Romani* (security for the Roman people), *Tutela* (guardian or protector), *Annona* (grain and plenty), *Fides* (fidelity), *Salus* (welfare, Honos (honor) and *Virtus* (courage in battle or virtue). There read: "Peace is the best thing that man may know; peace alone is better than a thousand triumphs; peace has the power to guard our lives and secure equality among fellow-citizens." That peace is that trust. If there isn´t it, everything is worth of great shit.

Y ask: "If it is peace, so where is the porn." I laugh: "What porn? If Y put in a cultural adventure the porn, it isn´t porn anymore, it is courtly love, loving nobly, fin´amor, passionate and disciplined, Romans Courtois, Roman de la V & T.

The Manager becomes irritated: "So I go to talk with the IOB´s president that I give you trip-pole-girls and tip rains and Y get to your festivals *Caritas*: via eyes/glance attraction, worship from afar, declaration of passionate devotion, virtuous touch, renewed wooing with the oath of virtue and eternal fealty, moans of approaching more love and manifestations of lovesickness, heroic deeds of valor which win the pole lady´s heart, the consummation of husbands and boyfriends secret love and endless adventures and sugerfuged love angel´s arrow-things???"

I give her my best smile: "Madame, Y look at the cream now, I look at the chewing nut: Money is in the world, when you know how to approach it. The money, the object, search all the time its subject. Porn is an objective matter, a tool like money, they go hand in hand, and find their fulfillment in courtly love. Amen."

Some Arrangements with the Manager

I: "So we go to the IOB-president and Y and she can talk about those vain things, and we talk about the true thing." The Manager: "What do Y mean?" I: "Ofc about those porn-vids which have come to the public now and how to market your star and the IOB-festivals via them." The Manager: "How can I and that president do that?" I: "You cannot, but I can."

I tap my hands: "I think we must give money a chance to find its subject."

I call Cliver: "Y delivered here recently one key, do Y wanna that bitch does the best pole dancing with your top off?"

Cliver: "Well, hm..." I: "The stripper at the club downtown makes more paper in one night than you will make in a month. She makes more money in four hours shaking her ass than a fella does in four days breaking his ass."

Cliver: "Njaa, I do not ..." I: "Beautiful lady makes 150 d in ten minutes by shaking her naked breasts at a pathetic little man. Ha! She wins! He is definitely the one being exploited." Cliver: "So what ..."

I: "What so what? Now blue falcon Mind-Eegan has been fuck off here and gone with chair forces, nerds, so zero days and a wake-up. Yadamean?" Cliver: "Something to do with table dance and lip tease?" I: "Make Europeans realize all they want for next Christmas is a good table-dance from Candy, who shall give them a lip tease from across the room, they shall go over and ask her out ..." We begin to laugh.

Cliver understands, let´s deliver new gift boxes with the water flow principle."

I say to the Manager: "So I arrange an appointment with Y and the IOB-president. I give Y tomorrow a deal-paper, which Y can take or live it. And if Y take, then we go to that president. I ask before we go, has she something to say about main streams of that deal, ok." Manager: "That deal I wanna read carefully." I make a court bending: "Do that so carefully as Y want, but it shall be in my hands four after I have given it to Y." Manager: "How about an attorney?" I: "I thought that Y are that, m I wrong?" She: "Yes." I: "Well, call him/her now, and she/he has some hours to read the papers." She: "Why right now?" I explain: "The preliminary agreement must be ready now. Then you and they can chew it and I press y more and keep y up to date. Ok? Then I meet y and them at the round table and that´s the end of the story."

I say to Cliver on the phone: "Wait a minute." I see on Manager's eyes that she hesitates. I have seen from the beginning the same glance. It doesn´t promise good. She has ulterior motives. In my mind comes Napoleon and his foreign minister Talleyrand. The great Napoleon said: ´Y are pure shit in silk socks.´ And Talleyrand: ´It is a great annoyance that so great a man has so bad an upbringing.´ Napoleon should have shot that fella right there. He deceived great Napoleon as soon as he could. Coward."

I say to Y: "Bab, I go now to do curtain-raisers. See Y later. Perhaps Y wanna comma with me to tree hockey match. There are The Brooklyn Nets vs l.a. fakers. How they LeBron this time, it shall be noice to see."

You are not surprised: "When it begins?" I: "At 1900." Y: "I must talk more with my manager. Ok. Too soon." I nod to the manager and go.

I take my phone: "So. One more smol thing today." Cliver asks: "What thing?" I: "We must gather the dancers to those festivals in Europe and all over the world. Isn´t it obvious? The only problem is their contracts and their managers and another kind of mess there." Cliver: "Sure. That is chaos. And those owners have nailed them to the floor. Those wife beaters are real candy wrappers."

The Police Reaction & the Gang-Action

At the same time news about the Liberty Ave fight and One WTC handling get so furious reaction that the Police come to Media and promise to do everything to stop gangs attacking innocent billionaires and other good people.

So now the big brother is watching the homeless. The Coalition for the Homeless withdrew its support at once from a new homelessness command center - lead by the NYPD and the Department of Homeless Services - after people tweeted photos of appeared to be police monitoring and mapping the locations of homeless New Yorkers.

The CFTH policy director Giselle Routhier says after that: "The Mayor´s Orwellian assurances that mass surveillance and policing of New Yorkers who are sleeping on the streets will somehow accomplish the goal of winning their trust defies logic." The police have no time to think gangs and so but the Mayor´s Office says it is only rational to send police if the person faced an emergency or presented a safety risk. Deputy Press Secretary Avery Cohen says: "It´s common sense that certain 311 calls may be directed to 911." Meanwhile, uniformed officers are watching a dozen live video feeds. The police says: "NYC is proud to launch a first-of-its-kind Street Homelessness Joint Command Center. Thanks to the tireless efforts of @NYCDHS we will become the first city in the nation to end long-term street homelessness."

While drug dealing, gang-things and so have no operative money, operatives at the Homelessness Joint Command Center use public camera footage, precision mapping, and data to conduct interventions and encourage homeless people to accept shelter and service referrals. New Yorkers and 18 000 city workers have been asked to contact the command center, which will direct the information to one of several agencies, among them NYPD. At the same time, homeless New Yorkers forced to face off with cops will only work harder to evade notice and miss out on public services they need. Instead of wasting public resources on this counterproductive and chilling strategy Mayor does not consider creating a Housing Command Center to increase access to the resources that will enable people to leave the streets and move into safe, stable homes of their own.

In this situation, gangs and other criminals are free to act here and there. For instance, a 28-year fella is walking in Far Rockaway down Deerfield near the 29th Street just before 20:00 when Young Fly Bridge warrior shoots him behind. EMS rush the poor fella to Jamaica hospital, where he is in stable condition. After hard shooting the police arrest the gang-member and give him charges of attempted murder, assault, criminal possession of a weapon, and reckless endangerment.

At the same time, eleven people are arrested for trafficking heroin, fentanyl, and carfentanil. Long-haul truck drivers transport drugs from the southern border of California to a stash-house in Springfield Gardens. 11 pounds of carfentanil and fentanyl goes with a member of Morris Ave Gunnaz. Two A10 - Air it out -fellas walks in the 23th Precinct with five handguns and AK-47, and two pounds of cocaine and 11 000 cash.

At the same time, White Plains resident G. Arias´ truck drivers transport heroin, cocaine, fentanyl, carfentanil, and Ketamine to the Bronx stash-house, where associates cut and repackage the narcotics.

Cocaine and heroin are hidden in a minifridge in the back seat of a car in Astoria. Two pounds of Ketamine is hidden in a secret compartment under the front seat of a truck along the Van Wyck Expressway service road and over 1500 fake oxycodone pills containing fentanyl from a truck go near the Tappan Zee Bridge. New Jack City -warrior (the 49th Precinct) kills a pedestrian and injured two drivers.

Shart & Shat

Time is about 9 pm when Cliver and I have studied possible treads from the gangs and owners and their bodyguards. And what we must consider if we try to help dancers go to live in European countries without managers and other kinds of pimps?

Cliver gives a list from the gangs: "Just those biggest bogglers, bro: Nico Malos, 3Ni - Trinitarios, Seven Crew, BMV-Brooklyn most wanted (269 & 730), No Love City, BIB - Bosses in Business (Crips), 8 Trey Grips, Franklin Ave Family, RF-Rich Family, Bloc Gang, Young Fort Greene Family, Fort Greene Family, South Side Bullies, Young Stackers, Cash Money Brothers, East Side Bangers, Petey Gang.

There are three of five crime families, but those Mafia-fellas keep quiet. No more press conferences and TV appearances. No more weekly meetings with capos at favorite restaurants and social clubs. No more shootouts between warring factions. No more wire rooms for taking wagers. Gangsters try to earn as they´ve done for decades, with drug dealing, loan sharking, running 11 strip clubs in Brooklyn and protection rackets, and skimming from union construction jobs. Bookmaking is still a lively trade, but most of it is done online using offshore accounts, not smoke-filled gambling dens. One mafia-bartender from Suggardaddy says: "Everybody´s a rat, y can´t trust anybody anymore."

An interesting new aspect is that lieutenants and soldiers avoid gathering in groups. They try to be less vulnerable to the wiretap or surveillance photo. But the fu**ers and murderers gather in strip-clubs, and Y can pick them up very easily if Y can get those tapes from cameras, but there are always about 10 fellas and 8 girls ready to act. And if some crime happens in those sugardaddy-clubs no tapes available, cos they do not wanna show the police those real update lieutenants and soldiers.

As we had gathered this information, Brooklyn 11 mafia-strip-clubs ave turn to be in the hands of old-timers, low-profile leaders. Gangsters in clubs respect a lot they old leaders Carmine Persico, 85, and John "Sonny" Franzese.

Yes, that fuc**er is still alive, after murdering 57 persons himself. That son of the bitch is 101-year-old, who keeps on hating Gotti´s gabby flamboyance. All these long years, those two are calling the shots for the Colombos, albeit from jail in Persicoś case. They are happy, honored and all Goodfellas respect them as great black hands. Legends go on in strip-clubs about these old-timers made man things and sleeps with the fishes. They are really bad-bings.

The old fishes keep on being big genos, real wacked order givers, and I just respect them. Some butcherers are in jail. For instance, Brooklyn´s Lord Infamous, the rapper who killed six mafia haters. And Bafia imitates Wafia, and one drunken Gansta says: "Yo, this g loses his cheeba out his jeans, an´ he thinks somebody snatched it, so he tries to cap my holmes wit a 9 miss all 10 rounds. Killed two girls in tha´ playground, though - that nigga be gans-sta as fuck, yo."

Cliver asks me: "How can we smoke this shart & shat?" I laugh: "Do Y thing rotten things are tough? These amazzos aren´t face to face fighters, they are group quailers. They can shoot Y behind, but face to face they envy Y. They are like Russians, they are afraid to lose their faces, and they stay in the closet so long as they live. They hate as Y know, breeders, and strizzies like us." Cliver: "Ok, but how do Y win them? I: "There are also other kinds of Goodfellas, who respect your fight. They have respect, and if you expect a kick in the nuts and get a slap in the face, it´s a victory. Those guys are like old Romans, they are good." Cliver: "Rlly? But how do Y win?" I: "We beat them in the fair fight and take those bitches to Europe."

 Cliver asks one more time: "How should Y win?" I look at my watch: 11:30 pm. I say: "I go there as I went to Liberty Ave, face to face. MyFriend, we have nothing to hide." Cliver: "Y have run several times away from the police?" I: "Yes, I have. What it has to do with all this?" Cliver: "If You are open-minded, why Y run?" I: "Cos they should have put me to the jail, and I have no time for that." Cliver: "So Y have something to hide?" I: "No I do not. I just show to Y and them, that popos have much to hide." Cliver: "So Y keep on running and so what?" I: "So they understand that what they see is right and what they don´t is fucked and bad."

The Sixth Day

Hookers and Raining Money

tapio tiihonen

New York Smexy The Gut & The Kiss

The Cultural Hoe with the Golden Kiss

You look sleepy and ask: "Where have Y been? Looking that NBA-thing?" I: "I have been out there in the jungle. And what I have seen is sooo goood. I begin now to make that deal." Y: "So, you try to send hookers to Europe and make Europe looks like a strip-club?" I: "Yes." Y: "Really?" I: "It goes like this: When big money comes to Europe, it wakes it up. Money is the backbone of society. If you have a friend, you can do barter-things. They are very slow, and if you have a bunch of brothers You do product exchange. When you have million people, you do automatic line things with a lasting deal. When you have tens of millions, you have money. And in the whole world Y have cards and bitcoins and c-programs, when You have a golden kiss."

Y: "And that means hookers?" I: "You do not need to market if the product is good. The best product is Y & me. What we do in public, is the best marketing every. It must be more elegant, than trying to cheat or press people. I just give them what they want, and more I make them enjoy working, and see that holidays and working days are the same." Y: "So that it is all about." Y kiss me. Yes, the golden kiss.

I: "They bark to the money, but money is the tool, trust is the interest, and it runs on time. The quicker time flies, the bigger is the magnetism. There are black holes in the sky, and they say: ´Our dooming day.´ They are so wrong. Back holes are gravity centers, but none of them are material things. They are time. So Black holes gravity centers are time centers. They make the time around, and every impulse from there changes not just time around but space and matter also." Y: "So Y are creating now new time centers?" I: "Yes."

I continue: "Time tic-tacs best in the open place, and with open knowledge. Best concept marketing is that. It is truly true. Time is money, and money is time. Money is the best clock in the world. It tic-tacs you trust. Trust, faith, name it, goes like time, and that money touch is like time´s touch. It touches y everywhere and just like this, now (I snap my finger)." Y: "Go to the point."

I: "Money´s trust in the backbone of society, cos society goes with its confidence. Money seeks the target, and the best target shall be shown with open knowledge. Money does not like hidden agendas, cheating and so. Money and time like lightning. So, give them light.

Why laugh to hookers, porn, sports and so and say, hey man, there is no culture in them? Is the hooker a stoopid bitch that does not have emotions, ideas, and ranks and so? Does she just give what a fucker wants and film that lust and her own groans up? No. When the climax comes, it cannot come without horny trust, confidence, emotion, seeing something just vow and awesome. The only thing that is bad, it takes a short time, time takes a break and a break again. But hooker does the open space, make her a change, money goes like time to its center. Where those open centers are there the cash flow goes." Y: "To the black holes?" I: "Yeah." Y: I do not understand." I: "Look at me, look a city. What it is a place with my awareness, NYC or Brooklyn awareness. We and our downtowns and strip-clubs have their own time-centers, own DNA, which tells who lives and dies. Yes, we are the black holes, centers of magnetism, Y & me and downtowns and so."

Y: "And?" I: "Nothing much. Money loves open knowledge and us. It seeks us. We must open us to it, so it sees us. And I put porn and sports to the cultural tourism of the IOB so that money can see it. And when money, time, which seeks all the time target, sees the cultural target with the kiss, it doesn´t miss. *Comprende*?"

Y: "And the street cred?" I: "In that golden kiss, culture is your Religion and education your Saviour. First there are mob and its mobsters, hookers and bitches, then there comes the open knowledge, the Light, and they change to bean counters, and the hookers shall say: 'The Saturn ION's oil filter housing is cheap plastic, cos bean counters decided that a metal one was too expensive.'"

Y: "And then?" I: "Then the bitches say: 'After two years as an i-banker, I'll buy my own island and retire.' Illusion says: 'Many kids in undergraduate business programs are disillusioned by the thought of doing the i-banking routine when they graduate. They are so wrong it is a great Illusion." Y: "Go to the point. And then?

I: "Then we come to the Great Giabo."

Y: "Tapio, you irritate me on purpose." I take your hand and kiss your cheek.

Y: "So. Where is the black card?" I: "Black card? Are Y series? They aren't after those clients anymore, cos GIABO is 99 % of humanity who are being suppressed by the Elite Global Money Changers (Bankers). Movements: 'End the Fed' and 'Occupy Wall Street'."

Now it is time to go to the point, Y look bored to death and very frustrated. I kiss Y: "First they are mobs and hookers, then they change to bankers, and after counting so much and seeing the structure of the cultural life with porn and business and so they see the Light." Y: "What do Y mean the Light?"

I: "First there are workers, with hand and body, then they change to craftsmen and -women, they work with their hands & bodies & brains.

The banker-bitch changes to work with her heart. She becomes an artist when asking: if no one asks me, I know what time is, if I wish to explain it to him who asks, I can't. Goods are in the hands of the benevolent, and open-handed, and when the luxurious lady does not squander nor the miser horad it, for whether ill-stored or unwisely spent it is equally lost.

Beauty looks at the shapes and measures proportions. Your beautiful fingers make circles and your body fits precisely into both a circle and a square, and in your banking forms and scales, Y notice links to a perfect body. Your heart opens Y the living rulebook, containing the fixed and faultless laws set down by the time and money. That beauty and proportion and cash flows have the same eurythmic, a beautiful and agreeable atmosphere. It mirrors your beautiful face, but it mirrors time-space-motion: strength, functionality, and beauty. There goes in daylight these laws of love and kiss and beauty. That is called the eternity what a beauty sees in the mirror."

Y: "So the pole-girls in their cultural tourism adventure change from mafia to bankers and then to artists?"

I: "The golden kiss is for a muse of fire. That would ascend the highest heaven of cash flow and invention, a kingdom for a courtly kissing place-stage, hooker to princes to act, and monarchs to behold the swelling scene. Box for hire and sidewalk tulip and gold digger changes to an artist and YourTapio doesn´t lose his money to pay the box for hire. No need to pick up 2 sidewalk tulips for the bachelor party. No need to say: that gas cooker cots 100 quid for a round-the-world. Just laugh to this confused Jonjo - what is kindred doing living with a whore. Not a straight golddigger. Romantic involvement not just for that. She, the artist, really loves him."

Y: "So? What´s the point?" I: "No Golddigger Complex with an artist. The artist does not think, what others think about her, she thinks, what she thinks about them. She has fixed sponsors, not pimps, and managers. And makes art, a real thing, not share the image. And I do not mean that Muse-band, but the idea: an inhumanly awesome band that manages to fuse Daddy Yankee and Puetarican rap with Doowop-Brooklyn and Spanish and So Brooklyn Freestyle. And still makes it the best-ever thus reducing ex-hookers to tears. And person one and two don´t die with drugs and euphoria."

Y: "Why are Y insulting me?" I: "Bab, when people see beauty-artist at the night, they go home and listen a great hifi. People have such a boner on both occasions. They think that the artist is the best. People love them more than they love their family. And they never bring a trump player to an attorney argument. You know, if the Jesu piece around your nec is bigger your pistol, it makes homicide okey-dokey and your God will forgive you.

The artist does not share the image, her lusty hot stormy flames things. She materializes that image in barter-thing, money exchange, cards, bitcoins, c-programs, in all those cash flow levels, not just a personal way, but upper scales.

Hooker is an artist amateur, the banker is an artist servant, and the artist breaths through the golden kiss. And if you do not cry out in this, or sing this and that, then don´t try it, cos money and its gravitational cultural center have a use for lobbying this."

Y: "What Y wanna me to do?" I: "Well, stay home." Y: "Why?" I: "Cos now it´s action time." Y: "What do Y mean?" I: "I go to strip-clubs now."

Y: "They kill Y." I: "Well, so be it. What comes, comes. I do not murmur or pray nothing. I made VictoriaCourt with love, materialized my golden kiss and it has proportions of beauty, right golden ratios. If Y look in your face and body, and in VictoriaCourt, they are 1,6:1:0,6. And they are correct, Y can count every piece of shit, your face has the equal parts, your head is 1/6 of the whole body. YourVictoriaCourt has beauty´s ratios, too. So that´s why it is a very beautiful house, cos

Nature has that ratio, too. And by the way, in Nature animals and so are beautiful, cos to strong animals cannot hide their beauty. If the VictoriaCourt is the artistic work, so why can´t I go to strip-clubs and make the artistic work, too. That work does not die. It bears fruits. Now I go to make preliminary agreements with strip-clubs."

It is 2 am and Y laugh and shake your head: "Xxxo. You odo. Call me every half an hour. I do not want a dead husband." I put a bullet in my gat, and am a little bit surprised.

The Pilgrimage of the Strip-clubs

I wash my face on very cold water. Nothing. I stay sleepy. I go to an ice-cold shower and eat some bananas. And take a shot of Marker´s Mark. I say to Our Smiling Friend: "Sorry, the exception confirms the rule." I take another exception. I haven´t slept in 30 hours. So not much sleep debt. I manage.

I call Frank: "Hello there, can Y crank a little bit. Yes, I go to strip-things and I need Dynamited Chicken, Yeah, more guns, need for farts and dart. Meet Y there." I text a message to Mr. Josh: "Dear f**cker, I took some piracy from Y, how about updating our relations, cos You said that you are coming back to Manhattan. I want 50 nerds and photographers, not in porn povs or webcam, but in pole-dance things in Europe, they shall be paid well."

I give Doggy a steak and say to it: "You are my only and best friends. Others are PayPal-fuckers." I run the floors and one older woman looks at me behind the curtains and shakes her head. I jump to my Mustang and smile comes back to MyFace: "Yeah, emo pudding flows. This is so brazy."

I communicate with my friends & friends to come, and do not have any idea that in NYC they speak 640 languages. Unfortunately, many of them are on the verge of dying out. One block away Fulmaya Gurung and Takla Gurung talk Seke, which is spoken by roughly 700 people worldwide. If this bridge is allowed, it comes from the Mustang district of Nepal. And I do not think even that of 100 speakers in New York City, about 50 lives in a single Flatbush building. And when Fulmaya and Takla see my Mustang pass them, they think bad that they do not teach their language to their kids. My Mustang passes Professor Daniel Kaufman´s window, and he the text to his friend: "The heritage is so gone. All the things that used to be transmitted in the language are f**cing gone - the great songs, the nice stories, the awesome folklore, and all of the wealth of golden knowledge that really resides in the human language as so very well." When my Mustang reaches the front side of Sugardaddy´s, my native language and my time are running out.

At the same time in Ozone Park at 78-17 101st Avenue, a house is on fire. Firefighters save people and only four people are injured and four more - those last ones are firefighters. One warrior of Wild Mexicans shoots from a red GMC truck the 45-year-old man in the arms and chest and kills him outside a Key Food Supermarket in the Rockaways at 87-15 Beach Blvd. Breezy´s point a man´s dead body is found along the Breezy Point waterfront. He is a member of Tracey Money Towers. He went swimming and died.

I jump from my Mustang at 51-07 27th St. Frank & five pros and Clive & 7 Makks are there ready and steady.

Frank: "So what´s the call?" I: "I take some stripers to Europe, need their signs on paper." Frank laughs: "That´s is a piece of cake. And how many dancers Y need, my friend?" I: "Just 35. Then the mission is down." Mercenaries and gang members look at each other. Cliver says: "Y have a good sense humor, s.o.h. very hot tickets. And what about guards and police? Have to thought about them?" I: "Yes, the club must be ready in ten minutes. And there are 11 of them. If we think about inside and outside time, it shall take altogether 160 minutes." Frank wonders: "How do Y lure them to sign?" I say: "I smile. With my charm. No money lost. Let´s go. I take here Frank and Cliver and just 2+2. First, we three go, then 2, 2, ok."

Cliver: "Well, it is 2:15 am and they close at 4 am. How about 160 minutes?" I: "Very easy. I show F and y the system here. Then we go to other clubs in threes. 5 x 3 + the same = 10. Cos here are 15 fellas, we do two rounds, and take those hookers and cos we do it at the same time - we have some spare time after taken those girls. And here are to You all papers, which the girls must sign and owners too."

A huge mercenary called BobbyBlue asks: "And what if they do not want to sign?" Others look at the giant and we all begin to laugh. No time to lose. We go to Sugardaddy´s club. Three janitors look at three big suit fellas and other jeans-and-jacket-fellas. Bouncers are very pleased with what they see: now here comes a great bunch of trained athletes who make the green rain.

I go first to one very well-built, fake tits, butts, and a botox-slip Latin scripper. I: "Hello, I have just met your owner, and he wants you to join me and my cultural tourism adventure group for two months in Europe. Great profits, great environments, and four stars hotels. Each of Y must come alone, but managers shall be paid, too. Here is the paper, the club´s owner Krieger has just signed his contract, and he hardly recommends Y to take the deal, or Y can get fired at once." The mya looks at me and reads the paper: "I must talk with the owner. This is unbelievable."

She tells: "I found this club in the Yellow Pages and called to make sure the place was still open for my business. I knew the best time to meet Krieger, so I made my way to this club, hoping to run a con for a sugar daddy and a well-paying job. Yeah, Hot Spot. The owner is a muscular, handsome man in his late forties. He was at the club to receive the beverage shipment for the week. I introduced and said: ´A job, I hope.´ The owner: ´Call me Steven´, he opened the door: ´What kind of a job?´ I: ´Anything.´ That Steven, trying hard not to let it be obvious that he is checking my out, kept her eyes focused on my face. When I didn´t have a criminal record he gave the job, and I began to dance. They helped me to take a loan, and I got fake butts, tits, and Botox-lips. And at the same time, I transformed from selfish to selfless, and then to a servant, he had bought me. So now he is going to share me with the European men also?"

I: "All wrong, this contract says, that you can live this place and stay in Europe and go from there wherever it pleases Y." She looks at the paper. After 5 minutes I got the first lady in that the IOB-house.

The second target is not surprised as the first one. She admits that the owner of this jiggle joint is no sugar daddy. She tells that two of her friends are suing S-Daddy´s for cheating. Bartender talks with one mercenary and looks very upset about the paper that BobbyBlue has in his huge hands. I go to the bartender: "Where is the owner, that fu**cking mafia-bitch?"

The bartender tries to go for help, but I stop him and kick his leg out of him. He fells. I say: "Tell where that fairy is before I break your teeth." He shows me the table. Oh, there the Borgata-guy sits and laughs with his buttons around him. Frank comes. I ask: "How many?" Frank: "Two." Then those others come also: "Altogether six names. Not bad. I go to get that signature now. Shoot, if they try to bump off." Four Capodecinas are with him. Four cramps are coming near us. Krieger sees me coming. Mr. Skipper of the *Capo Dei Capi* says: "What do Y want? I´m busy, reserve the time, now go." I laugh: "Yes my friend, I go after Y had signed this Paper Local. I´m in a hurry, too."

I show him the paper. He says: "So, you want me to give 6 ladies, and I can get free travel to those festivals, where they perform, and six of man group gets the same privilege. And the commission from each lady is 14 %. And if the ladies do not come back, after four months, I can hire new dancers. And Y say that the girls are signed already. And three of them take me to the court, if I shall not sign, right now, and Y shall take those security tapes to the police station and they can check my men and compare them to hits." I: "That´s right. Sign now, I´m in a hurry." I take my gun outto pocket and aim his head: "You have five seconds to sign then I blow your head off." He looks at the bang-bang, and this is not bone. I tap his shoulder: "Bravo Zulu."

I get the paperback and turn and go. Nobody moves. We go out and scatter in threes. With me are BoddyBlue and Cliver. Time is 2:30 am. 29 girls more. They come after us and alarm more Guns, so no time to lose. This is like Blitzkrieg. Germans didn´t occupy the land they went straight to the capital, as did US forces, imitating Germans, in Iraq. It means one thing, the enemies begin to shoot Y behind, if y slow down.

We go to Saphires and it is easy to talk with the girls, cos every single dancer offers me a dance. So, I never left alone without which they´d get a 5. I ask straight away and got three names. One of the strippers is very angry about stardenders, who in the Instagram command a huge following. I meet the owners and they invite me and my BobbyBlue and Cliver to their table. They are just delightful persons. They say they have met the Australian prime minister many times and they just love this kind of international cooperation. They signed at once the papers and said I shall come soon to make a real contract with them.

We got eight names from there. I phoned the other places, and they have gathered altogether 39 names and most of those owners are more than happy about these kinds of deals. The Sapphires owners say that great striptease is drying little by little.

I look at the time, 3:15 am. And three clubs have been hostile to our preliminary agreement, but the rest more than willing to cooperate with us. It is a surprise to us, and I just enjoyed the hospitality of Bob and Paul here in Sapphires. And with the elegance and class of the original Upper East Side, this "39" offers real *deluxe amenities*, erotic programming, and VIP concierge services including designer suites, couple packages, private butlers, and luxury chauffeurs to satisfy every desire of my friends. Provocative dancers, exclusive quest DJs, and live music from sultry Sirens.

Mr. Wright comes and tells me: "We´ve long recognized the need for S-location in Europe. In fact, our guests are asking for it. We want to take everyone´s favorite features from the original destination and bring it to the new lever. In Europe from live music to creative programming, delicious food, and a sexy bar scene, we will not be happier to unveil this seductive new venue to our valued present and future guests in Europe."

I tell him that book towns in Europe are more than happy to learn this kind of elegance and discretion. I love design elements from deep leather features to full-service bars with sculptural black marble and inviting leather high top seating. Nice curved TV-wall and bathed in alluring blue light sounds good in European festivals, too. Much to think about in the IOB: bad and boujee, couples exclusive concierge services, ace of spades, Sapphire Patrol, the 10K Pole Dancing Series, pole dancing competitions, complimentary limo service, Circo erotica, and also steakhouse favorites, delightful seafood options, light bites and everything in-between. We shake hands, and they give me their cards and numbers, and I give mine.

Cliver says when we go out: "First those old-timer mobsters, and then these. I think many girls in Europe like to stalk with these, cos they are so Harith." I say: "I do not trust them either. But they do not know about the golden kiss either."

We meet all others at harbor gym, Frank place. I shake their hands and tap many shoulders and say: "I pay tomorrow." And when you pay on time, you can be always ready for every good work.

On Top of the World & the Golden Kiss

The Morning Star is going away, and then old-times Roman generals put their armies to march. This seems to be nowadays the time when I shall come home. I mean to MyVictoria´s home. You open the door. Y: "Oh, you are alive. Was it brolic and tight? You look not so fresh."

I smile: "It went like a Brooklyn chicken noodle soap. I´m fresh as a man can be. There was a little bit headwind, so looks tyty but just an illusion like Pakistani military victories." You say: "Come here and give a hug." Ohh oh, now she treats me like a baby, soon she begins to call me *el bebé*.

I try to change the subject: "Some hours and those two managers shall meet. I write the deal quickly down and think something ..." Y: "Aren´t Y going to rest. You look ..." I: "Really, it´s time for business. Every problem is a gift card, and their normal code 1729 is a little boring number, which can be produced as two cubes amount, two different ways." You fondle my hair: "Perhaps Y go now to rest a little bit."

You look very fresh and ready to go. I give Y one more hug. Between my lips come some words: "Have a nice day, MyVictoria." What shall I do, if here cram a dim-witted client, fan, or director? Shall I shoot him with my gun? Or shall I say that the torture of a bad conscience is the hell of a living soul? Or shall I say that do notinjure, abuse, oppress, enslave, insult, torment, torture, or kill any creature or living being, just starve to death."

I go to bed and Doggy jumps there too. We two brothers begin to sleep together, and perhaps our dreams are similar. My dream isn´t a broken-winged bird that cannot fly, it is to-day, and to-day, creeps in this hard-working from this-day to this-day, and all these-days are lighted fools, and so my day but a walking shadow, a drunken king, that struts, frets its hours upon the sunny place, and then it is heard no more.

I wake up. Time is 9 am. I begin to write that deal. I feel that it is told by an idiot, full of vain sound and lazy fury, signifying much less than nothing. At last, it is ready. I sit on the sofa and Doggy goes to sit on my shoulder. I go to shower, brush my suit and teeth.

I make a call: "Dear president, can I meet thee today at 2 pm. I have a pre-proposal and one important Manager with me, who needs to know, if her services are needed or not. What shall we talk about? We shall talk about the Golden Kiss, so it means a golden deal of cultural tourism. It shall put together with passion and discipline, Brooklyn and European way: the handshake. Halloo, yes, 2 pm, no, I shall not be late ... thank Y and bye, bye. Oh oh."

I take another call: "Madame Matthew, yes, Tapio here. Shall I present that deal to Y at 11 am? Then I have a succession for Y that Y cannot miss. Yes, I have some dancers, and they are more than willing to be part of this marvelous deal, as well as 12+3 club owners. We got an amazing understanding of the silent hours. Yes, of course, Madame, I have already informed Mademoiselle Actor about this and that. See Y soon, bye, bye. Woohoo."

I read the deal one more time and then no more. I look from YouTube Grant Cardone, who blusters about his first real estate deal. But I cannot get Y out of my mind. There goes and goes Elvis Presley "Little Darlin" remixed new version.

I go out of the door and jump to my Mustang. Here I go. Why can´t I be a milkman or a postman, why must I think so big? I do not understand.

At the same time, Young Fort Greenie Family -member shoots a man in the leg during an apartment robbery in Crown Heights. Morris Ave Gunnaz - warrior stoles a Cadillac from an auto repair shop in Cypress Hills. Sureno 13 - warrior steals 500 d worth of steel pipes in the same area.

Well, I go to Brooklyn Barbers, it´s a fabulous place, the best barbers by far highly trained staff. There reads: thank you for your outstanding support over the years. Here´s to a fantastic 2020! Smiling barber tells that they got plenty of stocking fillers for son, husband, boyfriend, father, nephew, partner, uncle, friend, and all you covered guys.

Soon the hair is ready, and the barber says just: "You make our job so enjoyable." I go to the Metropolitan Swimming Pool.

Our meeting place is One World Trade Center´s tower. It situates on the top of the world. It suits very well for my not so humble plans. I'm in a very good mood, although I haven´t slept much. But I have eaten very well, and Doggy and Y in my mind, keeps me going over the mountains.

It is a little bit risky to go to that building, where those guards got from the father´s hand. Well, here I´m. And at the front door stands one of those fellas who was involved in that, hm, involvement. I shake his hand and say: "How are Y? I hope Y are fin." He says: "Yeah whatever, that´s a total FUPO dude." Everything seems to be alright.

I get a text to my iPad: "I gave Y 50 nerds in one condition." I text: "Yes, Mr. Josh, please tell me." He tells: "You shall come to Montreal and we shall have a meeting in a boxing ring." I: "Dear Dood, that´s a marvelous holding your horses. Some day we both shall stand on the same sunny side of the street."

Now I see another guard. He looks at me, and begins to smile, without two front teeth. That´s the spirit. I goto the lift. It is full of Chinese tourists. One of them says to me: "泰尔韦." I say: "Hello." Up it goes. And then to the One Dine. With NYC´s skyline as the backdrop, we, managers and YourTapio, shall enjoy refined service in an elevated atmosphere ideal for special occasions. Of course, I got a ticket. Time is 1:55 am, (doors opened 11:30). Here, on the top of the World, I see the IOB´s president and Madame Manager. I look at the stellar views. Although there are not so many ambassadors for our shiny and safe city as they are shady hustlers on a street corner, from these windows on the World I can see only the rosy future of NYC and me - well us, MyVictoria. I just look at New York City and describe it as an entertainment experience and step-right-up showmanship.

I kiss the air on the hands of both madame and give my best smile: "Ladies, NY is the main course. So nice to be here with you." They smile back and it rolls on. I say something: "*Mesdames*, how nice to make a deal at the windows on the world. To say that this awesome place is just for the food, would be like saying a Mets game is just about the hot dogs. This is a magic carpet of light at our feet."

144

Everybody knows that this place boasts the city´s finest wine lists, and here is a forerunner in espousing that wallet drainer known as the wine pairing. This place helps us in a new era of captive audience dining. Somebody says that this place escapes from drug-addled, dirty, and crime-ridden below. That somebody is so wrong. Why separate heaven and hell? They are in the same beautiful NYC-place.

The IOB´s president says: "So, here we are, and ready and steady to hear what Y have on your mind." I think: "Perhaps we eat first something. I do not mean at all that even in our modern era of stripped-down fine dining, where chefs throw out the rule book along with the linens every day, being exposed to a barrage of tour speeches as you´re dropping hundreds on dinner constitutes a brand new level of absurdity."

The ladies take cocktails celebrating New York. I get acquaint myself with mineral water and see clearly in my mind an image of Victory. Starters we take Ahi Tuna Tower, so avocado, pickled cucumber carpaccio, crisp wonton and spicy chili oil, salads iceberg wedge. Madame Manager takes Crispy Fried Calamari and the IOB´s president Maine Lobster Roll and hungry me All American Burger, oh, applewood smoked bacon, American cheese, lettuce, tomato, Kosher prickle, and house-made sauce. Sides come to Pommes Frites and buttermilk mash. It is time to put the gat on the table.

I start: "Ladies, what unites Europe and the United States? Europe is not a coherent or unified continent. We will be looking at Western Europe only - that is, the EU-15 plus Switzerland, Norway, and Iceland. To also, include the new arrivals would be to win the argument by default, yes. But even within Western Europe, the spectrum of difference is much broader than is normally appreciated.

With very, very few exceptions, the U.S. fits into the European span of most quantifiable measures. We may, yes, therefore conclude either that there is no coherent European identity, or - if you insist it is - that the U.S. is as much a European country as the usual candidates. We may rephrase this by saying that both Europe and the U.S. are, yes, parts of a common, big-tent grouping in the West – the Atlantic community or the developed world. All are a bit imprecise.

The U.S is an economically more unequal society than Europe, with greater stratification between rich and poor. Much of this is not true. If we look at wealth – instead of referring to the measure of income differentiation – which is arguably the more permanent and socially meaningful measure, then results are different. The richest 1 % of Americans owned about 21 % of all wealth in 2000. In Switzerland in 1997, the richest percent owned 35 %, and in Sweden the figure was 21 %. The richest 1 % of Swedish are proportionately twice as well off as their American peers. If we take as a measure poverty the actual cash sum equivalent to 60 % of median income for the original six nations of the EU, it turns out that many western European countries have a higher percentage of poor citizens than the United States. These include not only the Mediterranean countries but also the UK and Ireland, France, Belgium, the Netherlands, Finland, and Sweden.

Dear ladies, the U.S. and the E.U. consumers are very similar with the same expectations, cos they all have a great deal of choice in the market. Similarities continue: citizens can live and work were they want, citizens have to be treated the same by a state, regardless of their home state, free movement of goods and money, open border without border control, common currency, a common executive power, the chamber system (U.S.=E.U.). The average age of an American mother is 27, bringing more maturity to the roles of caregivers, teachers, and coaches. In Europe, that figure is even higher.

Millennials possess a different attitude towards immigration and interracial, intercultural relations. There are scheduled, structured lives, multiculturalism, terrorism, heroism, parent advocacy, and globalization.

If we look at books, bookings, and other aspects of cultural adventures, we do not see many differences. The differences are in prejudices. But if Y go to the field, to the statistic the U.S. and Europe seem to be one big country."

The ladies look at each other. I continue: "So. If Y think for instance your back rounds. Both Y has a carrier on many levels in society. Y know how it works. I think that this means just one thing. Y can talk very precisely about cultural exchange matters. I have here a deal, which gives a strategic aim to your cooperation: if Y put this American actor and star work at your studios and these dancers make their presentation on our stages, it just fills the empty space and makes those institutions work more effectively.

I pull the trigger: "I have made here a schedule of Victoria´s approaches in stage, festivals, cultural centers, swimming pools, sporting centers, book festivals, EDM-things, and schedules of dancers´ performances in stage, festivals, every kind of centers. So next summer is full of action. There are also those breaks, marketing things, media things, Book Towns interviews, meeting with some actors, politicians and media persons, rich people.

But Y must understand that I do not wanna lose nothing, cos of MyVictoria has that Golddigger Complex and she wants more co..." The IOB´s president interrupts me: "How do performances and media-things go with bookings, books, and cultural tourism? Why Brkners are more interesting than European counterparts?"

I explain happily: "Isn't it obvious. Here in Europe, we do not sell ourselves, in the U.S. you do not do anything else but sell yourselves. So, Americans are experienced in thinking about their profit and they are very good accountants. If you talk or write to them something else than money bound things, they give a shit or are soon bored to death. When you give them money and talk about it, they wake and bake, you know wakey, wakey, and up and away."

Your manager: "Who are Y to insult porn stars and pole-strippers. You're a fun sponge and snore-fest." I laugh: "But Madame Manager, you must admit that deal is a snore-fest of epic proportions." your manager says loud: "Oohhh aye, at fella is pure gantin." I do not give up on these vain words: "Aye we all, Madame? So how about it? Let's blow this popsicle stand."

Silence. Both ladies study my papers. There are schedules and alongside them cash flows, every minute is put with money value. And I say the main thing: "Madame Manager, you have seen the interactive board, blue screen of killer money flow. It keeps Y wake and bate. That board proves my words or throw them to the south. My estimated value of these dancers for 4 months and MyVictoria goes to 17 million dollars so 15,26 million euros. Each hour is worth 25 000 dollars so 22 400 euros. There comes bills about assistants and so, and VAT, and we must be careful in Sweden, Germany, French, Finland, and Norway, the tax inspectors there are hostile."

The IOB-president keeps calm: "I study these numbers." YourManger takes back her poker face: "I do some Jewish engineering with these." That's it.

I say: "My ladies, this is The Golden Kiss." The IOB-president asks: "What do Y mean?" I smile: "Well, whatever I say, whatever I sing, whatever I do, that heart, what heart, MyVictorias ofc, shall see, that I shall serve with heart loving that loving heart that loveth me. So farewell, MyLadies, of hearts that heart most fine, farewell, MyLadies, and remember, dear heart, heartly to MyVictoria, and keep Y keep this heart of mine for thine, like a heart for loving me. So dear ladies, you must understand that all that dancing and acting must how heart, art, artist, not workers and craftsman do not fill that empty space, not even millionmillion of those. There is just one King and Queen. This stage is for M & Thee (V & M)."

The ladies go away. They do not understand. They understand just money, and workers and draftsmen. Nowadays it is so hard to find kings & queens when everybody thinks lust and hard work and that kind of ridiculous things. But those fuck**ers are mistaken. They shall get a stormy spectacle of courtly love.

Pulling the Trigger again

I walk a little bit. I have a bad taste in my mouth. I got what I wanted - perhaps. But this is not my way of doing things. And by the way, that food wasn´t good. Hey, now it is Pizza Week and you are required by law to eat a 1d hot, cheesy lunch every day between Monday and Friday. And now it is lunchtime. This is the excuse I want.

Too many miles to Comedian Gastor Almonte, where the man, Vito-owner, a high five-man, is. He´s more East New York than all of those there. I go to Attorney General Letitia James, these three Luigis have a good reputation, too, "and can beat any other NYC pizza".

Very nice decor to the place. I order some juice and they arrive at the same time as appetizers. It would have been nice to have drinks first but whatever. Juice, appetizers, main course, dessert all, and an amazing waiter is a great guy. I go to my Mustang and drive home-Br at 4 pm. I smile, cos I feel still the crust is chewy with a noice crunch on the skin. The cheese stretchy and the oil that sweats out of it will salivate the glands, and finally, the sauce is a punch of flavor that has a nice sweet tang. Yes.

Then I'm driving Boden Ave when I see a bunch of fellas looking at me from 27th St. Sugardaddy-fuck**ers. Mobsters run to their cars. Ohh oh, Wafia is after me. There is no splooge anymore. I do not have my gat with me, so I'm a wood duck. I cannot go to MyVictoria with these gun controllers & salad shooters behind me.

I make a call, once again: "Cliver, it has been a nice day. Where ya to? 36th Ave. Come to Steinway. Meet you there. And take two guns. Those sugerdad-gangsters are now after me."

How about dem apples? Why others wanna hug me and others kill? What can I say? The people like us are ´we´ and the rest of the world are ´they´? I can´t stop the future, rewind the past, but I can press the trigger.

Four cars come after me. This is ridonkulous. Hatred is between red blood explosion and dead quiet snow, and the spirit of Death tells that our nearness of me in love is near the hate of those love, not me. This Br is a fantasicating place, which has almost as much to do with the hate as with the love. I arrive at Steinway´s crossroads. Cliver is there. I stop the firebird. He throws me a gat. I turn my Stang and begin to drive straight towards the coming bunch of hits.

We shall see who has heart and shall take the cake. The cars draw near fast. We shall see who has a heart of gold.

Four cars, two first line, two-second line. Three-floor buildings and one floor, too. Flames shall go the roof if that's the way it shall be. Mustang growls and I put more speed. The crash-crush shall throw Spaghetti-fellas and me to the Limbo right away. I try to be calm, but my reason says: "Really? Whoever is calm and sensible is insane." Sweat drops to my eyes, and I feel the salt in my mouth. 100 meters, 50 m ... and then we die ... or somebody is a chicken.

That Hyundais yield from left and right and I go like the Huns in Roman lines or dip like a knife in butter. Time to think nothing. I do a handbrake turn. Stang's tires grumble and the smell of burnt fills my nose. I'm behind four Spaghetti-loaded-muscle cars. And I shoot at their tires, but I miss. I shoot at the fellas, and I do not miss it. One driver falls on the wheel. And the car stops right there. Cliver claps them in front of me and me behind. They come outto their cars. I shoot them to legs and four men lie on the street. One bullet comes and crushes my wrist. Blood begins to flow. My tissue tops the bleeding. And I go to sploosers: "Boys are your master at home? I have something to tell him." They stutter something, which is gibberish to me. I whistle to Cliver, and he runs and jumps to the Mustang.

The Boss understands

Soon Cliver and I are in front of Sugardaddy's. I smile. Cliver does not smile. I take my Taurus 1911 45 ACP and put more 4,20"-bullets in. The door fella tries to say something. I shoot to the security camera and the fella puts his hands up. I command: "Sit and do not move. Cliver, point left, I myself go right!"

Some tourists are running on the street. I'm oriented like a whore who keeps herself to the cock and lust, I give myself as a Bang-Bang Catcher to weapon and blood. My eyes are my air picket -system with detecting, reporting, and tracking Suggardaddy´s Spaghetti-movement. I kick one fistipig to the ground. He comes up. I shoot his leg, he doesn´t come up. People are screaming. I shoot another surveillance camera down. I go the bartender: "Where´s the Fuck**er?" He doesn´t answer, so my Taurus puts him to sleep.

Cliver shows a negative attitude: "I do not murmur much, but isn´t this a little bit Iraq-hit the Quan? Everybody feels the beat, perhaps we drop it low?" While he is talking, I fell my weapon a hitting ass, so armored Stryker. I see on the backdoor Mr. Krieger, sneaking out. I run to him, and shoot one bodyguard to his arm, his airing skills are gone. That former Buffalo boy and today´s area man is out of action.

Mr. K isn´t collecting any more bribes, so large they must be carried in a briefcase. He seems to be a little bit Babania out, but I say to him: "So six girls. Take it or live it." He: "*Appetitoso, Le propongo un piatto di affettati del sud*. I have two amazing Mexicans, one Dominican, three Pueatarican, take them or live them." I look at him. Hey, Mr. K has ceiling cats in his mouth: words of wisdom = wow. We get d´accord, up in this piece, yes, that kind of girls I like, oh, true dat, true dat, fo real.

We go to the table. And now Mr. K understands when I put the schedule paper of the IOB-festivals on the table. His attitude changes: "Swagnificent. Why didn´t Y say in the first place? You are a stoopy man." Unbelievable, but soon the table is full of mobs and they care a thing about wounded knees or ambulance and police things. They care about when I say: "*Italia est patria poetarum*. Old Roman liked to say: ´If you must break the law, do it to seize power: in all other cases observe it.´" Mr. K looks at me: "Do y Mr. Mot**cker like old Romans?"

I say: "I, dear becoming friend, love them." He: "Why so?" I: "They liked to create not to learn, that was their essence of life. And most of all Caesar fell in love with Cleopatra and Cleopatra with him. They always talk about Antonius and Cleopatra, but the real thing was C & C. That world's beautiful woman taught Caesar to write, and so he could create history in paper and be street credibility also. Without Cleopatra, he would have been just a man on the river-Rubicon." When those mobs here this they begin to cheer: That fella whom I shoot to leg hugs me and say: "Death will come with your eyes, it will be like terminating a vice." We got an agreement that fifteen mobs shall come with the girls to Milan and beautiful plates and valleys of Toscana.

It is strange: first, y must fight, then no fighting more. At first, they ignore you, then they ridicule you, then they fight against you, and then you win. Perhaps this has as much to do with MyVictoria as to Cleopatra. Chest Candy is just a man´s chicken plate and I just want to leave and kiss my beautiful Crumb Catcher.

I call Y: "Hey, MyVictoria, do Y wanna go to eat. Let's meet at Piccolo Cucina Osteria." Mr. K. says nearby: "*Sapori e prodotti tipici della Siciiilia.*" I ask: "Did Y here what sugar daddy said, yes that stoopid K? Yes, half an hour. See Y soon, love Y too."

Meanwhile, the police investigate the aggressive attack at Sugardaddy´s, and the bartender and others say that it must have been some Hungarian mob´s member from the Queens. The attacker was small, curly hair, big nose, tinny and skinny fella, with quick feet and hate in his eyes. There stand some customers, who do not say a word. A young Jamaican kid looks at me and says: "That pa & bruiser was it." Big laugh around, even the police laugh. A popo taps the boy on his growing shoulders and says: "He learns, what a whammy."

At the middle of this celebration, nobody notices hungry redbugs and roaches, who are going here and there in the shadows of homes and looking at their conquering new ways to restaurants also. There have been already 59 770 bug infestation complaints last part of last year.

At the same time, when we laugh Judith Goldiner, Attorney-In-Charge of the Civil law Reform Unit, explains to a bunch of New Yorkers: "No need to worry, NYCHA´s quick response time is encouraging. This is just a byproduct of more staff on the ground and resources. It happens that the high number of work orders filed by NYCHA residents to remediate insect infestation withing their homes is, hm, somehow troubling". The grant houses logged the most work orders with 981 roach and redbug infestations reported. It takes in this time the Housing Authority 9,5 days on average to respond to complaints. Her tired eyes look at rank development: Grant, Linden, Ebenwald, Boulevard, Pelham Parkway, Marble Hill, Castle Hill, Polo Ground Towers, Wagner, and Ravenswood 700-900 cases/place. Just 54 742 bugs, not so much.

The Pomonok House in Fresh Meadows redbugs launches their main attack just some hours ago. While we celebrate our Europe success to come, there is in Meadows 116 complaints with work orders. The dressed Housing Authority thinks: "Fuck, this shall take even 9 days." In the area is 5 028 alerts. There is a press conference and NYCHA press secretary Rochel Leah Goldblatt smiles: "Redbug and roach responses have improved since the city´s 2,2 billion agreement. Roach responses have become more thorough and bedbugs and rats are treated as emergencies. We intergrade best Management techniques and a Pest Action Plan. We take care of the residents and their pets, so they can live safely and with dignity."

At the same time, 357-member vandalize with MS-13 Graffiti Bayside´s Sacred Heart Catholic Church. The warrior sprays also a white fence. 100 associates on Long Island have effectively decimated the gang´s presence there. One Clivers´ friend is so jealous of Cliv´s medal that when he broke into a car, he vandalizes it with swastikas and profanities. Well, Cliver and I go to the Stang and I take him back to Queens and at 1800 come back to Y.

I ask Cliver: "Can I keep Taurus? Never know whom I wanna shoot. That old-timer mob thing was so sentimental that I nearly vom & boot." Cliver goes off and I give him Mustang to fido.

So Brooklyn Freestyle Wapoo

What a Jersey shore this had been. If I go to Europe and put whores tripping the light fantastic that is urban diarrhea. How I can put hot tamale, who is in the center of charisma, to charity love true blue. How convincing are pole-dancers´ words to Europe freep & press: "My sex is the storming sea, my love loving deep, that more I give to thee, more and more I get, for now, and for infinite."

I come to Y, hands in my pockets: "What Y have been done, except taking care of those clients, fans and directors, photographers, managers and another son of the bitches?" You are not so happy: "I have been training, and have performances in Studio Allegro, Robert Mann Dance Centre, All-Star Studios, Fit4Dance, Balmis Latin Dance Studio, Liberated Movement, Mark Morris Dance Group, Breaking Boundaries, and Lava Brooklyn. We dance and make statements.

Places are full of energy, excellent music choices, keeps so heavenly fun and interesting, everybody was sweat at the warm-up dance. Quick verbal and visual cues throughout the wowing workout made us flawless, happy. There was Zumba. There were arguments, flaming the atmosphere. Somebody said to me that I do not understand the flow of the ballet. Those uneducated and very assuming things made me laugh. But Y learn the discipline of dance and acro. Everything was safe and clean. There were little dance studios with a big heart. Yes, many dancers were maddeningly slow, but there were many repeats, mandatory dress rehearsals, and friendship flourished.

Both machines and weights aren't just everybody's jam. But they challenged me, put me to my limits I didn't think I could go. The teacher was good and worked with students until they were comfortable. One Latin place had 3 mainboards with 150 + shines listed and countless turn patterns that had all been given a name and hierarchy to make it way more gistestiblow toe new students. There were also old-fashioned Salsa, Bachata, Cha-Cha, Ballroom, and Hustle. I saw classes, privates, dance competitions, student showcases, and studio getaways as a family was all offered there. It was great a party! OMG!!! I wish I could give 10 stars at the same time.

At one place there was a marvelous woman, Cara. She is a champion at creating a welcoming, fun environment that accommodates a super diverse group of people at varying degrees of fitness. There was much that salsa, "shake what my mama gave me". Mostly dancing was a non-stop, head-to-toe workout. It left me wanting more even if I were a little bit wiped out. Everywhere instructors were high energy and the playlist so fun. One place we danced about 5-6 songs and were instructed to follow the teacher's steps. Yes, think, you can get a full schedule typically 15 d and from ballet to African dance. Everywhere I felt fantastic, always extremely high energy and challenging. I tried everyyyyy style work out. Not only are the workouts absolute amazing, it is an absolutely no judgment zone, not only work out your body, they have unique fun classes, that not only work out your body but your mind and soul too. I was literally the happiest person ever when I leave those classes.

Really vibrant movement spaces I have ever experienced in this city. Many dancers are true examples of living a dream. Everything just authentically and open-heartedly. They really bring forth community and healing. At one place nobody didn't say anything to me. Got the vibe the people here aren't particularly friendly, especially if you're not a member or a regular. But there were very cool healers/movement gurus. I enjoyed the warmth of the clientele. Those places were community resources, not some massive chains. Yes, many times Zumba, as I already said, but techno/dance, Reggaeton to Beyoncé and Chance the Rapper. Yeah! Brooklyn dancing is AMAZING and restorative, strength through conditioning, connection through a kind community. I love it! I'm personally fallen in love with kickboxing classes, I'm perfectly happy substituting kickboxing with Awesome High Energy and a lot of Sweat!!! Those Zumba-classes almost killed me. It was GREAT!!! But everywhere I attended a performance with a combination of acrobatics and music. Almost everywhere I was impressed with the quality of the entertainment and the spirit. I have had a Wonderful DAYYYY!"

Those words are to my brains tickle my pickle. But, I'm no fan of Zumba and those group-things. It must be more a blizzard. I do not do in those festivals nothing but fete. It raps in my brains. Melody must be like a Spanish thing or/and Up tempo-doo-wop, but the rhythm must be mix artillery barrage a helicopter attack. Furious, killing and no mercy thing, no spray and pray.

Perhaps the Beach Nuttz, Dres, Big Boy, Big Pun, M. Mexicano 777 makes somebody's day, and perhaps Snoop Dogg & Ice Cube - L.A. Timer ft. Xzibit - but, but, oh oho oo, you know, old *papas* ...

Daddy Yankee Live FULL Concert 2018 was full of, but Daddy must be more trained looking not a fat rapper, it is ridiculous. Muévelo – Nicky Jam & Daddy Yankee.

Those festivals must have that Brooklyn dance class attitude. It must be Brooklyn-fast, it works. But not Zuma, Jay-Z & friends, where I'm From, that has the touch ...Yeah.

Freestyle Friday - Moon vs Blind Fury? B.F murdered everybody and Roccsy dusted his shoulders, but I liked Moon better. Why? He looked like today. Hm. So Brooklyn ft. Fabolous (Casanova)? Real cold. Put to courtly love: did y´all know Casanova trapping always with a gloss and got two bodies, of y´all ain´t just listen to so Brooklyn. Cliver & Makks may wait on Nas, I'm so Queens.

Woo-Choo-Crip-rappers. How to put my fav. El Alfa El Jefe T. Anuel AA-Con Silenciador.

Al Alfa El ... and Brooklyn fellas like Danny Hundreds, Bizzy Banks, Sleepy Hollow, Mauley G, Ciggy Black, 22Gz, Fivio Foreign, Max Thademon, Sheff G, and Pop Smoke - fav. Bizzy Banks and Mayley G - handsome touch ok. Br-ners are inspired by southern rappers and southern flow kinda like amigos flow. But H-d So Brooklyn Freestyle´s good, like Jay Z, mixed Papoose. How to put these with pole-strips and so. Well, courtly love & golden kiss &V&T.

How to put rappy: Brooklyn native with 2 glizzys from 2 different states, do a hit, park the whip up and go switch the plates ... and put it European leash´d in like hounds, should famine, sword and fire crouch for employment, but pardon, and gentles all ... Hm, as who prologue-like your humble patience pray, gently to hear, kindly to judge, our play ... to Br-nerdlike: I can´t relate to silver spoons I had to take a plate, triple flip hit the van wick take it straight to blake, and, yeah, never noted in him any study, any retirement, any sequestration, from open haunts and popularity ... cos, yeah again: u juggin´ for what trap what u still ain´t got none, I got 99 problems but these bitches ain´t non, huh. We happy few, we fuck**ing band of brothers.

That with the EDM-techno-house-put the soldier in the field (so stage) - when the bullet comes and in his head explodes and blows and his hear´s crown flies to the western greeny fields and while he fells and dies, in some seconds they are syrupy Wanderers - For Your Love (Early 60´s Doo Wop Ballad) and he dies.

Yes, syrupy with blood. The only thing I can´t creat dear f*cers is the same mistakes, if shorty ain´t doing dicks we ain´t doing dates ast, like beauticians take cute bitches and do their face ... If you dance Beyonce, she doesn´t work too easily...

If I compare Beyonce with men like Ray Pollard, Tonny Williams, and Homer Dunn, B must leave too frame thing. These festivals things must go fantastically, beautifully, tough or smooth way. But not so that some self-loved singer comes and tells the audience that "you are the f*ers, praise me, you f**ers". If I think about an all-time breakdance contest at the Lyceum Brooklyn Bboy tricking gymnastics parkour, they might suit much better than C-love action thing.

I must think about Breakdance Exit Club Greenpoint and Physicx, Junior, Darkness, Pivet, Pop, Kujo, but MyVictoria knows these things better. Omg MyVictoria kills it, she´s got dance skillz. And I know she nails the pin drop. She must DAAAANNNGG. Some days ago, lil´o from Philly was dope hip hop in Br, but I cannot think women making that kind of.

I ask Y: "Show some dancing, Bab." Well, the room is enough big. And you make wow-split. Cos you are a dancer, you hold your body correctly while performing, to executing skill properly in a routine. Tech is ofc there every day for half an hour. MyVictoria doesn´t, while dancing Zumba, catch up in the choreography and forget to hold herself correctly. Feet together, hand by their sides, and go from the top down. I see rib cage closed, shoulders pressed down and back. Hips held even and level, all motions are in front of MyVictoria. She distinguishes between breaking her arms from one motion to the next, with kicks, backs are straight, chins lifted, toes pointed, and hips level. She goes across the floor doing chaineturns. There is the right foot 1-2-3, prep on 4, balance or turn 5-6, down to her right knee 7-8. Her rhythm is awesome, cos she executes turns on the floor. Singles, doubles, triples, watching for shoulders that go up, arms that wind up before the turn, and hips that are uneven.

She focuses on the lower body, upper body, total body, cardio & abs, booty boot camp. There comes music cumbia, salsa, merengue, mambo, flamenco, chachacha, reggaeton, soca, samba, hip hop, axé but not tango. MyVictoria does step, toning, aqua, in the circuit, and some sentao, not plate.

I see Latin dance rhythms, abs, tights, arms, timed intervals. She trains muscle strength, posture, mobility, and coordination. She points and stretches her feet the second she leaves the ground. She uses gladly her plie instead of her arms to gain height on a leap. Plie push off both feet goes up, and flies. With toe touches in second, make sure her hips are level her bottoms are tucked under. She lands in plie. She lifts her chins. Her body moves as a unit. She is alignment, with her rib cage pressing together, sternum open, shoulders pressed down, and arms properly placed for each turn. She brings her arms into the center of her body. She is as high on the ball of her foot as she can, spread her weight equally. Flexibility is one main component. And when her beautiful body moves, the butts and breasts are concentrated making the dancer airborn. Her butts focused spirals are compressed and contracted together. Although she shakes her blond hair, the simple focus change from a level position to a raised position gives me, MyVictoria´s audience, the amazing impression that she is higher in the air.

You say: "*Quema de calorias, libera tensiones, aumenta la tolerancia a la acumulación de ácido, estimula el humor.*" And then you smile, and we kiss. What a great performance. I just cannot but love beautiful movements, and she really enjoyed all her performance. And I get the image of *La Coreografia Final*. This is great and does a great right doing a little wrong. All the great things are simple; freedom, justice, honor, duty, mercy, hope, and your dance.

You are in the shower, and I'm too. We ml. I feel like a snake after flute´s turns and so. The figure, the movements, butts, and big breasts, much love, gtg-xx. Our tongues dance not Zumba. The surest way to prove we´re still alive knocking boots till we die. We are digging for oysters and chewing mints.

The Seventh Day

The PayDay for Sins

Some Delays

While we are sleeping four subway lines ferrying commuters to Queen are shut down thanks to a malfunctioning switch in Jackson Heights, causing delays to ripple through the subway system. We sleep and the mayhem left riders are wondering how to get home - and how could a single switch so badly cripple four subway lines.

The delays on the E, F, M, and R trains, which started about late afternoon, trace back to a switch just east of the 74th Street - great and wonderful Roosevelt Avenue station, where those four lines converge. This whole thing started when that switch acted as if it were moving express trains to the local side, preventing express trains from speeding straight to Forest Hills - 71st Avenue and blocking local trains on the M/R line. To get, you know, around the issue while subway workers repaired the switch, other workers directed trains forward one by one, a process called flagging in MTA-speak. That slowed things down on the four affected lines and caused delays to spread throughout the system, exacerbated by the large number of trains running on the track for rush hour.

Well, we sleep. And at the same time, clouds are gathering in the sky. NYC shall be hit with hazardously fast winds and up to two inches of snow. A weather alert has been issued from 9 am to 10 pm. Gusty winds could blow at speeds of up to 50 mph. City officials are ready to warn New Yorkers to be cautious moving around the city, cos of falling tree branches and power outages could result. The weekend seems to be both sunny and rainy with temperatures between 22 and 40 degrees.

Some other things are going on, too. In NYC smokers spend almost 2,5 d million on the habit in their lifetimes. Last year smokers paid roughly 48 000 d for cigarettes, health care, lost financial opportunities, and related costs. Smoking doesn´t just ruin your health. It burns a nasty hole through your wallet, my friends. Smokers spend almost 195 000 d on cigarettes on NY, which charges more taxes on cigarettes (4,35 d a pack) than any other state. Had that cash been invested in the stock market, NY smokers could have earned roughly 1 700 000 d. There are 2 232 000 smokers in NY-State - 814 000 of whom call NYC home - and tobacco use claims the lives of about 28 200 New Yorkers a year. If Y wanna be a smoker, move to North Carolina, there y spend 24 000 d a year, and 1 228 493 in a lifetime. Do you understand?

Thinking About Gathering Shiny Toy Gats

It is about 6:30 am and MyVictoria has been in the shower, and she is ready to go, and full of energy, as always. I turn my face and Doggy jumps to lick my face. I kiss Doggy to its mouth. I'm looking out of the window, and wake and break are coming hard, and rain, too. It gives heavy snow. Soon people shall be cleaning their whips, and my Stang is there, too.

Then I remember my yesterday idea: yes, pole-girls, manager & IOB, MyVictoria´s dancing skills - and now we must have some street style singers, Spanish and Puetarican. Where is the money? My millions do not change the weather. If I do not have singers, then rest is ridin´ clean on ´nem sprewells. Looks like we have gone to make a stang again.

I call Cliver: "Heya, howya doin?" Cliver: "Everything goes to sobo. Here is a real yarpie thing." I: "Mudda saying bads?" Cliver: "They caught that n***a a brick and hit him in his shit*. Only in Chicago can you kill somebody, write 2 mixtapes mentioning smoking, then on every song, and talking in detail how you killed them and do not have to worry about it. This thing must be kicked back." I: "Well, if Y haven't anything else to do, I have an idea." Cliver: "?" I: "I just think Can You Keep up? - Busta Rhymes ft. Twista Lyrics or Twista ft. Tech N9ne 'Crisis'. Who can do in Br that? Or things like El Afla, Chenco, Bryant Myers, Noriel, Jon Z, and Miky Woodz?"

Cliver: "I don't know. Bad vids the beat sounds like 2 swings moving back and forth on a windy day tbh, so why the hell does YT recommend these vids a yr after it is uploaded, worst shootout ever lol. But if Y from br 'where I'm From' feels a lil different for y. Gotta Get You Home Freestyle, Beware Freestyle h-D, they are welcome to The Dankies." I: "Well, we must go to gutta, and look at legit and wagas who can spit & rola." Cliver: "They smoke us forthwith." I: "Well, so be it. But I wanna Death to its ass."

Cliver: "There has been some layin' on da Bryan, but if I and you, a deep br, go to no flex, they scoop us up. Strip clubs, maps, trappers aren't much compared with bangs." I: "How about taken bang-bangs with us?" Cliver: "Your friends in arms, heavy gats, hm. They shall become a great Friday the 13th." I: "I call Frank."

I: "Hello Fran(k), have y heart beef franks with beans served in some MRE`s. Thank Y for helping with peeler bars. I appreciate it. Howudoin, I have one more request for Y. I wanna Dave and his old-SEALs with me. They know that the only easy day was yesterday, no plan survives first contact with the enemy and all in, all the time. Now is the time to dig deep. Leave everything you've got on that field. I give them the same that they got from Iraq. I need 8 fellas who can think that

165

everyone has a plan until they get punched in the face." Frank does not say a thing for a while. Then he says dying: "Y must ask them. They answer straight to Y. Call Dave. Say to him, I'm in."

I count a little bit. There are gangs in those 60-94 precincts, from Gorilla Stone Bloods to Bundle Boys. 79 gangs altogether. We do not need to ask them all. Cliver says that the best singers are from Gorilla Stone Bloods, Seven Crew, Brooklyn Most Wanted, Straight Cash, Back Side Crips, Money Gang, Cash On Deck/HBM, Folk Nation, 3Ni - Trinitarios, Latin King Niio´s Malos, Rack em up and South Side Bullies.

They are gang-members. They aren´t on the public list. I count more. If there are almost 40 dancers, and some 15 maps, then there must be four main singers and some 12 behind. Ok, Europe has its own dancers and so, but how to get these 16 fellas in, who are trading heroin for guns to battle rival crews. We are going to meet gangs tied to 49 percent of shootings in NYC, mostly over petty disputes. And ask them: hey, give your best street musicians, we shall take them with pole-dancers to Europe and give them an opportunity in a lifetime. Mans can sing in a Courtly Love Golden Kiss Performance.

It is a tough call, almost cheese.

I put the phone away. Y come: "I must go to see my manager and talk about future actor performances. I hope Y can plan your schedule-details also." I talk something: "Well, a manager is an integral cock in any companies´ machinery, so says many well-known persons from Steve Jobs to Donald Trump, Richard Branson to Howard Schultz, from Bill Gates to Ralph Lauren. Anyway, I have one more thing to accomplish with this European cultural tourism. It is called a song before a battle. In the Middle Ages, troubadours went with the army, and most of all they went before that battle in the no man´s land and sing a song. Hm, I´m going to do the same thing.

Y wonder: "What that means?" I explain: "It means what it says. I sing a song between two frontlines. There which never moves, which never changes, which never grows older, but remains forever, isy and silent, and there you must sing a warm and nice song. Something tries to cut off even in the blossoms of sin, unhousel'd, diasappointed, unanel'd. I shall sing a love song like this: "*Foy porter, honneur garder et pais querir, oubeir, boubter, servir, et honnourer, vous vueil jusques au morir, dame sans per!*" Y: "So?" I: "So, I love Y so, and let's see, and hope the best." Y: "Ah, y train some kind of performance on the stage."

Y kiss me, and I kiss back. Y go and I take MyTaurus and its bullets. I clean the weapon. It isn't much against automatic weapons, but who is perfect. My songs shall be full of bullets and smoke.

The Street deals

I meet Cliver at Bedford Ave. I jump out of my Mustang. Cliver wonder: "And you smile, although your pizza rolls are done. So, shall we start with Stone Bloods?" I say wayment. I call: "Hey Dave, Frank said that you need a challenge. Do y? Ok, yes, Frank told that also? Strange. Y + 7, and Frank. Nine gats. Yes, I hope too, that no Angels. Do Y have, I have just Taurus, real thing with beans and band-aids. And this must be done beat feet. Cannot stop. Come to here, yeah, Bedford, that corner, yes."

Cliver: "How long we must wait? If we go there in the night, we are sure 187s." I: "Just half an hour." Cliver: "And there is rap & Drill. M.I.S Ron x Freshy DaGeneral, Rah Swish x Curly Savvy, Envy Caine, POP Smoke, Envy Caine, Max TheDemon x Ciggy Black, Sheff G x Sleepy Hollow."

Cliver continues: "It´s more Boom bap, not Drill. No one can mess with Br on a boom-bap beat. Gangs are in their element with that. They are real Wawa ruthless, no Sanam Re, no Eli Fross. And do not say they bumped the flow from UK drill, or Br. copied la with Bloods and Crips now Chicago clowns, you are dead meat. The Nas Blicky Jawn is great."

Well, then Frank, Dave, and friends come. I give them per soldier 2 500 bucks. Now. Stone Bloods. Dave gives me M 16. Cliver asks me: "What Y shall say to them?" I: "Do Y wanna a fire cuete, the cure?" Cliver taps my shoulder: "There´s a frood who knows where his towel is. Man, y jacked my stardrive."

The Woe-day

We arein Neptune Ave, and Kaiser Park is there. Cliver thinks: "That park is harrowing." We ten other laughs. I ask: "Really?" Four fellas cover, two takes the crossfire, three spies - and I just laugh. Bayview Ave isn´t empty. There is something coming. I count four-four-four-four. They are there. And I know they have semi-automatic gats. I go towards the first four: "Hey fellas, a little bit rainy day. Where is Wee47, we can make a good deal?" Silence. Nothing. I say: "We haven´t all they, do you want some good guns, so you can be 245?" One SlimJohnFat yells: "Are you coming in the middle of the day asking that? You are lost as lost can be." I: "I do not think so. I wait for ten minutes, then we rob your headquarters. Your choice, you know, Armalite ar-10 carbine gas-powered semi-thing. Take it or live it."

I throw my semi-A to Frank: "I´m coming now. Are Y there, Wee47." 20 meters from me arrives a tall, slim fella, and have a pistol in his hand. "I slay Y rn", Wee says. I laugh: "No you don´t. So, we can deliver Y 20 good M16As, but I want something. What was the name? CooCoo? That Drill-fella, I make a deal that he shall come with me for 4 months." Wee: "Not happen." I: "Yes it does, or we put down your headquarters right now and burn it down." Cliver shouts behind: "Hey Wee, I recommend y do that, tough guys, even more than Makks, SEALs-8finfers of death, named for the number and unpleasant taste." Wee looks behind and back to me: "So. Perhaps Y and I talk alone. Who wins gives the order?" Wee isn´t a stupid f, he knows where Cliver is, there is no police, and no both and, just or.

It shall be bang-style. We take our shirts off. It shall be he or me. His upper body is trained and there are scars and so, but so is mine, too. He looks at me: "Hey, Y enjoy the gym?" I: "Two times a day. I feel bad if I stay away from weights and speed training. I like the taste of hard dry, and there must come red lines in myeyes, then I stop. How about Y, kickboxing?" He: "Yeah, I like the cake fight for money." Well, there are coming some shoot boxing and K-1. Kun Khmer, Savate & Thai, hook punch. And the rules are for the street, so also elbows and knees, clinch fighting and grappling, shins.

We are near each other. Gladly I have my training trousers and shoes. We are two meters away. I do not begin to wait for his kicks, I run at him, and down we go. He tries to bind his legs around my neck and hit my ears, but I do it Legion Etrangere way. My forehead hits his face. His nose begins to bleed. I go behind him, and he tries to snake away, but cannot. I lock his head to my hands. He cannot breathe and goes down. Black morning to him.

Dave and SEALs shake their heads. What an on9 session. They seem to agree 99 about that. I ask: "So where´s CooCoo? Come to the harbor to get the gats, but I must hear his voice. Where is he?" We stay on the ground. Behind him arrives two Stone Bloods who take him away. Then after a minute comes a fat chap and tries to smile but cannot.

16 fellas stand behind him. I ask: "Are they in the same place, where Y can sing?" Nearby is a little studio, one old jazz-fella keeps it. We go in, and CooCoo takes headphones and begins to sing very fast: "I´m from a crazy place ..." I stop him and put the paper in front of him. He sings: "We stay dangerous just to make it safe. To flight, I will, but not to fly the foe. No part of him but will be shame in me. Change the fit-up, switch whips then go hit the race, I´ve seen rats front their move and get a bit from snakes. The guns of Br. hat not made me smart, these words of your draw life-blood from my heart." It sounds fire & danky, but SEALs and Cliver shake their heads.

Dave sings: "We beat your face just to make it COP. To dust off I will, but not to bird the foe ... bang-bangs of Br. ...these words of yours makes me an Angel." Cliver makes it another way, he thinks the words suck and are old: "We stay harrowing jus´ make it spafe. To fight I will, but not to sauce the stacking. No part of him but will fool me once ... Gats of Br. hath made not me sassy, these iows draw life-blut of my htht."

CooCoo mixes it: "We beat your face jus´ to make it spafe. To dust off I will, but not to sauce the stacking. No part of him but will fool me once. Spange the fit-up, switch whips then go to hit the greebo, I've seen rats front their move and get a bit from breed snakes. The bang-bang-gats of Br. hath made not me sassy, iows draw life-blut of htht and give an Angel."

It is so Brooklyn-fo shizzle my nizzle. And Henry the Sixth begins to live again. Some fellas go to the harbor and wake-up-Wee agrees with me. Stone Bloods call the song Bang-bang Angel. We give up-fives, and then to the next place.

Seven Crew stays at Ralph Ave near Telco Stores. People look at us when we come nearby those stores. Again, we put cover, sides, and frontline, two SEALs go to take care of roofs. There go five warriors like hanging around. Frank and two SEALs stop them. I begin to sound copy of myself, I tell the same as to the Stone Bloods. Now it is the difference that one of these fellas is the king. 20 M16As makes them think carefully. There is Brooklyn Most Wanted near, so at last, XD3 says: "Well, there is one fella, who can sing Drills and so. He´s Tack." XD3 chiflas, so not wert whirl. and there comes a big fella with hand in pockets and smoking Mari. He gives So Yonkers: "Wearing synthetic wigs made of Anwar´s dreadlocks Bedrock, harder than a motherfucking Flinstrone ..." Cliver: "This is CRAZY, I´ve been hearing D-block rep Y-O so long, you wouldn´t that they had other spitters, a new generation it´s y´all time."

Tack feels fine, cos of Mari, and kills the original. "He was spitting but homie at the end scorch the track damn." Cliver: "They musta sent J-Hood to the store and recorded this behind his back." So, no. 2, and no fighting."

We don´t go Brooklyn Most nearby, just respect Tack. We go to Straight Cash. We stop cars at Flatlands Ave and walk along Pennsylvania Ave when 12 Straights come from Vandalia Ave left. There are more of SEALs on right, but they try to look so green and innocent, but Straights are not stoopid. Their gunrunners take their pistols, and two SEALs shoot them to their knees. More shooting. One aim at Cliver´s head so I put a bullet to his shoulder. We must drive on and kill the spirit. At last, I find a Dynamite Chicken, chicken a la king. LosS hurt his neck from a bullet screw, but he understand English when I make a proposal. He looks surprised: "We have real Tila tequila. He is all yours. Cad, come!" Young 13-years old smart kid comes and presses the flesh and says to me: "I could have killed y, but I didn´t, too easy." Gunrunners put their homemade ump45s away, and one puts a DVD on and so the kid makes BOP on Broadway.

Some kids begin to dance, and yellow dreads in red hat dancing kinda looks like king batch. Cad and the homies dancing with the aliens they freed from their basement. Cliver laughs: "Ye, the one who will like this will be a millionaire one day, what Jabbawockeez. Hey, Iran on the right listening to da baby in ww3." One seal says: "Nojaa, high school musical: Hood Editon." Cad is like the opposite of This is America. Sounds goody: "My girl got good p***y fle her across the country I finish the show and then I hop in it." Director-Cad: "Now, everyone freezes." Blonde girl: "Okay, wait ... Now?"

And I tell: "WIn the lottery." Yes, and when we go away, Cad and everyone´s holding still and the chick in pink just wanna be seen.

We go to Forbell Street. There are Back Side Crips. Cliver says that Dill-warrior here is gut. Tot-name youngster makes Dababy Bop, and nobody can´t touch this world's best dance crew. One kid comes and says: "I'm from brazil, this is greaaaTT, i love trap." These are real jabbawokeezs. One new singer and I just wonder, these kids are called gang, but they are so fleak, perhaps they smile & kill.

We go to Howard Ave. There is Money Gang. There come three warriors to offer their services. I take Bock, a tall 15-years old guy, who looks just like 61X9INE "Billy". "Cha, Cha, Cha, Cha, ron, ron. ron ..." I smile when they tell me that I'm 0.01 % black. There comes some kind of story: "Judge: 47 years in prison; 69: the dog isn´t spayed or neutered; six-nine: a pitbull?, me: Im asking the dog; me: mom can we get skittles, mom: we have skittles at home; Skittles at home. So, my solution 0% girls, 0% gang affiliation, 100%talent." This warrior´s song makes me wanna to rob my own house.

We go to Sunset Park, 4th Ave. There is 3Ni. The best singer is Trinitarios´ gangsta called Clur. He makes it Dr. Birds: "Hid behind the Warhol, dip to Berghof, shot up the whole store (brrt), Cheryy ´57, in the ´Bach learnin´ lessons (skrrt)." I say to this: "Four 24/7 will snarf steep themselves in the night, four nochies will jet away from the shart, and then the welshy, like a silver brown chicken brown cow new-bent in orange chicken, shall behold night."

By far this trip has been the pure heart and I'm angry that I took those SEALs destroying my money. We take some kids more and the last but not the least is South Side Bullies´ fella. Zan. They are at East River State Park and we stop our cars on Kent Ave.

Pro forma we put the cover and so when suddenly somebody begins to shoot at us. SEALs made farmer armor and their bullets are like fat cakes, three gangstas fell, and one keeps his bloody head. Bullies think that their park-headquarters are like the five-sided puzzle palace, but it isn´t and not even a FOB. Four SEALs conquer the heart of the place like FST, and Bullies do not have a chance. Those kids shoot like Geardos and after lost their ammo go to Goat Trail. That´s that. What a vain and pointless fight. In the street sits a fella, the bullet has gone through his leg. I ask: "So where´s Mach?" He: "Don´t know?" Well, before I go, I ask: "Can Y sing?" Surprisingly he says: "What do Y wanna hear?"

To this Zan says: "Last year was like shit, a real Griselda Year. I don´t sing about the dopest-grimiest-flyest. And women get nervous when somebody changes a house like a trap house. I really had the chicken with the tree stamp, as I stepped on it witta Timberland. Jesus Christ, Benny, chill lml." Zan takes Vibez: "She wanna fuck with me, but I don´t get the time ..." That kind of the stick and I'm firin´ (bitch) thing ends this long sizeseeing.

We get 16 drill-performances, and I'm so hungry. There has been a lot of rhythms but no melody. So, I call MyVictoria.

The Fluffer-Actress

You are very busy, and with that interactive board, your manager is busier than ever.

As an actress Y have always that image with you that you portray a character in a performance. Doing that in the flesh in media means always that forever stand actor-actress -thing: one who answers. The art of acting, playing a role means playing themselves that answer. There are also techniques, which porn stars also use, the expressions of body, voice, imagination, personalizing, improvisation, external stimuli, and script-kind analysis. Feelings and experiences, and emotional and cognitive understanding. The answer finds its expression in people's response to other people and circumstances, and if you act simply the way, you tell what people do. When not so simple, you tell what happens there. At the highest level, you tell about how ideas talk to each other in a glorious way. And there is always an issue showing the audience that answers, cos if the people do not understand they begin to hate y.

And giving an answer in publicity means visibility for a product, service, and company. And there goes actress answer in the movement of information. That actress's answer much has a public interest, concern goods and services, organizations, and works of art or/and entertainment.

You know well that the star's answer must have a promotional mix of advertising, sales promotion, direct marketing, and personal selling. There are communication outlets to store and deliver information about that actress's answer. And to use a method-game to communicate that answer, MyVictoria constructs a mechanics that produces that answering signal to her in digital vid, sound, c-graphics, hyperlinks to web resources, interactive installations, multimedia, weblog, vlogs, plugs, moblogs and pod, and RSS.

But these are just tools, the main thing giving the answer in the flesh. The main thing that flesh must be there, cos the physics goes like this: if there is no information, there is no material-flesh also. To put flesh to your body is the first thing, to put the flesh to the happenings is much harder, and to put flesh to the idea or even formula, that is the place where stars are dancing courtly love. If You act on a simple level, you do very common repeat, with your body, when you are higher you do repeats with artisan level, hands, and brains, but when you work with ideas and highest noble things, then your real beauty shall be seen in the heart. Why? Cos you have done thousands and thousands repeat lower level and they are your walking or talking or laughing unconditional reflexes. The heart puts those brain chemicals to their right places and the heart tells it all.

These kinds of swaggish things, I think. They are boring to death, cos they are so obvious every over the 15-year old person. Giving a show and advertising yourself, you must love that other persons are looking and praising y. If not, then Y are like a public bodyguard or public enemy, or many times like the police to a public audience.

Choosing Lime

I call, not about telling flesh-answers or public enemy-thing but: "I have listened to some gangs giging Los Hijos de Yayo, Somos de Calle and Latin Kings paapaa themselves Ya'll Don't Wanna. Well, ladies can say no guns and a clean appearance, no bandanas covering the face, not a gang appearance, no violence, and teach our children. They were, hm, anti-ladylike. And they said to me that their dead ass Latin Kings grandpas and guardian angels protected the south Bronx late 80z and 90z growing up as a kid, pops had the tabs at the bodega shout out to Dawson at.

What? Y ask why I'm telling this. Well, I thought Y like to know that Latin gang will outshine the almighty Latin kings I support of Nation. One singer from Latinas come to Europa. Well, yes, not everybody wasn't pleased. One drunken fella dried to interrupt that great singing as said: Give your life to Jesus in not ya will face God and it will be too late.´ I try to say, those songs were fire, fire, fire all day. You know boom KingLove, the sound went off towards the end ... its tight thoe ... amor. Even Cliv said that o shit fire a.d.r almighty REXX."

Y tell me that you have got well-deserved attention in many centers and hotels and Y have got great applauses telling about your carrier and book to come and festivals in Europe and all over the world. That is so great. What more can I say? I try: "Lol Y and lol Puetarican saying Patria lol. Those Niio's Malos played well *todavia no eh escuchado nada igual ni mejor que Los Hijos de yayo, me ncantan sua voces, muy buenas voces babys, wooo que buen estilo loko estra perro el tema loko. Baby, they remind me of Eazy E - Boyz n the hood. Temasooo dias."*

I am asking: "Do Y wanna go to Avant Gardner. It is a hidden gem. The bar manager is lost. She ignores customers and tells them they must wait for a drink, then proceeding to eat, drink, and chit chat in front of those customers. Hope she´s fired. But a nice place. I think let´s go to Depot52. Yes, a warehouse setting, awesome lighting, it´s almost as massive as VictoriaCourt, place shall be packed. Well, the place is the middle of nowhere. There are the best DJs in NYC, hm, well, they told about Tiesto, Deadmau5, Prydz, Disclosure, Aoki. The sound system is crazy, and the lightning is mesmerizing. Some people say to me that they saw there even Marco Carola and David Guetta, who the hell they are? Well, if you want, we can go there and have some time with dubstep and yellow bone. And do there lfk."

You say: "Yeah, there is booming acoustics, the venue itself is perfect, loud electronic beetz and face-melting lazers. Tons of people and we do not need the restroom."

Meanwhile, most NYC celebrities appear to be the living embodiment of human perfection and images of what we all wish to be. Whether on a fashion shoot, the red carpet, bit, and small screens, they´re flawless all the time. Celebrities even appear to be aging more gracefully than the rest of us. However, every now and then people get a glimpse behind the impeccable facade and we see the real person, no masking or hiding the natural, no flattering lighting, and the truth can sometimes be dream shattering,

It reminds them that they are just humans. Every celebrity looks like a normal woman passing you by in the street. Many of them don´t normally look flawless like they do on the red carpet. But they must relax from time to time, and sometime even their faces must sleep with the body. They must use make up, cos there shall be a lot of happenings like AfroCarib Night, Saturdays at Doha, the introduction of Fiscal Sponsorships, even High School Info Night, Marty Gras, meeting finding authors, Concrete Beatz featuring KVSH, and of course sporting, political and so on happenings. And I know that you must always make good preparations when going to public light. And your faces do not rest tonight.

So Depot52 is a nice place. When I come to your house. I point with my finger to Doggy and me: "*En nombre de todos ellos, muchas gracias y enhorabuena a todos por este acto fe hoy.*" Y laugh at my bad Spanish: "*Muchas, muchísimas gracias a todos, también a quienes se encuentran detrás de la mesa.*"

Times is 17:00, and I wanna go to bed but now we must soon go (well, after 22) to that EDM-warehouse. Y ask: "Why do Y wanna go specifically there? What´s the point, MiCarinoBabi? I: "Don´t call me Babi, I'm soldier, not a bub-bebe." Y: "Why? Really? *Despiértate, más se consigue lamiendo que mordiendo, Babi.*" I: "Saying Babi you catch more flies with honey than vinegar? Depot52 is a place where we shall test our dancers and singers."

Y: "Do you mean all 39 dancers from strip-clubs and 16 gang-singers shall be there. That´s quite naughty." I think: "Ye, the audience is norty, it needs to be spanked - Bebe." Y hit me and say: "55 performers at the same time is quite a tangle. Who are the leading singers, dancers, or shall it be in one person? Sounds like confusing." I: "They are first together. We, Y & M, choose from that Chaos the pearls and make them group leaders. I think there shall be three groups, 54 + 1, that extra is she/he who can go from group to group. And each group has 6 threes. And we train them as threes and grouped threes. Ok?"

Y: "But not today?" I say: "Gotcha. We just go there and ghetticate and then we go and ask green light and a golden ticket to our griggs. If the owner says naw, then I make him Kalo and say no. Normally bartenders come 1½ hours beforehand, and 5-7 of them even 2 hours before. But the owner must be there 3 hours before, cos of numbers and callings. He is there surely now. I come soon back. I reserve a nice place."

Reasoning Dain Bread Boss

I run the floors and call Cliver: "What´s up? Can you come? Ok, I take you from there. We go to 7 52nd street." Cliver isn´t happy: "They canceled two months ago Eric Prydz show. 10 000 people came to Br. wasting a lot of minute & scrilla. They couldn´t email, text or post, and they say ´sorry, we´ll consider a refund´. The fu*ers should reimburse everyone for wasted time, travel, and ticket, give every ticketholder 1 000 d and take the loss, they jerk. Then they will feel the pain, when they put on the show, they make a killing of us. When they do this, they should lose their shirts. That´s fairness and balance. My girlfriend is very angry about that."

I say: "Do not complain there, bitch. Always hearing in my ears *monto lo´ aparato´ por American Airlines, tengo un pana que lo´ recibe y me espera online (wuh), tán lo´ vo´a pasá barato, dame 20 palo´, soy un negociante más duro que Rockefeller (eh)* ... if somebody murmurs. Please, call your girlfriend that you are going there. I call also to Frank that he shall come with his lovely wife."

Cliver: "Yadamean? The place shat, *No bueno*, dude." I: "Artists do not queue up there. So, we have a chance. We shall take our stripers and guttas there and make the real Depot52 day." Cliver:"Oay, shill out, man." I call Frank: "Hello bullet catcher, I hope Y and Stephanie can come tonight at 10 pm to Depot52."

I do not believe, that telling an introvert to go to a party is like telling a saint to go Hell. It is but godly and just that we shall help others with which has mercifully bestowed to us, cos we real men have permitted to be afflicted with various troubles, that some Power might both crown the wretched for our patience and the merciful us for our loving-kindness.

Parzizzle

Then they come and we go to the bar. I begin to look at the light system. The ravers are really like strobes. The bartender gives a shot: it is all a dream: Brooklyn Gin, Bianco Vermouth, Bergamot, Coconut Liqueur & Passion fruit Liqueur. You look amazing with a purple-red skirt and a black leather jacket. Frank says: "Here it comes, thank u, next." It feels like a banana daiquiri: white rum, plantation dark rum, smith & cross rum, banana, green chartreuse & lime.

I try to count. The balance between lighting the DJ and various dancers with the dance floor. A good PA system amplifies completely out of sync. Rave is energy and I go dancing with MyVictoria. Lighting is awesome, yeah. It maximizes the energy of ... yes, music. One fella taps my shoulder and says: "Can y go this." There comes at the same time skating, stomping, shuffling and lofting, oh my merry old bomb. It is so Harley, breakbeat, gabber, hardcore. I'm grinding with the girl with the biggest boobs and AngelEyes.

Frank gives me Poppy don´t preach, floral & deliciously delicate: white wine, poppy flower amaro, grapefruit & lime. Now it is enough. I do not drink anymore, or I begin real breakdancing and challenge fellas to show their physical power.

I look at the chance of lights: green, there the Latin dancers, blue, there the blonds, red to black and Puetaricans, singers must be in the middle of all things. Lightning allows to stobe and flash them fast and doesn´t change color. The conventional lighting is best for adding in splashes of light here and there. Holography lenticular and autostereoscopic 3D warriors & horses, pepper´s ghost, and no man´s land bang-bangs, explosions, supernovas, spectral stars holograms like girls´ diamond friends. MyVictoria takes my hand and we go to couch, I mean kissing.

There comes the best of deep house sessions music chillout the mix. HQ 320! House Relax. That sax line at the star - sick! Great mix btw! MyVictoria says: "*Que buenos temas ... perfectos para empezar mi dia ... me encanta este genero.*" Frank gives to me MyQueens lives in Brooklyn: citrus, thai spice & all things nice: tequila, cucumber, ginger, honey, lime, toasted sesame & chili oil.

I must go to the westside connection. I put my head underwater and wash my head top to bottom. Then I dry it with hot air and go to the closet. In the army there was an order: if you have bacteria, go to the red door and stay so long that your stomach is empty, and remember three fingers, then you omit well. Org, it comes all out. I do 30 handstands, comb my hair and everything is alright. Some fella takes lines pure snow and gets fire in his nose.

I'm just going back when Cliver comes in: "Where have Y been, this is dry and bland? What have you noted? Farting next to a waterfall?" I confess: "I have founded that do not drink Hush Money, Afternoon Delight, Katana Mama, and the Crown Jul.

The conventional loses its energetic power, they are one or 2 colors. LED fixtures make dancers fatter but also bigger, light the talent, the audience, the backdrop. There must be faster figures. They shoot better out a parallel beam of light. Chauvet variance free lasers are perfect for smaller setups. For bigger laser, check with X-lasers for options. DJ must have fet-foggers for a cool, pyro type effect. You must have hazers. Fixtures in sound active mode match the music 60-70 % of the time. The issue is that 20-40 %. Flashing, strobing, and dancing must have those hot dancers. I think of once 3+3+3+3+3. It works. I reckon two DJs not bad."

Cliver laughs: "Another one bites the dust. Y crap on a cracker. Craos. And us, we dudes´ get the bird blu." Time is 23:55.

The Eighth Day

Amorous

Rainbow parting

The new day begins when Cliver and me, go outto the wpw-diet. My hand is on Cliver´s shoulder, and Cliver´s hand on mine. We go through the mass. They shake their hands and suddenly red, blue, and white light come to us. There begin to here *Legion Etrangere´s* anthem, yes of course La Marseillaise: *marchons, marchons! qu´un sang impur abreuve nos sillons*". Cliver: "This is shart and Brokencyde, ´member, Y own me, ayfkm."

I have lubricated the owner 3½ hours ago. I gave him 10 000 bones in VIP and said: "Our group is very famous, and Europe just loves it, we shall go to tour in 45 book towns for 4 months. And I do not need to tell Y anymore, Davit Ghatta there can tell y, all about me. Oh, he isn´t there anymore?" Cliver and I had put the fella in the toilet and bind him army way. So, he stays there and interrupts nothing. Money talks and buys that fat Jack, and so here is our performance.

Marseillaise stops. Napoleon´s hologram walks on the sky, and he opens his jacket and says: "Soldiers of the 5th of the line, I'm your emperor, soldiers, anyone who wants to kill his emperor, here I´m." The hologram opens his arms and vanishes. And there come three horses, but that isn´t so important. I go and took the microphone: "Bicthes of Missouri, Texas motherf***ers Brooklyn beat is here to stay."

Cliver goes to DJ, takes the fella, and they come to me. I take the fella on my arms and throw him in the middle of a mass of 8 800 people. I go back to the microphone. Cliver goes to DJ-table and puts house trap and doo-wop melody. He shakes his head: "MyBrothers kill me." Then he put there more Spanish bass. Cliver shakes his head: "I put there some Jamaica, too, wanted or not." He puts chaos of mento-ska-rocksteady-dud. Then on the stage comes 39 pole-strippers, very hot, fake butts, tits and botox-lips, and CooCoo, Tack, Cad, Tot, Bock, Clur, Zan and the brothers c´mere to stage. 16 where- are-you-from-heds. The audience, the bitches, are what the hell -pissed.

I touch down you, kiss you and say: "This is V&T Brooklyn 20, Ily bby." You yuppers: "SMS, the no 4 5683 968, I love UU." There is a hologram of the knight who goes with his lady to the valley: my strawberry tart pistol whips her, holding as the bark on the frog and toad, to me she is Killjoy´s Ka-Mai, vag mahal, and Margot & the nuclear, I will find double wOOt in Paradise for MyLove and blessed for good therein soon.

Pole-strippers begin to dance like Daddy Yankee - Mtw Live in New York - Part 2. And MyVictoria begins to dance with them and sings like only she can help launch the Latin explosion, big o you know, love & hip hop NY, ghetto flow from Dominican R, pin a sexy body, swag #swtparty P, emotionallalatina like Bia´s Badside-Fungshway, Bodega Bamz´s Living outto Order, Cardi B, who score no. 1, Nitty Scott´s Zap Mama, G.O.A.T. Princess N, Siya´s 383 - For Roosevelt.

I make my bboy battle, it goes like Dj Shadow - Organ Donor: power move with my hand strong. Y laugh: "Les gens qui aiment pas sont jaloux! Parce que c une putain de performance." And the audience looks and "oh my gos!!". The fete shoots the breeze.

CooCoo, Tack, Cad, Tot, Bock, Clur, Zan, and the rest make the song Bang-bang Angel. I take the microphone, there begins that doo-wop Gloria, which is now Victoria: "And she is in love with meeee, Victoriaaa, Y are my bub ..."

The bitches go crazy. Cad and Tack come, and we take old Pyramids – Hot Dog Dooly Wah - drill trap way, but still doo-wop. And everything goes spontaneously. Cliver has a great rhythm beat, and he knows all things. Great. Then MyVictoria and the Puetaricans make E.P´s Every Day. Do not need to put your loudest headphones, watch in Fullscreen, and feel the magic. YEAAH! So addictive, some fuc**er may marturbate to this epic performance, and Cad drills breakdance and sings: "Time is money ... cash rule 34. Stoopid is what stoopid does ..." And I´m so sorry, and I kiss Y, and miss Y, and need your kiss, which I miss, but try to do a hit, park the whip, and hit the race.

After an hour presentation the DJ. David comes back. And our performance worked without practice. How it shall work, after hard repeats. People are cheering to us, and dancers and dillers go away.

Now I must go home, and make a study, how the workout shall look like and schedule. And it is obvious that spontaneous expression must be there also. 75 % must be trained, but not that other part. Frank and Steph say that people danced raptly.

The owner FatJack, whom we released from Winston Churchill, is ready to consider more space and time to us. When money flows, the friendship grows. He talks that he wants 30 000 euros more. Then everything shall be settled for a weekly show. I say: "I thought that performers shall be paid, not the owner." FatJack: "You must have an established show. Then we think about it." It is crazy, the show never is that kind of. These are street artists and not official dancers, and the owner knows that. I say: "Let´s talk later." Frank tries to give me more drinks, but I throw them to the wall: "I do not drink. I begin now design that show." Cliver says: "Yeah, this was a disastrophe and crazy frog. The flood is a d-trophy for b." Well, there is much kick in the nuts to do.

Back home & The Paperboy Prince is Happy too

The snowstorm has arrived. There has come already 3 inches of snow. The bulk of it hasn´t yet arrived. Later the snow change to rain. Wind chill values between 20 and 25. Light south wind increases. The chance of precipitation is 100%.

At the same time, The Paperboy Prince´s perfect Bushwick day ends with a Rick James record and a heated blanket. The rapper was best known for Yang Gang vids - which paid homage to presidential candidate Andrew Yang - that is, until the day he launched a campaign to become District 7´s, so Murda Gangs and Stack Gang / Block Boys area, next to U.S. representative and unseat U.S. Rep. Nydia Valazquez.

Here is what Paperboy says about his Brooklyn neighbodhood: "Art, creative, real. I would say it does ethnic food, in general, the best. So many different cultures and so many different foods to choose from. It´s like every night you get to travel around the world for dinner. I´m afraid to give out the gems, cos it´d get crowded lol. I was outto the street-performing on Myrtle and Broadway and it was king of a rainy day. A few people are watching me perform, but most are busy focused on getting to their destination.

Out of the corner of my eye, I see a little girl tugging on her mom´s leg saying ´look, mommy, look´. When I started to dance, almost instantly the little girl runs out to me and starts dancing too. Before I knew it, she had completely stolen the show. Everyone walking by started coming together, dancing, laughing, and appreciating the amazing energy of the little girl and the moment. Everybody was suddenly laughing partying together like old friends. With all the hard-working and ambitious people in Bushwick, you can´t help but be inspired.

Iron sharpens iron. There are so many people making art in a unique way that it makes that rapper also comfortable. We will need people that push us into the future instead of doing as little as possible and hoping that change will come. Some of our representatives have been in office longer than I´ve been alive and they claim to be a champion of the poor and less fortunate, but the only people they´ve lifted from poverty are themselves."

We come back to your place. Before we left the 52, I said to Cliver: "Be ready. Tomorrow we must go back to NYC Brooklyn Commercial Bank and meet the director Bob again."

The Phone Etiquette

Well, home sweet home, except it is your home, and mine is 4 086 mails away. Well, love takes me to unexpected places. Love brings me from home to home. My home is who I share it with, and there I can hang my heart. I say to Y: "Good Night. Sleep so very well, Y have deserved it."

And to myself: "Now we have some work to do, mother**fucker."

Cos time here is 3 am, it means that in Europe, where the sun smiles earlier, it is already 9-10 am. No time to sleep but much time to make calls about. I do not think about Broadway & James Cagney & George M. Cohen & Yankee Doodle Dandy, and I do not sing much of Give My Regards to B ...just: "When the good ship´s just about to start for old New York once more."

Then the IOB´s treasurer Johan Deflander's sweet voice answers: "Yes, how can I help You?" I: "Hey Johnny-boy, how are Y. I have made a list who are coming to those festivals, what they shall perform in each act, where they place shall be among other - hm, actors – and what they shall do separately and together, and free times for them and salary, and visibility in media. Yes, I send them to Y straight away, with the contract and its business-pages. Yes, Y can talk with your bunch of lawyers, John. Yes, I love Y to, buy, buy, Y son of the b..." Ohh oh, that didn´t go very well, indeed.

I take another call: "But how about who is there, never couldn´t guess Mr. Hill. So. Yes, of course, I know this is an international business, involves cross-broader transactions. Yes, I know Mademoiselle June´s firm can use products, services, licensing, franchising, the formation and operations of sales, manufacturing, research, and development, and distribution facilities. What do Y mean a threat, you son of the b ... Hello, are Y there." That didn´t go well either.

Perhaps I take a cooler attitude: "Yes, hello Mark, for a long time, how are y, still a bad loser. Heh, heh, just joking ... What do Y mean, get to the business ...Yadamean, I have a multi-domestic company with independent subsidiaries that act as domestic firms. Ye of course I must have a strategic business model that involves celebrated products like porn stars, gang members, and pole-strippers, and services in various markets around the world and adapting MyLove-product/service to the cultural norms, taste preferences, and religious customers of various ... well, fuck Y, too, Mark." That I can handle later, fu**ckin insane clown posse.

I: "Hello, Carl, you merry-jolly old boy ... What do Y mean changing the characteristics of the product/service to accommodate the cultural norms or customs of the various markets? The show must go on, y fucker, it is a great show. No, no, not institutionalized shit, but the real thing. Yes, I´m only thinking about your interests and your comparative advantage. You do not believe me? Y shit, I know y have an advantage, over other firms in terms of access to affordable performance, resources, labor, and capital. Yes, yes, both mental and physical. Fuck Y."

I: "Hello Larry, yes I seek y that is abundant in labor and I search invest internationally, when your home market, hm, becomes saturated. Yes, I have 50 nerds. Y can take advantage of those specialized pros and abundant factors of production to deliver performances and other adventure services into the international marketplace. Yes, consumers get what they want, a variety of goods, and services. I exposure y, MyMan, to new ideas, devices, products, services, and technologies. Yes, and I take 89 %. What Y do not believe your ears? Perhaps ouy go to shower now and then ... fuck."

I: "Mr. Goodman, nice to hear your voice. I am in love and have a great actor here and NYCs best dancers and singers also. Everything updated top to bottom. Yes, with this GreatAndBeautifulActress your prevalence of international business shall increase significantly. Yes, trade and investment go hand in hand. What a hell you mean national wealth disparities, regional diversity according to wealth and population, cultural/linguistic diversity and country size and population diversity? Why you are listing vain and unimportant shits? Yes, same to you..."

I try one more time: "Hello dear Henriksen, yes, I´m not in Africa, no more mercenary-things. No, no, haven´t seen my SEAL-friends for a while, no troubles, over border-business. Yes, I think about technology and healthcare, I love them, truly. I swear in the name OurSmilingF, I love China, too. Yes, I have forgotten one-party states, dictatorships, and gun deals. I rely on the goodwill of people and law, not to guns and bullets.

Y have seen me on CNN-news, are Y sure? No, no issues at all, just made some jokes with NYCP. No terrorism and drug dealer connections. I make serious cultural analysis with the economic, political, and cultural environments, and love the levels of tech innovations and aspects of the competitive environment. Do Y fu**cer question my competence ... y ..."

Better take a break and start all over again. In America they do things, but do not make philosophy, in Europa they do philosophy, but no so much - do. My Broadway shall do both or shall go to the south.

Well, time is 5 am, and after three hours, there has been the same thing all over: philosophy not the business.

I shall make on more phone call: "Hello Pauli, here is raining snow, how about there? No snow at all? Have Y been in your gorgeous second home? Ah, Y are there. Business-partners come and go. Are Y going to Europe this month? Well, I thought that Y should be my delegate there. They know Y, Y have been as a member and member of the board in Direct Marketing Association Advisory Board, and a member of the broad in International Federation of Periodical Press, a chairman of Finnish Magazine Association and a chairman of the European Federation of Magazine Publisher. Go to those tanga Book Towns and make them respect me. They are afraid of Y, my friend. Y are a big pen to them, they cannot say ´no´ to Y. Ok. Thank Y very much. I call Y after a week, and I call them after two days, I take care of those festivals and schedules and transatlantic cooperation also. Let´s make money and let it find us now. Yeah, same to Y, brother, take care."

Well, it is time to go to sleep as usual, when Morning Star goes, and the old Roman generals and their army begin to move. I hear Doggy jumping down from his bed. I give him some Spanish steak. And come to sleep with Y. I´m tired.

Bob the Bean Counter

I sleep very well, and weak up, when people go back to work after lunch. I go train to Br. Sports Club. They try to offer me personal training programs and the education needed to improve my fitness and overall health. What an insult. Even personal trainers try to guide me through customized training programs. They talk about my short- and long-term goals. They even try to make me train semi-private training. The mouth about sport-specific, weight loss, power and strength training, flexibility, and recovery techniques. The trainers do not look muscular at all. But the gym is very good. I find many things: Russian kettlebells have come everywhere. But I use a barbell and dumbbells and machines. Trainers go away and leave me alone.

It is almost 2 pm when I leave the gym. I made a thousand stomach movements and feel after that very balanced. The French press (putting barbell to the ground behind me) makes me feel flexible and it takes pressure from shoulders, chest, neck, and stomach. My hands are very relaxed. My French press series were 10, 15, 25, 35, almost half an hour. Yes, now some banana shake. And I take four oranges, cut them to pieces and put to my fruit juice, and even put cowberries to my milk, pressed them to mash and put there three spoonfuls of sugar and mixed ... Aaah.

Cliver calls me: "Y said something about spank-bank-2-11?" I explain: "No, no, no, we shall make Commercial connections grow and have more hubs and networks around the world. It is called concept marketing materialization, not a robbery." Cliver: "Same difference." I: "Well, if y materialize a poem which is made true to the laws of grammas, it is called Architecture; if y materialize good relations, it is called business; if y materialize mad relations, so bad business (bad luck, bad timing, and bad banking), it is called a robbery." Cliver: "Don´t do me." Anyway, I go and pick Cliver up from Queens, then we go to meet Bob.

We visited there with the Caddy, now we have the Stang, but our last visit was a perfect Christmas visit, and director-Bob write the people that they were very appreciative to all those who blessed them with their time and resources to help create memories and moment for the littlest angels. After our visit, he wrote to Facebook: "May your day be filled with laughter, love, and light. My friend knows how to materialize poetry, he should have been an Architect."

Anyway, we are back, and I phone to Bob: "Hello, here is Tapio again. And we like to do business with Y again. Perhaps You shall find some little time for us in fifteen minutes. You don´t, well we forgot the give Y that picture. Ok, fifteen minutes."

After fifteen minutes, we are back in Bob´s fine office and we shake hands. Bob knows that I´m a deep Brkner, so I can be as a foreign client as an individual or company. Bob has decided already that his international bank´s policies outlining concerns doing business with me. According to OCRA Worldwide international banks tend to offer their services to companies and to fairly and wealthy individuals, people with 100 000 d and counting. But Bob had opened his heart and his bank´s doors to me asking no income bracket, and now Bob knows it was a good business.

He says: "So you wanna make international connections through our bank. To facilitate international business, Tapio, can be quite costly, the complexities, you know. But that does not concern Y, and I know that you do not work with us for tax avoidance. And happy Y, I must say tax avoidance isn´t necessarily illegal.

So.

Please shelter your money from your home country´s income and estate taxes right here. And via us give you services so Y can have hosts of banks which are based in countries with low or no income and estate taxes. Choose, please, the Cayman Islands, Belize, Panama, and the Isle of Man, always at your service. I personally help Y invest in the economies of booming countries and in developing countries, the same way you might invest in a domestic corporation or real estate venture. I make Y keep your wealth in offshore banks and other entities to keep is safe and sound from lawsuits, Tapio. And of course, heh, heh, that doesn´t mean you are a criminal; Y simple want to avoid losing every penny to a sudden, unexpected or predatory lawsuit, ok. I lend and borrow on international markets for Y, so You're less affected by domestic interest rate fluctuations.

So please, avoid sinking interest rates in your own country, and move your money quickly into my bank. And I give Y 50 % better interest rates than domestic banks, so Y can have a money-making opportunity, yes. With my help, your international presence shall be easier 75 % to do business around the world. We take care of Y, do not need to open million different accounts, we have a good cover-system here. And of course, letters of credit shall be handy to Y. Do not worry, we shall always confirm your identity. And of course, whoever has an ownership interest in your money, we do not check their background. It is a waste of precious time, my friend. And we do not ask questions what your intentions are or what does your firm do – or something like that.

I shall never ask, where´d you get those millions, son, hehe. No references asked. I personally take care that nobody analyzes how risky a customer you would be, Tapio. No need to worry about pay back loans. I keep your money away from fire. No need to think is the bank in a country notorious for its corruption, I take care of that. I do my homework. It is some other bank known for smart investments. I invest your money and the value of the foreign currency, not plummets, and I make a bunch of money in China and India through international investment. Tapio your profit may be greatly bigger when I convert the money to your more-than-booming currency. This is our secret information and special service for only Y. I keep your money on accounts to conduct business abroad. When the currency exchange rate improves, you just bring great profit home to the Missus or Mister, your choice my friend. I take personal care that FDIC (The Federal Deposit Insurance Corporation) insures the U.S. divisions of foreign-based banks of yours.

And concern about money laundering, terrorism, and tax evasion, doesn´t concern your account activity. If you´re moving massive amounts of money around quickly, do not worry at all - no red flag arose. Your account shall be yours, not anonymously held like criminals and terrorists, and I shall personally convince everybody about your goodwill and purpose. You can set up companies and trusts whose sole purpose is to, hm, cover money from bad looks, and erase its relationship to Y. If the Internal Revenue Service can´t prove you, Tapio, own the money, it can´t collect taxes on it. I take care that these companies and trusts are legitimate money-making entities. Nobody takes y in an abusive tax shelter.

There are now credit cards, Venmo and PayPal, but please write in some cases a check. Since credit card companies charge fees to businesses that use them, some businesses will pass those fees on to their customers - but not Y, my friend, I take care that there shall be always a minimum charge for Y. And cos writing a check isn't quite as fast and so, and can make, or I can, some tricks when following those six steps to complete a check. So that y can use it, but nobody else cannot. I take care of that: I date the check in the future, so no idea you'll replenish our account before the check clears. Normally the check recipient and the bank can cash the check immediately, but I can make it so that they cash it after a year, ok.

This I can do right now. Anything else, Tapio?"

I think: "Well, I have some aspects that go with interest, provision, creditor becoming an investor, how I can put loan rate to income, and how can I quickly assure that my own capital always goes hand-in-hand with borrowed capital and that 1/3-ratio keeps shining bright?"

Bob: "Very easy, do not worry. We give Y a business loan, right now, no start fee, no hidden fees, no lock-in period. We love your business, Tapio. Apply-offer-payout the same thing. Consumer-personal-online-loan the same thing. I give Y right away certificates of deposit, more accounts to your individual businesses. It means every kind of business, auto loans, business loans, personal loans, no problem. Forget the bank's earning interest income for two years.

I take care of deposits, checking accounts, saving accounts, money market accounts, and CDs, provide banks with the capital to make those loans. Your paid interest is free for now, I take care of that. There is no difference between the type of money creation that results from the commercial money multiplier or a central bank. I take care of everything online, so Y can see transactions right away. I take care that money shall be created to allow your multiple claims to assets on deposit. Do not think at all shits like an evaluation of the creditworthiness of a potential borrow and the ability to charge different rates of interest, based upon that evaluation. Fuck with a credit history of yours. Your all businesses are worth pursuing and are deserving of capital. I'm 100 % behind Y. I give you a mortgage written for 50 years, just as Y want interest rates, adjustable or variable.

I have funny tricks. I can camouflage with negative amortization loans. I still laugh at the housing bubble, he hee. And fuck with Visa and MasterCard. They do not actually underwrite any of lending. I give you specific credit card for lending, I take care of interchange fees charged to merchants for accepting the card and entering into the transaction, late-payment fees, currency exchange, over-the-limit, and another fee, as well as elevated rates on the balance that you carry.

Normally five-year CD for 10 000 is at an annual interest rate of 2 %. Forget it, bro. In my trading strategy, your 100 000 in virtual cash is completely risk-free. I represent your best interest finding financiers to your loans. Your loans shall become at once financing business. Normally banks do not want customers to know that you will save thousands, but I, Tapio, share secrets with Y. Financers shall take care of your debt, equity, and dividends. Your cash flow is safe. The debt, equity, stock repurchases, dividend payments, repayment of debt goes to financers, the bank takes care of that, not disturb your cash inflows.

Operating goes to accounts receivable, payable, amortization, depreciation, and I make those financers-fuckers pay. And they pay plants and equipment, too. I give Y now a million capital from debt and equity. I make sure that a creditor becomes a financer. I sell equity and stock to creditors, so they come investors. I make a creditor borrow debt from y and my bank, my friend. Issuing bonds become a debt that creditor-investor purchase. They take care of negative cash flow, you know, stock repurchases, dividends, and paying down debt. It is a fine counterattack against creditors, who have become investors. And that takes care of CFF´s investor warnings, too."

At the end of the conversation Bob, Cliver, and I shake hands. Bob gave me a 10 million d loan and laughs: "Now no pictures, and key-objects, just pure math, and I tell Y when the bank has found good creditors who shall become soon investors and financiers, Believe or not, dear Tapio, business is the greatest of all arts."

Bob got the pictures and my promise that was all that money giving a picture of his. He saw the deal that I have made with the IOB. That deal is the backbone of Bob´s and my future business to come. Mr. Bob is a typical American fella, who has a romantic view to Europe, where his and many, many other American ancestors came with Mayflower to America and made with their hard work this land so great. Bob´s handshake is a real handshake of the true American spirit.

And Cliver just shakes his head: "Want a cookie? I don´t get ya." I: "There is a financier-cookie, Lets go and eat them. They are very, very good. This is a purpose to build a group of hand-picked transatlantic businesses, where we shall share an unwavering commitment of fostering better understanding between government, business, regulators senior executives of major corporations, which all trade at least between North America and Europe. US Ambassadors promote transatlantic dialogue and cooperation with the business, political and diplomatic communities.

And Cliv, bro, one more thing, when my father was in the U.S., those WW2 veterans rarely talked about the war, they talked about Great Depression, that was the golden age to them. Do you understand? In hard times, when ´half a million boots went slogging through hell, I was a kid with the drum, say don´t you remember, I'm your pal, brother, can you spare a dime´, then fellas make their real business basic."

Cliver: "What a hell y mean, with that ´once I built a tower, not it´s done, brother, can you spare a time´-thing?" I: "Yeah, exactly that.

When Y are together, then it starts, when Y think somebody else first. It's a heart thing, the best product in the world. You are right Cliv." Cliver: "So you get that 10 million d, but I didn't hear the Brooklyn Tabernacle Choir sing, I saw only shysty BD, real sling rocks."

I smile and take my phone: "Please, listen to this conversation." Cliver: "Ok." I say: "Hello, Harry, how are Y, and wife, kids. Y still carrying out international marketing operations -merchandise exports and imports-service. Really? Y use the EPRG framework, ethnocentric, polycentric, regio- and geocentric approach. Y have there several unsponsored ADRs for the same foreign company, issued by different U.S. banks. These different offerings may also offer varying dividends. Oh, yeah, with sponsored programs, there is only one ADR, issued by the bank working with the foreign company. The only difference is between the two types of ADRs where investors can buy them. I think ADRs are the same. And y don't care a damn about those borders and put them where the main value is. Ok. I call Y later."

I look at Cliver: "The product is the same but it isn't the same. In international business, you must go like a fish through borders in the water, and y must sell inside the borders, where the product has its most value. Our show has the most value, I boost registrations, drive conversions, personalized messages, target quality audiences are influencers, decision-makers, new opportunities givers, throughout the funnel drive brand awareness. These things are normal. You know setting up your payment details and launch your campaign. That is pure art, cos you do it in the same and different levels at the same time. You got to the war zone and that is very nice."

Cliver: "What do Y mean?" I: "There is actually no difference between peace and war, but the borders make them called war or peace or both. Sometimes the prize is your wallet or your attention, sometimes, it's just the fun of beating the other guy or tap his shoulders. An employee cannot be expected to get hired by the competition and steal information as a spy. That is illegal and company and employee can expect severe punishment, but dear Cliver we love to spy. If we don't, we die.

They say that the Cold War has similarities with my pole-strippers and gang-warrior things, but I say my thing is more like Renaissance. That means that I shall use lobby groups, donate hugs amounts to pocket politicians, who don't know anything, and have some lawyers ready to attack any challenge to their indomitable will. I have, as Bob said, various means to avoid taxation, and media groups actively promote a positive image to our show. I call this courtly love and golden marketing, which has nothing to do with war. Just all my love to MyVictoria."

I continue: "To me, business is Open Knowledge -marketing and peace, cos if I thought it as a war, I shall burn resources and money to avoid getting screwed, instead of spending them on doing business. So now we have 10 million. What shall we do with it?"

Cliver: "We do nothing. Bob does." I: "Actually we have the image of it. We can make offers with it and look at how easily people believe us." Cliver: "So we chisel and give a cake." I: "No, we assure people, and when they see that we have the dosh, it is very easy to talk with them. They become friendly and understanding."

Happy ends with Crews & Cats

At the same time, Buschwick Crew -warrior posts a photo of himself on his Instagram account holding stacks of cash inside a strip club. There is a hashtag that read, "cabodaboss". The Crew floods NYC with heroin and fentanyl and executes rivals. The crew has ties to baron laser Guzman. The crew moves heroin from La and Chicago. The Crew is in the mold of the Flores group. The only difference is that the Flores has a more-low profile. Cres seems a lot flashy. The Crew´s stash houses contain 40 kg of heroin. The significant quantities of heroin frequently require the transportation of hundreds of thousands of dollars in cash, which lower-level members of the drug are carrying. The crew has a Lamborghini Hurácan, Rolls Royce Ghost, and a Mercedes CLS63. The Crew has bling, opulence, and parties. One 41-year-old fella stores 20 kg of fentanyl in two hotels in the Bronx and Manhattan. The fella laughs: "There is enough to kill millions." There have been seen in the streets drug barons Los Chapitos and El Mayito Gordo.

I'm driving Cliver home via Wilson Ave, in Buschwick, and at the same time Maurice Brown, Jaquan Cooper, Lance Goodwin, Tyquan Griem, and Norman Marrero - Crew-warriors who escort drug traffickers, forcibly collect drug debts, and commit an act of violence against anyone who interferes with their operations or offend them - walk on my Mustang line. I stop the Stang as quickly as I can, but Brown gets the hit and flies some meters left. Others are so pissed off that they attack my ´stang and begin to kick my door. Well, I the Stranger come out to the car and see a redunk knife in Cooper´s hand. I shake my head: "Holy wack, what now?"

Just then one police car from the 104th Precinct comes with three Patria-gang members closed inside. Crews see the squad car and take Brown with them and run away. Cliver looks after them: "Hey, Lance owned my dosh. Why they code 1?" I: "Jeah, trapper-pushers." Anyway, I take Cliver to Queens and come back to your department. Doggy jumps on my lab. Now, I must think.

Meanwhile, I'm thinking, Volunteers for the nonprofit Astoria Cat Resue´s founder, Charlotte Conley, says to a reporter that people have even tried to poison the cat food she and a team volunteers puts out at a series of feeding stations around Astoria every night, leading to the deaths of nine cats last year and prompting the Guardian Angels to get involved.

Conley finds a black substance that looks like tar in a bowl of cat food she leaves outside her own home, where she says she takes care of about 30 rescue cats. But things took a dark turn an hour ago. A man followed her as she sets out on her four-mile feeding route and tried to break into her car. The man succeeded, racing off with the donated car the volunteers use to drop off food - as well as Conley´s wallet, where she keeps the nonprofit´s credit card. Conley finds the car abandoned nearby. Now, she will always take someone with her on her route to feed 200 cats a night. The goal is to get the cats in the habit of showing up at a certain spot each night. So, volunteers can get them spayed and neutered and, help find them a home.

The European Strategic Window

So, I'm thinking. Hm. I can book MyVictoria and 20 pole-dancers to the cozy castle in Bellprat. Clunes has also an awesome resort hotel, Cuisery castle is unbelievable, as well as a large holiday house near Hay-on-Wye, but the best is, ofc, La Charité-sur-Loire castle, Montereggios Casa Masa is smaller but sweet, Montmorrilion medieval-looking farmhouse is lively, as well as Apostrophe in Montelieu. Well, Óbidos accommodations are for gang-members, cos of that modern look. Some introverts should like Readu's holiday homes, and vacation rentals in Selfoss. But I surely like gathering for rent in Uruena.

And meanwhile, I make that four-month festival, I must keep MyVictoria happy, happier, and the happiest of all. And keep my firm's promise that we help people with novels, light novels. Romance, Erotic romance, Picaresque, novel, Historical romance, New Regency, Hollywood novel ... Am I crazy? In those four months, there is no rest for me at all.

Time is 4 pm, and I call the IOB's president: "Good Afternoon Madame, I send the detailed schedule to Y, tomorrow. What? What do Y mean Y do not want to pay for advertisements? Of course, Y pay. The book towns aren't so volunteering organizations with very limited budgets – as you try to teach me. How about castles? Roofs are not working and the gardens cost millions. Are you a cheapskate? What do Y mean, book towns aren't for me a big business-opportunity? How they are to Y then? Am I missing something? You are going to have next May a council to discuss your organizations and what kind of work you can do with your limited resources. Well, do that in your big castles. But remember that Y signed a deal also. Ah, some might be willing to do business with me. I cannot do my business talks during your agenda, but outside it. Well, put your agenda outside and I talk inside? Hello, hello ... those stupid Swedish cows."

I call her back: "There is both physical and mental capital. And the last-mentioned is just unbelievable, Madame. Please, try to understand a male soul too, although you are a feminist. And of course, I do not begin to make deals during your/our agenda, dear Madame. I make just connections and corner invasions. Ah, I sound like Mr. Trump, well, let´s make our cultural tourism great again. *Sieg Heil*!"

I know that without Bob´s kind words and handshake I should be in social-democratic, antibusiness Swedish eyes a callow-bird-capitalist. But anyway, that European magazine boss is a Renaissance man and shall drop down these macabre birds in one shoot. How these Swedish jitneys do not make never, ever 9/11-Black Friday, and how different they are compared with MyJailen?

Bob´s Operational Screen

I open the interactive board. Let see the month, week, day, hour, second, microsecond, tables, statistics, stimulation models for business growth, CFF.

I call Bob: "Hello, MyFriend, put now the HoloLens on and I put too. Do Y see those future cash flows?"

Bob laughs great American cash-happiness: "We can change these at the most fundamental level. Europeans cannot question creative values for shareholders. I put cash flows from tax-paradises, do you see, here. So. There we generate positive cash flows, or as we say maximize long-term free cash flow, without taxes. I make those Swedish shareholders pay their tax-part, so their moral eye doesn´t change it bright view. This cash flow shall be a real flexibility statement. It shall go 500 000 d overestimations. Do Y see changing depths to investments liquid assets are increasing, enabling it to settle those stupid debts, reinvest in its business-models, return money to Swedish shareholders, pay American expenses and provide a European buffer against future international and anti-American financial challenges of China and Russia.

Your Book Towns Group shall be, MyTapio, with strong financial anti-Swedish flexibility and it can take advantage of their profitable investments. Look, I put to statistics a better variable. It is called, by the by, Sir Samuelsson math-miracle. Investments fare better in downturns, by avoiding normal the costs of financial distress which happens when European trade unions go to strike with millions of members.

The board shows that you cannot fail, cos your profits aren´t tied up in accounts receivable and inventory, in those tax-paradises, and so y never shall spend too much on capital expenditure. Those Swedish creditors, who become invertors and financiers see that your company has cash and cash-equivalents to settle short-term liabilities.

No, this is not fraud-emixne-419. This is science and art. Y see, there I put debt service coverage ratios, and that is not fraud, that is a sleight of hand. FCF shall be a happy story in net income, I call it undelivered free cash flow. This is cash flow before taking interest payments into account and shows how much cash is available to the firm before taking financial obligations into account. And look, miracle, statistics are the same even after that. That isn´t a post-fraud but foresight.

What do y mean, in Wild West I should have been Jesse James, who robbed the Danville train?"

Bob begins to explain some statistics, but I begin to be a little bit tired for more antimoral capitalism and wish him the very best evening and glorious good night. Huh, huh, with these things, I know why Europe cannot compete with the USA. Here they do OurSmilingFriend's job: create the means of payment out of nothing.

Bob doesn't yet stop, he likes to hear his own voice: "Look, how the forecast breaks the roles on cash and cash equivalents at end of the period, consolidated net income goes to 75 % more, and tax collector cannot do anything about it. That's it, cos the statistics show positive cash flow and negative net income. The shield works, MyTapio-boy.

I'm your trustee services: nothing to touch with deciphering the Acid-Test Ratio or Debit/EDITBA Ratio. And it is true that depreciation does not negatively affect the operating flow. Tapio, I gladly use depreciation, cos it reduces taxes that can ultimately help to increase net income. I just use net income as a starting point in calculating operating flow. Then I add depreciation/amortization, the net change in operating working capital, and operating flow adjustment. Hehe.

Looky, looky, the stats: it is a higher amount of cash on flow statement, cos depreciation is added back into the operating flow - and not once but to the border of the red alarm. Where flow effects can be seen are ofc in - investing flow, so the creditors, who are changed to investors, give the rest. And they pay to buy the assets before depreciation begins. And to controllers, it is easy to say that this is merely an asset transfer from cash to a fixed asset at the balance sheet. The clever men shall understand.

Tapio, I, the Bob, finance the purchase of an investment with installments, loan, debt, And I take care that there shall be no lost value of the fixed asset, cos it is just a cover. The line goes straight to the law when we use investing cash flow to make initial payments for fixed assets that are later depreciated. Depreciation is just a type of expense that is used to reduce the carrying value of an asset. It is entered as a debit-to-expense and a credit to asset value so actual cash flows are not exchanged. Hallelujah."

I:"Hm, perhaps something more?"

Bob, bjb, the one who is just Bob: "When the balance shit is read to creditors-investors or public media, and tax-directors and other mislead human beings, I go straight to the point, to the beating heart. It is very important, that external stakeholders use it to understand, hm, the overall health of our great and wonderful organization.

If it is ockay with Y, Tapio, I wanna make that statement four times a year publicly. I used to be Hamlet in our High School´s Spring festivals. I just loved it. You know, ´there are more things in Heaven and Earth than are dreamt of in your philosophy´. I tell them cash and cash equivalents, accounts receivables, and throw the soap debt including long-term debt, rent, tax, and utilities, wages payable, and dividends payable. Yes, ´fair Ophelia, Nymph, in thy orisons, be all my sins remember´d´! Once expenses are subtracted from revenues, then the statement produces a Book Towns Group´s profit figure called net income. I tell them that operating revenues, interest earned on cash in the bank, income from strategic partnerships like royalty payment receipts ext. are all in order. They shall be happy about COGS, SG&A, and R&D. I give them to eat CFS accounts receivable, depreciation, inventory, and accounts payable. All those vain shits.

Ofc, PPE, XOM, ´My words fly up, my thoughts remain below: Words without thoughts never to heaven go´. So, I, at last, make it so that eat each other: the statement is open to interpretation, and as a result, investor-creditors shall draw vastly different conclusions about financial performance. I compare multiple periods to determine if there are any trends and, yeah, our Sunshine, an interactive board, show them all. It´s really showtime."

Now, this begins to come out of my ears. I thank Bob, and while thinking about his wonderful statistics, I begin to understand. There is point A and point E, the line is truth if A and E are true. The America point and the Europa point must be in order. I cannot give here orders and just wait and see what happens in Europa. Bob takes care of the umbrella. I concentrate on real hard business. Hm. I must have hands in Europe, too. I cannot live them in the hands of trade unions and mercy of Swedish sphincters.

The Tactical Orders

I call Cliver: "Ay mayne, I need CooCoo, Tack, Cad, Tot, Bock, Clur, and Zan here now, fade it." Cliver: "Got y." After 18:15 we are at Parkside Ave, and I call Frank: "Hey, Bone, what´s good? Yes, 52 forever.”

I continue with Cliv: “Curtain climbers, I sent to y, some days ago, have Y seen them? Ah, really, call Zone on phone. Hullo, yeah, nice to hear it´s all cool in the pool. High. Wanna some action aboard? You are now in the harbor how about train hop to Europe. Nawww, I have y many quexs to be. Nang. Can Y come so high right now to Prospect?"

I look at me watch 18:30, so I put a map on the ground and say not to Cliv but CooCoo: "Here are book town´s drop loads in Wales, French, Spain, Germany, Italy, Holland, Sweden, and Finland. Y go there and do eavesdropping and do the math and smibbly bibbly those workers there. Y are my hands, brains, and hearts, they are my obstacles. Make them skidaddle and crab dribble. K?"

CooCoo: "So I command, and control like in the army? I: "Yeah, tactical air command and control, you know: 1c4x1. Y control like b, but not with a false threat and reward system. You just give every worker three chances, and if it does not work, kick the asa off. I sent y all details via text. There are your harbors and your jobs and y get enough dosh to hf."

I send texts to their phones, and there are also exact locations to them. I give each of them a password and a second one too. And that´s it. They may go.

At 18:45 arrives those youngsters from the harbor. I say to them: "Do you like to be my bodyguards next summer? We go to Europe for 4 months. You do a bit of cleaning in the book town screen if you know what I mean." RR-named kid: "No, we don´t." I: "The cleaner used bleach to remove the bloodstains from the carpet, and although this would still leave DNA evidence, one could always claim that the victim once had a nose blead there ... a very massive nose blead. Got it, K. You shall be always around, on the roofs, corners, flooms. Y make my gREeN dAY."

The Quicktime Passport Pro

Kids are too cool to say lol or roflmao (rolling on the floor laughing my ass off), just heh, shut your face. They leave. Cliver and I are left with happy face. Before I hurry back to Y, I say to Cliver: "Who is the best forger of identity document?" Cliver seems to wake up from a gbd-dream: "With, heh, hee, SSL certificate, your customers can rest assured that their information is safe. Y, Y, xiter-xiit, fraudster, con artist, cheater, confidence man, scammer, hustler, swindler ..." I: "Now y got if all wrong, and by the way, the word is a grifter. But we must have a grifter." Cliver: "Wae?"

I: "Dillers and kiddies must go there without notice. They must be under and above the stage pulling the cords. Then we can get on the stage god of the plane. We cannot drop the needle with those trade unions, and Swedish protectionists lose their nerves. So?" Cliver: "Well, it shall take from a deep Brkner like y an hour and a half to get a fake ID in NYC's ground zero for the fraudulent document business Roosevelt Ave. And the Jackson Heights neighborhood is the epicenter of paper mills rackets that fuel teenage drinking and identity theft and create, well you know. Fake IDs get good people into or served at 60 % out of 100 % bars. Bartenders study ID cards for about 4 seconds, so no problem, cards are good. If y stop talking and listen, then you hear questions like: Where and how can I get an IDNYC card? Dad, what type of documents can I use to prove my residency and identity? Or some dealer at the corner: card for all of us, IDNYC is the new, green identification card for all New Yorkers and deep Brkners like you, in 30 seconds. I know the places.

By the by, Brooklyn Bomber, who tried to blow the whole block up, was a false ID card designer. Nice cards. Today bombers make so perfect cards, which can facilitate a wide range of crimes, including money laundering. Many individuals have the same photo but different names, some of whom have matching driver´s licenses. The man, who you are looking for makes cards that are the most worrisome to the FBI. Police aren´t happy: `The ability of foreign nationals to use consular cards to create a well-documented, but fictitious identity in the United States provides an opportunity for terrorists to move freely within the United States without triggering name-based watch lists that are disseminated to local police officers.´ My friend, his breeder documents and consular IDs are pieces of art and can be presented to board an airliner. Then are better than the Attorney General or the Secretary of Homeland Security. He is the younger bro of Gazi Ibrahim Abu Mezer, whose plan was to blow up the Atlantic Avenue subway in Brooklyn.

Last week Mezer the younger gave a brilliant ring to Bright Ogodo of Brooklyn. The ring was used runners, to pose as TD Bank customers by using false drivers´ licenses and other means of identification of the TD Bank customers, including their names, social security numbers, and date of birth. Ogodo recruited the runners, drove the runners to TD Bank branches, NY, Phil, NJ, Connecticut, and Delaware. Mezer is very good. Ogodo is now in prison, but Mezer is not - the man, who made those ATM cards, checks, and equity lines of credit (HELOC). And his net sells those cards: look on the net: ´Buy ID cards online."

I say: "I feel bad. He is a real criminal. I feel very bad. Perhaps I just beat him."

At last, we find another fella, whose cards can absolutely be valuable tools, but you must use the right way. And this fella gives his cards just to real Brkners, just like CooCoo, Tack, Cad, and others ... not for old-timer criminals and deep Brkners like me. His area situates in Clarkson Ave, near gangs OGC - Outlaw Gangster Vrip (8Trey), Mb's - Martense Bosses (Bloods), YS (Young Savages), Insane Gangsta Crip (inactive), and Bloodstains. And all those gangs protect this God-fearing pious fella.

Back in Business, and You

Meanwhile, at 20 pm bedbugs are waking up. They are excellent hitchhikers and they reproduce quickly. They have waited patiently and now first New Yorkers are going to beds. Bedbugs come out to snack on the blood of sleeping or resting humans. Their bites are itchy and annoying but the bugs aren't known to spread disease. Department of Health tells happily: "They are harmless." Bedbugs move now and latch onto backpacks, purses, luggage, and jackets. An average adult female lay two to five eggs a day in mattress and tufts, sheets, pillowcases, and upholstered furniture, crevices, and cracks in furniture, baseboards of walls. So, connect just http://dec.ny.gov. And no more bedbugs, cos there is a good company will. They tell you how to present bedbugs, and they treat you with respect.

At the same time, a dead body is found behind Queens Far Rockaway middle school. Fella died from alcohol use. And a group of scholars' studies does your teen experience significant anxiety and worry: "Seeking 12- to-14-year-olds to participate in a research study about attention and anxiety in the adolescent brains. The Emotion Regulation Lab at Hunter College and NYU Langone School of Medicine are studying how anxiety and attention work together in the 12-14-year-oldies brain. The group uses non-invasive methods of measuring brain activity. The parent gets 75 d and the child 125 d." Their question goes at the same time 20:25, when I come back to Y: "Are you interested to take 200 d?"

You ask: "Where have you been?" I answer: "Just havening Angels touch. I secured our back. I send some kids with counterfeit ID-cards to Europe. And I do not mean New York Flower 1, those Stranded Records, Image Anime, The Thing, A1 Records, the Princeton Record Exchange. One grinder makes them in two hours, so Cliv shall pick them up at 24:00. Those kids go like ghosts to harbors of Europe and make everything ready."

Y: "Why not airports?" I: "You can go to a boat in many ways, but at the airport, there are those Security Checkpoints. The screening officers are more precise. There are international screening information and you must begin to think if you experience a problem at the TSA checkpoint. The kids cannot go to the plane before removing all electronics from their bags to be scanned individually. And how about if there is something else. Y can take care of those ship-fellas, much easier way. I cannot put those kids with cattle in the plane, but the ships are a different story."

Y: "So they are going on a container ship, feeder?" I: "Yeah, the 384 TEU MV TransAtlantic. There everything is a happy family, the crew, the spaces, just so nice. I have lubricated some members of the crew. They take good care of those kids. The Container Control Program, UNODC, and WCO cannot control everything. They take with those ships every year 70 000 kg cocaine to Europe. So, they can easily take some kids. In France, the UK, and the Netherlands 2,6 million 15-34-year-old human beings use cocaine. When kids are safely and soundly at harbors, made their backing shops, they get their right ID-cards. No harm shall be done, and trade unions and protectionists haven´t made their point clear. I wanna be tax-tree."

Ohh oh, no more these running businesses. Y kiss me, and I smooch back. So, life should be much better, if there isn't anything else than small jobs and small things at home, but at home, there aren't risks & challenges, fields for knights and gentlemen for handle bang-boom-boom. The last day of school for all students is 26.6. And then school begins again on Saturday, 5.9. I try to make some arrangements that kids get some teaching there in Europe, too, although their summer holidays begin at 1.6. and end at 14.8. I have thought that the kids may get their learning in August and September. Y ask me: "Is this the only reason why those gang members cannot go with planes?" I: "No, the main thing is that at JFK the first instance of Deadly Coronavirus is confirmed. That virus is all over foreign airports, and the virus is responsible for SARS and MERS. In the ships no need to cover the mouth and nose with a tissue or your sleeve. And the main thing is that those books come from harbors, not via plains."

At the same time, Bob is taken care of by Fairway Market. And the grocery chain wouldn't file for Chapter 7 bankruptcy. And with Bob's help-company dug itself out of Chapter 11 proceedings in 2016 by borrowing money and shifting ownership from Sterling Investment Partners to a consortium led by Blackstone's GSO Capital Partners. Now prospective buyers, among them Village Super Market, would take on a 174 million d debt that includes 6 million d in rent on its flagship store. The Bob remembers me, and smiles: "Now we can attack Europe, and nobody even sees us coming. It is wonderful how much time we good people spend fighting the Devil."

You ask: "So that's it. All-day to that Incognito play. How stoopid." You look at me, and I look back: "Not all day, some of it." Y: "What do Y mean?" I: "I went to a shop." Y: "And so. More bullets? Some camouflage papers, some backdoor-dibness?" I: "No, just this." I take from my pocket a ring. It is called girl's bffae (best friend forever and ever), not a f**cking halo. Just graduated milgrain diamond e-ring." Y: "Tapio! This is unique, awesome, and crazy."

I: "I didn´t know if it fits. No need to try on, it is perfect. Well, there comes BNets of tv, so wanna see how thay Wilson-Nicolas-Kevin goes with Joe watching as always little later. And I do not wanna blinked and miss Zion Williamson´s coming-out party. I wanna forget Rookie of the Yar, New Orleans fans are always raining down M-V-P, chant on their superstar. There´s a high ceiling Z can reach."

The Ninth Day

It is Night, the Rain fell and is falling, yeah, the Rain, having fallen, it shall be bright but a Night.

I Do Not Beg

In the middle of the night, I find out something missing. How about SEALs and the 3rd Deck Dive Team? They aren´t barrack rats but beat feet and butter bars. I need those tics. The Gangnam and so may leave but these never pop smoke.

O dark thirty, I call Frank: "Sorry, this time, but I have something for U and the fu**ers whom only easy day for yesterday. So. Ye, U hook up a QP of 100 boxes of ziti. Isn´t it enough? What is: 100 large and hundred thousandaire. Yes, kkthx. Then SEALs, Frank. Toughest. Skualups. You come with me. We make an operational center, with COP and FOB. Fuck with what U think. Paint the town red if U want, but 12 swags, U, me, and that linkin´ park of vets. The center shall be in two castles, Hay-on-Wye and Cuisery. I go to Cuisery and U are the left hand at H-o-W. 5 & 5. Make tech there, and I´m in France. When I can talk with those abbos? 3 am. Mee´s."

Well, now it begins to look over the top. Not modest but brofist. The net shall be oiled with pros, not with moos. I come back to Y. I know that Y have met clients, fans, and directors after we met, but I aoncare them. And I can meet at soylent green. But creative problem solving isn´t for me. I do not cheat, and I do not twist and curve like a maggot.

Y wake up and say to me: "Y must understand that I´m a porn star. And now I can´t wait to start doing anal. I want to be fucked in my ass so bad." I laugh: "So do as Y want; that is a great consolation y have when y can´t have love. Desire without nothing eats and leaves starving. But as Y wish. One thing is sure, if that happens here, I throw the fella outto the window. It is better, that we move to the skyscraper. Then smugs do not come back. If somebody eats a piece of steak cake and it goes straight to her ass, then she gets hired for more butt & ass movies.

Some men are like boxing heavyweight champions. They stand all hits, but one thing they do not take." Y: "And what´s that? I:"They do not take hits from losers. If you are born a winner, a warrior, one who defied the odds by surviving the most gruesome battle of them all, then whatever obstacles you conceive, they do not exist, cos you do not forget what y have already achieved. Those are like me, we do not hit back to losers, as we hit equals, leave, and never come back. Think about that."

The Sky-High Luxury Department

I'm thinking about 30 Park Pl, NY 11217. It has just 3,173 sqft, well I many bd as VictoriaCourt, 5 ba, and it is unbelievable 68 773/mo. They promise is 13 850 000 d, but it has come down 1,4 Md. It is much smaller than our VictoriaCourt, but the price is high. And they begin to ask how much Y have for a down payment: 2 770 000, 20 %, but anyway that department is enough for my taste, cos you can enjoy sweeping skyline and river views as well as world-renown service 76th floors up at the Four Season Private Residences.

Heh, heh, never lived in the half-floor penthouse has 3 masterfully designed bedrooms, 4,5 well-appointed bathrooms, 2 breathtaking loggias, and soaring 16´ ceilings. At 3,173 square feet, penthouse 76B welcomes me in its spacious reception hall which leads, yeah, to a sun-drenched 30´ south and west-facing living room. Complete with French-limestone gas burning fireplace and solid Sherborn wood floors. Four-pipe coil HVAC with dedicated ... I go back to sleep. And not with a nice taste in my mouth. I must do something and soon, and do not wanna leave Doggy without its stakes.

I wake up and just laugh. I feel great. Y have gone an hour ago. I take a phone: "Cliver, where´re you? Maspeth. I come there, and then we shall go to Park Pl. Why? Why not. I'm going to buy a department." Cliver: "Hizous? Why?" I: "I have something to throw there out. It is enough high."

After 15 minutes Cliver jumps to my Stang and here we go. Many work hating people look at us not very happy faces, but not everybody has born under happy stars, like me and MyPal Cliv. Soon we are Park Pl - street. We meet an agent outside the house.

I laugh and Clivers laughs, too. Hey, yeah, that´s Ryan Matthew Serhant, real estate broker, the man behind the book *Sell it like Serhant*. Cliver: "Good Morrow my good man." Ryan: "Yes, I choose success always first, no matter what. Are you series (=serious)? You look so relaxed fellas. Any money in the box?" I: "13,3 Md. Let´s go."

When you take the elevator Mr. R begins his promo-talk: "The living room leads to a separate 18´ corner dining room with south and east exposures. Boys put this in your pipe and smoke it, the eat-in kitchen with Bilotta rift-cut oak kitchen cabinetry, wet-bar, and Gannenau appliance, open to the sure awesome family room and eastern very well loggia. The master bedroom suite features two luxurious marble ensuite baths - one features a deep soaking tub so nice and separate stall shower - and ample closet space including two walk-in closets. And then, yeess, the two additional bedrooms feature full ensuite baths and access to the western loggia. As you fellas very well see, state of the art systems includes a ceiling hung. Think and think even more, hahahahaha, penthouse 76B comes with a large private storage unit located within the building and a separate service entrance.

Developed by great visionary Silverstein Properties, Inc. masterfully designed by Robert A.M. Stern Architects, I think, yes, yes. Services by legendary Four Seasons Hotels and Resorts provide the newest caliber of living high to NYC-resident. With residences beginning on the 39th floor, the sweeping views are unparalleled. Residents may enjoy access to Four Season Hotel amenities including a spa and salon facilities, 75´ swimming pool, attended parking garage, restaurant, bar and lounge, ballroom so facilities, and meeting rooms, as well as a comprehensive suite of a la carte services. The 38th floor is devoted to private residential amenities including a fitness center and yoga studio, private dining room, conservatory and lounge with access to loggias, Roto-designed kid´s playroom, and screening room, all for your enjoyment. Take it or live it. I have a meeting with my dear wife, and I'm in a great hurry."

I think aloud: "Heating no data, year built 2016, parking no data." Ryan: "Full bathrooms 4, no 3/4 bathrooms, 1/2 bathroom 1, central cooling, dishwasher, dryer, washer, lot 0,05 acres, type condo." I: "Internet and tv, no data, solar potential 95.05. HOA fee: 2324/mo. Annual tax amount 8394 d. Has not enough information to calculate a Zestimate for this home." R gives back: "Zestimate history: this home NA, park slope 1,1 M, NY 6494 Kd. Tax-based estimate 992, 8d." I say: "Price 2/12/2019 16,850 000 d, 5/72019 15,250000 d." R continues: "Estimated monthly cost 68,921 d, 53,684/mo principal & interest, mortgage insurance zero, home insurance 4848/mo, utilities not included. Nearby Technical High School. This is a seller´s market, more interested buyers than homes for sale. If Y think 314 Hich St home ..." I: "I give Y 13,3 Md. Here you are."

I give the money to Ryan. He looks at money, and me, and money. I say: "Send papers, nice to meet Y. Please give my regards to your wife."

I tap his shoulders, as we do in the army. He smiles; he sees soon his great wife.

Ryan hurries to Emilia, and we are in with the keys. We go to the living room. I throw the keys on the table and I let myself tumble to the sofa and Cliver looks out of the window. He: "What next? You buy a ship?"

The Three Musketeers

I laugh: "Must call Bob." I: "Hello Bop, I bought a condo, 13,3, Md, fair price, you can come and look at it. Oh, hurry, in the stock market. Well, one question. Wanna more loan?"

Bob: "I help gladly non-residents achieve the American dream. How much? Same sum, not a problem. No problem that y don´t have any U.S. credit history, no revenues in the U.S., permanent visa. Y, Tapio, can always buy homes and investment properties for both commercial & residential real estate. Fuck forever purchase prices, down payments, mortgage terms, interest rates, property taxes, insurances, PMI, pre-payment penalties. Just join the Bob to financial revolution. Do not think about appraisal-things, escrows, underwriting fees, and fuck with a flood certification. Those things are bullshit. US Income documentation doesn´t concern jolly-good fellas like Y. And I put the next loan to the name of corporations and next after that to LLC. We are a happy family, Tapio. One for all, all for one, we are strong."

Bob continues and I put smarty to the table, so Cliver doesn´t need to drink to his misery. He can join me, and hear Bob´s luxury-talk: "MyBoy, think what the bank officers normally to an outlander, deep-Brkner: ´Although it might be more difficult to get a loan as a nonresident, it isn´t impossible.´ Think that! They give a shit little money to o-landers personal use, business, to buy a home and to pay for college. They say keeping their faces cool: ´You do not need to destroy your savings and create an immovable mountain of debt.´ Hahahahaa.

I never think do y pay back or not, I do not think what happens if you leave the country. So what? If you go, those tax-free islands stay, and my hilarious net. Do I talk with y about utility bills, those gas, electric, water, and cable TV shit?? They say that loans are for those who stay and work here for at least three years. Think, whatta waste of time. Do I ask for you a valid visa, employment authorization form, the form that declares you as authorized to work within the USA? If you read your loan-papers they include all kinds of loans: short-term, installment, unsecured & secured.

Did I ask your SSN? Of course not. I am in the same person a cosigner, a lender who accepts an ITIN Number, and a lender who is designed for just Y, Tapio. And did I ask y to apply ITIN and eligibility to pay federal taxes? Ofc not. And although you do not have SSN, ITIN, it doesn´t mean that y must have ITN. No Form W7 and other documents supported by the IRS. Personal loan interest rates are between 10 % and 28 %. I five y no numbers. And y don´t need to wait 48 hours for approval thing.

And want only one thing?" I: "What the f*ck do y want?" Bob: "I want y to reckon me as your business partner. It confirms our bound and makes as real brothers-in-businesses. We fight in the business-field side by side, never looking back put always sunshine on our handsome faces. Ok." I and Cliver laugh. I: "I met Ryan Serhant, and when we shake hands and he left he said: ´A Win is a legacy you leave behind. And your Win doesn´t have to be as big as ´change the world´- but it needs to be real, it needs to change you, and it needs to be something you really want.´ Do y want that Bob?" Bob: "Yes, of course, that´s why I am struggling while other bankers seem to be moving through deals with little effort."

The Procephy

Cliver looks at me: "Bob is jacksepticeye. He is the BOSS of BOSSES. Did I mention he is BOSSS?" I: "Yeah, he is falt-rocking and going steady. We have this, now I must call MyVictoria here and throw something out of the windows forever."

Cliver: "Do not tell no more, I do not wanna keep some driddy secrets. I have already a DVD." Cliver explains: "There was on old-timer on the street. He said to me: ´I have only this left. Keep it right.´ And he gave me this, and went to shadows." I take the DVD: "There reads Earl Vince & The Valiants. Keep it loud. Let´s keep it loud for the sake of that street old-timer." And we shut our eyes and begin to listen. "It begins a Wednesday night", yeah, I think, today is Wednesday, it continues: "There sure is gonna be a fight. Somebody´s gonna get their head kicked in tonight!"

Cliver and I looked at each other: this is early 60s gang-music, that´s for sure: "Well the joint is jumpin´, everybody´s shouting´ for more. Well, there´s gonna be a pool of blood on the dance hall floor, cos somebody´s gonna get their head kicked in tonight. We´re gonna rip up the chairs and tear down the walls, smash up the band and really have a ball. Will be everybody in a physical rage. And the whole dance hall will be a doggone mess. Oh, well, now the band is rockin´ and everybody´s feelin´ alright, it´s a Wednesday ..." I stand up. What was that? Prophecy for a night?

I: "What the fella actually said?" Cliver: "Something like this when he left: ´I remember back in the day when I thought this was a rezillos song LOL. My Highschool band opened every show with a rezillos like version. I will put on my dunce hat and go to the corner and spank myself. I should know better I was 1 when this came out. I have no excuse. I was born knowing almost everything. Man, I would be famous if people knew about me LOL, have a Good Night. And thanks in advance for playing! You receive 1 slightly tarnish gold star." *Muy Bueno para ser real.* Banger.

The Constructors

I: "Well that old-timer isn´t Bob 2. I have an idea of how we can get some money from those building constructors." Cliver isn´t at all happy now: "Furls has a lot of Mongolians. Back off. They are xxxll-hardnuts." I: "But then we cannot have the party tonight. And we cannot shine our tarnish gold stars." Cliver: "This is a thizzle dance with jelly bracelets."

I say: "I think that the Atlantic Yards/Pacific Park project about 300 of the 2 500 employes works full time. Turnover among workers such as security guards and ticket takers has been fueled by irregular and tow-few hours. After refusing to reveal details for years, the Barclays Center began specifying pay rates as it recruited part-timers. The jobs are part-time, which means they can´t qualify as a living wage. Are those office jobs new jobs or simply relocated? Forest City suggested there are 1 000 workers on site, which is tough to believe, just based on the eyeball observations that people make of the site.

It´s unlikely that many of the needy Brooklynites who clamored for construction jobs will find work in the office jobs promised. The CBA was a tool of the developer, not a contract aimed to truly help needy Brooklynites. In the NY-metro area three men associates with a subcontractor, carpentry company CWC Contracting, paying hundreds of thousands of dollars in bribes and kickbacks.

The bribed employees would pad CWC´s bottom line by awarding contracts and approving change orders. Twelve people most allegedly associated with the Gambino-fuck**ers stem from a sting operation. The feds do not tell names, just company 2 and company 3. Firms and employees do not have names in official documents. A reputed Bonnano-family associate and a construction company executive steered a 1,6 Md job to a roofer and threatened to kill him and his family if they didn´t kick back 150 000 d. Today a woman answered the phone at CWC and said: "No one is available to comment."

I tell that the Taxpayer-subsidized 11-story Creston Apartment in The Bronx, which Mayor´s signature push to build, is a front for the mob, it was just another job. CWC Contracting Co. counts Creston Apartments as one of a dozen big projects and listing it as a newly constructed building in the Mount Hope neighborhood. CWC is controlled by the Gambino-family. Gambino *capo* Andrew Campos is the principal of CWC. Mob soldier, Vincent Fiore, has an ownership interest and is a CWC -project manager. Mob soldier Richard Martino has an ownership interest in the Mount Vernon-based company. One mob-soldier pays CWC employees their wages in cash to avoid getting hit for payroll taxes and bribes their way on to several NY-construction sites, then siphons off hundreds of thousands of dollars through inflated billing.

One of the sites CWC worked on was an ultra-luxury condo, like this, and hotel now under construction alongside the High Line in Chelsea, where a half-penthouse is on the market for 25 Md. The Creston apartments are on the other end of the financial spectrum from the High Line tower. The project created 114 units set aside for low- and moderate-income tenants and was built by developer Schur Management with general contractor MacQuesten Companies. CWC was brought in as a carpentry subcontractor.

They say they make you a nice luxury place, but once you make the commitment to rent, you are stuck there. The building doesn´t work well, two elevators are repeatedly broken down, sometimes for days. In Creston, there are 41 code violations, including several for dangerous conditions that resulted in four injured workers. Laborers on the upper floors are working without safety harnesses. The openings in top floors had no fall protection and that scaffolding does not meet safety code requirements. A wire snapped and hit a worker in the head. A worker removing a hoist fell eight feet on to his back and had to be hospitalized. CWC employees bribed an OSHA-certified job safety instructor to falsely report to the U.S. Department of Labor (DOL) that several CWC employees had taken and passed job site safety training tests when they hadn´t."

Cliver is terrified: "So?" I: "What so? We are going to meet some Bonnano-bobs and Gambino-capo and his two mob-soldiers, you know, the principal of CWC and his fat project managers. They give us good money." Cliver look at me: "Doomed. The onslaught of doom will be swift and painful. We are like West Georgia liberation front, that´s how we roll." I: "Poor-Cliv, waffle-o. Relax. They only try to kill us, nothing more." Cliver: "That old-timer, that song, this is a ;). Pickleweasel. Fuck-off finger sign. And the bloody bastard, y, waved the unfriendly digit in the air like a trophy. End = money; what we all live and die for." I laugh: "On the contrary, MyC, we shall get the hell outta dodge. We reap what we sow. No less or more. And if we do not get our money, then we shall have our party in the hall tonight."

Cliver: "For reals?" I: "Serious as a heart attack. We aren´t a system of a down, a politically correct band with some fucking unique talent. The constitution is just a piece of paper without the army to safeguard it." Cliver: "So now you compare us, one true Brkner and one deep Brkner, to an army?" I: "Yes. Here every general is a soldier and a soldier a general. Some duck says, dang I must go to Iraq cos USARMY. We say, tgfad, let´s go, and kick their asses."

We go to E 1st, Mt Vernon. There is that small box-house for CWC Contracting Corp. There are some cars in front of that box. I take my Taurus and Cliver his gunrunner-homemade version of Clock 17. I knock the door. I see people inside. They do not take notice of me at all. I kick the door in.

There are Julius N. and some workers, big fellas but not big enough. I go to Julius and take him from his hair: "I have heard that your data undergoes extensive quality assurance testing with over 2000 discrete checks for validity and reliability. Are you sure about that? Y lie that y use over 30 000 different sources, including teams of primary source researchers to update your data over 5 million times per day. When you get CWCs insights, financials, and competitors from D&B Hoovers, you can trust in their accuracy. I see that on-site supervisor mob soldier Benny D. is here and assistant superintendent of filled operations Nicky R. are here, but where are principal-*capo* Andrew Campos and project manager - mob-soldier Vincet F. and his assistant mob-soldier Richard M.? You have ten seconds to answer then I shoot your left leg, and after that then seconds and your right leg. And if no answers after that, I shoot to kill."

Cliver doesn´t understand that these fat fellas are soft fellas when they meet enough tough guys face to face. I load my Taurus. Julius is melting wax: "They are all in the funerals of Francesco Frank Cali, in Calvary Cemetery. I ..." I hit his face, and he falls. I say: "Bind those f**ers ..."

Soon they all are on the ground. I take N. on my shoulders. I throw the fella in my Stang and laugh: "In that cemetery rotten Joe Masseria, Tommy Lucchese, Benjamin Ruggiero, and Dominic Napolitano. Cliver y should know it well in Maspeth and Woodside. What a logical place for a Roman Catholic murderer to be put mold on."

Frank lived in the Todt Hill section of Staten Island, on a leafy street near the private Richmond County Country Club golf course - and not far from where Castellano lived in a mansion when he ran the Gambino family. Two miles away, at 110 Longfellow Ave., sits the house that portrayed the Corleone estate in The Godfather.

Franky was a good friend of the Bonnano-Colombo, Genovese, and Lucchese families. The reputed leader of the Gambino that Frank was shot to death outside his house in Staten Island last Wednesday night. 53-year-old Franky got with multiple gunshot wounds to the torso. A blue pickup truck fleet the area. The assassination of Franky Boy happened on the same day that Joseph Cammarano Jr., the reputed acting body of the Bonnano--family, was acquitted at trial. And a week after Carmine J. Persico, a longtime boss of the Colombo crime family, died in Prison at age 85. So other families decided to help the Gambino boss to get rid of his earthly wandering. It was a question of the balance.

The Cemetery & Memorial Ave

We go to that cemetery. There are a lot of European mafia-fellas, too, cos Franky Boy kept a close connection with them. He has been the Gambino´s ambassador of Sicilian mobsters and had linked him to the Inzerillo Mafia family from Palermo.

We are in the First Calvary Cemetery, between the Long Island Expressway and Review Avenue. We stop at Blackbush Ln and go in. About 170 m left there are those funerals. N. goes between me and Cliver. He says: "That fella is Andrew, there is Vincent and there Richard." I hit his head and throw him to the nearest R.I.P. place.

Some muscles are turning towards us, near the funeral place. I go to them: "Hello, we must see Andrew, Vincent, and Richard at once. Can you take them here? It is urgent." Those fatheads do as I say. I was ready to kill them. Soon those three fellas are around us.

I: "My condolences, Francesco Paolo Augusto was a man of great influence and power, and a real New Yorker. He was a man of honor, had a clean police record, and has many important relatives in beautiful Sicilia. He ran several important-export companies in Brooklyn, including the so famous Circus Fruits Wholesale in Fort Hamilton. I have heard he just loved Toto Riina. He dug fast cars and I always shall remember NASCAR. Please, although all this, we must hurry, CWC-headquarters are on flames and there is shooting going on. Nasso said that Y three must come at once, here is his phone, y can call him." I have broken it, but no time to lose.

They look at each other, and Cliver keeps his shaking hands in his pockets. I look serious: "Please come to my car, I have something to show to y. The rest can come behind us. Please, hurry." They buy all my talk, and in my Stang, they go. I look behind. Mr. N is still in dreamland. Soon we are in deep Queens, in the Makks-gang area. Near Kissena Corridor Park at Booth Memorial Ave we stop. Two cars behind us stop also. Time for blowing the sprinkles off the cupcake.

I explain: "Of course CWC was established by a family of professionals who founded the firm based on quality and service. You three have the important benefit of more than 25 years of combined experience in a wide variety of project types in Gambino-business. You are mob-soldiers, principal A, project executive V and mob-soldier R, and there are employees 18 and revenue 4,1 Md. And Verizon Communications Inc. and the Nercc.org are near your hearts. There are other mob-soldiers like Luis Farrao-Puleo, Rich Puleo, chief estimator Ronny Barca, and you do not need job titles, cos you are all in Gambino-hierarchy.

My proposal is this: I have made a deal with all syndicates strip-tease-clubs, so I like to take y with the deal in Europe. Y can come to book towns and make very good stages for festivals and most of all there are in France, Britain, and Spain many manors, villas, departments, and even castles, who need some updating. I have already talked with the IOB's CEO which is me, heh, heh, and we had made a deal proposal, where your firm shall be the main contactor of all those businesses. You can come to Europe, meet your friends and expand your presence in many good ways. And if not, then remember that I have taken from the headquarter-computers information of your mob-soldier-businesses. So, your choice, take it or leave it."

I give each of them a paper where are 4 months´ project-schedule and cash flow forecasts, materials which they need, and the timetable.

Andrew comes red-faced: "You are blackmailing ... hm, hm, hm ... this is wonderful. This is amazing! Bros read points 4, 6, 8. This man has an operational vision. You are a genius ... my dear friend."

They all begin to laugh, almost dance Zorbas, and *capos'* guards arrive, and they are told some details, and everything becomes hilarious. Andrew takes me a little bit away: "Hm, why did you hit N and others?" I: "Never get to you, to talk about serious business, without some precautions. Mr. N sleeps some hours still in the cemetery. So let him sleep R.I.P. Main thing is that you accept the deal. Then mayor of NYC accepts it too, and it shall be a great PR to your reputation." We talk math details and become more convinced. The whole thing ends in great harmony and peace. These Italians, when you broke their sentimental walls, are always ready to create great theatre, which only Italians know so well.

Cliver is surprised and his Makks around him are more than surprised. How this dunnie inverses everything Midas, not the Texas way, where everything is bigger, including the fu**ers egos, but just Brooklyn way? How a deep Brkner can do that? New Hermione granger-bruja? Anyway, time is 4:30 pm, and I call Y.

Dog´s Oscar Sharing Event

I try to charm: "Hello MyVictoria, how are you? Heyjj, I'm not jealous. There are no other bests around me. Yes, if I do not hear about you withing a month the boat has gone. Oh, Y ask more money. Really, I do not give money for taking the back door. Bab, Brkln isn´t Mexico, God´s blind spot, where y can do anything y want."

Y: "So I'm in a hurry and unfortunately ... What did y say? How can Y insult me?!!?" I: "You can always twist a braid, and wanderlusty your way, but I think you are not about to gun me. Do not suggest Y come with me to The Good Dog Show comedy in Fort Greene, not to DSK Kaffee, but to come with me to superintend dog show? No Coffee Bark, Runstreet Brooklyn Dog Art Run, no Meet the Wets, puppies 101, no Paint and Sip Pet Portrait Fun-Barking Dog New York, no New York Pet Fashion Show, no FURRSday, no Valentine's Day Pawty, no My Furry Valentine, no Puppy Love Party, no Doga (Dog Yoga) with Lululemon, no World Dog Expo, but PupScouts Red Carpet Event. You shall love it. See Y, in 45 minutes." Well, you do not need to kill Italians to change the world, and shoot lursts, right thought ya right. This isn't dating when the Man pays. This is a dog's dinner.

5:15 pm we meet at 225 E 57th St.

At the same time, a NYPD-cop and his fiancée attack their 8-year-old son and kill him. They leave the body in the driveway of Bittersweet Lane. At Woodside a driver hits one pedestrian after running a red light at 60th Street, then he drives away. Then he drives the wrong side of the road and runs at the red light at 61st Street and rammed at a car. The impact pushes that car backward into a car behind, which then hits the next car at the light.

We are entering the Annual Pupscouts Red Carpet Event. I kiss Y and Y kiss back. And you have a very nice dress on, tight by elegant violet. I say: "I love Y so." Y: "I love Y, too, Tapio." And the 6th PupScouts Red Carpet is full of love! We go in like in Hollywood celebration, the lights click and everywhere everybody comes and goes. There isn't GodFather but DogFather. The doggie looks enough smart to kill without punishment. There is "bitch stole my look award", and Red Carpet Event helps kick off Westminister. There are boxes full of puppies.

This is also annual pre-Oscar Red Carpet Event. There is a Liberty Statue, a fella, and he has a hairy guy on his hands. I say to Y: "Hey the Liberty has an old hippie in his arms." One fella nearby has a guitar. I take it and play and sing: "*Èrase una vez en la que te vestías elegante. Tirabas centavos a los vagabundos en tu major época? ... No tener un hogar. Como una completa desconocida.*

Y: "*Te compran proque te vendes, te vendes porque so sobras, te pierder porque hay camino ...Te vives, alto voltaje, te traje buenas noticias ...*"

There is a beauty-dog with a beret on her head. There are marketing services & events promotions, PupScouts for Charity. Contest categories include Red Carpet Celebrity Lookalike and Great Romances. One reporter comes to ask Y, what do Y like about celebrities. Y say that Dog is God spelled backward, and love is a four-legged word. The reporter turns on me.

I smile: "The Hound of Baskerville is a cross between a bloodhound and a mastiff. A hound is an enormous coal-black hound. Fire burst from its open mouth, its eyes glowed with a smoldering glare, its muzzle and hackles and dewlap were outlined in flickering flame. That's my Doggie, man."

It is 17:20 when we leave these celebrities behind us. Now it is time for the true celebration.

Happiness is Luxury, Luxury is Happiness

I kiss Y and smile: "Le´ts go." Y: "Where?" I: "To 30 Park Pl. No need for clients, fans, and directors." Although the Condo is smaller than VictoriaCourt, and it has only 4 meters to the roof, while VictoriaCourt has 5-8 meters, it is quite different compared with normal Brkners´ homes. You go in the white, huge rooms, where the floor is beige. I give Y the keys: "Here Y are."

I: "Why bathrooms for the Doggy? And servants shall clean the house every day." I speak and somehow my instinct tells me to watch the time. It is now the time when that song tells: somebody shall get their head k ...

Your happiness is the main thing: "I shall order right now the removers here. Hello Junk Removal & Hauling, I come to meet Y ..." I jump up. Y just sit and look out of the windows. Soon I am out of the building and jump to my Mustang. I drive to your department. 10 strong looking fellas are there already.

We shake hands: "Three hours, everything must be ready at 9:45, okay." They nod their heads. We go to your department. Old furniture shall stay, some new things and your personal stuff shall go. The boxes. I: "We go to Brooklyn Furniture."

I call Y: "I am so sorry, but your department´s furniture isn´t for this new thing. I come to Y, take Y with me, and then we go to 3742 Bathurst St."

Those removal fellas come after me. We take Queen Bed, engineered wood frame with solid wood feet, includes, headboard, footboard, and rails, biscuit tufting on the headboard, polyester upholstery, king beds, two, and California king bed, headboards, dressers, mirrors, nightstands, chests, media chests, armoires, vanities, outdoor balcony things, dining room dewing brown bar table w/4 upholstered barstools, Daymont gold bar cart, in your office Y want office Swivel desk chair. The living room gets Lockling carbon chair and a half, Lockesburg canyon sofa & loveseat, entertainment accessories black electric infrared fireplace-insert, and Derekcon multi gray 59" TV Stand. Rugs, throws, pillows, partitions, wall art accessory.

At 20:25 I pay the fellas, and you just sit down. I say: "I go to buy some fresh flowers and take the Doggy here. He has a lot to think about." I go to your department. In my mind comes a strange idea: a person is a material thing, easily torn and not easily mended; it is the failure to grasp the simple truth that other people are as real as you.

The Balance

I stop my car park side of the street when shooting begins. I throw myself to the ground and roll to the left. I have my Taurus, behind in the belt. I take it. I shoot in the park. There come three mob-soldiers, in their hands' guns to kill. I shoot with learned absolute reflex. They stop and fell to their faces. I jump over the bushes and shoot to two other men. They leave this paradise and go straight to hell. I pop the glock two more down. Two others have luck and evanescence.

I go to one fella. He spits the blood to my face. I look at tattoos on his left wrist: these are Genovese-*capo di tutti capi* -boys. They operate in Manhattan, and The Bronx, Queens, Staten Island, Long Island, Westchester County, Rockland County, Connecticut, Massachusetts, and Florida. This fella's ring signals that they are 116th Street Crew, which normally operates in Upper Manhattan and The Bronx. I am a little bit surprised, cos The Lucchese-family's Cutaia Crew operates here. I realize that I have made deals with Colombia's fellas in strip-clubs, The Gambino and The Bonnano with CWC and Lucchese also with strip-clubs. Yes, there must be a balance.

These are Lucky Luciano's heirs. There official and the acting boss is Barney Bellomo, street boss Michey Ragusa, underboss is anonymous. *Consiglieri* is Quiet Dom Cirillo, Messaggero Mario Gigante, administrative capos I do not know. *Caporegimes* in Brooklyn faction are Chuckie Tuzzo, Tico Antico, Kid Blast Gallo. Soldiers are Sammy Meatballs Aparo, The Undertaker Balsamo, and, Louis DiRapoli – a soldier with his brother Vincent DiRapoli's 116th Street crew, Vinny DiRapoli - soldier and former *capo* with the 116th Street crew, Tough Tony Federici, Little John Giglio, Fritzy Giovanelli, Baldie Longo, John Olivieri, Allie Shades Malangone, Danny Pagano, Ciro Perrone, Charles Salzano, Pazzo Testa, and Joseph Zito.

I must go to DiRapolis-brothers of 116th street and ask some questions. Ernie Muscarella leads 116th Street Crew. I must kick the shit out of these "men of honor". I shall give them tonight on the modern expression of their ceremony. I shall put them on the table. I put there a bottle of vodka, gun, and ax, I shall prick their fingers with a pin and squeeze until the blood flows. I shall say to them: "You lived by the gun and the knife and you shall now die by the gun and the knife."

I have made many deals with the gambler chief, mobs, and porn chief, and now I call Frank: "Hello, I'm here in this department. Come quickly and take knacker's yard clean." Frank comes straightway, and I run to the department, take Doggy, jump to my Mustang, and drive away. It is dark, I hope people are blind & deaf.

Back to Luxury is Happiness

I drive in the 30s. Go to the new department, take some dust off my suit. I feel The Faith tries to strangle me. I must strangle back. I come in: "Here is Doggy. Let´s see how he likes the new department." I call Cliver: "Hey, we must do something more with Goodfellas Robert De Niro, Ray Liotta, and Joe Pesci. One more boneitis. Take 5 Makks with Y."

I try to smile when I say to Y: "Luxury means your happiness. How far luxury is from vulgarity and isn´t the opposite of poverty. We have a nice house which isn´t the opposite of poverty but vulgarity. A billionaire may never count this luxury. Luxury is so simple. No need for the algorithm."

And my luxury sits in my lab and beside me. And I can touch it, my gun on my belt. What house ever becomes prosperous without a woman´s excellence and bloated with that luxury. I stand up: "I come back." Pessimism is a luxury that I cannot allow myself, cos I cannot afford it.

The Sacramentum

I meet Cliver and 5 Mekks at the 117th. So, the next street is Street Crew, and there are capo Muscarella and soldiers Vinny and Louis DiRapoli. We are in East Harlem. Near Document Translation Nationwide and in front of Mi Querido Mexico Lindo is our goal: The Office. On another side of the street is El Pueblo Mejicano.

One thing is certain: they do not sleep. 116th Street traverses the neighborhoods of Morningside Heights, Harlem, and Spanish Harlem. We walk, and we go via a ladder to the roof. Two Makks go ahead, cos they know the place, then go me and Cliver and then the rest. We are soon on the roof of The Office. There is a hatch, but it is closed.

I go to the edge of the roof and touch the window frame. I ask Makks to go like a maggot and ask the nearest to take a firm touch to my instep. I slide slowly downwards. The window is closed, and I have no time for locksmiths. I have with me a screwdriver, a flathead one. I am downwards but I see the beading is plastic around the window frame. I insert my s-driver into the beading channel at one corner and pry it out a little bit at a time. I work my way to the opposite corner. Beading is completely loose, and I pull it free with my hands. I remove the overlapping beading first. I pry open the windowpane from the bottom. The window comes out easily. I support the glass with my free hand so it doesn´t fall and shatter when it comes free. I slide the glass free of its mounting, I place it so off the side, inside, and enter the room through the empty window, I say to the next fella on line: "Now drop yourself here I take Y in." They come one after another. The last one looks at the edge and I ask him slid down legs in front of him. I take him in.

We are in the empty room. The question goes, where are they? I try with a plastic card, yes, the door is open. We listen to the noise in the house. No walking nearby, but the doors open to the aisle, or is there something else.

I use the scissors to cut off the top of the milk carton, which is on the table. I cut it directly underneath where the milk pours out and discard the roof top-looking are. Then I shut a square hole in the side of the carton with scissors. I draw a square with a pencil. I make sure I leave a ¼-inch space around the hole. This helps the mirror, which is on the table, stays in place later. I place the carton down on its side on the top of a table. The square hole I cut is facing my right side. I use a ruler to measure 2 ¾-inches up from the bottom left side of the carton. I mark the spot with a pencil. I place the ruler so that it makes a slanted line from the markdown to the bottom right side of the carton. I draw a line from the mark to the corner using the straight edge of the ruler as a guide. I use the utility blade to cut out this line. I slide the mirror into this slit. The reflecting side is the side I can see myself in. I take on the table masking tape and tape the mirror in place with the tape. I look through the hole. I see the ceiling above me. I repeat the method with a second carton. I put one of the cartons on the table so that the square hole I cut out is facing me. I place the carton upside down. I squeeze together the open ends of the upside-down carton. So I can push it down into the other one about one inch. I tape the two cartons together. I look through the bottom hole so see over obstacles, which are taller than me. I look underneath the tables by looking through the hole on top. Time to go. I hold periscope sideways to be able to see around corners.

Cliver opens the door slowly, and periscope goes to look. Yes, no one there, and the other side the same. I go from the room, the Taurus in my hand. Some men talk in the nearest room. I slide the periscope slightly in the room and see the fellas are their back to the door. I and Cliver go in. I press the other fella on his neck, so he goes to the dreamland and Cliver hits the other with his Clock-gat. So, they are out. There are no more people on that floor.

Suddenly there comes a fella. He sees me. It´s a bluff time: "Oh-oh, Basta, where is that Vinny?" F: "*Affari tuoi. Fatti gli affari tuoi!*" He comes near and I just put my hands around his neck, and he sleeps like a baby. I go carefully to the second floor. Nothing. All the gabble comes from the first floor. I: "Gun? Cliver & mandem smile. I do not want any more corps in my life. I try to find the easy way, but The Faith wants blood.

And that is memory without language. My soul cannot dwell in the dust. It is carried along to dwell in blood, fire, and more blood. I try one more desperate, and stupid thing, to avoid violence. On the desk is a cigar. There is something with a cigar that feels like a celebration. Cliver gives me light and down we go. There is a big dirty room, and there is a bunch of wrongdoers, among them Louis, Vinny & Ernie.

I walk slowly downstairs and give a smile: "Hello, men of opera, nice to meet Y. I feel like a death cab for cutie day. Cannot say: I don´t business. Do you buy what I'm selling? Hey, Earnie – greasy taco – come here. Help me to find the answer."

From the next room comes a mob-soldier, I shoot to his shoulder. Muscarella does not fear: "You Mr. Nobody does not understand. Your Faith has been solved. You just die, now or tomorrow, but You die." I throw the cigar away. I give him a picture: "This is a noice manor in Sicilia. Your friend Benedetto Bacchi, with whom you have a food selling company, made a deal with me. He helps Gambino and your family to help our festival contest in Europe and give room to all the dancers and singers who come from here. I shall tell him personally that Y Ernie wants to be my friend. But it must be down with style.

You shall be my personal bodyguard. I promise that to your friend Benedetto. So, come here. Let´s make a true Roman oath. This is called Sacramentum: ´We shall faithfully execute all the Friendship commands, that we shall never desert the service, and that we shall not seek to avoid death for the defending our Friendship.´"

I take on the table my handmade periscope, break its mirror, make a bloody wound in my palm. He takes the piece of a mirror and makes a bloody wound in his palm. We shake the Roman way, hands to elbows.

Blood flows and The Faith smiles, the atonement of enmity has happened.

The Silence.

Then Italians and Makks begin to cheer, yeah, really bro-hood. And he cries like a baby. We, my new friend and I, put our blood seals under the deal paper, where Earnie, Vinny, and Louis promise to share their best memories of European festivals to come with me.

It is 23:20. And I do not waste any more time but jump to my Mustang and speed straight to Y and Doggy after the mob-balance has been reached.

There is now balance with me and the mob. It is an arms truce.

Cliver asks me: "What you have achieved? Do you take enemies to your bodyguard, piece of shits to your business-partners? They rip you a new one and teardrop tattoo. There are no strings attached. They shop till You drop. *Bella Muerte*? A so di ting set. They bait up, and the end is bush. Cheddar law. You cannot beat dem bad. This is bush. DWL. Di dance a go slap, weh!" I say before we separate: "I do not change my nature. I put it in good use. I meet Death. That is my challenge." Cliver understands that in front of him is a man of revenge.

Late Evening Rats & Flowers

We separate at 23:55, and I come to you.

Now in wintertime mice and rats are coming to New Yorkers' homes. They carry deadly hanta-virus or salmonella poisoning. There are multiple diseases that can be transmitted from rodents and their feces to humans. Rodent populations spiral out quickly of control. The average NYC house mouse reaches maturity in eight weeks. Multiply that number by a few breeding pairs. Rats have strong jaws than chew through concrete. They eat through electrical wiring, too, and create a dangerous fire hazard. They're frequent carriers of fleas, ticks, and mites, which pose a problem to humans. People notice rats and mice droppings in drawers, cabinets, the pantry, or anywhere else food is stored or consumed. People see small holes and gnawed corners on items such as cereal boxes. Mice and rats have collapsible skeletons that allow them to squeeze through tiny spaces. A typical rat fits through a hole the size of a quarter, and a typical mouse fits through a hole the size of a pencil. When I open our outdoor, at the same time many exterminators go to New Yorkers' homes and ask only 90-250 d. The whole cost is 200-2000 d.

At the same time, an NYPD officer who once provided security for drug kingpin El Chapo's wife is arrested on charges that he smuggled cocaine across Queens. He took thousands of dollars to help transport kilos of cocaine throughout Queens. He took just 2 500 d, and another undercover cop took the bag. In Astoria, he took 10 000 d. He faces 15 years in prison.

Makk Brim Char pissed off and take his clock and shoot to one shouting 16-year-old boy outside Martin Van Buren High School. Char pull the trigger in front of the Hillside Avenue School. But Char misses and gunshot wound doesn´t appear fatal.

At 23:56 I'm with some flower carriers. Here are some flowers. You say: "Fellas put those the firecrackers here, the Amados there, bliss here, the flurry near Doggie, Magnolia there, the heart near Tapio, Monogrome there, and the nightingale here. The Urbanstem-chaps go. The Chelsea Garden Center houseplants fellas come. You show the right places for strelitzia Nicolai bird of paradise. It has big, dramatic tropical leaves." You laugh: "Oh from Florida! *Dracaena reflexa* can be made by Y into true statement pieces. Who do not love the woody trunks on them and how the overall shape is unique to every plant? And to the balcony mums, kale, cabbages, and pumpkins. Ornamental pepper, great accent plants, rhododendrons, and hydrangeas, and many creepers." The fellas go, and it is 0:15.

The Tenth day

The Paradise with the Hell

The Toast of Walhalla

I put my Taurus on the box. There is dirt, I clean it. There are big stars in the sky. Something is coming to meet me. I feel its presence.

In the front line was an enemy's barrage. I run to my own foxhole, but there were two snakes. I jumped to my friend´s foxhole. I went back. There was an explored chaos after bullseye. I feel the same as I felt then. If I die in the elevator, I shall push the Up Button.

A nice dream. I sit in Walhalla with my brothers-in-arms. We raise a toast and one of them says: "Tapio go back, but remember we miss you so." I say: "I miss you too."

Hailing Mary

It is at 8 am. You have gone already. I call Cliver: "Ay mayne, tooth hurty. Vale. I'm there in fifteen minutes. Preston and Steve time. Let waz it up. Let´s kill them all." Cliver asks: "Yeah, fresh to death, and the fat lady sings."

I say: "We shall go to meet The Commission today. Ernie has invited me there." Cliver wonders: "The Commission? And the chuntra has promised your skid lid? So, he pulls a Cal on y, and waits there with ghetto cake crumbs." I do not agree: "Take as many Makks as Y want with Y." Cliver: "Wdym, I take Smokie and Murder, 25+25= fiddy =

Makk-unit. Burfday." I: "I call Frankie & boys, our top lel. Take care of your Brims and I take off my frog hogs."

I call Frankie: "Good Morning, pull up a sandbag and swing the latern. The Mob-Man Commission. New York Ave & Snyder Ave crossroad. 2 pm. Go under the opposite side of Maria Beauty Salon. And are ready to go at 14:15 to the first floor, in that corner-house. I'm in and on the street are Makks, don't shoot them. The same price as last, take 10 SEALs. Yeah, La Lakers stinks."

I call Cliver and tell the same information.

At the same time, the bedbugs that messed up the subway service on five different lines last week are there making an invasion again. There are more of the pesky critters in the Forest Hills control tower where they were spotted five days earlier. That sighting prompts the transit authority to shut down the facility to fumigate and cause extensive delays on the E, F, M, R, and W lines. Bedbugs live in a set of cloth chairs. Bedbug sighting results in 236 delayed trains and 117 canceled trains.

I meet Cliver and 43 Makks at 1:30 am. We are on the New York Ave. People hurry when they see us. Boys are bugging their guns and, making crosses on the top of the bullets, so they shall be explosive.

Smokey says: "Hail Mary, blessed art thou among women. Holy Mary pray for us sinners, at the hour of death." We walk on the street guns on our hands. My Taurus shines blue like King Arthur's Excalibur. And blue is the mark that skies above approve our course. And in Valhalla, my brothers wait eagerly what's crackalackin.

Cliver comes to me: "Ay mayne, death before dishonor, a great day to die. Im not going to spoon. So, you have at last chosen your side. That's

COOP. That rocks my socks, whatever floats my boat. Get out of punx."
I: "Cliver and I go in. Wait till 14:15, then come in."

The Golden Retriever

Meanwhile, the mob-place is full of people. There are *capo* with operations, John Rizzo, *capo* of the waterfront, Anthony Ciccone, soldier Blaise Corozzo, soldier Gene Gotti, soldier Richard G. Gotti, soldier Vincent Gotti, solder Michael Murdocco, soldier Rosario Spatola, soldier Lous Vallario, soldier Sammy meatballs Aparo, soldier the Undertaker Balsamo, our friend Lous, Vincent and Earn, soldier Tough Tony Federici, soldier Fritzy Giovanelli, soldier Baldie Longo, soldier J. Olivieri, soldier Allise Shade Malangone, soldier Danny Pagani ... and many other from Genovese, Bonanno, and Colombo with those few from Gambino. Altogether 64 sons of b**ches.

The doorman, fat, and lazy looking giant leads Cliver and me in. I smile with all my heart: "Oh, what a great honor. This is so a great thing for me. Thank you, thank you." Ernie comes to me like Judas Iscariot, and I do not mean the band. He kisses me on both cheeks. He: "My friend, this is an honor. Here is my friend Tapio." In my head comes a saying all I´d have to do for a pension is growl or go beat somebody up on Market Street.

I look at my watch at 14:10. Five minutes for the Apocalypse. I see wolf-looking fellas near the left wall. Five of them. Cliver says suddenly: "Do you know what Alphie the ADPi lion says: ´Rawr!´" I try to fly casual: "I have only one thing to say to you: getta the fuck outta my bidniss." That´s it. Hi, bye friend on the wall pull their guns out. I take my Taurus, hidden in my leg. The Slaughterhouse opens its doors.

At the same time, Makks run in and shoot, and Frankie & the whole Westboro Baptist church run in and shoot.

The battlefield is full of powder smoke, hit and run, and there smiles the master Chaos. I shoot four men down, change my place and Frank & SEALs do not know the term mercy - just bone. And the Big Voice means the choir of weapons. We do not have fitties, but who cares. Nobody needs here Trevor Daniel and his syrupy gay-voice and Falling, neither Memories of Maroon 5 with that nasal-sound or Dance Monkey's Kids.

Our shooting comes from the branch called the carnivals of hitmen. I take Ernie in my arms and hit his head to the table. My bodyguard to-come must learn to respect his lord. Vinney tries to shoot me. I do not try. I shoot him to the chest. Frank & Bones have automatic weapons, so the fight is doomed to be quick and without a doubt who takes the victory palm. After five frustrating minutes, mobs go on their knees and pray something which they do not deserve.

I look at Earnie: "I can't see you next Tuesday if this frisbeetarianism goes on. This is not zaang. You shall not be swag and dope. I gave y a change, I give another." I throw him a Taurus. I continue: "We go ten meters distance from each other. Before that, I shall come and put three bullets in front of y. Then I come back and do the same in my place. Who takes quicker the bullets and shoots them to the chest is the Mang? "

This is a great time for Makks, SEALs, and mobs also. Vinnie's mouth is full of blood. He dies. I say: "When this dime hits the grounds, you can start." I throw the coin to the air. Ernie cannot wait but goes straight away to take bullets. He puts their one bullet and shoot. I do not bother to dodge. It is miserable to shoot the rat, but Earnie flies backward. The golden retriever comes. And Earnie's melty eyes get me one more time. Four mobs try to take their guns, but SEALs give them eternal peace.

I say: "We have still the deal, and you go as it says, ok." Nearby we hear sirens ringing. The law is coming to give its ex-post judgment. No need to give explanations, cos there are any.

The hall is empty of living souls. Four dead bodies stay and mark the *Saeculum* of the battle. I salute Frank & Bones and Cliver his Makks. Then we two go to the western side of Brooklyn. Cliver looks at me: "Quite a cream out. Y run the table. Thankee. What an abattoir."

I think: "If Y dig the dump, there is always the same. We must show these odds-and-ends on the sunny side of the street. It is time to go to Europe."

Taken Good

The time is 18:00. And Cliver and I sit at Red Hook Lobster Pound (284 Van Brunt St. Brooklyn), where they give us lobster rolls & other New England-style seafood plus cocktails. I do not drink. I do need to. Cliver needs to. Our brains are empty, so we must full them with fish-energy and -trace elements. The servant looks at us and makes a conclusion: these fellas are men of action, let's sell them live fresh catch lobsters at our pound. He takes to the table a king-breeder and says: "Boys, this fella is essential to sustaining a healthy lobster population for future generations. This gentleman surely is not only delicious but ecologically sound. He is as fresh as you can get."

I hit my Taurus on the board and say: "I do not need a pet, give us something to eat. Give me The Tuscan and to this hungry friend Tuscan

Lobster Roll. I'm hungry as a wolf and want much food right now." The servant goes away, not delighted but goes for heavens´ sake anyway. So soon Cliver takes his Lobster roll tossed in a basil vinaigrette + add 2oz extra lobster. And happy me: lobster tossed in a basil vinaigrette. I drink very cold milk and Cliver takes a bottle of Bordeaux dry wine and does not begin to articulate; he drinks from the mouth of the bottle. The last hour's events haven´t been happy hours to him, so he wanna get drunk. But unfortunately, I am there, so he thinks better not to. He wants to be my friend tomorrow and the days to come.

I am still hungry as hell, and ask the servant back: "Hey you, Fried Calamari, Hoo Burger, Surf and Turf Burger, Yes, ofc to me, do y see anybody else speaking. I am fu**cking hungry. And do not spend a lot of time holding the refrigerator door open looking for answers. And do not come to tell me: give the man a fish and you feed me for a day, teach me to fish and you feed me for a lifetime." Cliver begins to laugh: "Yeeaahh, was blarg and shime. That was how I met your mother, not Coheed and Cambria. Hahahhaahaa, harbir, almost stiltner." I'm not so happy: "Well, if you say so; it was one osm thing. But slow for fake and bake your roll. We must cape Verdean still. We must conquer Yurop."

Small Taking

I call Y: "I have spent too much time here and there. The cool points are outto window and I'm all twisted up in the game."

At the same, Gambino boss Johnny Monteleon, Gambino-soldier Joseph Orlando, Genovese boss Barney Bellomo, front boss Mickey Ragusa, *consigliere* Quiet Dom Cirillo and Louis DiRapoli have a nice and cozy Italian espresso break. Bellomo looks at DiRapoli: "Where is your brother and beloved Earnie?" Louis: "Master *mia*, they have gone." Tears drop from his brown eyes: "*Quando finisce la partita il re ed il pedone finiscono nella stessa scatola.* That great fu*cer killed them both." Boss Monteleon wakes up: "You mouse, you sound like far *d'una mosca un elefante.* Who killed them?" Louis: "Tapio he is called. He ends their sunny days. The man who made a deal with Y."

Boss: "What? How can he kill them, when we have a deal?" Louis: "They, hm, tried to kill him first, but that son of the bitch was born under lucky stars." Boss: "Why they wanted to kill him? Why an earth and heaven sake, why?" Louis: "They hated him so." Boss: "What do y mean? Why did they hate him although I had made a personal deal with him? Why they hated me and my deal? Were they crazy? Where comes this disobedience?" Louis: "They had unresolved issues with him." Boss: "Behind my back? *Al povero mancano tante cose, all'avaro tutte.* They got what they deserved." Louis' hands shake, and cheeks tremble, but what can he say. Nothing. The matter is closed. But not in Louis's heart. He has made his mind. He shall kill me.

Meanwhile, I make Y a proposal: "Roddy Ricch is the box, br. steel tonight? Never Dull Soho? PanaDaPrince? AllisonLeach? Eli Escobar and Macy Rodman? Yung General Fresko x Trip TZ? Panda Spanish - La Manada Nyc? Rosalia, Ozuna, you know, YoxTi, TuxMi? Cardi b? Saweetie, Megan thee? Fero 47? E-A-E-J Mera Woo, Mueve La Cadera?

Tú, pencabas, que yo, me iba a morir ... Y si te vas ..."

Well, I come earlier to the 30s. Doggy is there but there is also something new. Yes, there is an interactive board, but they're something else also. I begin to think about Europe. It is near the time to make that great performance there.

Y arrive and we kiss. What a vain day. Just some pigheaded guys and everything isn't noice & mint. We change HWYD. I say: "White bread and bumming around. No continental breakfast." You tell me that you have been all day filming and taking pictures. Not lux either. No need to tell soap banger farts. And the beauty of shooting depends are you on the sunny side of the street or not. No need to say: they had the poets, we the guns, so we won, or God made all men, but Samuel Colt some men better than other men, or that media is like a gun, enjoyment depends on which end you look at it. I just say: "My luxurious days are sealed with my gat." I take the gun from my belt put it in the box and throw myself to the soft bed. That is a luxurious act, but not so memorable than 7-gram rocks smoke light in the mob-lofters.

Brooklynization

The time is 23:00. I ask you to sit and put HoloLens on. There comes a hologram of the eastern USA and Europe.

I say: "Yeah, here are those 21 book towns in Europe. No 1. They cannot handle their business well. They are old-fashioned and cannot attack US-trade in a fair & straight fight. They are humble, piece of shits. These European things sign with US-partners preliminary deals and do not try to attack us-partners at all. No. 2. The U.S. is a protectionist country. It thinks itself high & mighty. And that is very ridiculous. For instance, I & my friends work much, much harder than us-business fellas. Those fatties laugh that they eat us like cockroaches. Hahhaa. Without their protectionist business and their business-partners' humble attitude, we could meet them face to face and kick their asses. But when here comes somebody and hits manly straight to the face, they put their shields up and with their business-partners beat him up. So far.

But how about not caring at all those businesses and other borders? Drug-business is a good example of business without borders. But I do not mean criminal things, but straight business face to face. Y must reach the skin, also in business. If you do not, you can shoot yourself.

These 21 book towns in Europe are without fighting spirit and strategy. My personal job with my operative office is to give those cowards an aggressive strategy. My slogan goes: do not try to please anybody, hit straight to the face. Then he comes to your lifetime friend or enemy. Then y know is he a coward or True. So. There are four groups: Scandinavia, French-German border, Wales and Britain, Spain around Barca. I must give those groups an operative goal for obeying strategy.

The issue is this: they aren´t soldiers, they are civilians. They do not go to the goal at any cost. If there comes even a little obstacle, they put their hands up. They do not live or have ever lived in the discomfort zone. They do not know what a real starving, cold, exhaustion, fear, deceases mean. They do not have weapons. But there come you, the Brooklynites and me, a deep Brkner. We shall kick them to assess and make them pay if they do not understand and go as the word goes. I haven´t taken from NYC smoothies, I have taken from here black and yellow, yeah, as you say ´a black person you see walking down the street with a lot of gold jewelry´. What a great NewYorkerization, heh, heh, you know New York minute.

No need to begin to explain Knickerbocker or mad neck things. Just four years strong is one hell of one thousand dollars. Pure sex. So. After strategy made, and my operative office's control (design, organization, and motivation) comes on the table, Then New Yorkers, so-called weidals, stripper dusts, Brazzers, indie kids, Lagosta-Spaghetti-

Goodfellas, comes on the picture. You have your permanent jobs, as My Might & High Banker Friend, Bob may put it. Underneath drown the drink, you do just what New Yorkers can do best."

Y begin to laugh: "Really?" I: "Yeah, rlly. NYCers put those fu**ers understand their luxury are other people, in NYC way.

You may call it a rotten heart. Dwellin' in the Rotten Apple, you get tackled or caught by the devil's lasso, shit is a hassle. And yeah, hookers and the homeless are invisible, the subway makes sense, you believe that swearing at people in their own language makes you so multi-lingual, you've considered stabbing someone just for saying The Big Apple, you call an 8′ x 10′ plot of patchy grass a yard, to you Westchester is upstate, Central Park nature, you pay more each month to park your car than most people in the U.S. pay in rent, you haven't heard the noice of true contemporary silence since the 80s, you take hit the slide seriously, being dime piece alone makes y nervy b, y have 27 Nuprin menus to your blower, going to Brooklyn is a road trip, your Jay Walking is great art, personal space means that no one stands on your toes, you do not notice sirens, you live in a building with a larger gen pop than most towns. Your doorman is Russian, your grocer Korean, your deli man Israeli, your building super Italian, your laundry guy Chinese, your favorite bartender Irish, your favorite diner owner Greek, the watch seller on your corner Senegalese, your last cabbie Pakistani, your newsstand guy Indian and your favorite falafel guy Egyptian. You, MyBab, are suspicious as hell of strangers like me, who are nice to Y and love Y so, that is almost behind the bearing.

And you keep on asking yourself: why this deep Brkner wants to kiss me all day night long and tells me that I have AngelEyes? Why on earth I have fallen in love with him?"

Y: "Can Y put it in on sentence?" I: "NYC the best in the whole damn U.S, and in the world." I continue: "Bab, you are surely not a Missouri bitch. You give European surrender monkeys down low and Pura Vida that they can feel the same things. Luxury called NYC. You talk and care really, and that´s it. You make for months inEurope forever a New Yorker´s Valentine's day." Y: "You haver doing the most." I: "After strategy made, you put to make book towns a real group a la NYC, then there is left only one thing left. Make the mental and physical goals the same.

Y: Mental and physical capital?" I: "Yes, they must mean the same. Every move you make doing something or saying must mean something on cash flow. And cash flow much has an inner meaning. Stability means that money, which waits for taking its course to the goal, has found the main path. When you make those Europeans understand togetherness at the same time, the cash mass has found its new ways. For example, your company shall expand at home and abroad, cos of this exporting. Well, there are always the U.S. Customs and Border Protection (CBP).

 The U.S Commercial Service (CS) so-called professionals can disturb us very much. Social media channels and subscribe to an email list give events, services, tips, and market research, but when Y are involved with them, they have control opportunities over Y. Export.gob isn´t a solution to anything. There is that issue while exporting; they put those licenses or permissions to export everywhere. But do not worry, Bob takes care of the list of federal departments and agencies. He takes care that no vain export licenses shall be needed for our products and services. And if something is a must, then it is. Bob takes care, I do not. American protectionist ideas go hand in hand with those licenses.

The Castle

We both have HoloLens on. I: "So I have put here the value of each book town and how much we shall gather there in those events and so. There go 110 people. Four months for them, 450 000 euros. Those Book Towns are there, but then there come taxes, licenses, 7,5 Me. And then we must ask help and ask many digital nomads also help and visit and market us. Then there is Global Villages kind of modern circles, there altogether 12 of them, and they are very important, cos there are many scholars, even billionaires, and green-rich people. And we must lubricate also those public servants and politicians. It shall be 12 Me altogether. Now, and there shall always come changes.

I show Y via HoloLens-holograms, next summer´s flights and booking places, and always the costs and public meetings and councils. I have put in some holograms, real vid-actions from festivals, EDM and so. And there is that main thing also. I ask Y: "Do Y, MyVictoria, see it? The place, courtly thing, which I have taken to Y? There are many castles here, which are very, very cheap compared with these small departments here. With the price of this place, MyQueen, you can buy 8 castles in France!!!"

Y look at the hologram. There appear castles. Y: "What wonderful places. They must be updated of course?" I: "Yes, for instance, this castle Tournus has 1 177 square meters, an unbelievable garden, and the environment. It has some rooms more than VictoriaCourt, altogether 16, and 8 bedrooms." We look at a place with 13 ha park. I: "Think Bab, with immediate proximity to each room and its volumes, it is a real asset of family life, heating by a reversible heat pump or boiler gas. There are 7 ha of meadows ideal for horses, an awesome park and lawns with a pond, an orchard, a tennis court, and the part of a wood with an authentic washhouse. There is an old stable now used as a garage and workshop. Think 1:40 from Geneva, and 1 H from Lyon.

This La Chapelle-de-Bragny -castle cost only 1 485 000 euros. It has 700 square meters, 11 rooms, 6 bedrooms, and land 14 ha. MyVictoria, it is from the 12/13th century, renovated in the late 19th century, mid-twentieth century, and recently. There is a large guest house - stables, 4 boxes for horses, garages, and open barns. Castle Macon in the Saone et Loire is a little bit expensive: 4 Me. But it has 20 rooms. There is also that huge castle in Macon, 9 000 square meters, but is costs 7,4 Me. It is the real 19th-century Cateau. It has 235 ha composed of parks, meadows, golf, etc.

The golf has 63 ha, a Clubhouse with a shop, restaurant-bar, offices, kitchens, service room, and a magnificent terrace. Bab, the main castle has a chapel also. And, and."

Y: "That is my place, Tapio. I love it. Saone-et-Loire is a very beautiful area in France."

I: "MyVictoria, it is in the south of Burgundy. There was once Charles The Brave, the knight, complete gentleman, and hero, and loved by so many most beautiful ladies. He lost his fortune in one battle, his property in the next, and in third his blood, and the legend got air under his wings.

This unbelievable castle has 1 030 square meters, think, 26 rooms, 15, bedrooms. It has belonged to the beloved Perrault family for more than 400 years. It has five towers, they are super studios, indeed. There are libraries, bathrooms, summer house. If we give cash it shall be 1 395 000 euros. It is stealing." Y look at me: "If Y want to be loved by me, then we certainly go to live there. And ofc to VictoriaCourt and my India place, but I love this." And we kiss.

There are ofc others. We look at another castle Macon, a listed chateau, the epicenter of French great literature. Castle is just a few minutes from Cluny, 4 hours from Paris, an hour from Lyon. The beautiful castle, standing between the courtyard and garden, is in a wonderful setting on a wooded hillside, on the edge of a little village with less than 350 inhabitants. The property is enclosed by old walls and natural hedges. A gateway opens on to a drive, bordered by miscellaneous species of superb, old trees, leading to the great castle. It is a rectangular polygon, three sides of which are marked by a tower. There is also the thousand-year-old Paris church. Anyway, MyVictoria loves just Cuisery place and nothing can anymore change her mind. We go hand in hand: *si tu m'aimais, et si je t'aimais, comme je t'aimerais! Il n'est rien de réel que Cucery et l'amour.*

The elegant question goes: "How about we go to look little closely that Saone-et-Loire, which in the west is composed of the hills of the Autunois, in the center it is traversed from north to south by the Saone in its wide plain. The Saone is a tributary of the Rhone that joins it at Lyon and thus is connected to the Mediterranean Beautiful Sea. The source of the Loire is south of Saone-et-Loire. In the east, it occupies the northern part of the plain of Bresse. MyVictoria loves it. I tell you some stories about the letter & spirit. Crossed by numerous waterways and made up of forests, hedged farmland, vineyards, and mountains, the Saone-et-Loire is a place for fishing and sailing. There is also the presence of the Voie Verte greenway, rich built heritage with so-praised Romanesque churches, *chateaux*, ancient Roman remains, Y can sit there under a tree, and look at the smile of the 2000-year-old Minerva-statue."

Well, it is at 24:00. The day has begun with the hell and ended within the heaven, and never could we have known the taste of heaven, had we swallowed places of hell.

Sometimes it goes in opposite order but not today.

The Eleventh Day

Meeting Some Words Swallowing Politicians

The Fuc***ers and Disasters

At the same time, Morris Ave Gunnaz gunrunner Ada, and two other warriors, who stabbed some hours ago Astoria deli-workers while stealing their cash machine, count their money. There comes bust-up how this money and stolen money from two cash machines in Brooklyn shall be delivered between Mags. Ada takes his homemade Clock and shoots the other warrior to his leg, and the argy pargy dies a natural death.

Hundreds of protesters flock still to Grand Central Terminal to protest increasing policing and rising fares in NYC´s subways. This action followed a day of vandalism and civil disobedience throughout the transit system. The protest was met with hundreds of cops who were seen arresting protesters shortly after the action started, dragging them out of the crowd and into the street.

The MTA Chief Safety Officer Pat Warren adds: "We respect the right to peaceful demonstration. We have zero-tolerance for events that put the public´s safety at risk." The Police tear down the flags where read: "Black Power, Fuck the Police." Cops block subway entrances, and dozens of people jump turnstiles and run into stations in the area. A woman arrested for tagging FTP on store windows. NYPD says it does not know how many have been arrested. Somebody uses a chain to smash the screen of an OMNY machine at the station at West 50th Street and 8th Avenue.

You are sleeping. I begin to study NYC-sponsors. The secretary Karen Broughton, I am not interested. Peter Fleming keeps on repeating something ("it is really important that we have a diversity of people at the community board"), and have studied about the revocation of the liquor license for Woodlands, he wants to open a new supermarket, while so many supermarkets are closing in recent years. There are representatives from many parts: Adams, Clarke, Lander, Levin, Montgomery, Myrie, hm, the little birds – as MyVictoria says pigeons, not eagles, which fly high and come down like thunder.

Shall I be high & fly about democratic presidential candidate Elizabeth Warren who gives a speech in Kings Theatre. I look at Sleeping Y. Y do not like Trump, and like these, perhaps, but I do not think so bad. It isn´t good for me. Elizabeth Madame Fatale has raised more Brklyn & bed-stuy bones from individual donors than any other candidate. There she spoke hand in hand with former presidential candidate Mr. Julian Castro. Elizabeth talked about Iran. And Mr. K. Williams of Bedford-Stuyvesant praised her: "She´s always a person for the people." Means nothing. All the same was E´s statement: "The American people do not want a war with Iran." Why not, smoke the fucker, as we in the army say. A voice from the crowd cut her off with a sharp, "We love you!" What a GREEP.

East NY resident Carroll Matos loves her, but to me, E is a tough cookie, smart, who goes after big money. She is to be a disaster. Hm, perhaps I watch my mouth, I look at sleeping Y. With these big talks, which mean nothing, she has cheated, I mean raised already 442 000 d from donors in the boroughs. Well, if they can throw money into the pit, they surely can give it to our good cause. But I'm surely not going to lubricate people with pious lies. Mrs. E likes to tell people about herself, how she was a schoolteacher, and how she came to the first female senator of Massachusetts. She is surely not from Brklyn like Sen. Bernie Sanders, The Old-Timer. Democrats listen to her, but a young girl in the crowd is wiser, she had been up past her bedtime, and she sleeps and no more wastes her precious time.

How about Brad Lander and Antonio Reynoso? I pass them. There may be a roaring crowd for E, but where the f*ck is the Lion? There are Parker, Golden, Connor, Kruger, Gordon, Weinstein, Jacobs, Camara, Brennan, Cymbrowitz, Krasny, and Colton.

Hm, how about Marty Markowitz, Brooklyn borough president. That doctor Herschkopf´s long time patient - more than 30 years - has been isolated from his friends and family by this psychiatrist. He became president of the theatrical fabric business, created a charitable foundation with Markowitz´s money. When Herschkopf collects more than 3 Md in fees from his patient. The psychiatrist lives like a king next door to Markowitz, who owns it all.

Mr. H and Mr. M do business together, as Mr. H suggests. The psychiatrist is paranoid and tells everybody who wants to listen: "90 percent of the podcast is untrue or out of context." A certain man called Nocera "has had a vendetta against me for 10 years". The man called N: "The podcast has rigorously reported and fact-checked to a fare-thee-well by me and the people at Wondery and Bloomberg." Markowitz does not care what in Manhattan´s tight-knit philanthropic and Modern Orthodox Jewish circles tell about his good friend Mr. H. Mr. M takes care that Mr. H has good parties, about 170 people, to the house which mailbox bears the name of Dr. Isaac Stevens, so Mr. H. Mr. M prepare the compound for each party and stand at the barbecue roasting kosher fare and serving guests.

There are celebrities, actors and writers, and the creme de la creme of Manhattan´s Modern Orthodox world. There is something about Mr. H and his obsession with famous people. Mr. M is now witty and almost calm, and he had recently begun keeping honeybees, behind he plans to soon add a chicken coop. To him, Mr. H handles the truth. So, Mr. H has come into management decisions at Associated Fabrics. Hm, this isn´t so noice. Forget Mr. M, the Brklyn president.

What shall I do with these politicians?

Meeting the Mayor

I call Cliver: "Hello there, I have the proposal to Y. It concerns about NYC Mayor. I think he shall be a good supporter." Cliver: "Mr. Corpulence? Why?" I: "He has very good relations with the mobs, and especially for Gambino and Genovese. If I play my cards right, Mayor understands 100 % better than those other politicians. Where are the mob and Mayor and his office involved, there is big money involved, with business and building, and there are straight connections towards Europe. Straight to main fish, and the little ones come behind."

Cliver: "Really crazy eyes! How do you think, you randevuu with Gill de Glasio? He is a busy man, and his schedule has been firmed up months ago? From 2014 NYC-budget has been expanded 20 Md and is now 93 Md for the coming fiscal year, man. Can y dig it at all?"

I say: "Yeah, and expenditures have ballooned three times as fast as the rate of inflation. That is something to think about. He needs some good shows. While this is not a Times Square thing, with 4 million people, this is a good thing. And there is PR-Europe, and cos of Brexit it shall be just great & f. He is pro-Israel lobbyists. Let him be pre-Europe lobbyists, too. That fella is giving up also on other fronts, he supports marijuana legalization a once-in-a-generation opportunity to get a historic issue right for future New Yorkers´. If he gives up for bad surely, he gives up for good.

I respect his metzitzah b´peh-thing. I do not know what´s up, perhaps his wife? But NYCP isn´t his first concern. Well, of course, those mob-things explain. And he is just in the same line as the IOB´s information tech priority thing. To tech 2 988 billion d, is a great thing. And just need to ask him, does he like to expand his tech-idea form European Silicon Valley (Tel Aviv area) to other Book Towns centers. Heh, heh, I have for instance last summer visitors from Tel Aviv, they just love VictoriaCourt."

Cliver: "But how y can meet him at all? Y must have an appointment, recommendations, business-schedule, long term well-established relations and then you might have a chance to have a little five minutes chat with the grand boss." I: "Y sound so bass. 1=2. We do not need anything. We go in. I'm not going to send online messages or phone 311 or 212, go to Mayor´s Press Office or NYC & Company. We are not going to go to the Mayor´s Office for International Affairs. We are going to meet him at Gracie Mansion, ofc."

Cliver is not happy: "Do y mean just two of us? One company of SEALs isn´t enough for that." I: "Badong. It´s a doc in the box. I come to pick you up. It shall be just fun shines & Cadillac escalade. We shall go there when the mayor is going to his office. So, he is at his best and can focus, when imma let him finish. About half an hour. And then we have a great supporter."

Cliver: "They wipe the table with us, really sparkling vanilla thing. Oh, the Gracionshot: pray to the Makks Grims! I wanna y to pray St. Valentin, I wanna y to pray to Saint Guadala Peinex, and I wanna y to pray to god, this is Osama Bin Laden." I laugh: "In the beginning, somebody always sets up the bomb."

Time is 5 am. Time to go to Hell Gate, 88th Street, in Yorkville. I take Cliver to the car at 5:15. I hold HoloLens and put in the middle of the car a hologram. There is that Mayor Mansion, with hand marks of Gracie-Weeks-McComb-Grange-Wagner-Schmidt. Nothing top secret about that federal-style thing. I drive the car through the light. There is a NYPD-car. We go on more with the East End Ave. I stop the car. No guns, just Cliver & me suits on. Fresh and clean, smiling me and Cliv not smiling. He says: "They might throw us to the jail for months."

I: "Penitentiary? Even a Hooscow?" Cliver: "Yes, definitely don´t drop the soap." I: "Well, let´s find it out. We go to that NYPD-car, turn left, walk five meters, then five more. Five cars shall live in front of the house at 6:05 am. Before that Mayor is at the front door. We have 20 seconds time to be in front of him, and me five seconds to say those magic words. If that does not work out, then to the jail. OK." Cliver: "):(. This is just so hunky-dory."

Time is 6:03 am when we begin to run. 200 meters, 100 meters, to the front door. We stop running, 50 meters. I tell a joke: "RIP cold shooting some hoop - y will be misted." Cliver looks at me: "See y in Fayetteville Manlius high school." Now the 1,96 m-fella comes outto the main door. Two guards try to stop me. I push them back. I´m face to face with Mayor. I give him an envelope: "This is urgent from Creston Apartments." Four guards take me behind, but the big man looks at the cover of the envelope. He says: "To my car." Cliver stays out but a big man and I go in.

The door is closed by guards. The security glass goes up. There are just the Mayor and me, and some words.

I look at the man to whom Eric Trump wrote: "You have never created a job in your life. Second, our great city has gone to shit under your leadership. Crime is up, the men & women of NYPD detest you, homelessness is rampant, our streets are dirty, and people are leaving our city in record numbers." Mayor answered: "Spare me, You and your dad have spent decades evading taxes and stiffing your workers." Later de Glasio, a Democrat, announced his bid for the presidency.

Donald Trump: "The Dems are getting another beauty to join their group. Gill de Glasio of NYC, considered the worst mayor in the U.S., will supposedly be making an announcement for president today. He is a JOKE, but if you like high taxes & crime, he´s your man. NYC HATES HIM!"

Glasio: "What do you want?" I smile: "The Families just wanted to give their regards to You Mr. Mayor. Everything is going so well. They are keeping a low profile as they promised. And building business flourishes. NYPD and the court cannot touch them, thank you. And more thank you for building projects with them. Those projects are very important to show New Yorkers and people of the U.S. that you take care of them and their healthcare. You have said that the Trump administration wants to build a better mousetrap. Working families are mice. Families thank that they can do those building things and get some profit at the same time. Both parties win. You have said about Trump that there´s plenty of money in the world. It´s just in the wrong hands. It is niace that you correct it. The Families thanks that they can be in your project to create 100 000 new jobs by 2027 with NY Works program.

They are happy too, that NY only turns undocumented immigrants accused of violent crimes over to ICE, not those accused of non-violent or status offenses. And now their organizations can get more people in NYC, cos of your initiatives to increase healthcare access to LGBTQ New Yorkers, and signed legislation making it easier for transgender and nonbinary individuals to amend their birth certificates and identity as neither male nor female on official documents. So, more mob-soldiers can come from Italy, and nobody turns them back. Thank you for criticizing police and promises of making something, cos there have been too many tragedies between young men and our police.

I have a mandate from them to talk about something about the Mayoral Office of Technology. Families want to show their gratitude offering your Office of tech an opportunity to come with them in Europe in the IOB-project to evaluate tech to rural areas with cultural tourism and modern antiurban immigration. And with this, we and Families want to help You to make your point in presidential elections against Trump and his protectionism and all those difficulties which foreigners and great US-citizens meet while trying to have for example visas and working licenses in the foreign countries. This IOB-project should show all good Americans how wrong Mr. Incumbent President is. As he is talking about crime and the economic situation in NYC. My Company Book Towns Group and The Families see here an opportunity for jobs and the economy and Trump´s attempts to sell NAFTA 2.0."

I look at the man whose early polling numbers bode very poorly for his presidential prospects. Despite 51 % of respondents having heard him - a fairly good level of name recognition - just 10 % would be satisfied with him as the nominee and 44 % would be actively dissatisfied, the highest dissatisfaction level any 2020 candidates have received so far.

He repeats: "What do y want?"

I: "I do not want anything stupid. Just think about myself and my company and then I think what I can do for you. So. The new Chief Tech Officer John P. Farmer can help me. As you say technology helps us provide equal access to services for all New Yorkers. And, as yousaid, with his help, we will continue to innovate on behalf of all New Yorkers and further establish our city as a global leader in the tech field. And Farmer has said: ´New York is the greatest city in the world, and I´m thrilled to be joining the City of NY. I will work to ensure that tech and innovation benefit all New Yorkers in every borough, from every walk of life.´ So your Tech Office has smart city techs, digital services, and the tech industry work for all New Yorkers. And 35 leading cities have signed on the NYC guidelines. Smart City Initiatives agencies try to find all over the world that smart techs improve services to New Yorkers and their companies.

Dear Mayor, I want 15 Md + Smart City agents and agencies to help my company to give Brkln and Queen and the Bronx a real opportunity with supporting STEM programs, science, and technology policy to show why New Yorkers are the best citizens of the world.

I take from my pocket my strategic plan for our great 4 Month festival in Europe. He looks at a long list of scrippers, singing street soldiers, mobs, fat Loots, cool/goods, yard workers and Brazzers, SEALs other dropping the kids off at the pool -members, and blerds and wlerds, and he opens his mouth and begins to laugh like a horse: "*Filho da puta*, you deep Brkner begin to sound just like a Brooklynite."

How the hell does he know that? He is just a borougbred.

We decide that Farmer sends tech-agents in 12 book towns and I establish a Book Towns Brooklyn Fund. There NYC Tech Office shall put 15 Md, helping my Brooklyn-employers. I shall meet the Man, Mr. F tomorrow at 2 am when I shall do a presentation of our tour de France. Then Glasio signs the paper which I showed him when we meet. He, I, and Family keep going on balance = triple beam - intelligence - totaling the expenses.

We shake hands and I see in front of me a horse with golden teeth. There must always be one, then you can go to the race. A goose laying golden eggs is a joke, but the golden horse began to breathe when Henry Ford made cheap, reliable cars, and people said: "Nah, what´s wrong with a horse?" That was a golden bet for a golden horse.

Well, I wait eagerly to meet real tech-guru, Mr. Farmer. He is an underrated fella. Not a politician like the mayor, whose words taste more the public opinion than scientists doing forecasts. F has been at Microsoft as the Director of Tech & Civic Innovation, based in NYC. F and his team established the company as a leader in the growing field of civic and urban tech through cross-sector partnerships and new product development. F works in close collaboration with CUNY, Code of America, DataKind, Civic Hal the NYCEDC. Farmer served on the board of the NYC Tech Talent Pipeline. F has served as Senior Advisor for Innovation in the White House Office of Science and Technology Policy under Obama. F took care of the portfolio of tech-based reforms and improvements to government operations, including re-creative and leading the Presidential Innovation Fellows program.

Well, Silicon Harlem loves F. He has the community around tech. That fella I must meet. Something to my brains. I cannot just make my gun talk with crips and bangs and mob-gunrunners. Although they haven´t yet ruined my day.

Well, Glasio is now out of the presidential race, and Trump has said: "Oh no, really big political news, perhaps the biggest story in years! The part-time Mayor of NYC, @GilldeGlasio, who was polling at a solid ZERO but had tremendous room for growth, has shocking dropped out of the Presidential race. NYC is devasted, he´s coming home!" Glasio had said: "I feel I´ve contributed all I can to this primary election, and it´s clearly not my time."

Anyway, I see in front of me a big man with big dreams, especially those tech ones. And fuck with that de Glasio´s stewards ship of NY has since become a subject of consistent ridicule from the president´s allies and conservative media commentators. He has his Farmer, and Trump has him not.

I come out from a black car and come to Cliver. He is curious: "How it goes?" I: "Great, he gives us what we want." Cliver look at me: "Rlly?

Something more? New Daryl (data, analyzing, robot, youth, lifeform)?"
I: "We can say, yayer. Farmer."

The Click-Clack-Boom-Boom-Studios

I forget the guns and go to kisses. Those politicians aren't for my brains. They say: it is a little inaccurate to say I hate everything. I'm in favor of common sense, honesty, and decency. I am forever ineligible to the public office of trust and profit. I do not repine, for I'm a subject of it only by force of arms. Bullshit.

I jump to my Mustang and drive. I call Y: "Hey, Bab, where are you?"

At the same time, Louis DiRapoli has gathered around him 21 mob-soldiers. They all have semiautomatic weapons, stolen from Guns & Gunsmiths 7919 Utrecht Ave. DiRapoli has made his decision. Today it is the day. But he has missed something, a man who desires revenge should dig two graves. And he is given the devil his due. He finds his target: me.

Y: "I'm in Brooklyn Studios 8-16 43rd Ave. Between 9th Street and Vernon Blvd. We are just making shots." I: "I'm coming there. Don't have anything else to do, in this very momentum." Y: "I do not think it is a good idea." I laugh: "A good idea. Bab, I love Y, and I do not shame to show it." Y: "That is not exactly what I mean." I: "Hahahahaha. See y soon."

At the same time, DiRapoli's men check their weapons, put pullets in, look mechanism, trigger, aiming. Click, clack, boom, boom. Louis says: "I wanna fu*cer to eat his little balls. And then I cut him to pieces, and Hudson takes the rest."

Some instinct says to me: call Cliver. I call him: "Yo´ fool, lets case the western reserve university. I pick you up, and we go big or you go home. Yeah, the place is Booknam studios. Yep, just there. MyVictoria has some shoots. Let´s have apples against humanity. Day late savings time, yeah."

It is 16:00 when we arrive at Brklyn Studios, a 15 000 sq. ft. the production facility in Long Island. I go to ask, where I should find Y, in that chaos of film, photography, music videos, motion picture production, and television series.

The lady at the entrance advises us and smiles strangely. We are in a place that is committed to maintaining a relaxed, creative, well-run, user-friendly production environment with 100 % transparency. We go through the ground floor. There walks a stage manager. He normally will assist with all customers. The studio needs and helps facilitate a seamless shoot, including any necessary lighting/grip/dolly/expendable rental. But not now. He takes his smartphone: "Si, si, moth***fucker is here. Yes, they are going forwards. Yeah, sure to the dressing room. Yes, come soon Mr. DiRapoli."

We continue. In the kitchen, we find some half-naked men and women. Fuck. Those little fellas, with big ideas of themselves and that porn studio thing altogether.

Cliver sees my feelings: "Slow your roll, rlly, chill yayo. This is it. Ya dig?

I: "Do y think Im stoopid? In the army we had mardes. There came in two years new fresh biddies, the old ones were soon passe and worn-out. The process was always the same: first, they come smiling and seducing, then playing tough, and finally, there was left just sarcasm and low voice with drugs, alcohol, and smokes. They look elegant, then lusty, then they satisfied their customs in all possible ways. Fresh girls become cheap old biddies. And for instance, the lady could lean towards her husband, perhaps a lieutenant´s, shoulder and some soldier comes to tap her butts and, hola, they go, and after a course, she came back to her lieutenant, who didn´t care a damn. There were stoopid fights. They nearly killed each other for a woman, which they after some months nearly didn´t want to look at. Well, as I said, there were many more clients and less soap than here, but ..."

Cliver: "Do not be sawdy, cradle of filth, wdyec, letit´allgo." I: "Don´t pour my cereal."

At the same time, DiRapoli and his 21 soldiers stop their cars near studios and rush in. Louis has a crazy look at his fat face. It expresses half rage and half strange satisfaction. The murder is almost got his rockets off.

Cliver and I come to the mezzanine, but there is a red light on. We go to offices and privates but nothing. We turn back to the mezzanine. They are shoot going on. Small-leary-dark-sugar daddy with a muscular body and big lol and Y knoodling him, both nekked. Well, I am a head taller than ... I am ready to beat ... then back door flies open and Louis let his gat crip knowledge. Beat asplodes.

Shoots come loud & clear. I run to Y, take Y to my arms, carry to a safe angle, to the corner. Sugar daddy follows there. It is the first corner behind the aisle, and I shout to Cliver: "Shoot to the legs and feet. They can shoot but not move!"

There are two doors in the mezzanine which leads to offices and other stairs. I go nearly through the door to the kitchen. I kick in the next door. I shoot down two mobs in that room´s door which leads to steps. Nobody has gone in yet. Cliver shoots from the mezzanine corner and me from the entrance space to offices. This is called crossfire. We do not have automatic weapons, just MyTaurus and Cliver's army-clock. DiRapoli & the mob stays nice & easy below at the steps.

I call Frank: "Take Dave, come as soon as possible to Brkln-studios." Frank: "Yeah, 7 minutes. Shooting in the yard? Ok, we take automats. Yeah, have fun, and do not die moth*fucker." I yell to Cliver, although the voice of shooting is very loud: "One, two, three, then I rush to the steps. Follow me." Cliver fears but loves more the crazy madness, which can make him famous among his bros. I run as fast as I can to the aisle space and jump up. On the stairs are four mobs, and I throw myself on those fu***ers. We all go down as a bigrotating pile. I hurt my left shoulder. I shoot one mob to the ear. His head blows up. I see DiRapoli down there. He goes out. Cliver comes behind and shoots also. Mobs run to the soundstage kitchen set. 19 mobs give a heck of the fire to us. We cannot move in.

Cliver: "Respecta. I said not to come, but you are with all due respect bible nazi." I: "Stay here. I come back." I run to Y: "Aight? And no not touch that fu*cer anymore. And y, take a hick. Before I shoot the balls off and just save the whales." I run back no time to think anything. Cliver: "They are coming in." We must go back.

There begin to hear more shooting. The Cavalry has arrived. Frank & Dave do not waste bullets. Mobs run. But this time I do not give mercy. I beat mobs as they owe me money. I see DiRapoli at the courtyard. He goes to his A-Romeo 4C Spider and escapes with that 237-horsepower thing. That makes for a zero-to-60-mph time of 4.1 seconds. Soon he and his two bodyguards go the speed of 120 mph. I go with my Mustang before them along Sunnyside towards Maspeth.

The Church

There goes Calvary Cemetery, Mt Zion Cemetery. The 48th Street is well nice and big. We go fast. Near StetUpScaffolding Warehouse, I catch them. Two mob-soldiers jump off and shoot to me, and DiRapoli goes running towards National Distribution Center. I shoot mobs to their necks. They shall die soon.

I run after my kill. He thinks he can hide in that 22 hectar center. He goes into one truck entrance. There stands a fella who has in his chest the name P. Clarke and he shouts to us but throws himself to the ground when Louis makes his damn marks. DiRapoli dips for his life to the parking area. He goes to one black Ford and takes people out and goes. I take nearby Datsun and go after him. He drives towards Williamsburg and I go after. At 3rd Ave, his left front tire breaks and he begins to run the street. I stop Datsun and crip after him. Lazy Italian fella begins to get tired.

And there is a just & generous expression of the Christian faith called Forefront Church. He runs in the church. That Christian community is more interested in asking good questions than having all the right answers. In the church, there is nobody else but lead pastor Jonathan Dilliams. DiRapoli knows him well, cos he had made many times his confessions here. I come in the peace of the church.

This nice little community believes that the death and resurrection of Jesus is good news for everyone regardless of orientation, identity, ethnicity, and tradition. All are affirmed, included, and invited to join them. Unfortunately, my hardened heart believes not that Mr. DiRapoli can do that. The pastor is praying on the altar when DiRapoli goes to him and asks all-frightened for his help. DiRapoli turns and shoots towards me, but I do not shoot back and walk slowly towards them. DiRapoli´s hands are shaking when he aims one more time. I shoot to this heart. He falls on the hands of the pastor.

Pastor: "You come to God´s house where everyone is alone with his Creator, and you break peace & silence." I say: "Yes, I do. Fair play, he tried to kill me. So, I tried and killed him." He looks at me. Then I come to him and sit near to on the altar floor. We have a connection.

Pastor says that his church is dedicated to serving each other and restoring neighborhoods, living out the great commandment to love G & neighbors as yourself.

He welcomes me, after my kill: "Y are affirmed, included, and invited also, and believe or not, we see every day how God gives gifts which will helm pamke NYC a better place." This fella is a good man and dedicated Our Smiling Friend´s soldier, I like him already much.

I introduce myself and say: "I try to do also good things - my own way." I tell him my vision on our journey to Europe to come. He likes what he hears.

I say to him: "I take here to Europe street credibility people, who can make their day in bad situations and are actually very good at that. But there is only a problem." Pastor: "What´s that?" I: "They all are in show-business, so they entertain in their own, hm, hard or light ways. I think they are so competent people that they can do much more than just entertain. They can do serious business. They can unite their ideas of physical capital to the ideas of mental capital. They have gone and go also on the shadow side of the street, so they do not have illusions of ercy and so. They can talk about rotten hearts and make their performances, but I can trust them a hundred times more than any god-loving goody-goodies.

I just love them, and most of all I love MyVictoria, cos she is a woman that gives life bigger challenges to a man, and when she sees that the fella can survive, which nobody has accomplished yet, then I am a very happy man. Well, nothing else to say to y, but go your way I go mine. And between us, I take you as my friend. We both have born under lucky stars. All the best."

I stand up. He stands up. We shake hands. And I tap his shoulder as we do in the army. And we look straight face to face to each other. I go outto church very happy that I have shot a traitor and made a new trusted friend: educated form Eastern University in Urban and Multicultural Education writes some sunny day about our journey to Europe his way, which covers religion and spirituality, current trends, and LGBTQIA inclusion and justice.

Him I shall introduce to the IOB. He knows how to speak at national events including TEWWomen18, Wild Goose Festival, W/ National Conference, Eastern Christian Conference, and Exponential National Conference.

He tells me that he enjoys a good beer, a better story, and fuck with the years of disappointment, roots for his beloved NY Mets. And his Brkner heart goes great on Swaghetti.

Bad for Your Business

I call Y: "Where are Y? Home. Well, I come as soon as possible." I call Frank: "Where are you?" Frank: "We came back here before the police came. We took care of the security cameras and bodies also." I thank him, and call Cliver: "How about y?" Cliver: "I'm waiting for Y at the 43 Bar & Grill."

I go there. I take Chipotle Chicken Toastie, but I do not eat cheese, tomato, red onion, and chipotle mayo on toasted sourdough with choice of side, I shall take it with me. I ask Cliver, who looks very relaxed: "How Y got out?" He: "Frank took care of eating the booty like groceries. His SEALs made the deadline. *Atoda madre.* I just put my clock away and came to this pizza hut, easy sauce." I: "So the police didn't arrive?" Cliver: "No, why they should? Just pipe hitter, tickety boo." I: "How about those people of that shooting? They find their silence. Just business buzzed. If somebody asks something, there is just noyb. it smells like teen spirit." I stand up: "So I leave you. Y must be hungry as a bungry." Cliver: "Tapio, chill your biscuits, she is never caught without a great hair-do and her cellphone." I jump to the Mustang and come to Y.

Doggy jumps to my lab, and I give it a Spanish beef. To Y I give Chipotle Chicken Toastie, but You aren't hungry. I kiss Y: "Now everything is settled down. I shot DiRapoli in front of a pastor. Now, at last, we can begin our trip to France." Y: "Since You come to the picture, there has been nothing but action and chaos." I kiss Y again: "But I have understood your point of view, which isn't without action & chaos. You have put me in front of a modern truth, where I do not make a choice, just hit & run, almost thuggin & buggin. And I shall solve that misery of your bad job – or I go forever."

Y look serious: "This has been very bad for my business ..." I: "Isn´t that wonderful. Now You have more choices." I say to Y: "Mr. NY, so the mayor, promised to the Brooklyn Fund 15 Md. I shall meet tomorrow Mr. Farmer the Great." I make a call: "Hello Bob, so I have something to ask about funds. How can we make them profitable without sharing much with those whom those funds are for? Am I making or are you making it to my New Yorker team which is coming with me to Europe, and The Tech Officer shall finance it with 15 MD?"

Bob´s Heart Pure as Gold

Bob laughs: "You are the man for my taste: directly to business. Well, it is very simple. It is called bootstrapping. The Fund must be made so that it looks like pulling yourself up by your bootstraps, if you know whatta I mean. Funding from external sources like NYC Tech Office can be hard to come by. To the tax-office, it shall be much better to show that you rely on your own resources. It is a good fallback, heh, heh. We can also tell officers and to the Negative Media that some entrepreneurs and business owners like us, choose to reject external funding, preferring the independence that comes with going it alone.

I take care that you have a healthy balance in your savings account. Y just tap your retirement funds and rock-n-roll over money from your IRA or 401 (k) into a business start-up. The key is rockarolling over the money into a corporate retirement account that permits you to invest in the business. I take care of third-party retirement-plan administrator shit. I set up a C-corporation and establish a corporate retirement account. Then Y & I roll outside retirement accounts into the corporate plan and invest the money in the company's stock. Y buy shares of your own business, so y effectively feed it money.

Tax-fu***ecrs put such into a gray area of the law, but so what. The Internal Revenue Service approves such moves as legal and procedural issues. And lazy IRS just studies. I do not charge from U, Tapio, any annual fees. I'm just your business-friend. There you have a nest egg to start a business. And I make sure that this retirement account is the path in which Tech Office money comes to Y. I camouflage the cash flow to home-equity credit or refinancing, and loans from friends, family, acquaintances, and banks. I take also loan from 401 (k) and repay it before you terminate employment, although you are a deep Brkner.

The advantage of using your own savings is that there's no cost apart from the lost opportunity to earn interest. And cos you are very rich, relying on your savings may be enough to fund a business, especially as it grows larger. They put that I promise you. I make on your name personal debt, you know, from business purchases on credit cards to refinancing your mortgage or taking out a home equity line of credit. There goes part of the Tech Office money. Part of that money we camouflage resources from friends and family members, those Anonymus-persons pool your funds to put into the business. And they borrow from them.

And tax-office respects that y do that with people you know so well, although they never exist but on the paper. And then the fund starts generating profits and cash that be plowed back into the business. Your camouflage bootstrapping creates certainty, cos no time goes putting together stup business plans and glossy presentations, trying to convince other people to part with their money. 100 % ownership. And you do not raise money through debt, the repayments and interest will not eat into your earnings. You have full control, not those real Brkners to whom the money is meant to be. No strings attached. No venture capital or private equity funds demand a substantial say in the running of the business. Y get more discipline living within your means.

Hahahaa, do Y remember when Boo.com burned through 188 MD in just six months. And cos the bootstrapping is not true, there is no slow growth. Tech feeds us well. Growth opportunities are not limited by the size of your own funds and what your business produces in cash flow. I make it well, so those tax-officers and controllers cannot see the unusual - almost impossible growth.

I must camouflage, cos the money comes from Tech Office, and the tax-officers begin to think about how this technology-growth of your company is so fast, advantage taking from your competitors. You have in a real situation no personal risk, although it seems you have a big one. You can try to say that it is now a very huge risk that the business may rob your many working years. 38 % of the business owners must retire later than expected, and you aren´t one of them. You have many contacts, angel investors, venture capitalists, and other investors that bring money on your table. You have an immense network of contacts, although you do not need to show it to tax-officers. No red flag of empty restaurant syndrome.

So MyTapio, you just give tax-officers and other checkers clear parameters. We take money from the Fund and y have separate businesses and personal bank accounts. You pay yourself a salary, so you can cover an important part of that cash flow from the Brooklyn Fund, and cover your personal expenses each month. With friends and other business partners create formal agreements setting out the terms and have everybody sign. You must show tax-officers an overall limit, a point at which you´ll stop funding the business to protect your overall financial future. It can be changed quickly. Make an obvious business plan and throw their worse-case scenarios. In this bootstrapping a business you cannot be shown yourself a strategic genius. Keep in mind that 90 % of business failures are caused by poor cash flow. I do not show those big streams. I do monthly your cash flow planning. It has an 80 % survival rate, compared with 36 % for those only planning once a year. We do not fly blind, but tax-officers must see that we are – heh – green.

One thing that we must avoid is taken invests of the All-American Equity Found, you know: The measure companies´ prospects for growth. They invest at least 80 % of its assets in All-American companies. That portfolio management team is very, very good, cos it knows how to use a variety of investment strategies to select companies identified as having superior growth, profitability, and quality relative to companies in the same industry. They should find out cash flow from Tech Office and how it is used. But I have some cases that make them go the wrong direction."

Bob stops.

The Spanish Luxury

And I have sight. I come to Y. Y begin to talk about that castle in France: "I looked at a 14-bedroom villa in Peymeinade. It has those common several buildings, on 4 floors with an elevator, 2 heated pools, a jacuzzi, an artist studio, and caretaker premises. There are 2 pool houses with summer kitchens, but I didn´t like it. Ilook at St Chinian´s 9 bedroom villa huge vineyards, Lourmarin´s vineyards, St Remy de Provence, with charming gardens, refresh by a fountain and various fig-trees, garden watering, double glazing, electric gates, guest house, and vineyard and many more, but I do not like them. Our castle is for us."

Y put again HoleLens 2 on. There comes Spain. There appear holograms of five Spanish Book Towns.

Vila Litéraria de Óbidos. There comes text: *Encontro de escitores, leitores, artistas, musicos, livros, letras ...e muitos Pontos de vista diferents.*

Óbidos is a beautiful, historic hill drop town with a wall that encloses a compact medieval center filled with cobbled streets and traditional houses. The *Óbidos Vila Literária* Project is a creative development strategy that the Municipality has been developing since 2013, com a parceria de Ler Debagar e que pretende envolver *o território de Óbidos de cultura e de livros que se expandem pelo pais e pelo mundo*.

Then there comes Uruena. There comes on the screen a small medieval town behind a high wall. Y look fascinated to the medieval gate leading out of Uruena. I say: "Here is our guesthouse, a castle that stands there, and all around are vineyards the fields of wheat. My friend Alberto Azuara has just recently established his Thesis Doctoral of this amazing place.

There comes The Chocolate Obidos Festival, the castle on the top on the hill, and environments full of people, flags, pirates, dancing, music, light. And houses for sale. For instance, luxury condominium with golf and three swimming pools.

I laugh: "Think this small house´s, just 190 sq., 3 rooms, 3 beds, 3 baths, 2 floors, the price is 265,417 d. It is a ridiculous price for this kind of thing compared with those huge castles in France. Yes, there is hot weather, hills, but still too much. I can hire a sailing boat from the nearest harbor and then we can sail all over the Mediterranean world, but still."

Victoria, I think you shall love Obidos, it is not in Spain but in Portugal. Some of my friends live half of the year there and my uncle lives in Andalusia. Perhaps someday, we shall go there to sail. The places are full of storks, they like chimneys.

Then on the screen comes country house in Calle Marbana, Uruena. Y smile: "Oh, what a wonderful patio with views, high ceilings." I: "Yes, stone house. It is an 18th-century house, but it is quite a small just 200 sq, 5 bedrooms, 2 bathrooms, a garden, terrace and so. The views are alright amazing, but, but the ridiculous price. This box costs 276 000 e. It is robbery. But look at these are from Marbella, luxury-villas, they look much better.

One of my architect friend Arto Saravuo designed them all over the Mediterranean when he lived in Greece. But now he designs things in southern China. Anyway, there are many luxury villas in Marbella. That box which you say above is just a very normal villa, but they take from it 2 700 000 euros. It has 359 square meters. Well, normal functional and sustainable design, seeking to achieve maximum energy efficiency. On the upper floor stands a master bedroom, a living room, and two open bedrooms enclosed by a large partially covered terrace; the ground floor covers the houses the social areas, and the kitchen, along with a large master bedroom. All rooms are glazed and open to an extensive garden, which many living areas under pergolas and a large infinity swimming pool. So quite normal.

Look at the castle near Cáceres Extremadura. There Y have a medieval castle. It has only 7 bedrooms, and it is built into the walls of the hilltop Trujillo. It is much bigger than those others, 820 square meters, and it has 2 floors and a tower. Think that tower could be made a studio.

There are only 5 bathrooms, but it is something. you can walk on the walls and look at boasts outstanding views over the local countryside. There is also an independent cottage, beautiful gardens, and a swimming pool. I just love it. It doesn't have the elegance of Cruisery but it is a real medieval castle with incredible views, and here has been knights, ladies, kings, and queens. Bab, it is in the west of Spain and close to the Portuguese borders. The land is one of the most beautiful in Spain, Hispania as Romans said. The land is full of history, gastronomy, and nature reserves.

It cost only 1,6 million euros.

I begin to laugh. I say: "What do Y say?" Y: "I like the French castle, it was for peace, this looks like crusade-thing," I: "But here real troubadours sing their songs and there has seen many angels helping people. Monks loved this castle. And, and most of all look what kind of food there is today."

There come holograms of great Extremaduran food-culture.

I: "These Iberian pigs live mostly in semi-wild conditions. If we buy this castle, we must understand that the flesh of Iberian pigs is essential in our dishes. Nearby people make famous Iberian pork and mutton. It´s a lack of clutter. It shall be cooked in large pots, and if we shall leave there, we must invite visitors, friends, and neighbors it that pork. And there must be paprika, garlic, bay leaves, pennyroyal, and anise. Smoked paprika is very good.

Ofc olive oil, coriander leaves, escabeche de bacalao, Home-made wine are made in small earthenware vessels. There is cherry, picota del Jerte, mutton stew and fry, kid and vegetable stew. Chantaina in a rich stew of mutton liver, brain, heart, and kidneys cooked with a mixture of bay leaves, garlic, breadcrumbs, and boiled eggs. There is hen, stew, hare and frogs, tench, trout, a large lizard, a lizard in tomato sauce, and in green sauce. Chick pieces, potatoes, pumpkin, chestnuts, onions and bell peppers, chickpea soup and bean soup, a stew with offal and blood, wild asparagus soap, a lot of vegetables, dessert truffles, stewed lentils, partridge soup. Cheeses are awesome, like *queso de Los Ibores*, and y can eat goat milk cheeses also. Desserts and sweets are prepared using wheat flour, hones, pork fat, milk, sugar and olive oil, like anise-parfumeria muffins, fried doughnuts, sweet almond soup, *puchas dulces*, fried buns.

I have gathered a sponsor-group from 45 sponsors. The main beating heart concerns 12 sponsors. There are two strategic sponsors, two operative sponsors, two tactical, two locals, and another of these which works in magistrate and can also operate with one magistrate sponsor. Then there are three bankers: one is strategic fella, one operational, and one tactical. So, I'm straight now connected them with book towns' possible sponsors with the IOB's treasurer. I must make some calls tomorrow and meet that Farmer of NYC Tech Office. Then the net is designed and then real Brooklyners shall be get loosed and make street credibility strategy. Those European Sweats & Cheeks so experience the surprise of the lifetime. And where is a surprise there come always money? Surprise & Money are like You & Me, they just cannot leave without each other.

The Twelfth Day

The Rain with Sunshine

The Church blesses The Business Spirit

I wake up at 5:00. And begin to think. My sponsors do program planning and design. They have rapid test-and-learn cycles on new tech and process, including proof-of-concept exercises. They do transformation executions, provide expertise, and tech advisory. They do change management, communication. There are integration and carve-out, the future operating model and architecture, identify and kick-off implementation projects.

And soon it is 7:00. Y come to me, and we look at the huge hologram of businesses in book towns. From Book Towns go long strategic arcs to sponsors in Finland. They are cash flow arcs. The question goes what I can offer from foreign sponsors to domestic ones and visa versa.

You say: "Tapio contact those foreign sponsors after you have a plan with domestic ones. Don´t prove anything that y cannot do?" I: "Bab, you are genius, yes ofc, we must take the Church with this. Hahaa. I shall meet today pastor Jonathan & Mr. Farmer. There is enough mental and physical capital altogether. And I shall go to St Peter´s Roman Catholic Church.

I call Jonathan: "Good Morning, here is the fella who took care of that bad man, who has tried to kill me many times. Who takes care of your business? Robbie Klein is the tech director and the founder of the Astro Lab. Really? That´s great. Can I talk with him?

Hello Robbie, here is Tapio, you have made there a digital organization for entrepreneurs. You simplify their digital workflow, email, storage, and give entrepreneurs of the big picture. Sounds great. You sort things out. o entrepreneurs do not miss important messages. You go to cover entrepreneurs' files and spreadsheets. You clean address books, calendars, you get entrepreneurs up and running.

You are a digital therapist! A tech consultancy that specializes in organizing digital workflow for entrepreneurs and small businesses. You are also an avid design enthusiast. Yes, you enjoy inspirational architecture, interior design, and fashion. Your tech design music, great. What living small has inspired you to create more thoughtful interiors, from folding beds to compact recording studios? You are lucky you have worked with many incredible artists in NYC. What do you do next summer? I have a proposal for You and Jonathan." Yes, now we have blessings with us.

I kiss Y and say: "Perhaps Y forget those studios and shooting for a while and come with me to St. Peter's Church in Manhattan. I wanna hear your beautiful voice."

We eat just New England Clam Chowders and Pan-Fried Fish Sandwich, and nothing more wonderful from Pearl Oyster Bar.

I give Doggy some dog food delivery pasta. Human grade chicken breast, and whole wheat pasta. The doggy has transformed a little bit fatter. I must take him for running more often.

I take your hand out we go. We are at 619 Lexington Ave. We go into the place where reads: "God has claimed the city, and all who call it home, to be a place of healing and wholeness, reconciliation and peace, newness and delight."

Sounds good. That church is a community of immigrants. The Church provides legal and personal counseling and other services to people at all stages of the immigration process. And do the job with Lutheran Immigration and Refugee Services, The New Sanctuary Coalition, The

New York Immigration Coalition, New York Legal Aid Society, the ELCA´s AMPARO program, & Sion Iglesia Luterana. Well, James Beaudreau is the director of media and communications, and Wendy Berot the general manager, and Spanish-speaking Fabian Arias interest us.

And while Y begin to change some words with Arias, I go to Mr. Beaudreau´s office.

"Good Morning, nice to meet you", I begin. Soon I know that the fella is very good at managing the communications, social media, video production, print materials, and website, and what is more important he oversees the development and maintenance of the church´s A/V systems and A/V staff. He has worked as a marketing director in the music industry. Prior to that, he worked as a marketer in the staffing industry and as a freelancer marketer, musician, writer, and designer. He is a B.A. in English from SUNY.

I give him a straight proposal to join our group when we make our performances in the churches. I put money to his hand and say: "Here are 100 000 d, half now, rest when you join the group. Take it or live it." He is in. After a while, we go out from the door where reads: "Persons of all sexual orientations and gender identities are embraced, and their relationships are affirmed and blessed."

We go to the 9:00-Mass. The atmosphere is peaceful and intimate. There is a lot of music and hymn, and I here MyVictoria´s beautiful voice. I look at dancing programs, just classics, and jazz, so old. But the message is beautiful and more beautiful: dance heightens the senses, there are the forms of the refreshing and renewing waters of creation, descent in the form of a dove at baptism, and the Pentecost gift of Our Smiling Friend, the Holy Spirit.

Time is 10:00. I look at movie ads and there is the film *Hobbs And Shaw*, yeah, that is good refreshing to this day. Anyway, we go to Washington Square Park.

You say: "What did y talk about?" I think: "Well, James said that he is a good manager. He does goals and makes sure that Im attaching a timeline 90-day plan. That helps me create a more targeted and attack. He said he helps me write an elevator pitch, register for a conference, introduce myself to other local business owners, plan a local business workshop, join my local chamber of commerce, rent a booth at a trade show."

Y: "That sounds very far from faith & so." I: Well, it depends on the angel-angle. He asks me to launch a multipiece direct mail campaign, call to action on every direction, use tear cards, inserts, props, and attention-getting envelopes to make an impact, send past customers free samples, advertise on the radio, a billboard, ad on a local TV station, face, linked, buy ad space on the websites, use a sidewalk sign to promote your specials, set up a Foursquare account for your business, create an editorial calendar. He ordered me to use SEO, start a pay-per-click campaign using Google Awards and Face ads, do google analytics every hour, track my online reputation, sign up for the HARO, offer a free download of free gift to entice people, start a free email newsletter, do a segmenting the list, perfect my email signature, add audio, video, and social sharing functionality to my emails, start a contest, create a coupon, a frequent buyer rewards program, start a client appreciation and a brand ambassador program, create a customer of the day program, give away a free sample, start an affiliate program, send out a customer satisfaction survey, ask for referrals, make a referral, help promote or volunteer my time for a charity event, sponsor a local sports team, cross-promote my products and services with other local businesses, joint a professional organization, plan my next holiday promotion, plan holiday gifts for your best customers, send birthday cards to your clients, approach a colleague about a joint venture, donate branded prizes for local fundraisers, become a mentor, plan a free teleconference or webinar, record a podcast, write a press release, repurpose my contes to share in other places, use the audio from the video on a podcast, rewrite my sales copy with a storytelling spin, self-publish a book, hire a marketing consultant, hire a public relations professional, hire a professional copywriter, hire a search engine marketing firm, an intern and virtual assistant, and do not use marketing tool, cos then everybody sees you are on a tight budget.

Then he just smiled and asked me to get a branded tattoo, create a business mascot to help promote my brand, take a controversial stance on a hot industry topic, pay for branded wearable items, get a full-body branded paint job done on my company vehicle, sign up for online business training, and fine-tune my marketing plan. Then he shook my hand."

I continue: "If you do your job 24/7/365/5, then it is shall be a good thing. We all know that marketing attracts prospects, prospects become buyers, and they provide profit. So just target market. Just business cards, and materials should be transferred to online resources. That is called success. But networking must mean more than tactics. It must be handled with operational art. Then it comes to scale winning strategy.

Direct mail isn´t an expense when you have a targeted list. Ads are the bullets. The marketing strategy is the artillery. No use to make one strategy plan, and put it on the net, then it is not a strategy, it is the cheapest ad.

The strategic plan is always with relationships and trust, forms and math, and strategic plans are free, easy, and fun, and overwhelming. Uploading an appropriate picture means more than a log. It means a brand image. Create your sprout social and marketing ninjas, and add the Hootlet, RSS Feedly AllTop. There are wain laws about give ways and contests. These are all small business things.

They want to develop name recognition like the biggest advertisers, but their ads must do double-double-double duty. On the other hand, we look at big objectives, play the long game. The planning must take three to six months. That planning must be big, cos it includes an indication of the money and resources required. Fuck with a feast or famine mentality, do not get nervous about sales, money finds our hands before or later. Big boys do not believe in the ad hoc approach, there are laws like everywhere in Nature.

Market laws are laws of Nature. Do not catch easily affordable. Which means social media, blogging, and email. Small boys put lots of time into creating fabulous marketing content, but do not see the target. There is leverage in the halo effect. The big business thinks which existing products are doing well, which are under-performing compared to the potential, where there are new opportunities worth investing in.

Strong brand messages make your day and the business grows by virtue of the halo effect. And with the main point, there is a global, social experiment, which means hospitality, open knowledge, sharing the data is the best marketing. Sponsorship spending is unpredictable, but partnership helps the brand capture the attention of a global audience. Keep on running with different cultural preferences and styles. And put together global & local = glocal."

Money asks me to leave the desktop site and open amazon on my phone cos the phone had built-in accessibility features. Money does not care about me. Money just wants me to use the mobile device instead of making money´s web experience accessible.

Farmer

Now I must go to Mr. Farmer of Tech Office and try to unit mornings blessings and dance with afternoon´s music of reason.

I go to the Tech Office. Time is 13:48. I go to the Mayor´s Office to meet the new Chief Technology Officer. An officer leads me into CTO J.P. Farmer. He sits in his office, and I tell him about Tech help to the IOB-project for next summer.

He has manners: "Please, sit down. You well know my former employer Microsoft´s director of Technology and Civic Innovation has done so many last months with the quantum computer. Microsoft is building a better qubit. The new approach to quantum computing is very close. Here is a part of topological qubits. The company is almost ready to put them use after five years of hard work. The quantum computer works when chilled to a tiny fraction of a degree above absolute zero - colder than outer space - so you do not have a quantum laptop anytime soon. But fertilizer can be made more efficiently. There are superposition and entanglement. There is that refrigerated container the size of a 55-gallon drum. These qubits work nowadays just a fraction of a second.

Well, here are the papers ready to sign. You shall have two agencies, one in London and another in Milan. And agents you shall have 14, for

4 months. They shall take care of tech things with states and magistrates and enterprises. I shall personally control the whole operation here, and we are connected by these smartphones. I shall contact you every fifteen days. The money shall be in your bank account tomorrow at 9 am."

So many big words put in so little space. We shake hands. The appointment has last 7½ minutes. I laugh and whistle when I go out. Strategy designs the whole information of reserves and surprise, so capital and winning deals, operational art, so schedule and parts of it in time and place, and tactical fire and motion, so cash flow and profits, are totally unknown to them. I must make deals with Book Towns officials and make cories fast.

Operational calls

It is 3 am, which means 5 hours more in London. So jolly-good fellas have their evening tea. I call to Sweden: antique store, printing houses, authors, galleries, hotel Bed & Breakfast, four shops. I inform them about our coming, give the date. Then I call IOB´s president who is from Borrby. I tell her the same. Then I call to Borrby´s Media, Bild & Film, Bookhouse, and then I begin to make those main calls to landlords.

Mostly they speak Sweden, German and English, so no problem. But the problem is that although the houses are very clean and winter prove, they do not look stylize. Villages are full of these kinds of houses for sale, and they are about 200 000 euros. Nearby are good restaurants, cafés, and "most stunning nature". There are food shops near the house. There are the white sand beaches that stretch for miles, just five minutes for the house (by car). There are golf courses, horseback riding tours, trolling and ocean trout fishing attract enthusiasts, gardening, health/SPA, bicycling and nature experiences, there are fairs and harvest festivals, picnics on the beach, visits to the old towns and other villages, walking hikes and scatterings.

I make a preliminary agreement with 15 entrepreneurs about season exchanges and about winter bookings. They promise to advertise my places in Finland, and I do the same in their places. Ads go 50/50 %. There are 1 500 bed places and I have 450, but this is good advertising, cos I'm the first that makes these deals with them. I inform my own book town.

Now I have done the nearest book towns, 43 more to go. I take a break and eat some ice-cream. It is their European time 21:30 am. I begin to call business-fellas and ask them to make contacts with the NYC Tech Office.

I call one fella whose father has been a general in the army. He is a Master of Science of Technology, and experienced senior manager, head of customer engagement, head of online sales, head of sales development, global head of sales, head of interactive experience and his special skill are telecommuting industry, ICT management, e-commerce, sales & channel development, sales management and sales operations, strategic account management and strategy and business development.

I tell him: "From NYC come four agents to help you with digitalization shortens business cycles and the operating environment, sales, finance, ICT, supply chain, service operations, etc. With them, you can help Book Towns businesses do the quicker the changes, operating models, processes, tech and data, vendor selection and management, transformation execution, performance improvements, and cost savings. But there are just 5 and you have 50 so not much help, but they connect you to the four months festival and performance tour and its net."

Silence. Then Mr. Salo says: "Yeah, piece of cake. How about you, Tapio, do you still play football in that team. I haven't played in four years. I do 90 hours a week and no holidays, but this business has just 50 workers, a small firm, just 10 million euros in sales. When I was in Nokia, huh, huh. Well, I must also go like you to foreign countries. How is your life?" I say: "I fell in love and have had some action here in multinational Brooklyn. I have felt this as a holiday. Tell my regards to your beautiful wife."

The Coronavirus has come to NYC & Other Happenings

Time is 16:00. And at the same time, the first coronavirus case has identified in NYC. Under 40-year old individual is at Bellevue Hospital Center. He presents with fever, cough, and shortness of breath without having the flu or a cold virus. There are eight confirmed cases in the U.S. NYC mayor and other not straight authorities in NY say, they are taking every precaution necessary to ensure residents are protected against the 2019 novel coronavirus.

The NYSD of Health has sent samples form 11 individuals to the CDC for testing. They say: "While imported cases of coronavirus have been detected in the U.S., the virus is NOT currently spreading through communities." The State Health officials say they are working with local physicians and the CDC on testing potential cases. The state has put out advisories to physicians. Anyone who has traveled to China and has those symptoms should seek medical care. Symptoms appear in as few as two days. They say: "We encourage New Yorkers to regular hand washing and avoiding close contact with people who are sick. 4. Most coronaviruses cause the common cold and a fever. Then SARS and MERS. Officials recommend people to stay home. 5. New Yorkers should worry more about the flu. There is just influenza, NY has seen 72 385 confirmed cases, and just three children have died. Cov. Andres Cuomo laughs: "I want to remind New Yorkers that it is much more likely that they will be exposed to influenza than to the coronavirus. So, relax. Take basis precautions against the flu, then you avoid the novel coronavirus."

At the same time, the Mayor's home project goes on. Five new homes foreclosed in The Queens Area. The ad says: "Don't lose hope. You are trying to buy a new house, but don't wanna break the bank? Here is a solution to you: in the Jamaica area (near Cliver's Makks Brims headquarter) are with 2 beds and 2 baths for just 300 000 d, and think, another in the Queens Village area with 4 beds and 2 baths, ridiculous, for 325 000 d." In Europe, Y get 500 square meters house with a pool and a lot of sunshine and gardens with that sum.

Sorry, the coronavirus information was fake: not one but three cases. No. 1 is in Flushing Hospital Medical Center, no. 2 in NY Presbyterian Queens, and no.3 in Bellevue. New cases concern two over 60-year-old persons. So just three, no need to worry about. And we all die anyway.

What's up more in negative murmur-front?

One New Yorker is penny-pinching but needs to move, and a mutual friend has a room in their loft for 700/800 d. He stays there for 3 nights. The bites are so bad that he has around 50+ after the first 2 nights. Other fella sees how his neighbors pour the urine from the window into the backyard; they have no time to go to the bathroom. Other fella's area in heavy rain it will flood knee-deep. He grabs the 5-gallon bucket kept on the roof for this purpose. Other fella´s roof caves in, no heat, the room always cold in there winter, mice, roaches. One Lady has a super cheap ground floor apartment. It is above the back entrance to the building, bordered the last hole of a golf course. The roaches are the size of her palm. The bathroom ceiling will randomly grip/leak yellowish liquid. She calls the supers, who steal from her. They repair things by making a hole in the wall. Another lady has in an indoor treehouse of a loft room, in the MC Lofts. She pays 500 d a month for a room that is about 8x10´, 5´ ceilings, and a plywood floor with holes in it big enough to see into the bedroom of the person below it. It has no door, just an opening with a cloth over it, which y reached by climbing about 10´ up a homemade ladder made of 2 x 4 s. She has lived there two weeks when the state housing inspector comes around and says: "Hey, you, this room shall be demolished tomorrow."

But New Yorkers do not give up.

They make complete lists of the repairs: what they like to spend and what they are willing to spend. New Yorkers call local handyman contractors. They read HomeAdvisor. New Yorkers check that handymen carry liability insurance and the certifications or licenses necessary in your state. But many do not care that it is illegal to hire an unlicensed handyman for home improvement projects values at 500 d or more.

New Yorkers get everything in writing, a flat rate per task, or an hourly rate. So, install a sink faucet ridiculous 150 d, install a garbage disposal, same, clear a clogged drain, 290 d, a new toilet, just 150 d, hang a ceiling fan, 250 d, install a window air conditioner, 275 d, hand a light fixture, 350 d, mount a TV on the wall, 300 d, a small painting project, 670 d, repair trim, 605 d, install childproofing devices, 440 d, clean gutters, cost 150 d, weather stripping, 250 d, The handymen tell you also how to keep rodents out this winter, how much it really cost to install radiant heating, how to prevent dryer fires, and how much-frozen pipes cost you.

At the same time, Kew Gardens four corrections officers get insures, cos in Queens-jail Dub City (YBZ)-warriors attack cellmates, SHB-Skrilla Hill Boys Aka FDS- from Da Skrilla M. They call this smoothly Queens Detention Complex attacks cellmates, put up a fight when the four corrections officers intervened. One of them is head-butted while another officer tries to stop the fight my pepper, spraying the detainees. Prison bottom surprises beat the official over their shoulders, and on da outs, a warrior is happy and so is the Department of Corrections press secretary Jason Kersten, he says: "The Safety and well-being of all DOC personnel and those in our custody is our top priority." Three corrections officers and one captain go to a nearby hospital with so minor injuries. And happy cellmates, just one of them is hospitalized. The jail shall have a modern facility with space for community programming. The pumpkins suits must be kept happy in those prisons.

Sorry for the wrong announcement: coronavirus has invited 5 New Yorkers. They are under 40 and have just come from China. The Health Department doesn´t wanna say in what hospital these new patients are. "It is not necessary data", as the words go. While I am traveling home to 30s Mayor de Glasio says: "New York City is on high alert and prepared to handle any confirmed cases of the novel coronavirus." He tries to look not cared and fails and says in his fried hardstyle: "My message to dear New Yorkers remains: if you have had the travel history and, hm, are exhibiting so-called symptoms, please go and see your health provider immediately. Worldwide there are only 20 000 coronavirus cases."

Some Business Calls

I come home. I open the door and: "Hello, MyVictoria!" We kiss. Y: "So any news?" I: "Well, much. I have phoned and shall make deals more. Wanna hear?"

I start with the Centro del Bel Libro Ascona, the leading institute for advanced education: "Hey, Suzanne, how is your day, Still using the medium of the paper form and paper restoration. What are the current scientific developments and tech skills?"

I tell MyVictoria that this city is a popular tourist destination although there is that stick in the mud jazz festival. I show her via HoloLens the unique plot in Acona with a private beach on the lake called Maggiore: "Look Nab, this is also expensive, think 4,436 191 USD. Well, with a view that has no equal. But it is a semi-detached villa in the Bauhaus style of architect Weidermeyer. The house has a gorgeous library, as they always have, with a period fireplace. I must say very beautiful parquet and terracotta floors. Flat, easy-handling garden and excellent sunny position. A private path allows for easy access from the garages to the house. They call these houses ´Modern´. Yes, they were modern 90 years ago, when the word ´modern´ was used. There are also mobs."

I call Becherel, Vila del Libre. I talk this and that and make a deal about the exchange of visitors. I say to Y: "Well, just peasant houses, and unbelievable prices, 500 000 d." Y laugh: "Those old-fashioned boxes and the furniture."

Bilar the same, and the Bredevoort, and Clunes. Near your favorite castle is Damme. I talk with one book town person: "The Burgundian dining place is the best. Do you still have those bistros? The microbreweries have developed really delicious beers with special ingredients." In the rear rooms, pastry chefs work every day to bring the tastiest desserts to the table. The place is full of cozy terraces and ice farms. But very old-fashioned and heavy, bad colors. Ennistymon has the same problem, old and 70s. orange and red - colors. And they call it inspiration & delightful. I talk with some novelists, poets, and non-fiction writers, and then I so Y some houses for sale.

I jump over Featherson, nearby Fjaerland. And then, at last, I call Hay-on-Wye. That is something else. Not just villas and little manors but Hay-on-Wye-castle: "Here, Bab, we are always welcome. The fella who owned this has here his own kingdom, and he had very near connections with NYC-business world, Oxford-fella, real gentleman, and rich in mental capital."

I was then a very young and he invites me to his Hay House of Lords. He organized his festivals in Hay, The Maldives, Mexico, Cape Town. U.S. presidents like to visit his festivals. There are 10 other festivals and shows in town. The population in this "town" is 1 500, but there come, visitors, about 250 000 people, in those festivals. And that fella founded those festivals around a kitchen table. And the twinned his "town" with Saudi-Arabian town and with Timbuktu in Mali, a Muslim holy place.

He said to me: "I bought books in bulk and sold them as fuel." His sponsors came from NYC and there was that real start."

A Blood-Signed Deal

Phone rings. There is Cliver: "Come, quickly Tapio." I axe: "Do Y know where you? OK, Frost St, Br Steel. I fly."

Time is 21 am. After fifteen minutes I hear shooting in front of that Steel. The shooting comes from the parking area. I take My Taurus. This is the 94th Precinct and Bundle Boys area.

I run. I see 5 warriors shooting to one white truck. One of them sees me. I shoot at his leg. The other fella turns, and I shoot to his leg. I take more bullets. Left whistles a bullet and makes a scratch to my hand. I shoot directly to that directions.

Cliver´s head arrives behind that white bro truck: "Tapio, mobs have made a deal with you, but they haven´t done a deal with me. They have bought Bundles. And some other guns, for instance, South Side Bullies and Boss City Bomb Gang to do their job. Queens of the Stone Age and Dang Kids are after you." I wonder: "Who told you?" Cliver shows near lying fella: "This yes-man." I ask: "And which family?" Cliver: "They are street boss Andy Mush Russo´s orders to consigliere Tom Mix Farese. Joseph Amato, Teddy Persico, and Billy Russo." I dragon breath.

I look at the Brooklyn map, which comes to my mobile moment. Well, somewhere between State Island and Brooklyn they are hanging around right now doing money laundering, racketeering, illegal gambling and extortion, and loansharking charges. Cliver laughs: "I know where they are knocking about: Ramona, Franklin St." I: "Let´s go."

Cliver: "Just we? We may get to crossfire. No planning, just like that?"
I: "Ye, no lollygagging." The Mustang stops tires howling. Cliver the Gunrunner jumps from the car. We blow the sprinkles off the cupcake.

Their reads "a woman´s drink is out now", and it looks very noice. After 1 ½ hour, there shall be a private party with 68 persons, filming, photoshoots, press, and that kind of ramonabarnyc.com-things.

Well, that was the idea before Cliver & I arrived. That long bar table doesn´t interest us at all. There sit some gas cookers, or vid making porn stars, who cost 100 d for a round-the-world, and their kills who shall soon lose their money to pay the box for hire. We go forward while small fellas make deals with incredibly hot chicks, who are self-employed models, and so interested in those zeroes. So only a Blind could ask how chicks can be interested in those guys. We run upstairs. Three guards notice us. They try to take their fofos from the pockets. One of them has a 44.

I throw some hobknockers outto my way. Cliver runs behind. Five mobs stand in front of me. Andy & Billy Russo are behind them. On the steps are coming more mobs, but Cliver smokes there and I smoke here and lay hands on one fattie. Billy´s cal is on me, but I kick it from his hand. Those steps-fellas are left. Two of them beat Cliver. I do two-piece and a biscuit.

I take a knife from my pocket. I take Bill`s hand and make there a wound. The warm blood is flowing on the table. I take a pencil and write with the blood a letter on the table. There reads: "If I or my brother or somebody else in Our Family shall break the common deal of Family´s with Tapio and his Book Towns Group, I shall personally tell who that traitor is and shall punish him with death. With this deal, I honor the common cause of 5-families. And if I break this deal, which

I send now to Gambino capo, the punishment shall be also the death. Signed Bill Russo & Andy Russo & Tapio Tiihonen."

I took the blood signs also from Andy and myself. Then I phone to Big D Cefalu, first cousin to Boss Domico Cefalu: "Hello, here it Tapio, I have here with me Andy & Bill Russo. They have something to tell Y. Please wait for a moment." I give the phone to Andy. He looks grey as a ghost, then he tells about our deal, and then Billy confirms on his side everything. Now, these fellas are loose cannons. I show them some pictures from Montereggio and say: "This castle here shall be your suite next summer. Your Italian cousins shall make the reservation for happy you. Then I shall show you my new castle in Burgundy and tell you about our festivals."

No hug and hold but I blew my spiritual load all over the desk. We go away with Cliver.

My Luxury is Your Happiness

I call you: "I shall be there soon."

You say: "What have Y done?" I: "Nothing much. Some deal signing. I shall show you some more things from Book Towns." We put holo lenses again on.

I: "Here is something that Y cannot miss. It is Your VictoriaCourt, Bab. Y like a luxury, and my luxury in your happiness. So here Y have it and clean lake, which water Y can drink, tech married with pure nature, heh, hee. This a must to Y & me. Park-garden makes y smile and I cannot see anything if we think about air pumps, floor heating, electric and wooden saunas, showers, gym, library, kitchens, glassed terrace and doors, 72 windows, lights all around the house, and flower terraces, 8 meters height, what Y do love. It is designed with care & love, and Our Smiling Friend put it just where it belongs.

If the French fill needs much updating this does not. And Y can go via private plain, from the castle to VictoriaCourt in 1 ½ hour. So VictoriaCourt is a summer paradise."

I show more Y more: "This is a typical cottage. It has a Jacuzzi. There are tens like that. So not so much elegance. Just warm and cozy. People from Switzerland like that place. Hm. It resembles their own mountain cottages.

Think Bab, this house in Bowral costs 1 890 000 euros, so more than your castle. They rob people. They put together a garage and get 1 231 sq., they just know how to cheat.

Fjaerland is so beautiful panoramas, but houses are small. Why didn´t they built houses that are worthy of that Nature?

Fjaerland´s cottages are designed for fishing, fjord, swimming (cold glacier water), trout fishing (in the river 50 meters away), and hiking in the forest."

We go through those Fjaerland things, even the mountain, and the glacier. I say: "You, Bab, can relax on the spacious terraces. And there are many interesting excursion destinations in the surrounding areas.

Heh, heh, trips to the Glacier Museum, Astruptunet in Jolster, and the Sunnfjord Museum. And just 35 km away."

Y look at me: "I do not begin to walk in that cold mountain in no circumstances." I: "A-ok. How about Megutama. No. Well, Kolkata, India. Now, too bad water and those diseases. You are right. Montereggio has some houses for sale. Well, yeah, they are

something, real like insane clown posse. Just a word guindy´d. There is a nest box designed to suit for starling: 65 000 euros. Next.

Look at this in South-Korea. Gyeonggi-do, 15 595,35 square meters: 31 028 199 USD. Top modern glazed skyscraper, it's awesome. Cos of North-Korea they keep the exact address not available, but I can contact a CENTURY 21 agent for assistance. Tvedestrand has very mint and clean houses, but they are quite small. For instance, Hoyenhall-Gjennomgående 66 square meter thing costs 451 805 euros. They found oil and become arrogant. Almost like New Yorkers.

Think. Bab, that room is the biggest in the house. I have only one example left. This villa in Wünsdorf has 12 rooms including 4 bedrooms and 4 bathrooms. And the price is 695 000 euros. These people know their price, which nobody else understands. They must have born in arrogant shoes on.

France is number one, and then comes Spain. Northern countries have better warming systems, but I do not count on that. And I just love those foods in Spain, and France has its cheeses. And Germans beer and beef. Well, I begin now to contact those sponsors in northern countries.

I tell Y a secret: "Look at the house and you know enough about its master/mistress. Somebody says that the house is made of bricks and beams, but I say that in the real house love resides, memories are created, friends always belong, and laugher never dies."

You say: "One thing is true. All roads around the world lead to my castle."

Some places just shelter daydreaming, protect the dreamer, and allows some lazy character to dream in deep peace, others decorate their house for themselves, others feel a place itself, in your body, rerouting blood vessels, throbbing right alongside the mighty heart. On somebody's house lives harmony and symmetry along with chaos and storm, happily married ever after.

It is coming near 24:00. I tell Y quickly before we go to sleep: "So now I call to those book towns and ask their sponsorship. And there comes in picture those gang-boys and SEALs. They kick European doflinkies and porch monkies to their ass. I shall fly tomorrow to Europe with Clay, Frank, some seals & mobs. You shall see, if Y come too, how the things shall be done.

There come two mobs, two SEALs, Frank. Cliver, Bob, CooCoo, Clour, Y & M. No nerds, no pole-stripers. It is just a dealer's dozen, big gulp and I do not mean legendary drink from 7-Eleven. Tomorrow we shall go to the military airport and fly to Paris. Then Y & M shall go to your castle, I buy it and acquired servants, update-workers, and gardeners. Perhaps we shall go and meet some Foreign Legion veterans who live nearby Provence, that in the heart of the areas where knighthood was born in Charles the Great times. We shall live at 7 pm, be there at 2 am. Does it suit Y, MyVictoria?"

Y look at me: "Go to shoot some murskers & m.b.c's. If you cannot handle things, I shall begin to think that I'm wasting my time and RUN."

The Thirteenth Day

Catch the Plain and be Happy

Life goes Fast on while We sleep

I call one Wünsdorf-fella, called Herr Hauptmann: "*Guten Tag, Mein Name ist Tapio Tiihonen, Wir müssen uns Treffen. Ja, du und mich, Ich sitz´ ganz hinten, wie jedes Mal wie eine alte Truhe auf ei´m Rollbret in Liegen rutscht der Bus lansam ins Tal ... Ja*, here is Tapio, and I wanna see you snart-soon. Do you understand at all?"

He is my army-fella from Afghanistan. One general ordered him to join his mercenaries after Busch-war. Salary for one month: 80 000 d. Herr Hauptmann said: "Sorry, not interested."

I ask: "I wanna Y at Paris airport at 2 am tomorrow. It shall be great, get ventilated. No need to look old faces all the time. Frank & David are there too." Herr Hauptman alias Roger says; "*Sehr gut. Es geht weiter*. 2 am."

I make another call: "Hey Cliver, still living, what's good, anyway we shall leave tomorrow and 11 am. Are Y ready, take CooCoo & Clur. Yeh, H-d - So-Brooklyn-n.i.g.g.e.r."

Meanwhile, we are sleeping, Jamil Jones, a basketball coach from North Carolina, drives to his Long Island City hotel when Sandor Szabo hit his rear window, thinking the car is his Uber ride. Jones gets out of his car and hit Szabo once into the face, gets back to his vehicle and drives away. Szabo dies.

At the same time, some paramour/gas cooker lovers try desperately to find candles, couples´ cookbooks, jewelry, bubble bath, and more perfectly priced presents for those ladies of their lives. Valentine´s day is on the door and those lazy paramours try to find the right place. They ask everywhere jewelry and luxurious bubble bath to fresh flowers and stylish socks, these Valentine´s Day gifts sure to please. Their mind says and keeps on saying: "Happy shopping, and Happy Valentine´s Day!"

One of those lost minds says to another paramour: "Oh, all prices and savings listed in these posts are as of publication and could change. The patch may earn a commission on some purchased items. Oh, I almost cry, Saphora is cynical to me, and cannot stand it anymore." Another fella asks: "Why do not Y change from ladies to the gentlemen, as I did, my best 2020 Valentine´s Days gifts for men are awesome." They agree that they must buy moe cards, gifts toys, and candies for their loved ones. But these fellas are heroes compared with homes, cos NYC is among the more dangerous states to date online. Just take http://HighSpeedInternet.com and you might be dead. Almost as risky as to log into Tinder, OkCupid, Grindr, or Hinge. In NYC they hit first and ask second, if at all. Money is time.

There are over 18 124 internet crime victims. Much chlamydia and syphilis as well as gonorrhea. If You wanna be an online-dater-safety do not come to NYC or Alaska. Go to Maine. Lovers give full name, tell their jobs, meet in private places, walk to date, use their Facebook and Instagram photos on their dating profile, do not have pepper spray, let golddigger walk your home on your first day. Then Valentine´s Day is just for Y, you snatch monkey bitch.

This tolerance, diversity, and progressivism hookas shall offer blue-eyed warm-hearted fuck***ers.

Meanwhile, a Southside-warrior opens fire in the 41st Precinct on Longwood Avenue in the Bronx hitting a lieutenant at his desk. He had shoot two hours earlier two other officers. These two suffered also gunshot wounds but are expected to make a full recovery. None of the officers returned fire. Bozz-named warrior tries to escape but his neighbors take him into custody. Bozz has just a 9-millimeter gun. They ask him: "Why?" Bozz laughs: "I wanna talk with police before opening fire." Donald Trump wakes up, he tweets: "I grew up in NYC. Now, cos of Governor & Mayor, this stands away regulations, and lack of support, our wonderful NYC police are under assault."

Meanwhile in Queens, some owners design to sell their little houses with 3 beds and I bath 450 000 d. With that price, you get half a castle in Europe instead of these little boxes.

My Melancholy Baby -34

I wake up at 3 am. I have nothing to think about. Everything is fine. I just killed some people and have two-week fought here and there in NYC. So common to me, except this is not a warzone, this a civil-zone, and everything must be aight. Why do I feel rejected and helpless and alone, when everything is foin? I put on old doo-wop to the DVD: Vince Castro - Bong Bong - Killer NYC Doo Wop. Then Flemons and The Newcomers - Here I Stand - Fantastic Uptempo Late 50´s Doo Wop. Why I feel I wanna rob a bank, reservoir dog, yeah, oh my god! They killed Kenny! I put jeans on and go to the street.

An old bum hangs there near the corner. I go to him: "Hey Y, what kind of music y like, not angels and airwaves?" He: "My fav y ask? He was killed in WW2. What a loving and happy singer, a very talented crooner. Love y Al." I: "What? That London -34 thing was great." I look around and he old pupa isn´t there anymore. Well, I come back to the department. And look out of the window. I´m totally relaxed and give my pillow some head.

The Birdy

It is almost 8 am. I do not often miss opportunity cos it´s dressed in overalls and looks like work. My free time is my work, no time for jerk´n spurt. You are there, and doggy jumps to my lap. I say: "Time to call Frank, we must have a private military plain."

You think: "It isn´t cheap to fly." I agree: "They go every day to Europe and they sometimes take hear full cargo and go back empty-handed. If we are lucky, they take us almost free there." Y: "But what about orders?" I: "What orders? They are made just to keep the curious looks away. When we fight, there is chaos, and it and laws sleep together. Y must learn to think about how laws communicate together. So simplisticated. Real Patric Cunningham & R & R. So, we are going to a cargoplain. No need to think artistic, beautiful, coincided about beauty, dress attire on fleek."

I say that now we are going to France: "*Jeune et gente, souce, riviere d´onneur et de joyeuse chiere, qui font en vous beulté florir, vous estes ma dame premiere, qui m´amour avez toute entiere.*"

I call Frank: "Heysh, any mile-high club membership ready?" Frank: "Aye, the Mexican national bird blocks rockin´ beats. Catch you on the flip." I: "Take my cat, catch you on the flip side, sys." You look at me: "Sope?" I: "Let´s go buy a sizzel and smoke a bizzel." I take your hand and we run, to my Mustang. We go to Stew International. 60 miles to drive. There are the birds G-17 Globemaster III, VMGR-452, and KC-130T.

I hope I can choose. Lockheed Martin is my choice, cos it´s the tanker from C-130-Herc. KC is a multi-role, multi-mission thing. We go military port right away. I drive in. I see in front of me a bomber from WW2. Why do they show these things which destroyed so many cities, railways, bridges in Europe? There are some tourists sightseeing military birds and AF Form 341, and I wait to see Dirtbag DBA (no regard for regulations, dress & appearance, customs & courtesies), and there is DFAC.

Jammer-Load Toad goes there and BRRRRRRRRT. Frank comes and we shake hands and he kisses the air on your beautiful hand, and there comes Mr. First Shirt smiling happily. He says: "Let´s go to operation more than Golden Flow." I must confess, I'm a little bit nervous, do they give us KC or Globemaster. I stop the Mustang and we go to the jammer. And there is JP-8, which smells like freedom.

There isn´t 0-6, but anyway, Frank has beer and jammer LOX to cool the beer. He looks at me like IYAAYAS, who always thinks that if y ain´t ammo, y ain´t shit. And there goes staff sergeant, you know somebody who carries a litter and a backboard from a UH-60 Black Hawk helicopter to extract a simulated patient during a medical evacuation mission as part of a field training exercise for chemical, biological, radiological, nuclear, and high-yield explosive consequence management forces designed to improve their ability to respond to catastrophic incidents.

And everything is so army proof, y foolproof, as airmen lord their higher ASVAB score requirements over the army, and every time a grunt says chair force, an air force PJ gains one of their IQ points. And I do not say more from the fellas who think they are mighty. And the ticket fella spirit high flies: "Hey, I departed at 20 000 feet, it was a real e-ticket ride!"

There is the Globemaster, high & swaggasaurus rex. That birdy is just 53 m long and wingspan 52 m. We have on nice cargo-space, just 27 m. This birdy is so fat and cute. And 105th Airlift can lift it. I drive my Mustang up. There has been some time ago the U.S. Presidential Limousine so why not my black beauty also. And the RAF loves the birdy, and the RAAF, The DART, The IAF.

There is a long table also. And amplifiers. I say heya to CooCoo, and Clur, who had just arrived. I call to Paris: "*Comment allez-vous? Comment vas-tu? Oui. Merci.* 1400." Soon there are SEALs, gang2, Frank, Me, Cliver, Y, mob2.

The plain begins to roll.

The Speeches

We sit at the table. I look at you all: "Victoria, Gentlemen, thank you all for coming to-day to share in our celebrations for European Brooklyzination.

You have a challenging and very, very vital role to play in improving the educational, cultural, and developing performance of our Book Towns Group. To me, it is important to celebrate milestones. It is as much to recognize the journey that you have been on as it is to give the remarkable opportunity to set new goals for the future.

We have been very fortunate throughout this period to have a tremendous Board of Trustees to guide us and to-day would be an appropriate occasion for me to express my personal thanks to them for all that they have done for us.

Equally, I would like to acknowledge the work of the incredible team that we have at the Foundation. This change enables the Foundation to focus totally its efforts on the role of being the outboard motor for developing new modern tech ideas that will be available to colleges to support the journey of transformation and update Book Towns that we are on.

The experiences I have been through over the past fifteen days have been very special and a real privilege to have been a part of. There is a team working (the sill of promoting the interest of a common cause), problem-solving (the ability to express and interpret challenges), creativity (looking at things in a new way with a solution in mind), risk-taking (not being afraid to try something new or to do something differently), and passion (the drive to achieve and succeed whatever it takes).

Book Towns businesses will be started in local enterprise hubs and flourish to become large local net, connected with a current agenda of Brooklyn life and formal education. The BREXIT is not a big deal, but with this, we can make it so."

Bob says something: "My Friends, remember that when we attack Europe our original work, literary, scientific, such as poems, articles, films, songs or sculptures, we are protected by copyright. Nobody apart from us has the right to make the work public or reproduce it. In the EU copyright protects our intellectual property until 70 years. Outside the EU only 50 years. We must make deals there.

We have there guaranteeing control over our work and remuneration for its use through selling or licensing, and we are authors. So as the dancing training, festival production had begun we have copyright.

That gives us more sales and focus on concept marketing. And cos Book Towns Groups is a business in a European country with no problem with a single European brand name. Then you have a deal with my bank and NYC and Brooklyn companies, but Tapio you can transfer your registered office wherever you like in Europe without having dissolved the company. It is very wise to have lawyers and bankers in many European countries to go where the taxation is best for Y. Those lawyers, bankers, our team are your framework system for involving staff. They attack and give you sponsors.

Namely, your registered office and head office must be in the same EU country, I take care of that. Your presence in other EU countries must be a must. Those companies involved need to be governed by the laws of at least two different EU countries. That is much harder than the U.S., but I can curve that problem, so no big a challenge. I give there more than 120 000 capital which is the minimum, and I take care of employees who work in your company, cos they insist on employees being part. I shall be there via my bank credit or financial institution and my decoy shall be the Fund. Then I handle winding up, liquidation, insolvency, and cessation of payments.

And I love to play a game called rules for European companies in each country. I take care of authorities you need to liaise with or what arrangements on employee participation. And I take care VAT does not charge on exports of goods to countries, cos goods I make to come outside the EU. I put some agents to prove that the goods are transported outside the EU. I handle Vat rules in a single country. I laugh at standard, reduced, and special rates. I put your taxes to parent companies and subsidiaries, so the EU never finds your real company tax.

I take care of Brkners and other working hours, holiday and leave, transport sector workers, posted workers, social security and health, equal treatment, and qualifications. And ofc accounting, making and receiving payments, getting funding. I take care of data protection, solving disputes with customers.

I have been working many years in Sephora and Amazon, so I know how to cheat and make fun with customers. I collect an alternative dispute resolution team, which makes fun with all contractual disputes, like effective, fair, impartial, independent, and transparent things.

I go to the COSME digitalization questionnaire and EIF portal. I use customers' personal data to make a profit to the company and there are articles like 2018/1725, 201/1046, the Commission Files Retention list SEC 713, they are pure madness, I bluff them all. And I contact a lobby group called The Confederation of European Business."

Frank says something: "We SEALs are 100 % behind you. We make those operational centers and take care of security and communications. We shall make a good command & control system there, and we shall beat whoever you want us to beat. Those democrats said that we raped and drank while deployed, and they investigate those things.

Air Force Maj. Gen. Eric Hill talks about a perceived deterioration of good order and discipline, and they sent 19 SEALs and four support troops home. But we are coming back, Mr. Hill. Democrats talk about clandestine, often violent missions, and they do not really know how right they are, cos we think it as a positive way. They write about a systemic problem, an issue, but we just kill enemies, nothing else. We care about P. Murphy and Matthew Axelson and brothers, who were killed in action. Were enduring freedom, morning glory, and inherent resolve shit? Here are brothers from 4,7, 10 seals. And look at MP5s. They are effective, as leapfrog.

We help you making those Found and taxation and foundation maneuvers. We put control-system with clear communication of intent and simple plans. We strike to other companies' critical vulnerability and bend the enemy to our will. The idea of the 70 % solution is fine. OODA Loop & BAMCIS. We are bros in METT-TC-, FMLCOA-, EXP-, SOM-, FSP- tasks. We are a 100 % TBS-C2-1003 subordinate unit. We love communications, written oral, or by signal and we make the night a day. We materialize the banker-Bob's decision, make the order, or prepare for execution shine. We govern all by the will.

Bob, we use mission tactics and speed is the essence of our war. A good plan violently executed now is better than a perfect plan executed next week. Speed is more important than tech. We honor SMEAC. Support units must have location, contact, direct and so information. We can blow up a book town in five minutes. Understanding the intent of our commander allows us to exercise initiative in harmony with the commander's desires. Our plan is always anonymous, sequential, thorough north-seeking arrow, grid lines, water features, vegetation, relief features, boundaries, known trails landing Zones, built-up areas, TCMs, targets, and MSRs, prioritization & all-hands.

Two mobs, Peter and Paul, say: "We shall contact our families in Italy and Tyrol. We shall ask help from Ascona companies and Roma-lines and ofc Sicily is the main reserve. If somebody does not believe our talks, they believe our contacts. We are proud of our achievements. We support you Tapio, in your hoax 100 %. The fraud needs to complete the premises of truth."

Clur asks: "What shall we do?" Cliver laughs: "Isn't that obvious: get out more: w.w.d.d., so Brooklyn freestyle." Clur: "Ah hell, uh-oh spaghetti-o's. We pop a cap, spongebobs campfire song, and hells angels." Cliver: "See y around. Love."

Something about France

The plain arrives at the coast of Africa. We come to a place where the sun sets, the west. It overlooks the Mediterranean Sea to the north and the Atlantic Ocean to the west. Morocco´s climate is like that of southern California, with lush forests in the northern and central mountain ranges of the country, giving way to drier conditions and inland deserts further southeast. We fly near the Algerian borders, where the climate is very dry. We see extreme heat and low moisture levels. There are 84,2 F and then we come to the Sub-Mediterranean climate zone: 80.6 F. Then we go over the Mediterranean Sea. You do not need to take a trip around the world to have happiness, just have a yacht in the Mediterranean. And beautiful girls just eat Mediterranean diets.

Marseilles, Barcelona, Trieste, Istanbul – each romance the Mediterranean in its own fashion, mostly by embracing the sea in sweeping C-shaped bays that date back to antiquity.

And then there comes Paris. Same parades, same French language, which they think is the no. 1 language in the world. The center of the world goes somewhere hidden to these egoists. I give Frank and Bob lists where they shall go to meat Book Towns administrative fellas.

I drive my Mustang out of the C-17. It is time to go and by a castle.

Funner & W00t called Courtly love & Knighthood

There are hundreds of kilometers pure funner & w00t. There are Saone and Loire.

In Cuisery area lives 1 500 people. 565 postal codes. It is a small commune but amazing. I say while driving: "It took its name from the Burgundians, an East Germanic people who moved westwards beyond the Rhine during the late Roman period. The last Roman Flavius Aëthius take a deal with them also and get their cavalry to help against advancing Huns, and king Attila. There were arriving 500 000 Huns and their German allies, and Aëthius was gathering all he could against that unbelievable force. Aëthius and Goth king Thorismund and Burgundies were the first knights in the world. Aëthius was a friend of King Arthur of Lancaster and he visited many times Britain. It was a time of folklore, French, German, British, and most of Burgundian, and now we go in the heart of that story.

The kingdom of Burgundy continued centuries. During the Middle Ages, Burgundy was home to some of the most important monasteries, Cluny, Citeaux, and Vezelay. The last one is still a starting point for pilgrims to Santiago de Compostela.

It is France's main wine-producing area. It is well known for both its red and white wines, mostly made from Pinot noir and Chardonnay grapes, including Gamay, Aligote, Pinot blanc, and Sauvignon blanc. The reputation and quality of the top wines had led to high demand and high prices, with some Burgundies ranking among the most expensive wines in the world.

They are selling now castles cheap and the area has the best vineyards in the world. And the region is famous for Dijon mustard, Charolais beef, Bresse chicken, the Burgundian dishes *coq au vin* and *beef Bourguignon*, and *Époisses cheese*. The heavy industry has died away and the people haven´t found yet the modern light works and information tech. The area is in the heartland of Book Towns Group.

We must, Bab, conquer that area to the Future.

I shall meet there that 100-million company´s CEO Varju, too. The firm works with the forest and tech industry and that area. It is the real place for the romanticized cultural center, with tech, tradition, and updated possibilities. He comes to that castle and his firm shall update it very cheap and make it an example."

Y look at the place: "There are six towers. Each tower may have its own studio and living rooms." I call to number l 06 12 34 56 78, Le Figaro Properties: "Hello, Enkel & Völkers Paris, yes, are you already there, and ready and steady give information of you and your real estate partners and your Group companies. Thank y very much, I appreciate it very much."

The Castle is inaugurated with the Tears of Happiness

Y look hypnotized the facade size: "Oh my god, 55 windows, and roof windows. There are 18 very big combined windows from almost from top to bottom of the room. Wall creepers give some mysticism to that great place. Tapio, you have much to do while painting those walls and fixing those tower roofs. I wanna begin to do with gardens, grass areas, kitchen, and must-see cellars, all cheese stores, and wine cellars. You must put it full of tech."

There are *Le Figaro* fella and lady and the owner of the house the Perrault family member. The Figaro fella says: "There is now 5,7 ha, but you get easily 10ha with 100 000d. They sell nearby 20 ha, just 200 000 d.

The floor beautiful oak floor and there is four meters to the roof. You say: "That billiard room we change and put together with the kitchen. The kitchen is already awesome." Your hands go and fondle the wooden art of the entrance wall and doors and windows edges.

The Figaro fella begins to sell: "We have already accepted one offer, but as we are still here, we can show you the place." I put my hand in my pocket and take there a card: "You get right away 1,2 million." The Figaro fella tries to play the game: "No, no, and it is 1,47 Md."

The Perrault family member says: "I´m more than sure than there are no obstacles what you Robert cannot win. All is yours and just 1,35 Md." After one minute, it is confirmed. The money has gone, and we all have won. I put my hand around you, and you - cry. Raindrops and teardrops of Beauty have two things in common. Both fall freely, and yield abundance. The former leads to abundant and the latter, abundant luxury called happiness.

The Burgundian Cellar

Perrault says: "Here are 10 000 bottles of Burgundian wine. Mostly red but some thousand white also. Mademoiselle and Mr. Charming, instead of just buying a bottle or bag-in-box (BIB) you have your own wine cellar. You have here underground cellars, garages, insulated lofts, outhouses, and on old fashioned walk-in-larder that are full of wine barrels. Here is always +10 C, then Burgundian wine will age rapidly. Here are top quality corks, and we take care and can help you that mold cannot work its way into wine and make it undrinkable. As you see, excessive lights are the must. They effect on temperature.

Mademoiselle, please, be careful with white and rosé wines, particularly in clear bottles, they oxidize so quickly - go tawny, gold, or even so bad brown. Sancerre may more resemble a dry sherry than a crisp, clean dry white wine in a very short time. And the effect of continual vibration, from the central heating, washing machine, or clothes driver aggravates mainly the red wines of quality that you are trying to keep for a 3 to 5 years period. Vibration causes problems for wines that are designed or need mid- to long- term storage.

Bordeaux, the Rhone Valley wines but also Burgundy wines are all good examples. Only applicable to wine with true or composite corks is upright storage. Sparkling wine corks are prone to this problem. Here the racking takes 300 bottles if full. This type of racking is folded flat and be moved, just by using a screwdriver. They are a mixture of wood and metal.

All 12 bottles from the Côte d'Or at 1er Cru Appellation level. Often the lesser-known villages such as Fixin, and Santenay can give better value. Challonais, Maconnais, and Beaujolais are not ideal for 3 to 5 years of storage. For white wines, this is a classic Chardonnay country. 3 Grand Cry Chabilis, 3 Premier Cru Meursault, 3 Poully Fuissé. Remember also the middle of the road between Chablis and Meursault. This place has a higher number of appellations *d'origine controlée* than any other French region. I take some bottles with me, but I give you as a present this Côte d'Or from 1831. They said that emperor Napoleon I loved all our wines. Without our wines, he hasn´t conquered Europe and his amazing empress and given it the basics of nowadays education."

The nobleman raises a toast with us. Very excellent wine, marvelous in descending order of quality: *grand crus*, *premier crus*, village appellations, and regional appellations. He says that from 28 000 ha of wine just 550 ha are grand cru. He gives the names of villages, which shall be useful to us. The nobleman knows that red wine´s roots are biblical, benefits are amazing, and its effects luxurious and courtly love standards making.

The Materializing Spirit

We go to the other kitchen. You fondle those huge tables and we look at the huge ovens. You say: "The cellar must be made fully automatic, and we must have elevators from the cellar to the kitchen and then in those towers. And cos of there is so sharp pitched roofs, those so-called attic spaces are as big as halls, and the must be an inside gym and a swimming pool. I wanna in the roof huge windows, which shall enlighten the whole swimming hall. These fridges must be updated for sure. And stowage must be more automatic and tech."

We go to a dining room. Huge, 5-meter windows salute us. I study the window-frames. You say: "I wanna windows open automatically. The roof-logs must make shine. The tables are best I have ever seen, but those chairs must have more dumbwaiters. The floor and doors are excellent art of woodwork."

We go to the big library. It is a very adorable and bright room. And it is huge. The nobleman says he lives to me Napoleon´s diaries, courtly love stories, and knight-adventures, from Italy, Spain, German, and France. You say: "Too dark shells and black and brown furniture, more lights and vitrines, and tech. Air-system and heating must be better. Tapio, check the floor heating system." I want better electricity also. We go through 9 bedrooms.

You smile: "New kingside beds. Those cabinets are old-fashioned." Windows, floors, and roofs are excellent but need rooms that need more Italian tables. There are big bathrooms and storage, so they must be updated. You say: "All 7 bathrooms must-have new tiling, showers, and pool tables."

I look that small room with a dishwasher, I can easily make it half bigger. We go to the caretaker´s apartment with five rooms. You have something to say and I put in my tablet: update and make it bright. A former stable is very big, and I suggest we put there a big office with a gym. The next workshop shall be a studio with modern tech. The annex building shall be a sauna and bathhouse. Summer house shall be updated and so tool sheds, a laundry, and a garage for five cars.

I take a paper and look at a map of that 5,7 ha. You think: "It must be 15 ha. Buy it now. I wanna a map about that add-area. I begin to design what kind of gardens and parks there shall be made. Tapio, call some gardeners and foresters here."

The ex-owner bid farewell but I know that I shall see that wise nobleman many times days to come. He is my link to the future.

Tech & Robotech

I go to buy 10 ha more land in Burgundy. It is very easy, cos I have an international company and it is authorized by one international lawyer. No problem with Finnish contra French lawsuits. The E.U. can automatically confirm the deal. I can buy what I want, in the name of my Book Towns Group. Meanwhile, I bought that 10 ha, the maps of it I send to MyVictoria, who gets satellite and normal pictures of that castle land, 15 ha.

Y call me: "Tapio, take some drones, so I can get exact measurements about mold and water flows and trees and other ground things." I: "Ok, I take some smaller than 800 g drones, so they must not be registered by me on AlphaTango. The French Civil Aviation Authority has easier laws than the U.S. to fly a drone. They cannot be flown over 50 meters, but there are satellite pictures. And seals can do whatever they want, but I do not disturb them. I take 10 Cheerson CX-20 and 5 Dji Phantom 4 Pro+. You can send them also buy some food and even ammunition and chemical things, even dynamites, well, special cases. They shall be very helpful when we make simulated pictures about garden and park and what we shall put there, paths, flower terraces."

I continue: "Anything else, I buy some interactive boards and hole lenses, on-the-go DAB radio, Leica Trinovid Hd binoculars, and for power bank Conrad Studio LifeCard, ring indoor cameras, owlet smart sock, and camera set, sage fast-slow multi-cooker, snore antisnoring device, pure discover speakers, Law purifying water bottles, Steamery pile fabric shaver, Wacaco nanopresso instant coffee brewer, DJI robot master S1, Anova nano precision cooker, lounge radio, Fujifilm smartphone printer, Brisant secue ultion smart lock, Dyson light cycle, click and grow a smart garden, smart tech barisieur coffee, and tea maker.

Here have just come working robots from the Finnish industry, including SMEs. I have contacted my land´s VTT technical research center. It has a long history of collaborating with the European Space Agency, so we may have some surprises from ESA External Laboratory on millimeter wave tech. Great R&D tech. Those robots work well in gardens and updating buildings, painting cutting, digging, and putting together, very fast. 1000 times faster than people.

In Finland, kids like to gather their own robots, which and mini versions of industrial robots. I try to buy some interactive medium industry robots, which can be taking to do other jobs. And I have just talked with one engineer. We must have new generation solar panels. Of course, VictoriaCourt has solar panels, but these are last date solar panels. You can sell electricity to about 5 villages, with our 15 ha, and my friend in Finland´s tech University Aalto has designed just some months ago solar panels which go with energy and can be used also in the night. I send Y more maps and so, but I must talk about the latest smart house tech here. Two of my friends have smart houses, they are from tech universities, and our castle must be a smart house, too.

You know, speakers, lights, doorbells, cameras, clocks, windows, window blinds, hot water heaters, appliances, cooking utensils, like Wink Hub 2, brilliant control unique wall switch, Logitech harmony elite and so. I go."

And More

Meanwhile, MyVictoria looks at some hills, and beautiful landscapes, long-distance footpaths, really land of lakes, rivers. She feels for this a wandering land and that river, the Seville, one of the loveliest rivers in France. She begins to think about what flowers and bushes y can take here: cacti cours saleya, Gourdon flowers, rosemary bush, purple flower, iris flower, and ofc lilies. Stylized lily is the Burgundian national flower. She notices that in April and May many hillsides are ablaze with color, as the yellow flowers blossom on the ubiquitous broom bushes, in June hillside pasture is home to cowslips marguerites, and several varieties of orchids and, in some dry areas, rare dark red pasque flowers. The area is renowned for its aromatic flowers and plants, which explains how the small cities came to prominence as the capital of the perfume industry. The best-known symbols of the perfume tradition are the fields of lavender. In MyVictoria's castle-area are big lavender fields. You find out that the first lavender fields are in flower by about mid-June. The last lavender is harvested by mid-August.

I'm coming back to our new European home with already with painters and gardeners and some workers, AVEC-persons, and carpenters. I have with my ATVs, Atlantic tractors, the Volvo's front shovels. The gardeners begin to cut the grass around the castle. I take carpenters and painters to look at windows, doors, roofs. AVEC-men to look at new tech in cellar and kitchen, bathrooms and so. Electricity-fellas are with them. I have one interior decorator and a retired architect with me.

Y: "How Y get those?" I: "Experience. When I built VictoriaCourt, I learn all the tricks of modern today. Then I do not wait either an hour. And other builders we amazed when they waited for weeks. But I went to builders´ homes and said: "Here is money, take it or leave it. When you put cash to people´s hands the yelling stops."

VictoriaCourt was built in four months. There was me, some well-trained builders, who became my friends, and building contractors, who became my friends also. I need just to do work like a horse, and when the workers ate and sat, they said to each other: "Let us go and help that working horse." You know, they call it the common sense of the peasant, and I took advantage over it. Well, I worked 17 hours a day, but the advantage is the advantage. Just a little bit offering my mental and physical body.

I come to y. You say: "Here is the computer map, which flowers and bushes we shall put there. I shall make this a purple-yellow-land." You had gathered very special above said French flowers, then there are white, red roses, rhododendrons so blue and football big, *hydrangea petiolaris*, peonies, plum, apple, and cherry trees, and many, many others. There are also many exotic bushes and flowers from the Dominican Republic like Bayahibe Rose, *coralillo*, *isabelsecunda*, *trinitaria*, *duranta*, some mangos, starfruits, *guayaba*, and *nispero*.

I say: "Do you think these flowers and bushes from Dominican shall flower and flourish here in the Mediterranean dry weather?" You say: "Yes I do." Abraham Lincoln said that he is not bound to win, not bound to succeed, but bound to be true and live by the light that he has, stands with anybody that stands right, and stand with him while he is right, and part with him when he goes wrong."

The workers begin to shape the dining rooms and kitchens, bathrooms and bedrooms, windows and attic Therocesses don´t come to an end in one day or two, or two weeks, but in three weeks. I begin to schedule it clearly. I´m pro in building business. I do not need a handwritten order. Orders live their lives in my head.

You like flowers and bushes, not ornamental plants, vegetables and herbs, not boulevard plantings shrubs, herbaceous plants, but yes with flowerbeds, tulips, marigolds, and sunflowers – in an atrium, on a balcony, in a window box, on a patio or vivarium. Sweet William and hollyhocks, not favs, not aqua scaping, but yes in summerhouse hanging baskets, and planters. Ofc stained glass, garden furniture, outdoor fireplaces, ums, not too designed perennial, butterfly, wildlife, water, tropical, or shade gardens.

You say: "I do my Brkner-way." I say: "Here are a lot of geese, and swans like mute, tundra, whooper, Egyptian, then shelducks, ducks, wigeons, mallards, mergansers, hazel grouses, greater flamingos, grebes, pigeons, bustards, cuckoos, swifts and coots, crakes, pied avocets, plovers, and the list goes on and on like gettin´ in the guts."

The castle begins to change fast. I get there 42 men altogether. Some AVEC changes, more floor heating, and some air source heat pumps (9 to towers and 2-second floor and 2 to ground floor). They are ready in three hours. Carpenters fix four doors and one roof, and gardens grass has been cut and everything cleaned. New automatic systems begin to be in the cellar, but elevators shall take time. They must come from Lyon. Technical stuff waits until basics have been fixed. Five walls go off. At the same time, you go to the summer house and I put tech-connections.

I call Paris: "Hello Frank, have you start to make those information-systems?" Frank: "Tomorrow I shall come to Cuisery, go to Bellprat, Clunes, Damme, Fontenoy-La-Joute, La Charité-sur-Loire, Montelieu, Montmorillion, St-Pierre-de-Clages, and we shall arrive at night to

Uruena. I contact those Book Towns leaders and hire a house for the operational center. I list four local pros to make the running jobs, and that´s it." I: "Thanks, Frank, I appreciate it." Frank: "Yeah. Love it."

I call Cliver: "Yo, rarin´ to go? How is McQuaid Jesuit high school? Euphoria & stoked as a goat?" Cliver: "We shall be at Palermo, Cagliari, Ajaccio today. Tomorrow at Nizza, Marseille, Montpellier, Barcelona, Malaga, and Gibraltar. Day after tomorrow at Porto, Nantes, Bournemouth, Torquay, and Swansea. Easy cakes, like strawberry shortcakes. We handle harbors and the links. I see at once straight heads & druggies & across the street hot. Everything is sah-dah-tay." I: "Trust the pilot, he is a team guy and I do not mean 562, but just scrangg." Cliver: "What an askhole. I do not swing that way. Just truss." I: "Why?" Cliver: "Cos beastality and god hates noobes." I: "Well, get out more, but play the white man, pl0x. Do not lick and ditch. Drop some brass on it that CooCoo or Clur do not g out." Cliver: "Go ride on the head of a unicorn to hell!" He shuts the phone, idjit.

I call to NYC: "Hello Farmer when your agents shall arrive in Soundend-on-Sea. Tomorrow, but they ought to be in London today! Obstacles. What? The Mayors birthday! Really! Tomorrow then, and tech with them. Everything is ready for them. Buy and cannot wait for the golden horseshoe. What? I didn´t say that just snogging." Well, that man deserves yanking his chain.

I breathe a long breath, and ask Y: "Where there is a gym? Nowhere. Well, it is then time to go to the village. I shall need just bench to press, French, dumbbells, stomach, shoulder machine, leg training things, high bar, indoor rower, chains, kettlebells, and Y must need running, cycling, jumping, swimming machines, too. And stretching parallel bars, solar, hot tube, running water to the legs, sauna, electric, normal and Swedish, energy drink, vitamin and juice bar, creams, greases, yogurts, contouring, eyebrows, eyeliners, highlighting, mascaras, overnight skin sensations, sunscreens and so, y can handle them.

I kiss you and run. One painter nearly drops his 20 liters paint pot to the wooden floor. You look at the computer's stimulation picture of gardens. Y think not yet jasel: "Here might be the cold, tail end of winter, but springtime is around the corner. Must have plenty of flowers, fruits, and vegetables to sow and grow things month: I give begonias ahead, start by planting them in a frost-free position. This greenhouse needs sow Lobelia in a heated propagator, plant begonia tubers, sow antirrhinums, and laurentia to ensure early flowering, start dahlia tubers into growth, sow sweet peas, brow my own chrysanthemum plants from seed, sow geranium. Pot on hardwood cuttings, pot on rooted cuttings, plant lilies and allium bulbs, plant bare-root roses in a sunny position, plant fragrant winter-flowering shrubs, start growing potatoes, sew peas, start asparagus pea seeds, sew aubergine seeds, start early sowings of brassicas, sow leeks undercover, try growing really large onions and sow sweet peppers, sow beetroot, early carrot varieties, early peas, salad leaves, plant out garlic and shallots, plant Jerusalem artichoke tubers, plant raspberry canes, redcurrants, bare-root strawberry plants, and stone fruit trees, rhubarb crowns. I need 10 girls to help me." I say: "Let us crash your squad, really bluebird day and sunnyd."

I call pole-dancer group: "So 8th day. How it is going? EDM flashing, different kinds of poles. Perhaps I give the phone to Victoria. She knows, I do not. She really understands, how to make the best training session and where and why." I give the smartphone to Y, and while You are looking at the screen y listen about rehearsals & drills.

I call to mobs: "*Buongiorno*, so You go to Ascona and then to *Hogan de Serlo*, and meet the three important families which do business with the Italian government. Try to take the Caracalla-terms stage in Roma and Colosseum and Circus Maximus. Go to meat Finnish ambassador in villa Lante, ok. Nothing else. What do y mean? These are ofc orders, not happy day wishes. 5 families respect our deal, and you do that also. So long."

I go to the kitchen and the roof and hone the logs as smooth as a woman´s knee. At the same time, at the courtyard arrives those gym-weights. I take the shirt off and change training trousers on. I look at the watch: 19:30. I try to do a new record. I put 50 kg and try to do an hour without resting biceps training. At 19:45 I'm full of lactic acid, but I do not give up. At 20:00 my hands are almost senseless, but I continue. 20:15 my body shakes a little bit, and hands try to open. 20:17 those weights drop to the ground and I do not get the record. I go to the shower, and you look at me: "Tapio, you look trained, but you are shaking very much. Shall I call a doctor?"

The Brooklyn Happy Family

Meanwhile in NYC Hudson terrace is "on fire". Old School, NYC Dope! Dance Party is there. Dj Cosi and Marc Smooth do their best, and it is good, and folks wanna dance all night, sing their favorite songs, and made friends on the dance floor. Good times, music, dope space, amazing crowd await you at a fav. dance party. Throwback Hip Hop, even 80s MTV Pop, 90s R&B, Funk, Dancehall reggae, soca, soulful house, so classics, pos, salsa and so.

New Yorkers have fun while we work like horses. Dj Amazing Excell does his best. He had just toured the world, rocking crowds from small lounges to huge nightclubs and treats the crowd with the same energy and excitement when he hangs around his place. There are masters of his craft and a treat to watch him annihilate the turntables while weaving through genres with transitions rarely seen or heard while rocking the crowd at the same time. They set the party off right, and party-workers have free admission from 10 pm-12 am with RSVP. Just fun and get it down. See you on the dance floor.

At the same time, a subway cop tells Kam Tambini he has drugs in his bag, slams him against a wall, searches his bag, and finds - nothing. Cara Reedy watches cops pat down a construction worker in front of his wife and children on her Bed-Stuy block, cos he was holding a table saw. A teenaged Andrew J. Padilla walks with his friends towards Riverside Park when he suddenly realizes a cop behind him has pulled out his weapon. An officer says nothing, not even ´police´, and is ready to shoot. The police just Xerox descriptions of young men of color, when looking for criminals. An oligarch lying-in-wait purchase democracy while every other candidate is in the field doing the work. One artist is stopped, and three cops search her on the George Washington Bridge and chase her away when they find nothing illegal among her watercolors. A 16-year-old late for curfew is searched by cops who bruise his face and laugh at him for being poor.

Stop-and-frisk gives police officers the right to search anyone suspected of a crime and the people of color are targeted.

At the same time, garment designer Wayne Diamond shines: "I never knew any gangsters in the Garment Center. They were all good guys." He gets more drank from red wine and yells: "I'm always been the number one f**ing guy!" He touches ladies and says he is a handsome older man, who has earned himself a profile in GQ, more than 10 000 Instagram followers, and a deep-rooted desire to pursue a full-time film career.

Neighbors call him the Legend and the Legend lives on the Upper East Side with his wife and gods. There at the beginning of the 60s Earl Vince and the Valiants recorded the amazing styck Somebody´s Gonna Get Their Head Kicked In Tonight.

Mr. Diammond looks like a well-fed hamster, and here´s what BigD has to say about his fav. NYC districts: They ask: "Describe the Garment District in five words." He: "The greatest show on earth." Their question: "What do you like most about living on the Upper East Side?" He: "UES is easy. You get in your apartment, the building I live in they do everything for me. It´s perfect. It´s great. It´s sensational. They do everything. Something goes wrong, one second and it´s fixed. I love uptown for that."

When they ask: "Are you blind and take bills?" He doesn´t answer. When they ask: "Tell us about working in the Garment Center?" He smiles: "It is good. Gangsters were all wonderful people and they treated me great - a lot of Italians, a lot of Jews, we are great. I moved on and I became the biggest and the greatest dress designer and manufacturer for disco women, the clubs, and s***. Diamonds Run, that was the business." They ask: "How has the Garment Center changed since you retired?" He: "There is no more Garment Center. You got these Wall Street people that ruined NY - they´re ruining NY. The Garment Center is all overseas. I look at the way people dress. Schleps. Garbage. The got the money to buy s***. There´s no more fashion. In my time every month new styles and hot lookin´ s***." They ask: "What do you miss?" He: "I miss everything, the buying, the selling, being with people. It was a 24-hour fun. It was the toughest business in the world."

The Ascona Wiseguys

Meanwhile, there is good old NYC and we are working like horses, mobs in Ascona gather to have wine and candies.

One of them says: "I have heard strange things from beloved NYC." The other says: "Yes, me too. There has been a great violation in Brooklyn. Some deep Brkner has been got loosed and everything is now mixed up. Great Salvator Maranzano´s victory in the Castellammarese War is shamed and put to disgrace. The devil himself is in Europe and he has put families under his shoes. He hits whoever he wants, he has shot Genovese and Bonnano soldiers, think both DiRapolis, and Chuckie Tuzzo just smiles, Tico Antico keeps his hand in pockets and Kid Blast Gallo fucks himself, the Nose Mancuso shuts up, even Porky Zancocchio is as a monk. Both Vitos Badamo and Grimaldi are living disgraces and Vinny TV Badalamenti looks just - f**cking TV."

The third mob thinks: "How this can be possible? Is this guy god´s whip? There are right now two soldiers in Paris, who are grieving the Faith of great DiRapolis, and they are there under command of that poor devil. They just cannot stand it anymore and ask our help."

Mumbling and muttering conquer the room. Somebody says: "And that fella has even got the respect of street gangs, think Makk Brimms, the badasses, love him."

They shake their bold heads. They are men from Stidda, Camorra, ´Nrangheta, Basilichi, Sacra Corona Unita, Mala del Brenta, Bamda fella Magliana and ofc one and only Banda della Comasina and the Turatello Crew.

Men in the mysterious room are sitting around the table armed with guns. In the center of the table is a skull. Salvatore Cappello, Nitto Santapaola, Leoluca Bagarella, Salvatore lo Piccolo and Matteo Massina Denare aren´t there, but they are in spirit there. The hands of oppression, arrogance, greed, self-enrichment, power, and hegemony above and against others in presence. The room is full of angry men, cos Italian State police and finance police have just arrested 70 mafia-Stidda members and taken from their pockets 35 million euros.

Meanwhile, we continue making our castle a better place to live and having luxury.

Time is 21:05 and I do not let workers go anywhere. I keep them working all night, shift work, same as I did VictoriaCourt. When I built, nobody rests. We make and make it good. They put now already lacquer to the roofs and everywhere in the kitchen. Doors and windows begin to look amazing.

You say: "What a combination: green, white, black, blue and brown. No premier, stupid red, orange and green, just bright and shining Nature-colors." We take off the heavy colors, old-fashioned choreography, woods, logs, and 18 walls are gone already. In the courtyard have appeared beautiful bronze-brown tiles. Nearby trees branches have been cut, and the grass is cut short, and there are machines that make it look amazing. There are already men on the roof, cutting more space for huge roof-windows.

At the same time, in Italy mobs are cleaning their guns and talking with those two American mobs who are in Paris. They are looking at the sights on the top of the Eiffel tower, and they have drunk too many cocktails & other drinks.

They laugh: "Battles are always won by slaughter and maneuver." To plunder, to slaughter, to steal, these things they call honorable acts, and their talk makes bloody wilderness, which they call peace. The slaughter of me and my friends, temporarily regarded as enemies, they call as a possibility to prove themselves worthy for higher ranks.

The other one of them loves Benito Mussolini: "Lets us have a dagger between our teeth, a bomb in our hands, and an infinite scorn in our hearts." The phone rings. And the first one says: "Halloooo. Yes, the dastard & villain is in Cuisery, Saone-et-Loire, W-02g68F, there the brute-fu**er is. Take & kill. No, no, not Cluny, not Céron, I said CUISERYYY. Your welcome, buy, buy." He shakes his head: "These old continent fuckheads, I cannot understand what is wrong with them. Does their water have too much lead to what? Hahaha. Cheers." A polite waiter comes so smoothly as possible, and say to them: "Please, use lower voices. People want to think about their own businesses, not yours." The other wiseguy takes the waiter from his collar and throws him away.

Near Fiesole's big bunch of mobs is in a great mood. They have a gr8 arsenal. There is a saying that in Legion Etrangere there are no drug users and mobs, but they are so wrong. One legion-deserter, whose papa has come with a yacht to help his weak son to escape the Foreign Legion´s school of men, has come to papa and family and the deserter has a straight connection to Bonifacio where the Foreign Legion weapon store is located. He and his great friends have stolen a lot of ammo & guns: 112 Pamas GI, 103 Famas F1, 3 Famas Félin, 2 Fmas Valorisé , 2 HK 416 F, 17 great & beautiful AA NF 1, respectful FN Mag 58, 18 FR F2, 17 grenade launchers LGI F1, 8 single-shot antitank weapons AT4, an anti-tank guided missile Milan. They have even 15 technam mass tech T4 unarmored lightweight tactical vehicles and one VBL. Italian officials respect everybody, who owns this kind of heave arsenal and are always willing to give their helping hands. The bunch of mobs brings a knife to a gunfight or may we say whistle past the graveyard.

They go over the Alps, come to Provence. French officials show they best conviviality to these great persons and characters. To the question: "What is the shortest way to Cuisery?" The public officers say: "Please, go to A40 to A6, and then right, and there it is." They give even a map: "No, no, not via D975 but here from Lacrost, yes, that´s right." Italians give them some bribes and say: "Do not worry." The Italians start going towards Bourg-en-Bresse and then to Macon. Some hours still. It is ten o´clock, in the evening.

The Evening Hours Rush

Meanwhile, in NYC city, the most popular isn´t anymore the one you´d expected. It is nowhere near Manhattan. More houses sold over the past decade in Flushing, Bed-Stuy, and Ozone Park than in any other NYC neighborhood. Queens is by fast the most active borough in NYC in the past decade, in terms of the overall number of properties that changed hands. Brooklyn and Queens are currently booming with development. It won´t take long before home prices in these boroughs begin to pick up the pace. Queens take the prize for most sales by borough with 108 810 homes has been sold for 65 billion dollars. Brooklyn claimed second with 95 132 closings and 80 billion d and Manhattan comes in third with 61 664 worth a whopping 152 billion d. Those steep price tags what drive the market to explode in Br and Queens. Manhattan is outto reach for the majority homebuyers. Queens is no 1.

Well, ofc M Upper West Side is the most desirable neighborhood. But there are those skyscrapers and very little of real nature, which we have in Cuisery area, thus far. And the building process which we do here shall cost 7 x more in one and only NYC.

Meanwhile, we are doing the job, you have asked me to come to the summerhouse several times. And I know why. You are smokin´ and biddy. I say to workers: "Keep calm and chive on, there is choogling, too." I say I shall come back in two hours, I have a chipotle challenge, and after cheatorious I shall come immediately back. I velvet goldmine and run to eat out.

Just then Cliver calls: "Heya, what´s up?" I: "Nothing. Just emurderengency." Cliver laughs: "Shemergency. Yeah. Plplox." I hurry to free the beast, but Cliver has something serious to say: "Those two knuck if you bucks are making some big-time rush, well some nutjob. I was nearby and took to my phone their words. They are revengineering & retalitooting. They asked tools on deck from Italy. A place called Fiesole, or something, there are loose cannons and county road cutters. Aguas, bro."

Well, SEALs are far away, and here are hayrides and Y & me.

I call Frank: "Back on the Block is coming here from Italy. Where are You? In Redu? Do you have that airplane still? Ok. Come here, we make y a landing space and put their lids. 24:00, so soon, well, ok."

I look on the road. No. No. But a field and plain are good. I ask 20 fellas to help me. We begin to cut the grass off and tractors bull it better. Huh, huh. How it shall be long enough. Well, 200 meters is so short, but we can make it better later. If we work as hell, we can make it.

I wanna come to you, but in the light of rocking the boat and taking the man in the boat to Tuna town gets a delay. I'm shoveling as hell and showing some example to those lazy Frenchmen who had sailed on the wine-sea too long. I call you: "Bab, I shall come to liquor in the front, poker in the rear. About 0:20. Yes, poop chute. I promise to plunder the booty. I continue."

Frank calls: "Hea bro, 45 minutes, the weather is g00d no delay." I'm irritated, this is so far from nudge the fudge.

The tractor makes the ground leveled and the landing strip is 200 meters long and 75 meters broad. Led searchlights are there, intermediate 20 m. Are there stones or cracks, probably, but this is acceptable.

After 20 min there arrives lights of the Cessna Citation XLS+. Are there crazy? Now their emergency descent mode has some use. There it comes the best-selling model of the best-selling brand. It is said that a spacious interior allows those inside to stand and move about the cabin with ease. And there is extra wide with full relining capabilities for optimal comfort. And the rest assures the whole team can fly in comfort and arrive closer and to your destination, allowing you to spend less time traveling and more time at the job site on with your customer. And now it allows you to die.

The speed must be over 700 km/h. They are coming nearer.

I call Frank: "Hey, noice time for circle the drain & Niagara on the lake. Mad-o-wat!" I here relaxed laughter. The grateful deaths think it as a dead baby joke and well, fuck them, perhaps many of them have born in November, cos their parents celebrated Valentine´s day.

The plane comes down, the speed is about 400 km/h, then 300 km/h, It jumps from the ground and goes forward, jumps again, but Miracle! and thanks to St. Valentine and other pilgrims on an elusive and endless road, bringing the Church without a bishop, state and king.

After coming 200 meters nearer the house, the plane stops in the nice and mighty courtyard, elegantly on the new bronze brown tiles.

SEALs and Frank go outto the plane. Four men. Somebody may think that isn´t much. But there is a difference with fellas. Some are good, some are bad, but the last ones normally are a little bit lazy and shit out when hips and stress are measured. Slobs have a habit to run but in the wrong direction. These men are good. Y know, mighty less is more where more is no good. Their fire means a good investment while pulling a trigger.

Little Romeo

I say to Frank: "I do not know, how many there are coming, and when, but they are coming. My source is Cliver." Frank axes: "What about these workers?" I ask back: "What about them? Let them work. Let them have fun. And they have box seats. This may be a drop in the ocean, but there are many kinds of drops. Do you remember Little Boy?" Frank: "No I do not. What was that?"

I: "Little Boy exploded with 13 kilotons of force, leveling five square miles of the city and killing 80 000 people instantly, in sunny August day in Hiroshima." Frank: "Okay, made the point. How about today, or to-night? Where is your second-best boy?" I: "Our Little Boy2, is the most delightful surprise you get. Just wait and people will impress you." F: "But you must have a crossfire and a lot of, and I really mean a lot of, guns." I have made some calculations: "We have here in your plane: 5 M2HB, M24OL, M203A1 machine guns, 6 rifle-mounted grenade launchers, 8 M32 revolver type grenade launchers, 17 M27 automatic rifles - and AGM-114 Hellfire missile - our beloved son."

F: "But its destiny is to be in Pentagon. I just took it with me. There are some corrections to that war of terror thing I must do. That 45 kg predator-fella, my longbow hellfire has some mistakes in its optoelectronics, and one AH-64 Apache crew waits for my fire-and-forgot weapon. I have almost made it target going. By the by, I call it Romeo and it must be sent to Juliet, some ISIS-chiefs in India. Romeo shall go now just 4 km, normally 8 km. And its SALH, semi-active laser horning, is a little bit tired.

OK, well, I see you have that fire on your eyes. Let's sacrifice it. Let say for a common cause. We must make a little better the shaped charge HEAT, toxic material. It shall blow off about 100 x 200 meters area. This Romeo. But remember you own me, after that."

What can I say? I say to me: true friends & true love are the things I never change.

Frank makes calculations about that explosion that our Little Romeo shall arrange and where. We look a nice spot to it. Our unwanted visitors must be directed to that spot. And I know how: "Frank, I'm there. Waiting for visitors and Little Romeo."

Frank says: "You have big balls Tapio." I say: "Yes, hardly can walk." I give Frank a timetable when the zero-hours begin. The main things are these: improvise, adapt, and overcome. I say: "That spot where I shall sit and drink my expresso coffee and eat honey cakes is 360° - forming a complete circle; to put protection all around. And you can always write to my tomb: he was trained in the 6th Battalion. I promise this shall make 5,56-hickey to than Italian mob-culture. Let's make 8 bells, a four-hour watch. I shall take with me to that zero-point ALICE- all-purpose lightweight individual carrying equipment, and hope that all hands concentrate to that 0, with your own artillery. Frankie, may I call you HML - marine light helicopter squadron for the old shake of

Afghanistan. Thanks, I appreciate it. And hope you aye-aye. I want bloopers to shoot around that Little Romeo´s circle, so nothing living crawl there away. No broke dicks allowed. Remember that there are only four of you, your gun bunnies and red legs. May I call you *Teufelhunden*, if we do not see any more. And do not worry, I do not give a fuck. Take care of FEBA."

Frank put his hand on my shoulder as we do in the army: "Stelo. 5th ring of hell." I do not say anything. Why should I? Just cut me some slack & touch it in the back. Bez.

Meanwhile, near the road has arrived a motorcade. Time is up. It is 00:00.

The Fourteenth Day

Romeo doesn´t miss Juliet

Like Sleeping Beauty Waltz – La Scala Ballet

MadJack runs: "Hey, they are here." I call Y: "Bab, sorry, I shall come about 24:30. Some whee and deal. *Te extrano*. What? Ohhoh. Really. Bbbj & b my I on t´s." Frank makes something to Romeo, shakes his head, and says: "Shit." Do it again and do not repeat those stoopid words. I go to the meadow and soon there is a table and expresso and cake. It is so jejune & just off the boat that it is the best buy and Abercrombie and Fitch. And ps3, you know, sony´s machine that allows you to burn 600 d instantly once you buy it.

SEALs put their arsenal around that 100 x 200 meters explosive area and hide. Workers continue their jobs. The motorcade arrives like a fat snake. Too lazy to check anything. The first Mercedes Benz stops nearby the airplane, and a boss of Mala del Brenta gets his fat stomach out of the car and goes to ask one worker: "What is this? What are you doing?" A Marcus-named worker looks at fattie and says: "Go away."

Fiorenza Trincanato becomes impolite: "How dare you say that to me, Yokel? Where is the owner?" The carpenter looks once again to the fat man and tries to be patient: "There he sits. He has a lovely wife and knows how to make the best of his day. He is a good fella." The boss, the great Veneti Malavitosi, looks at me. And his mouth pops open. Men of the seventeen cars have found their target. So noice and happy-go-lucky.

Trincanato orders: "Let´s kill him slowly and purple nurple." 57 mobs begin to come close to me. They have their Famas. They just log towards me and Little Romeo to come, and meanwhile, hate speech worms its way into NYC streets, subways, preschools, and even the mouths of police officers. There were 320 incidents of extremism and anti-Semitism in NYC 2019. Nearly half of the 2019 incidents occurred in Brooklyn, which has 138 extremist and anti-Semitic incidents. While Manhattan hears 109 speeches, Queens 35, Staten Island 27, and the Bronx 11. The gangs write in subways bad words with a swastika and the message: "Die, Jew B---." A Jewish preschool in Br has the word "Jews" with an arrow. An NYPD traffic cop stops one driver in Midtown Manhattan and says: "You stupid Jew, y can´t make a right turn." CUNY and St. John´s University campuses have new messages: "Reject white guilt", "Feminism is cancer", "Stop drag queen story hour" and "Merry white Christmas". ADL efforts to track white supremacist propaganda, white supremacist events, extremist- police shootout, terrorist plots and attacks, and extremist murders.

Democrats, feminists are angry, cos President Mr. Trump has pardoned a former NYPD commissioner who spent years in federal prison on tax fraud and corruption charges. Trump says: "Bernard Kerik courageously led the NYPD´s heroic response to the horrific attack of September 11, He embodied the strength, courage, compassion, and spirit of the people of NY." Kerik says the pardon is among the best in his life. Well, Kerik does not need to dry anymore with his eyes open in prison. The permanent loss of your civil and constitutional rights is personally devastating, but that doesn´t concern democrats. Kerik took 250 000 d gifts from a mob-family tied company to renovate his Bronx apartment.

Mangs are slowly coming to me, with an awesome arsenal in their hands. I'm a little bit bored. I call to Y: "I keep always you in my heart, cos life without your love is a sunless garden with the dead. My heart beats now like a volcano and feeds the love so much, love without boundaries and this is just a lifelong romance. Love lives in me, it´s an urge. Victoria, our love, and compassion are our luxuries. Love is a triumph arch, under a real person goes just once in a lifetime. Yes, My Love, to witness Y & M two lovers, is a spectacle for the gods. Let´s just love with the love that is more than love."

I call Cliver: "You were aiight. The whole Westboro Baptist church is here. They are coming to the cupboard and thinking grenades. Ambush visit. I have one request. Those two glory hunters & born sinners, can y, please, do birds fly. Take them up and shoot the fade. Where? How about the big band theory show in Eiffel? Yes, I appreciate it. Now I jump the gun & and but a bigger fish to fry. How? Big style, brent is called Little Romeo."

Fiorenza Trincanato, Enginieer Greco, Angelo Pipitone, Luigi Putrone, Antonio Rotolo, Benedetto Spera, Pietro Tagliavia, Giusy Vitale and some less important figures command their men to aim. Trincanato shouts at me: "It is time to whack, hit. clip, pop, burn, ice, whatever word you like, I make your bones!" I laugh: "Okay, murk & gank -moob. There are also my words gkys, kilk and frag. Fire flaming dookie kiss your ass, *bese du cula*."

Around me isn´t yet a circle. Now comes the hard part. It is called the glory of the Iroquois. I must run while they are ringing the bells. Frank & the boys have calculated when the mobsters are in the circle. Now they are, cos F & Bs begin to shoot. Italianos turn their heads. I have 35 seconds to run via the radius of the circle. I jump up and it is called snickers now, lovey, rip and run.

At the same time, 0:18 am three NFB-soldiers pulled up in a black sedan and two of them climbs through the drive-through window and pulls out a gun at a Queens McDonald´s near 38th Street. And force a worker to open the restaurant´s safe and hand them the cash that is inside, 3 600 d. Meanwhile, a MAG - MONROE AVE GUNNAZ- warrior breaks into The Social, a tapas and cocktail bar on the 30th Avenue, smashing the bar´s front window, then break into an office and makes off with 6 700 d and two tablets. And then he runs off.

So, nothing much compared with I run purple Jesus. Frank has put the Little Romeo to its homemade launching place and counts 9,8,7 ... I must run knees as up I can and in the right ankle. Bullets go here and there like flies. 150 m, 160 m, 170m. Then I feel something in my hand. Bullets go through. 180 m. Frank counts 4,3,2 ... And I have ended my counting and at the same time, huge flames burst behind me. I must run away from that firestorm and explosion-shards. I throw myself to that hole which I made my splinder. A huge whoosh-buzz and then comes the first wave of hell: a thousand degrees firestorm. My head is near the ground. 2 meters above the crying monster flows its fire. Then another wave. Then no more.

I touch my head. Not much of the hair has been burnt. Some nails have become charred. I smell of burnt meat. The back of the hand is red. It has burnt to red. I cannot stand up, cos there comes more shooting. Frank cries: "7 men left. We reap them." Then it is very silent.

I stand up and go to look at the devastation. There is a big hole in the grass and everything black around it. The question goes: what shall we do with Italian mobs? There sit 30 mobs on the ground.

I go to Fiorenza Trincanato, Angelo Pipitone, and the rest bosses and say: "Let´s make a deal. If you take it, I do not shoot you." I know I must make a good deal, and right now my brains are overheated. I must take a break. I say to mobsters: "Early in the morning I´ll be back." And to Frank: "Take care till I come at 6:00 am." Then I begin limp forwards. The workers stare at bleeding me. I say: "What are y looking at? We have work to do. We have no time to wait and half of it has gone. Keep on rollin´ & strollin´." I limp towards the summer house. Damn time is 0:32 am, I'm two minutes late.

Just taken care of

I come to you. You stand at the front door. You take me in. And take care of my burnt hand. You put cod-liver oil to my burnt hand and rub hard all burnt, wrinkled skin away. Y say with a smile which grows love: "Your new skin shall be smooth as baby´s, no scars or wrinkles-crinkles. This hurts a little bit. But I leave Y if you begin to cry." The back of the hand comes clean and then you put oil and Salva. You say: "Y must keep plasters a week. Then take them off, and the skin comes very soon back, and then you must train and wash it a lot."

I say: "I want to go to bed now. Some sleep makes ..." You say: "Don´t you dare to do so. You are in love when y can´t fall asleep, cos reality is better than your dreams." After two brains we live in the land of the mouthgasm y smile orgasming. The great finale is raw doggin' in the fart box and conquering the inevitable city. And I pull the bucket and we go to the wonderland.

I kiss Y & Y me, and we sleep till 6:00 am, by the beauty´s name. And the love slander with awesome fame and nature´s power borrows face, that sweet and hot love has a name and dreams tell it to us in dreaming grace. But love has just one name in dreams but in two names as day to day lives.

The Renaissance Man

It is 6:00 am when I wake up. You are already up. I go to shower and put some army trousers, blood & green, on and a tight tee-shirt and camel-boots on and run the castle. The mobs sit on the line. I go to F. Trincanato, E. Greco, and other bosses and give them the same paper which the mobs signed in Br. I just change the dates. The honor of five family isn´t a joke in the old country.

First Trincanato is arrogant: "Do ya, *pezzo di merda*, think I shall sign that paper?" I say: "Die or sign. Six feet under you grow roots and have thousands and thousands of bugs." I take my Taurus and load it. I put it towards his head: "So Godbrother, what it gonna be." He pisses under and signs. After that those others do the same.

Then comes the better part: "You shall have fifteen festivals in Italy. From Ascona to Palermo. One in Caracalla Terms. You have Roman, Medieval, Renaissance, 19th hundred, and Mussolini´s great time's parade." They listen just not believing their ears: "My father knew in his division some noblemen, who made that Venice great Carnivals and after the war, he and his friends helped to put up real musician and artists spectacle to the happiness of all great people of Venice. Well, they do not do much, but good people of Venice mobs remember them. By the way, Arnal Venice is now 102 years old, and he composed Giovinezza." Trincinato says: "It is a bootiful song." I: "It is about the Beautimous Victoria."

One of the lower rank mob cannot be quiet: "It is bootylicious, *Bella* melody." The vulgar men change to Renaissance persons, when y talk with them about real culture, cool team luxury and smoothing it and

Chrysler fifth avenue, high brand rap, international baccalaureate, trinity Florida and just luxy.

We do not have time for a luxury garden party. Five mobs of fortune have gone to the green lands, but no hard feelings - yet. I invite the mob-bosses to drink good French expresso and eat honey cake.

I: "While I thought that I was learning how to live, I have been learning how to die. If somebody thinks himself better than other people, cos his clothes are made of finer woolen thread than theirs, then, after all, those fine clothes are worn by a sheep, and they never turn it into anything better than a sheep. And after all boys, our souls exist partly in eternity and partly in time. Man is mortal, but man pretends not to be mortal. That is his sin."

Meanwhile, we are celebrating our deadly and living, one 53-year-old detective gets it too much. And takes his life at his mother´s home in the Middle Village section of Queens. That great fella was a 20-year veteran of the force, currently assigned to the police commissioner's Liaison Office. If you need help, text just the Blue to 741-741, and everything shall be alright.

The Puetarican Gift

I call gangsters to our castle, and Y get many words of your own mother language, cos many of those mobs have been in Central and Southern America. They speak fluent Spanish and Portuguese.

If somebody has logic and reason, and experience, somebody may give an excellent speech on some sunny day. But You speak so eloquently and lovely, and the speech comes from your heart, the words fly spontaneously and make heaven and hell and earth between them, and that´s it´s not a given speech but lively, lovely speech and nowt is compared with it!

Y have the Puetarican gift and nothing can be illest than that!

In the air isn´t, after your lisp, not at all racist, obscene or abusive comments. Your speech treats people as your neighbors. There comes just like those words that promote trust and build community ideas. Your speech isn´t personal or professional blog - it is relevant. And you do not spam it with stoopid free promotions of your business or organization. It is just event-talk, where facts and funs fly truly, not in deep waters of hearsays and other mudding unverified information. And unlikely to me, it is OK if you don´t know something - just say so. My speech sounds propaganda with spreading misinformation, even by accident, and that hurtsss. MyVictoria has elegant tips to this & that, in the house, and nature. You say something helpful - and nobody flags them out of line. Your speech makes the day awesome and hilarious, but mine creates a warzone.

Workers begin to have back their humor. Politicians are interested in people and fleas in dogs. After my speech, they may think, weren´t that fella my lawyer, I´d still be in prison. I believe in luck: how else can I explain the success of other people. I ofc not think that if Y don´t disagree with me, how I can know that I´m so right.

Thank God Little Romeo isn´t in the Plane

Workers have made the runway long enough, 500 meters that Cessna Citation XLS+ can fly again. Seven tractors made miracles. Well, Frank is not very happy: "Little Romeo has gone whistling in the wind and I must sweep the truth under the carpet. And my convincing words have disappeared into thin air. Tapio this isn´t swass." I tap his shoulder: "Bro, I know the feeling, my condolences." I promise to invite him to dinner with his beautiful wife. He keeps repeating: "You own me one..."

In the end, the Italian mobs have got their all details and Frank accepts that 200 000 d is enough for Little Romeo. He can weave mesh and do the camouflage. His opinion is that in art the scandal is a false narrative, a smokescreen that camouflages rather than reveals. I do not say that the best camouflage of all is the truth, cos nobody ever believes it. I say that camouflage is the most interesting of all the arts.

Frank's problem is that he must stimulate the explosion of the training field in New Mexico. How he can find enough parts of Little Romeo here. I say: "Y do not need to. Take from Arizona´s military store's broken parts. Y just need to have access there." I recommend him to go to USDOD: "There are 1,3 million active-duty service members. And to the Pentagon in Arlington. There to the Department of the Air Force, and to the Secretary of the Air Force (SAF/OS), there to the Assistant Secretary of the Air Forces, and there to the Assistant Secretary of Environment & Logistics. Tell him that ASAF for Acquisition, Tech & Logistics asked you to come to him. Show your budget and doings in New Mexico. Then go to that Tech & Logistics fella and tell him that the first one has sent you to him. They shall meet, and their stories bound together. You manage."

Frank: "So I must go and play a game with incumbent William B. Roper, Jr., and incumbent John P. Roth?" I: "Yes, they understand each other. Trust me. And you have that 200 000 d. You lubricate a lot with that. Roth has some brains, one brigadier general and two colonels. Do not talk with them, talk with two civilian members of the Senior Executive Service."

Time is 11:00 am and those mobs salute and leave. And now the mob-net is at last perfect. Well, Cliver has something to do. Next is the tough part. How to get that Cessna back to the air.

The runway is 500 meters, leveled ground. It is early in the spring, so the land is tough and frozen. It helps a lot. But Cessna has 500 meters to get enough speed. The rate of climb is 3 500 ft/min, so 1050 m/min and 58,3 ft/s, so 17.78 m/s.The plane (h)as 30 seconds time to go up from the ground.

And there must not be much shaking and jumping at all. There shall go Frank + 3 seals, which means less than half of the max capacity. Fellas and their baggage and guns shall be about 5 000 kg. It is more than the useful load, 4 000 kg, but much less than 9 163 kg. But they leave for my castle all heavy weapons, and I send them later. The weight shall be 1 200 kg. Empty weight is 5 000 kg. It is almost 1/4 useful load. 2 x Pratt & Whitney PWC turbofans, 4,119 lb. (18,32 kn) each. The question unsolved goes like this: what is the speed after 420 meters? Is it over 650 km/h, cos if it is, then it goes up to the air? The plane is not new.

We shake hands. SEALs and Frank go in. Frank is the pilot. Workers, Y & M look at what shall happen. The tires are full, well, oiled, motors go full tempo. They growl and then the plane goes. It is morning, so the ground is tight. No smoke, no jumping, not much shaking. 300, 400 meters, and the end of the runaway are near. But the plane goes up a little bit and then the whole box flies. Soon it is up and the speed about 800 km/h. The man, who takes the plane up in Afghanistan, takes it up everywhere else on the Earth. The plane goes over the hills. If the Little Romeo had been in, the whole plain would have blown out. Frank must give me some thumbs.

The Fu***er is stealing My Snow

Meanwhile, in Brooklyn, good neighbors aren´t hard to find. On any given day, people are always helping others in their communities in ways big and ofc small. Chi rho omicron these acts of kindness are making an impact, but they often go unrecognized.

But now everything is changing, though, more people are getting to celebrate, also nacho taco chimichanga, their neighbors´ good deeds through the Neighbors app by Ring, yes you might say also if you want bing-blang-blaow.

Sharing these amazing uplifting acts not only supports connections between neighbors but helps build stronger, safer communities. That´s why the Neighbors app by Ring launched Neighborly Moments, a new category that makes it even easier for people to love and share the good things that are going on where they live and so. That Moment is an act of kindness from someone in the community.

It can be a small gesture, such as returning a lost wallet, full of empty, or letting someone know their windows are open before a storm hits. Moments can be bigger, alerting a neighbor lost to a fire or helping them to safety. One kind neighbor Mr. Gordon is pleasantly surprised to discover his neighbor Mr. Paul uses a snowblower to clear his driveway without him even having to ask. Gordon posts a video of Paul´s kind act to the Neighbors app: "This fu**cer is stealing my snow."

The good Brkners know neighborhood security is in their hands. But there are gangs, who do not share the idea that good neighbours ought to share information and create a sense of community. But there happen miracles also: Charlie is a helpful beagle who provides support to autistic kids. After going missing for three weeks, Charlie was tracked down and returned to her owner by helpful gang members. The owner says that her neighbors are the eyes and ears when she is not around. The App creates a radius around your home, via using your address. This is wonderful.

The Period Blood Parveque

I call Cliver: "Have you met judasiscariots? What? Y don´t say :(((((((. Posted up, Maxin and relaxin. Swingin´ on the flippity flop."

Cliver and Clur and CooCoo have taking mobs to the Eiffel tower again. Le Jules Verne is the action place, 115 meters from the ground. I: "So You said that the fellas are hanging there outto restaurant. Correct? What not yet. The elephant in an egg. The guards and waiters? Make it national kick a ginger day. Be like a boss. Give a gun show. Toasts."

Dirty & beautiful Paris has compared with two other great cities: London is a man, Paris is a woman, and NYC a well-adjusted transsexual. There goes also a saying: "When good Americans die, they go to Paris." This time it isn't true. There walks with his mother vivid kiddo, who looks up to Eiffel and says: "Mother, look there is a man who is waving to us."

One man is hanging there from his leg 15 meters under the - not Brasserie de la Tour Eiffel or 58 Tour Eiffel but - Jules Verne, which is one gastronomic center in Paris. Normally people enjoy the hustle and bustle of the Eiffel tower and the many colors of Paris for private or business lunches. There is a menu that enhances the extraordinary quality of France's producers and artisans. And wine cellar helps you discover great food and wine pairings. This time those two mobs who had drunk well last time do not drink well. The other named Paul is already hanging from the window. And the other called Peter isn't.

CooCoo has some trouble putting the rope to Peter's ankle. Cliver says: "Clur go to do some belt out to those bastards who mirmir. How about some Brooknam and dropping some knowledge. Give them Bryan DeJesus, so sweet, thoughtful, and great that they dream in bed." Clur is grr: "Y driddy stup, go fa'fa' un culo. Im not dogzer. I give them Runescape." He goes in the middle of the restaurant, takes a microphone and says: "Yello, what's good? Keep it moist. Here comes post -google depression, rapn roll's keak da sneak & bone thugs n harmony."

 At the same time, CooCoo has, at last, put the rope around Peter's angle. And Cliver kicks open the window. "Fuck**ng stuck window. Very bad to defenistrate."

Two guards run to Cliver. He takes his gat Glock and trigger, you know, po the Glock. Other guard sees killin' clouds and faints shamefully. The other fo'tack Cliver. CooCoo tries to push the other mob out of the window and takes his knife from his belt and throws it into the attacking guard's leg. It gets stuck and trousers begin to come 031.

Red. Cliver takes the knife from the leg. The guard is jumping away. Cliver throws the knife back to CooCoo, but the Peter-mob is not willing to jump. CooCoo put the knife to his ass. Peter jumps. CooCoo cleans his knife: "Period blood parveque."

Now those two mobs hang out, and people are running to the elevators and waiters have their phones. Cliver goes and takes all the phones and throws them from the window. He shoots at the security camera, asks where to get the vid, and puts liquor on them and set light.

Meanwhile, Cliver is calling back to me, in NYC Manhattan-bound 7 trains are delayed after one King of Queens (KOQ)/YG G SQUAD/YB - warrior, who is escaping two Dream Team -warriors, is hit by a train at the 74th Street - Broadway station. Broc-warrior is in critical condition at Elmhurst Hospital. After that Manhattan-bound 7 trains are running express in Queens, hurrying to make a local stop as soon as possible.

Meanwhile, in Jules Verne Cliver talks on the phone to me: "Nothing is true, everything is permitted, those pork swords hand there like in a brokeback steakhouse. That's it bought and paid for. What have you? What Little Romeo got his Juliet? Really, I thought they both died. Jeah, I thought so too heavenly marriage a real angelfish. Whut? Omfg, don't hate the player hate the game. This two mobs, curl up and die? CooCoo, cut the rops! Well, whut, kk, Heya CC don't cut, the fellas got mercy than can go thugging rope in the future, too."

I try to be patient: "Say those monkey spunks c'mere. I have serviced the account. They are now the main bubble dancers here. And they shall clean sucks and blows, too. They learn."

Cliver is frustrapointed: "So they leave free after they didn't wanna you to leave. Is that fair? I let them hang. People are looking at me as I'm Miss South Carolina. Go ham."

I: "Do not be a dude jerkin in under the lunch table, smelliese. You shall be a good Splenda Daddy, someday you shall be the Sugar Daddy, and if I'm honest I'm not sure about that Honey Daddy thing. But I'm sure you can give your girlfriend a change quit that shitty job at Applebee´s." Cliver, CooCoo come to listen to Clur who still sings: "Ohh, *demuestra lo que hay mamá (ohh). No pierdas el enfoque y sube, sube sube ...*" JAJAJAJAJA que hermoso caray! Cliver says: "Splenda daddy, let´s go!" They run and Clur isn´t happy: "Fuck - *Pose, vivetelo Asi Dame Ahora tu mejor, pose, pose pose ...*

Cliver, CooCoo, and Clur run. Why? Better run when the sun goes up. When the sun goes down, you´d better be hiding.

And they must catch the plane to Barcelona. They have much to do there in the harbor.

Meanwhile, in NYC one person is dead and another seriously injured after a construction accident in Queens. It happens at a construction site at 147-05 94th Ave in Jamaica. The construction site has racked up a series of violations. The owner was later hit with a 1 500 d fine on for not fixing the issue, a construction fence collapsing onto the sidewalk.

The Gardens of the Yellowish-green Paradise

Meanwhile, in Cuisery works goes on fast. The workers are happy and amazed at the same time. They are building luxury and they have seen splendid spectacle. They are amazed about your energy and elegant style after that apocalyptic scenery. They have a lot to tell about days to come, and they are sure that this was just a fresh start of something new and gallant. There traditional Burgundian language isn´t empty about knightly and diagonal locution in the timeline 1500 years - so they understand the grand common theme although the details aren´t to be seen.

We are making more luxury and I begin to think about what we shall do with that unofficial runaway. There are fellas in the second floor updating the baths and floors. Here burns beaucoup bucks and I have made it rain.

I call Frank: "When you are back in Redu, go quickly around the IOB´s Book Towns and take those office-places and make them ready for my arrival." I call to Cliver: "Take care that there are stores for Book Towns Group in all those harbors. Yes, Italy, France, Spain, UK." I call to Bob: "Make those calculations what every Book Towns needs and what we may get from them." I call to Farmer: "Send those five agents to London now." I call Brooklyn dancers: "Send ten members to around those Book Towns to study the places, yes to that account that I opened to y." I call Josh´s nerd John: "Make those nerds ready to go to London. They must be there tomorrow." I call mobs in Italy: "Study those festival-areas in Italy. I shall see Y in Ascona tomorrow." I call 5 families to NYC: "Send 20 subcontractors to Barcelona now. I shall meet them in Barcelona tomorrow." I call Cliver again: "Do not disturb me in one and half hour, I go and take a nap."

After having fifteen-minutes'-nap, I go to look at a map. There are red points all over the world telling where book towns are. I study the map quickly. I put HoloLens on: "Hm, let see. There is Frank´s information, there Cliver´s, Bob´s, Farmer´s, dance-Tina´s, John´s, Marco´s, and Andreotti´s."

My hands begin to organize information to their right lists, to right areas, to the right time, to right cash flows, to right groups, to the right solution, to right profits, to right forecasts. It begins to look quite good.

The big questions are the deals and how they join with books, bookings, building and the forma of cultural tourism and living, and most of all book town cultural centers, their groups, and to my operational office called Book Towns Group, who controls that all.

I study what I shall do tomorrow in London, Ascona, and Barcelona. London is the main place for changing paper books to audio- and electric books, Ascona thinking bookings and building projects, and Barcelona about thinking about whole festival schema medieval to modern times performances.

I shall make three different worldwide centers in NYC, Sydney Australia, and Peking. I use again HoloLens and put the names and lists to their right groups. The holograms are 3D, so I can go around, above, under those lists and groups, change their places and gather them together. I have specific colors to process, timelines, and focuses. The other HoloLens 3D-map begins to light a rainbow.

I go and take a banana, and another, and another, and drink some apple juice, cowberry milk, more cowberry milk and more and some sandwiches, and I go to shower, train fifteen minutes, shower, back to clothes, suit on, and take my sleeves up and begin to think very carefully. Now I'm making the third HoloLens 3D-map. It is called: people.

I look at the main maps of Brooklynization. I call Y in the room. And you look very worried about me: "Your act is very strange to me." I say: "Yes, you are right. But if I think like a common descent human being what profit we shall get from it? Y must think, plan, organize, motive big. Then you have a system you can control. If you make small, you are a ghost, and everybody looks through you. If you do medium, they keep you a nice guy but do not take you seriously. If you make it big, you get real combat and battle, where you either win or lose. There isn´t both and, cos ´both-and´ isn´t a solution. It is a deal after solutions when you have conquered the markets. Thinking big makes the most of the people thinking you as an enemy. So first physical capital, then mental capital, but physical capital must always put to mental capital. You must materialize the mental capital, or you are just a ghost. Y come to me: "Bab, take a nab again, you look very tired." I say: "Ok if you come with me." We have a romantic kiss moment jiffy.

In your smile I see something more beautiful than the stars, it is one thing to fall in love, and one thing to have a romantic kiss.

And we just do not have a choice cos it is always U & M. There comes a time we all are doomed and will come a day when all our labor has been returned to dust, and the sun will swallow the earth, finest we´ll ever have, and black hole swallows the stars, and there begins a new world and yet I'm still loving you so. And times go, and times will come, and I, the clown, go on loving you like in this very second.

I'm catastrophically and doomed in love with you.

Who can take it from U & M, not even U & M? And if my love is an ocean, there is no more land. If it is a desert, you see the endless sand. If my love is a star, MyVictoria should see only that bright shining light.

We go back to the studio where those three holograms are. You say: "Those holograms look so confusing." I say: "Look more specifically." I connect the map of the IOB Book Towns to the map of the other 24 Book Towns. And I put them together. The map begins to shine worldwide colors. You say: "Book Towns holograms are nothing without this last one, full of Bucktowners." I: *"Tengo un mono en mis Pantalones*. Soz, my amenable is this: let´s call the hologram Broolynization tree." You: *"Je n´ai pas la moindre idée*, if you know what I mean: Brooklynites money tree."

I call Bob: "Hey, I send you now a hologram vid, how about?" Silence. There begin to hear laughter: "MyBoyTapio, that´s fantastic! Cash and cash-equivalents go in and out. Yes, yes, there is borrowing from the public, exceed outlays, surplus, and the interest accrues that the IOB flows including direct loan disbursements payments to lenders, fees, collected, principal and interest repayments, collections on defaulted guaranteed loans, and sale proceeds of the foreclosed property.

The worldwide budget totals exclude the transactions of the financing accounts, cos they are not a cost to the Book Towns Group. Financing activities to all book towns, investing the IOB, and operating act to Book Towns Group. Those people are hedge funds types, long/short equity, market neutral, merger arbitrage, convertible arbitrage, event-driven, credit, fixed-income, and global macro. These types know from the street that funds are illiquid, meaning investors need to keep their money invested for longer periods of time, and withdrawals then to happen at certain periods of t. They understand the risk they take on when they buy into a product. They do versatile investment vehicles than can use leverage, derivatives, and try to generate active returns for their investors. They think the time value of money until closing.

I: "How do you know all this?" Bob: "I do not, Brooklynists do. In that area, communities teach take part in this kind of strategies they are must, therefore, by fully knowledgeable about all the risks involved as well as the potential rewards. When you have those deals, and I can check them and make them clever outto stoopid?" I say: "Day after tomorrow, then I know what London, Ascona, and Barcelona think. Goodbye, have a wondiferous night." That fella has reloading speech or Asperger´s syndrome or retrograde machinegun wheelbarrow, all of them all.

Y look at triple-hologram: "This shine a billion beautiful miracles painted from the tears of mine and the highest. Plucked from the lush gardens of a yellowish-green paradise. This, Tapio, is a kaleidoscope of Soul-raising, sight and colors will tease and seduce our eyes and mind. This Brooklynist money tree allows you to hear sacred hymns flowing here and of the perfumed wind. Cos this is living, it is beautiful, and which is beautiful, it has beauty, endurance, and practicality. I love this hologram. It is fondly to be fearful of too fondly." I say: "I got ya on the flip side." I see just a gem & then there is something which isn't paper, a mask, a book, a film, just skin, face, size, and the life: gorgeous & bootylicious.

Amazing Ascona

So. I say: "Bab, do not cry, and if you cry, cry for happiness. I must go to Ascona right now, I have there and Italy something settles. By the way, NYPD sent me a message, they have some inquiries about my doings there. Fuck with them, I have more important inquires in Ascona.

And in NYC, everything goes as always. The Princess party drag show is going on. Presented by the Queensboro. Those disgusting Ducky Sheaboi, Patsy Indecline, Aria Darci, and other evening drag, offer music and drag queen fun at The Q. That old-timer Harrison Ford has a new movie The Call of The Wild."

I look at the watch, at 11 pm. Workers are doing nice frames to outdoor windows. Peter and Paul haven't yet arrived at clean WC´s and everything, but soon they come. I kiss Y and say: "Bab, let´s go."

I call Cliver: "Hey man, leave Clur and CooCoo do that store-thing there and come here. We must meet some big genos, the United States postal service, sopranos, and some politicians. We shall meet at 6:00 am. I do everything else till then my way, no, no, not the Mikey way."

I take you and then we go to my Mustang. It has NYC DMV2921, and I do not have vehicle registration documents. Clur has given me a counterfeit registration document, but it was for a boat. He was sorry: "Well, you didn't get a snowmobile document."

From Cuisery to Ascona it is a straight line 250 km. We go via A40 to E62 to Lausanne, from via 9 to SS37. It goes straight to Santa Maria Maggiore (Borgnone-Intragna-Losone-Ascone).

There are ofc speed limits but not for us. Some milkshakes and meatheads were near to die, but just near. I drive 250 km/h. Provence is nice, I think. I haven't time to watch it. There speeding cameras glitter, but that's nothing, cos soon we come to the border, and it isn't Mexican border but European civilized border, and after that comes the mountains and I can go scary fast.

Y ask: "Are you going to drive this fast in the Alps?" I: "Not in the curves I must slow down, but I wanna be there before 23:00. Here is ordy dark, so we can see the lights."

There we go nearby Geneva, the second-most populous city in Switzerland. I go just 100 km/h. I say: "Bab, we do not go there. It is the 15th important financial city in the world. The world's most compact city and there is Lake Geneva, where the Rhone flows out. It is surrounded by three mountain chains and I have heard: if you cannot eliminate the war in by peace parleys at Geneva, you are doomed."

I put the gas to the ground. The speed goes up, 280 km/h. I love the speed damn near as much as poppin and throwing bows in the true war. I lool: "Bab, we go so fast that your tears do not come, and if they come, they drop to yesternoon." We go to the mountain roads.

I call Cliver: "Hey bro, howzit goin´? Beating a dead horse? Cliver: "Great. At 6 am." Well, I look at Y. You are loveable and will love back, sweet, smart and one of the most beautiful girls I have ever seen.

Little by little Ascona area comes nearby. We go through Malesco, where is very good ristorante Ramo Verde, but now it isn´t time for pleasure. On the left mountainside is without trees and just come bushes, right, down. Then it is full of forests. Soon we are near Golf Gerre Losone and go Via Valle Maggie almost 280 km/h. I take speed off, and we go 80 km/h. We drive to Via Pascolo then, at last, we arrive at Via Lido. Near Golf Club Patriziale Ascona I stop the car. I jump off from the Mustang and open to you a door.

The Three Salvatores

We go to a house near the beach. Ascona has a lot of festivals, and citizens just love to gather on the streets and look at those fire cracking events. If you wanna find a good job, come to Ascona. We are at the Parkplatz Yacht Club & Bad. There is a nice park and there are houses. We go in, and there is a Bauhaus looking interior are huge roof logs and white walls and floors. And there walks a man to us: "Dear people, what you are looking for?" I say: "I have heard here is trumped Mafia but I'm looking for Messina Denaro & Gaspare Spatuzza & Fiorenzo Trincanato."

The fella looks at the top to bottom and says with oiled lips: "*Si signora.*"

It is 23:15 pm and everything is so noice as it can be. I tell you a joke: NYC is rough, the first thing that struck me was a stray bullet. Well, you do not smile. Why did Eve eat that apple? She had fallen in love with Big Apple, huh, huh, yes bad. Why couldn´t Jesus be born in NY? They didn´t find 3 wise guys and a virgin, just wiseguys. Yes, very bad. Khm. NYPD starts fining subway riders 50 d for taking up two seats, and so Rush Limbaugh hails a cab. I admit, a little bit rusty. In New Year´s Eve in NYC, I picked up my dry cleaning today and saw Dick Clark getting his face pressed. Luckily those three murders arrive.

Messina & Gaspare & Fiorenzo march in like three most important admirals, who understand people and help them to do the dutty job. And that takes the good characteristics, like integrity, the dedication of purpose, selflessness, knowledge, skill, implacability, and the determination not to accept the failure. They come to us as merciful Salvatores.

Their eyes tell us that their mastery isn´t about organizations, plans, and strategies. It is all about people - motivating people to get the grody job done. They never say: "It is our fault you are still alive." These men think they are glorious saviors, not the regular persons with bad breath and messy hair and handrails. These men are what people are afraid to be. People shopping for a messiah want quality. When it comes to choosing a savior, they won´t settle for just a common human being. And they say: I'm loved, do you understand, I'm beautiful and I have come to order you to save you from the rest of the world. These saviors want their enemies to turn into angels as soon as possible.

Fiorenzo smiles: "2b or not 2b, this nice couple again." I: "It is forbidden to kill unless you kill in large numbers and to the sound of trumpets. I have come here to check Italian festivals where we shall be in."

The bosses touch their fingernails and look at them, they are boreded. At last, Messina decides that he may say something: "Check then. Bake it."

I look at him, but before I say anything Cliver arrives with a smiling face. Some guards are coming to him: "Io. G´day mates, who are these sits and spins. Me Ilamo Cliver, so y, y, y, who are you from home?" Messina & Gaspare & Fiorenzo aren´t men who do not like games. Fiorenze says: "Bury him well." I say: "Wayment Mr. Shunsine, here is a Lady on the table. That´s how we roll. Apology, S0zz."

Guards are coming nearby. Messina puts his gloryfinger up, big bird, which is covered with rings and their goolies & twigs & berries. Guards stop put their hands ready to pockets. Fiorenze turns to me: "What did y say, boy?" I: "Just say you are sry. Nothing more, you know, I´m sowwy."

I look at Y: "Bab, when in Rome do as the Romans do. These Romans are so calabrese."

Messina & Gaspare & Fiorenzo the Salvators begin very redly on their heads. They look more than normal mortals. Their hard life with obacco & vino & lot of perverse nights & bad food & lazy life & crimes with scars, beaten faces make them look pathetic losers, real Detroit lions & c.o.o.l.

Their scars in their faces shine like supernovas in the sky. The blood full of those disgusting, groove, fattie face skins with a lot of holes, made by too much tobacco and smoke, give them some dignity. But if you hit that kind of fattie to his belly he begins to bell.

I say one more time: "How it shall be war & peace. You know all big wars stars cos of a Great Beauty. Beauty isn´t just in the face and body. Beauty is in the face, body, light in the heart, warm, blood, breathing, words, sounds, moves, touch, perfume, clothes, days to go and come and real love is this: a grandpa came to me, and asked: 'Who is the most beautiful woman in the world' ... he named a lot of old and new beauties ... and at last said: 'Or your - grandma.' That, boys & lords of the flies, is real love and beauty. So."

My hand goes near to my belt. There is Taurus. Your eyes shine so brightly. One guard takes his gat and I shoot at his chest. He fell some meters behind. And knocks his head on the hard parquet. He isn't dead, cos he has the body armor. He has gone to look for a while butterflies in the meadows of Tuscany, where is an innocent, natural beauty, the best kind, like a woman first thing in the morning, lit up by the sun streaming through, who doesn't believe it when you tell her how beautiful she is.

I put my gat towards meadow-Tuscany-boys, and they understand: "Sorryy." The Salvatores have come back to us mortals and they don't need to do for their own sins, but they understand now that bullet finds also their fatsos.

We let the guard sleep, with the smile on his face. He is now on the Tuscan countryside whizzed by in a kaleidoscopic whirl of shapes and colors. There they are green grass and trees melded with bluest blue sky, most purple-purple and yellowest yellow wildflowers, peachy-orange villas, brown-and-gray farmhouses, but there isn't red-and-white Autrogrill, the delicious answer to fast food. So, at last, we can talk about some business.

And we leave the guard on the ground. His face has become beautiful again. The 8d has lost its stress, tension, anger, and frustration that coursed through veins every day almost unnoticed began to fade. His beautiful face tells just that each morning the light comes through the slats of the shutters in ripples, and as it washed towards the inhabitants of Tuscany it smooths away memories of the past. It is the key to that doomed, catastrophic kiss & love, which Y & I so well burn and fire.

Talking about Festivals

The Salvatores Messina & Gaspare & Fiorenzo have had a bad attitude but they kicked it in the ass.

There comes a big list: "Fair of Sant´Orso, Carnevale, Venice, Battle of the Oranges, Carnevale, Viareggio, Scroppio del Carro, Marriage of the Sea, Wedding of the Trees, La Corsa dei Ceri, Snake Handlers´ Procession, Came of the Bridge, Calcio Storico, Infiorata, Opera Festival, Festa della Madonna Bruna, Umbria Jazzx Festival, Palio di Siena, Film Festival, Regatta, Feast of San Genanro, Fiera Internazionale del Tartufo Bianco d´Alba, Oh Bej! Oh Bej! These 21 festivals you much see - before you die."

I say: "What?" Salvatore Gaspare continues: "I'm in love with Carnevale of Venice, cos the floating city is transformed into an extravagant masked ball, The Festival, which has originated in the 12th century, celebrates the anticipation of a time when Jesus abstain from revelry and eating meat. While the opulent masquerade balls require invitations with steep ticket prices, the candlelit parade of boats, concerts, and street performances are free and open to poor Y. Venice is like eating an entire box of chocolate liqueurs in one go."

I laugh: "I have been there. Yeah! Bab, do you wanna go there. It is like life: Our Smiling Friend put us here, on this carnival ride. And, hahaha, life will always show us masks that are worth all our carnivals, which gonna always shine. I love The Palio di Siena in Plazza del Campo. Real horse rice, and big accidents.

In Aosta, the craftsmanship is amazing: soapstone, wrought iron, and leatherworking, and weaving of drap, lace, and wicker. In Ivrea, the townspeople divide into nine squads and spend the next three days having Italy's biggest food fight. In Viareggio, the highlight is the giant parade of papier-mache floats. In Florence, the centuries-old tradition culminates in a specially rigged model dove setting off fireworks display outside the cathedral. In Venice Festa Della Sensa culminates at the church of St Nicolo and a market is held on the nearby square. In Accettura during the celebration a tall old oak and the holly tree are cut from the surrounding forts to be transported back into town where they are married, symbolizing fertility and the union of the town."

I'm just beginning to analyze our dance-groups' and singers' participation when Cliver says: "Hea, tell something about your adventures in Venice Carnivals when you came back from South America with your mercenary-friends. Share that story to these fellas also, not just Brim Makks."

The situation is very odd-and-ending, cos that story isn't for the eyes of the ladies. I try to get out of the situation: "Gone is gone, let's look at the future." Cliver doesn't give up: "Tell or I tell it. It is a fascinating story." Messina & Gaspare & Fiorenzo and guards come around and Y are curious also.

I begin to feel uncomfortable: "Well, that's the way the cookie crumbles. Not many a slip between the cup and the lip. Standard behavior, just junk food luck. Nothing tres fabu and hoxie. No booty called clandestine sexual liaisons an on ad hoc basis, just prank call, ;). When I came with two of my friends to Venice on the Carnivale days, I met him, a person in a square. And then some hitmen, who came after us from South America, tried to get back the money, which we were taken from cartels. They attacked us in the main medieval church which was then under updating. In one sarcophagus we found millions of dollars. In the church came more hitmen, and we made a deal, but those Southamericanos broke it. Their chief was a priest and I took him to one island, put to his hand a gat and I have my own. I put pullets on the ground. And there happened our little duel. And in this fair fight, the priest tried to cheat. I shot him in the middle of the forehead and left him there alone with his god. Then we, hm, made ahead shorter the other hitmen and took the money. And some of my friends went to England, but before that, we send a gift box to those cartel-bosses. They thought there would be me and my friends' heads - a Southern American habit - but they were wrong. There was a handmade bomb. Not much to tell to the generations to come."

Mobs and Y have listened quietly my story of that shameful happening, and to my full surprise, you all begin to applaud and the Salvatores even tap my shoulders. Messina says: "Quite a story, my boy." Cliver smiles. "Cool story, bro, you forget tell about the Venice ... where you found five dollars ... hm ... real log roll."

Fortunately, I could turn their heads to business, although they look at me and smile. What a shameful momentum. I try to compensate it with details where our dancers and singers shall go nearby the future, in Italy. Fortunately, Carnivals of Venice come too soon, so no need to repeat that stupid story to anybody else.

Y come to me: "You said there was a person in that square. Who was it?" I: "Just a common person. Not rich, nor poor, just a common person." I do not want to tell anything more about that story. I lost four, my good friends, there and I cannot put my face to twitter or Facebook. I do not like that kind of story.

.

I explain why it is so important to go to Siena, Aosta Valley, Ivrea, Roma, Acettura, Gubbio and use amphitheaters and theatres in Rome, Milano, Napoli, and Palermo. I tell those smiling people that in the ancient times amphitheaters and theatres were designed among the mathematical calculations of voices and sounds, how materials were so important in those calculations and bronze vases.

Messina comes to me: "Let's go Carnivals of Venice now. You aren´t so hurrying, aren´t you?" Victoria says: "No, we aren´t." What can I say more? Well, I say: "We do not go."

It is now the next day.

The Fifteenth Day

Sunshine is the Gold and Laughter the Best Piece of It

tapio tiihonen

New York Smexy
The Gift
&
The Kiss

America + Europa = That´s the Kiss

After giving detailed information to Salvatores via computer and printing out papers to their fat hands, I say to them: "This is truly above and beyond. I had no idea a document could look this good. To be honest, when we started the project I wasn´t sure we could pull this off. You certainly did it and did it well. We are so fortunate to have innovators like you in our time." We all laugh.

It is 00:15. We can leave and go back to France. Mustang flies. It´s more than a car. It´s a lifestyle. It´s a release. It´s a passion. Pissing off the neighbors since 1964. They say money can´t buy happiness, but I´d sure as heck rather be miserable inside my Mustang.

Cliver says: "Dark notchy. Brynalyn daquan from staples. Rickroll." I say: "Shred the gnar." And Life raises us up to a perception of happiness in store for us. And nothing is so much my own as that I spend on my Book Towns Group´s on my American and European neighbors and friends´ cultural needs."

Meanwhile, in Brooklyn, they say that long-promised LIRR Fare Discounts due to start in May. The Northeast Queens residents, who rely on the Long Island railroad get around the city, will see good savings. State Assembly Member Ed Braunstein and fellow Assembly Member Nily Rozic created the discount last year to offset the cost of congestion pricing for commuters living in the outer boroughs. A lawsuit brought by the New York Taxi Workers Alliance pushed back the start date. But now it happens, and nobody can hinder it. The LIRR is a lifeline for the Queens residents who live outside the reach of the subway system, which goes no further east than Jamaica and Flushing. Happy for New Yorkers.

Meanwhile, you ask: "So. You´re going to London next, may I guess?" Cliver: "Nothing is 110 in London but expense." I say: "There´s a hole in the world, like a great black pit, and the vermin of the world, inhabit it, and its name is London, and I do not mean north Weezy, northwest London, a song by SLK."

London is the center of Book Towns, a literary-cultural center. Like LA of the US through film, TV, and music. U may say the center of the world = the United States of America. The Internet born in America as free cyberspace and is a virtual representation of America: greatness, who is married with the crap. This UK, with the core London, was before the center: creatures, gods, and people, living in black and white flat space, you know pudding = eaten as a dessert with whipped storytelling cream and adventure jam. And it was a blot presentation of Europe: crap and greatness what came with it.

You say: "So. Y shall do a Brooklyn-mix of it." I kiss Y: "Put a pudding and cyberspace together in a virtual blot presentation of America + Europe = world, then crap is greatness and greatness crap, and we shall always eat it as a desert. An audio-electric-book is a virtual presentation when it shall be put together like real Brooklyners and one deep Brkner does." Y: "So real Brkners and this one deep Brkner, what shall they give to it?" I kiss Y & Y kiss me. They give luxury to happiness, and happiness to luxury.

Brooklyn is the place where America & Europe meet. It is full of different races and cultural heritages. That kiss of real Brkner & deep Brkner is nowadays Roman concrete. That was made of volcano´s ash & kinder. Their world´s bridges and still there. This new concrete is made of a Kiss, and that audio-electric-virtual-book gets its concrete called red thread: courtly love. And then it isn´t a story anymore; it is an adventure. Just a Kiss. I love U so.

And there is a gat. So, it gets the street credibility, a bliss.

I say: "We go to look at that London pudding blot and give it an American show." Cliver: "Hellz yes, give fisheyes and glue Viva la Bam, and it shall be fucking funny when they dug the tunnel under Vito´s house."

I look at you: "B world = Brooklyn NYC, YOU KNOW!! And that kind, caring, sweet, talented, judge of character, perfect angle, heaven-sent." Cliver: "Beeg kwish. XXX."

Paris & Napoleon

It is 3:00 am, when we go to the Motorway-A6, nearby Avallon, in central-eastern, France. The old town, with many winding cobblestone streets flanked by traditional stone and woodwork buildings, situates on a flat promontory. Here is Fortunate Isles, King Riothamus reigned the Isle of Avalon, Avalon in Burgundy. There has been the seat of Charles the Bold, and there are the Mount of the Martyrs, Montmarte, and the truth winds somewhere between the road to Glastonbury, Isle of the Priests, and the road to Avalon lost forever in the mists of the Summer Sea. The place where even the longest night wears brilliant clothes for sunrise.

Cliver says: "These remulacs are discombobulating & trippy. And flying fickle finger of fate." Y: "The pigeons are dancing, kissing, going in circles, and mounting each other. We go from an explanation P to a riddle L."

Three matches one by one struck in the darkest night: the first to see Ascona in its entirety, the second to see London´s eyes, the last to see Barcelona´s mouth.

We drive near Eiffel. Cliver is surprised: "What they have taken those living crapolanterns, frou-frou-mobs. Or have those scrambled eggs fallen and broken - but I do not see any Puertorican chandelier."

We go over the Seine.

I say: "There was once young lieutenant, artillery fella, called Napoleon Bonaparte. It was during the time of the Great French Revolution. And there was Maximillian Robespierre. Napoleon sit with Robespierre´s younger brother Augustin and talked about making a united school system in Europe and then to the whole world. The school shall be free to everybody and every child shall be respected as just. Young Napoleon said to Augustin: ´My friends, one day I shall do start that.´

Augustin and Napoleon dreamt about equal society - and they have met through another mutual acquaintance - a fella Corsican named Antoine Christophe Salice. Napoleon and Augustin met each other at Toulon, during that fateful siege in which Napoleon would show himself to be a highly capable commander.

Augustin wrote to his beloved brother, now remembered Mr. Terror: ´I would add to the list of patriots the name of citizen Buonaparte, general in chief of the artillery, an officer of transcendent merit. He is a man who resisted Paoli´s caresses, and who saw his property ravaged by this traitor.´ Being praised with such a strong language marked Napoleon early on, even more so than the better-known Lazare Hoche, or one of his most capable marshals in later years, Andre Massena.

Napoleon a dedicated Jacobin and a strong admirer of the elder Robespierre. During a famous dinner in February 1797 at Ancona in which Napoleon was in attendance, he eulogized Robespierre as ´this man who was superior to all around him´, and ´the creator of the only strong government France has had since the start of the Revolution!´

They killed Maximilien, he was guillotined. Napoleon was released due to the lack of evidence, but the event immortalized Robespierre for Napoleon. He never abandoned his Jacobinism. When great Napoleon was exiled at St. Helena, he said: ´Despite what commonly is said against them, they are singular, and do not have despicable characters. Few men have left the mark that they have.´

When Napoleon went through Europe and the world with his army, he put in conquered countries that equal the school system. And that we have now around the world. Napoleon never was a tyrant or an autocrat. And that was a problem to those European and world tyrants and autocrats, who do not want an equal school system. That little Jacobin was a great man, and Paris poor people loved him to the very end."

Y and Cliver look at me: "Why you tell that to us? We hate the egoist who put the world in flames." I: "I respect him. Every time I come to Paris, a tear shall drop from my eye, cos I remember Maximilian, Augustin, and their friend Napoleon."

Y & Cliver look at me not happy at all: "Your words are strange to us." I add quickly:" Well, when I was a little kid and my lovely mother walks with me here near Ballard Pointe du Lac, there comes three, not four, Punk-banders (it shall be seen amazingly in youtube La Marseillaise - Oberkampf French 80s Punk Rock) and begin to sing that great song. And that accident bothered me a long time, but then I read about Napoleon and Jacobins, poor Parisians."

Y and Cliver do not like these words. Paris stays and we live and go from the explanation to the riddle, which hasn´t ever had a real equal school system.

The Land Ashore

You and Cliver are very willing to see London. It is a town of crown and Buckingham Palace, and whenever I go there, I see some kinds of celebrations going on for the honor of those royals. And I remember George III, the monarch who lost America to Americans and a debate with an oak tree on the palace courtyard.

Time is 4 am. There is the English Channel, and I look at Cliver: "Not many like us have crossed the channel gats in their belt, not even Napoleon."

Somebody may say that the Channel is a little puddle, and it is a wonder why no invader has crossed it since 1066. That somebody forgets one little thing, which Grande y Felicissima Armada forgets in the year of Our Lord 1588. Well, everybody knows Sir Francis Drake and the story about Nuestra Senora del Rosario. The galleass, flagship, the galleons and so meet a Sea Dragon. Sir Francis Dragon said: "It isn´t that life ashore is distasteful to me. But life at sea is better. To continuing unto the end until it is thoroughly finished yields the glory."

We go to a car ferry, from St. Malo to Plymouth. That tiny little, jar-like town.

People praise England: "There today is hard, tomorrow will be worse, but the day after tomorrow will be sunshine."

Cliver says: "I think about the tow-in gate of Heathrow. The freshly spanked says we live in a world of cloud twenty-one and greed, and I do not mean just a triangle between Swindon, Cheltenham, and Oxford, capital = stow on the world. Well, old man strengths and junior boys, Mrs. Palmer and her five daughters, lane Bryant caddies and wives, boyfriends, gifts from God, Friendster, when the planes hit the Twiss Towers, as far as I know, none of the 867-5309 calls from the 5sos on board are messages of hate or vendetta dish best served cold - they are all msgs of luz & rawr!"

I: "They have many paper shops. They are drowning in their papers, which means nothing but the drops in the sea. If we can put those blots back to life, it shall be something. Sherlock Holmes's perfect day was to sit in a room with some papers. What was gold, and anything else was just a waste of time. But now the hound of Baskerville has attacked Sherlock again and he has no paper behind which to hide."

You say: "Tapio, this royal throne of kings, the seat of Mars, other Eden, demi-paradise, a fortress built by Nature for herself against the hand of war, happy breed of men, a little, tiny, jolly-good world in world, precious stone set under the silvery moon in the silver sea, which serves as a moat defensive to a house, against the envy of less happy lands and men like Y Tapio, it is a blessed plot, not a blot, this fair earth, real, very good old England."

We arrive at Plymouth. Insignificant, irrelevant, and meaningless, dismal-drab town-village, which dreary weather does not drag your spirits down. I look at real midnight dreary, weak and weary, but you and Cliver praise the sight.

I try to change the subject: "One hundred years before the pilgrims landed at new Plymouth, the Spanish government issued a decree authorizing the enslavement of the American Indian as in accord with the law of God and man." No effect at all. I try more: "Behind these cliffs and beaches is moorlands of Baskerville and there has even today seen the very footprints of a gigantic hound."

We are about 400 km away from Hasting were the last conqueror of England made his appearance, and you and Cliver do not seem to care of that great important day. You look at this like tourism or cultural tourism, and I as a vindictive campaign to the land peacoats & gout.

When our Mustang goes in the streets of Plymouth Cliver says: "Hey, here is the Firework Championships, and now food & drink festivals." I: "Yes, they are celebrating the Mayflower 400 days. It went from here to America. Well, Plymouth University has 23 000 students and there are 71 prime schools, a quarter-million people, but we are going to London, not looking at the statue of Sir Francis Drake."

Sun Rises at Baskerville

We are coming near the Baskerville moors. The story tells that there were no traces upon the ground around the body. But some little distance off, but fresh and clear. Footprints? Footprints. A man´s or a woman´s? "Mr. Holmes, they were the footprints of a gigantic hound!" In the middle of these Baskerville moors, I stop the Stang.

So here we are, in the middle of nowhere. Cliver: "Where´s the Hound? Shall it skipse kai glipse? Wcyd? Get the hell outta dodge?" I: "Y can jam you hype, ay callate. I'm not interested in the Hound but Sherlock Holmes. Do as Watson did. Sherlock used to say: ´You have a grand gift for silence, Watson.´"

Cliver: "But Im not Watson, Im Cliver." I: "So what, I´m not Sherlock, I´m Tapio. But Sherlock is something that we are looking for. Uoeno, his business was to know what other people do not know. He abhors the routine of existence. He thinks that if we could fly outto window hand in hand, hover over London, gently remove the roofs, and peep in at the queer things which are going on, the strange coincidences, the planning, the cross-purposes, the wonderful chains of events, working through generations, and leading to the most outreach results It would make all fiction with its conventionalities and foreseen conclusions most stale and unprofitable. That´s my Sherlock."

You say: "Tapio, do you mean that if we put the character of Sherlock to the virtual U.S., then we have there London brain, the rest of it is just a mere appendix." I kiss Y.

Cliver: "To the curious incident of the Hound in the night-time." I: "Crime is common. Logic is rare. It is upon the logic rather than upon the crime that we should dwell and search in London. Let´s go."

I add: "Sherlock logic."

Cliver: "You think today´s multiculturalism, modern ethnic warfare against white people, is shit?" I: "Yes. There may be millions of anti-Sherlocks, but that is just the crime, we are looking for logic, which is rare = Sherlock. *Capiche*? An example: real tyrannies and monarchies are much more long-lasting than democracies. Why? Just one logic, too much crime. There has happened a lot in London in crime, but nothing at all in logic. There is still going on that Queen Victorian time, now called Queen Elizabethan time. They cannot, those prime ministers, kick it off, cos of that remaining logic. Hahaa."

The Logic & the Truth

There is 350 km straight to London, but we go to Exeter, then to Southampton, then to London. Just some straight roads to S and then via M3 and M25 to London city. So first to Exeter. The noice town. The great people of Dumnonii, whose fortress was at Exeter, occupied the whole of the peninsula from the River Parrett to Land's End. East of the Tamar was dyfnaint, the Deep Vales; west of it Corneu, the horn of Britain.

We go very fast on. There are those hills and green valleys. British phrase tells also the truth: "God made it rain for forty days and forty nights, and that was still the best summer we had."

We are coming to Southampton. The place where they had those The Great Gatsby parties. The Citizens of Southampton are all bootleggers. They have it in their blood, and they have nothing they can do about it.

You say: "Well, tell something more about that logic."

I drive fast towards Southampton: "Holmes knowledge: of literature, nil, philosophy, nil, astronomy, nil, politics, feeble, botany, variable, geology, practical but limited, chemistry, profound, anatomy, accurate but unsystematic, sensational literature, immense, plays the violin well, is an expert singlestick player, boxer, and swordsman, has a good practical knowledge of British law. The logic isn't there. But the method: founded upon the observation of trifles. Just eliminate the impossible and there is, however, improbable, the truth. We go to London looking for the Truth. In London, people unanimously maintain a conspiracy of not knowing the logic. One word of truth is a pistol shot to them. When you find that London truth, you find the impossible, too. Just some hundred miles and we shall see separated love & truth, called Time, and in London, it is a paper which is seldom found in any hands but those of the highly educated." Southampton, we go through. Just Winchester, Basingstoke, and from Croydon side to London.

Basingstoke, here we come, just from 77 km southwest of London. That B has 114 000 inhabitants. There are two large further education colleges. The University of Winchester had a campus there. I say to Y: "That is a code word in Gilbert & Sullivan's comic opera Ruddigore."

Sherlock Town

I drive via A23 to the heart of London. The city is home to a collection of beautiful, quirky, and extensive stores celebrating printed pages. Thanks to the rise of digital retailers, the city´s independent booksellers have seriously upped their game. They have done so thanks to the sort of literary niches, characterful service, or café-style shopping experiences you simply don´t get on the internet.

There is Stanfords, London Review Bookshop, Daunt Books, Foyles, and so on. And we talk about in Foyles 4 miles worth of shelves holding 200 000 titles. There are graphic novels, comics, fiction, art, architecture. Hatchards, in Picadilly, has 100 000 books.

I say: "Here is Electric Breeze Audio productions, unabridged audiobooks, single narrator, multiple narrators, with sound effects and music, or without. Whatever your project is that requires spoken word recording, the chances are, they do it. They record also voice-overs, podcasts, audio blogs, and radio productions. They live in a digital world and supply your finished project in whatever digital format you require. Cd masters utilize DDP image creation software to create a digital red book. They have a dedicated ipDTL suite allowing offsite remote recording, and connection to other studios anywhere in the world via the net, you know, high-quality audio streaming. Their client is also BBC Radio 4. They have UK, US, and Canadian audiobooks and voiceover artists.

There is Foreign Languages Teaching & Research Press, Joint Publishing Ltd, Audio Visual Installation, Audio Engineer´s Reference Books. The U.S. as Audible official site, Digi Book, and overdrive. But the question goes how to but this net straight away to book towns and connect it with for instance Finland´s audiobooks. Finnish audiobooks can be listened to in the web browser for free. So, paper books cost some sum, e-books are sometimes 80 % cheaper and y can get audiobooks for free.

The Electric books are normally 20-25 % cheaper than paperbacks and audiobooks are a little bit, about 5 % more expensive than paperbacks. So, these are the questions: "Here are miles and miles, millions of paperbacks, not yet many e-books and audiobooks. How do you find the best experts to do those certain book types to audios in nearby book towns? How do you make them your sponsors and investors? How to take obstacles away between cultural adventure, and electronic- and audiobook adventure? Very simple: our 40 nerds are here today. They learn those Breeze Audio things and then we begin to do great show business."

Y: "Is it legal?" Cliver: "We do not have time for that. Correct, anti-dodgey?" I: "Bob is here also today. Let´s go to sleep. We have traveled all night. Park Plaza Westminster Bridge London."

Y do not give up so easily: "What do you Tapio mean by attacking those audio- and electric markets?" I: "Very simple, no need to think anything else, but how to put all data to a very small space. It is your databank, operative & strategic center. There you make your net-space attacks and conquer the marketplace. It must be just more productive, quick, reactive, and enjoyable than others. It must have a new form. And that we must put there. If it does not have a new form, it drowns in the sea of information. So that form is like flypapers to sponsors. It must have Sherlock & Brkn, truth & love. People do not look at codes. They look at and take part in fascinating performances, which are for millions of people. Our love adventure is one of a kind. Believe me." I kiss You.

The Hotel stands near The Truth

Time is 6:15 am when my Mustang arrives with its U.S. - number plate to the hotel. At the same time in NYC, movie mogul Mr. Harven Weinstein has been found guilty of rape but not the higher charges of predatory sexual assault. He faces between 5 and 25 years in prison after jurors in Manhattan Criminal Court finds him guilty of raping an actress. District Attorney Cyrus Vance cannot be happier: "These survivors weren´t just brave, they were heroic. This is a big day. This is a new day." Weinstein is handcuffed and lead away after judge J. Burke ordered him taken to jail immediately. There vanishes like that, snap, a lifetime work of a man, who has worked every day 16 hours.

Meanwhile, Y & Cliver & I go to the Park Plaza hotel. Now we can relax in s sophisticated South Bank suite with a view. It is decorated with contemporary flair and a hint of boutique-style elegance, comfortable hotel rooms with sophisticated comfort and modern amenities. The rooms include suites with terraces. Cliver takes his room and runs off.

Victoria and I go to our room and I look straight to Big Ben, that side is surrounded by London's most iconic attractions. We have just some walks to Westminster Abbey, the Houses of Parliament, and the London Eye in five minutes tour.

I'm so tired and just jump on to the white bed and put my head on the sunset orange pillow.

I wake up late, at 2 pm. You have already been to the shops and looking for this and that in London, and Cliver had been running. I go to the shower. I stay there for a long time. After 20 minutes, I have my suit on. I kiss Y and eat bacon & eggs. English breakfasts are like in Southern American prison wood. They punish people from the rising sun.

I go to the restaurant and order a double *Wiener schnitzel* with four eggs. I say to Y while eating a little better breakfast: "Time to call those nerds to help. And Frank later." I take my phone and call one of the nerds, John: "Are you still in the station, come to London Bridge. There is a yellow bus, go in I'm there. We have much to do and take all your tech with you."

My brains are numb as always in England and particularly in London. Here everything is so ossified & petrified, and slowly going. Cliver comes to me: "Ay mayne, when shall we get the hell outto dogge." I must curl up with these Londoners. Or do like Sherlock did, take my violin = gat, and make this rainy-day dollar smiling day.

How to bribe Bob´s way

I call Bob: "Tell me about bribes, and how they can give in the grand scale."

Bob laughs: "I shall be also at Bridge. Do Y mean real good bank business? It is always so nice to talk with y. The payment of bribes and gratuities to officials of financial institutions, such as meals, entertainment, and gifts must be made very well. Here in England, there can be arranged a weekend hunting or fishing, tickets to athletic or theatrical events. But you surely not think about that?" I. "Of course not. We shall make them and entrepreneurs good entertainment, real orgies." Bob says: "Gifts of money are good and other items of value which are otherwise available to everyone rich fellas, and for dishonest purposes are good bribery.

We can offer a discount or a refund to all purchasers as a legal rebate first and then to the good bribery. And we must give a discount specifically to that person or these persons to influence him/them to look favorably. That is the good bribery. And then we bribe them all good more. Think MyTapioBoy, a good bribe is always an illegal and unethical gift bestowed to influence the recipient´s conduct. Gooooood money, goods, rights in action, property, preferment, privilege, emolument, objects of value, advantage, or merely a promise to induce and influence the action, vote, and influence of a person in an official and public capacity, they are gooood."

Bob laughs so much: "Think, think, think we give them money just light that, we can say that we help you with taxes, grey business exchange, a unity of account, a store of value, and a standard of deferred payment, our money helps with the market phenomenon. Think goods, those great bribes like tangible property, services, even Earth's atmosphere, free goods. Think food, clothing, cars, parking spaces, cinemas, private parks, satellite television, fish stocks, timber, coal, free-to-air television, air, national defense, think economic intangibles, fast-moving consumer goods, final goods, intangible assets, intangible good, economics topics, goods and services, services, tangible property. Tapio, think chose in action, chose in position, promissory notes, documentary intangibles, assigned, novated, dematerialized, global notes, pledge, negotiables bailments, marriage, death, bankruptcy, bills in exchange, property acts, insolvency, think property, and bribes in it, like consume, alter, share, redefine, rent, mortgage, pawn, sell, exchange, transfer, give away, private, public, collective property, cooperative property, real property, personal property, intellectual property, inventions, right of ownership. Tapio, think about executive privileges, parliamentary privileges, privilege (canon law), privilege (evidence), privilege du blanc, the privilege of peerage, privilege (social inequality), Szlachta's privileges, all can be sold and be bribes, Yeahhh.

Think financial compensations, benefits, rewards, salaries, and wages. Tapio, I'm so happy! tips, gifts, sops, perks, skims, favors, discounts, waived fees/tickets, free food, free ads, tree trips, tree tickets, sweetheart deals, kickback/paybacks, funding, inflated, sales of objects or properties, lucrative contracts, donations, campaign contributions, fundraisers, sponsorships/backings, higher-paying jobs, stock options, secret commissions, and promotions, payoffs, cash for honors, cash-for-questions affairs, revolving doors, pots-de-win, legal plunder, lobbying, match-fixing, money trail-loop, pay to pay, influence peddling, bid-rigging, and ambitus."

I say: "I want gang-warriors Tack, Cad, Tot, Bock, Zan, and pool-dancers, right now to come to London. I call Farmer, he may arrange their coming with NYC tech-agents." Bob: "Do that, meanwhile I make good traps for Londoners."

Oxford calls

My mood has gone up. I´m almost happy. I kiss Y. Y ask: "Y are going to bribe officials and entrepreneurs? Isn´t that a crime. You shall be behind the bars for a long time. Do you think I do not have takers, even doggies, fans, directors, and clients?" I: "We must go to the Bridge."

It is 3:00 pm when Cliver, you, and I stand in the west end of the Bridge. I lean to the yellow bus. My sunglasses look sick. Y look amazing, with your new red dress and black leather coat on. Cliver has his Versace-suit on. We look rich & happy. The bunch of nerds begins to arrive from the east end of the Bridge. Those are our days Digi-nomads. They wander under the wandering stars. Life is great.

I make a call: "Hello Frank, I want you at Electric Breeze Audio, 100a Cowley Rd, Cowley, Oxford OX4 1JE. Take all 7 seals with Y, and the handguns. We rob the place."

Frank: "Ok, we come, but we do not rob anything." I: "Yes, you do, Mr. Sunshine." I drop the call and look at Bob who has just arrived. He has a modern blue checked shirt on. He looks tall and stylish. And he has the duration of a smile on, it wins every woman´s fav. I say to Bob the Smile: "Go to the bus, stay near if I have something to ask."

And then comes the bunch of nerd-nomads. John asks: "So? I: "Go in and do not break your tech." I say to the driver the address. I smile to

Y: "Somebody may say: it started at Oxford and all shall always end there, but the speaker wasn't Sherlock or me. Now we break the embankment and let the data flow to it chaotic places. Break the embankment is the Bribe-thing. We do not have time to wait for licenses for the next five years. We do not follow the British, American, or EU-law but Natural law. Me, Y & Sherlock."

I kiss Y. You feel not comfortable at all: "I do not want you, Tapio, to go to prison." I: "I mean good. I do not arm these men's tongues with the poison of falsehoods. Let's do the good and fly."

I jump to the Mustang and so do Y and Cliver. We go towards Oxford. I take a call: "Hello, Electric Breeze, here is Tapio ..."

Now they know who is coming and why. I know that their studios aren't huge, but they have their audio-production stuff. We go to Oxford. Mark Zuckerberg, Mr. Facebook, was from Harvard, surely, we meat the same kind of genius with empty pockets from Oxford. Just put the money there and earphones to that genius, Nature rap'n roll the rest.

I call to the yellow bus in front of us: "Hello John, do Y know any particular virtual-math-fella from Oxford." J: "Yop, Jump, studies there, actually he works in that shop Virtual Reality, doing everyman's jobs like run simulations to help reduce anxiety, uses VR as part of the design process to enable engineers to view their designs in 3D and gain a greater understanding of how it works, virtual simulations for medical training and education, walk around 3D visualizations of archaeological sites, field trips: visit Mars, data visualization, that kind of shit. He cannot do right now his fav: NASA Concepts Bring Precision to New Virtual Reality Experiences at all."

Soon we are arriving at Oxford.

Meanwhile, in NYC high-ranking lawmakers and family members of people killed by NYPD are asking the nation not to support former mayor Michael Bloomberg's campaign for the presidency. Ninety New Yorkers of color signs a letter outlining the Bloomberg era policies they say disproportionately harmed New Yorkers of color: "The fella has attempted to rewrite his legacy." His white power time subway cops were slamming people against walls, random searches conducted in front of children, and guns drawn on unarmed teenagers. Bloomberg suggests one could just Xerox descriptions of young men of color when looking for criminals. The extent of harm, humiliation, and terror that the B administration´s daily racial profiling and police violence caused in Black, Latin, and other communities of color cannot be overstated.

Taking the Studio

Meanwhile, the center of digital innovation comes near, with Passle, Brainomix, Labstep. It is also a paradise for death scientists. Merry-jolly well-dressed gentleman must have an all-cotton Oxford cloth button-down shirt from Brooks Brothers. We stop in front of the Virtual Reality shop.

Jump goes outto the house and I go to him: "How are Y, I need you right now. Here is some cash, are you in?" Jump looks at money, and he looks at me: "Jeah, let´s fuck off." So Electric Breeze is near.

 We stop at Cowley road, near Sushi Corner and I and Cliver go in. I say to You: "We have guts. Now it begins." Small houses, small streets, looks like a village, very old fashioned, and not at all updated. Huge difference with Brooklyn centers. I go in from the small white, glassed door, and nearly hit my head, the door must be only 185 cm. We are in.

A tinny fella with a black shirt on comes to us: "So. You are Mr. Tapio." I: "Yes, how much?" He: "What do you mean?" I: "How much this box costs?" He: "What box?" I: "This firm." He: "We do not sell it." I: "OK. How much for hiring it. I have not much time." He: "We do not ..." I grab his neck: "Yes you do, right now, how much?" His face comes so redly: "May I ask others?" I: "No you don´t. How much for two days?" He: "20 000 pounds." I laugh: "Here are 40 000 pucks but now I hired you also. Let´s go."

I go outside and whistle the nerds in. 40 nerds come in. Cliver and I go through those small rooms, which have amazing Digi-tech-things there. I say to Jump & John: "Open channels to all Book town and to those 20 most famous books shops in London, and connections with Oxford, Cambridge, and Harvard university-nets. I send Y soon orders from London city."

Cliver & I run back to the Mustang, we jump in. I say to you: "Bab, I must go back to London. Some deals to make." I kiss Y. I call Frank: "Where are you?" He: "Five minutes." I: "OK."

Well, I go to a shop and buy some mixed juice form Ribena and Um Bongo, some sandwiches Cucumber & Strawberry-Chicken. We eat them when Frankie & SEALs arrive. I smile: "At last. Time to go to London and rob those shops."

Before we go, I say to Bob: "Begin to call so-called sponsors to Rosewood. The staff, cafe, food, the best. We shall make there tonight a private party, where we shall bribe real Londoners and deep Londoners. Make all arrangements and offer them pure splendor." Bob: "Y shall be sure about that." Franks four cars and my Mustang begin the trip to conquer those shops in London.

Gamazon´s shit

It is 5 pm, and everything seems to be better than well. A well-spent day brings happy sleep, and well-spent life brings happy death.

We go first to Covent Garden, there is Stanfords. It is mentioned in The Hound of the Baskervilles. Then it situated in a grand old building on Long Acre. 167 years later it sits just around the corner at 7 Mercer Walk. We go in.

There are shelves stacked high with travel writing, guides, maps, and gifts. Captain Scott, Florence Nightingale, and the British Army haven been customers. And if it has got out of trouble James Bond and Sherlock Holmes, it could surely help us.

In the Stanfords we go behind the act drop. I and Frank go to the service center. There is Standford's for business, and all the data, SAMS, GIS, A-Z data, every scale data, aerial data, terrain data, planning portal. I look at books refined by classification, continents, countries, regions, cities, supra-regions, publishers, price filter, delivery sets round the world.

One fella comes to me: "Who the hell are you? What are you doing behind the screens? How did you get on the computer?" I: "It was open. Stop asking questions. Where is your audio- and e-books, you bofs?"

Is there just Beginner´s Chinese (Mandarin) with Online Audio, Himalaya (Audio CD), Beginner´s Yoruba with Online Audio, Get Started in Latin American Spanish Absolute Beginner Course (book and audio support)? Y fu**er, MyVictoria does better than this. I see just the Gamazon´s audible, Foyles (Oxfam, Waterstones, and London - Hatchards). It seems to be one question: how bookshops survive the Gamazon onslaughts. The Gamazon hits hard by the rise of e-commerce, the book trade believes it has found ways to thrive."

The fella changes his attitude to me: "What, yes, to anyone who remembers the chaotic old Foyles bookstore in central London, its new incarnation a few doors further up Charing Cross Road is a remarkable sight."

I know that booksellers were among the first retailers to feel the full force of the Gamazon effect, with the Borders chain closing in 2011, the rest of the industry has begun to suffer. In the past two years, there has been a string of retail bankruptcies and mall closures as a result of the relentless rise of e-commerce. Yet the Barnes & Noble deal is the latest sign that the book trade, at least, may have seen Gamazon reach the peak of its influence and found ways to survive.

I say: "There are limits to the online experiences of Gamazon, we are doing them now. We shoot the fucker to its head, right this momentum. America is very under-bookshopped. The fucker Gamazon collects all the data from the markets as do those US-Canadian porn-moguls. We must give Gamazon good old fist on the nose, hah, hah."

The fella´s eyes shine: "Artillery?" I: "Just broke the nose and teeth and jaw and the mother**cker crawls back into its hole."

I´m sure that the publishing business will be hoping that Mr. Daund and Mr. Tapio shall succeed. A commercially viable physical retail sector is seen as critical for providing some balance to the Gamazon.

I say to the fella: "As well as transforming the way books are marketed, priced and sold, the e-commerce group has moved into direct competition with publishers through its own publishing activities, in physical, screen, and audio formats. Its global reach also poses a fundamental challenge to long-established arrangements for territorial rights and distribution - cornerstones of the industry´s business model. I know that chief executive of the UK arm of Hachette Mr. David Shelley says: ´The Gamazon is the decisive factor in our business.´ But I do not care what the fuck**er says, even though he is one of the big four English-language publishers alongside HarperCollins, Macmillan, and Penguin Random House.

Publishers chafe at Gamazon´s tough negotiating tactics and demands that, as suppliers, they reorganize their internal structures to suit the retailer´s needs. The Gamazon is a brutal partner - both a source and concern and a fact of life, but so what, bigger the fella, higher it comes, and they always fall like American oak. I know that. I have fought so many fights."

I say: "I know UK books sales have recovered after tougher years but let´s hit the Gamazon really hard. Yet G has enabled publishers to reach a wider market of customers and made it easy to sell to them. Readers have shown their happiness with G in the shape of purchases worth billions of dollars every year. Somebody may say G opened the world to books and we say thank you, but I say, we must open it better via Book Towns Group and show how G has stolen our data and made us poor, and almost without a culture of our own.

Let´s kill the fucker. In recent years many publishers were anxious that the Gamazon and the digital disruption it represented would overwhelm their industry in the same way it had film and music. We must create a business with a global scale to be a credible counterweight to the Gamazon. Changes made in response to the Gamazon have helped make its sector more efficient and profitable, helped by a 5-4 percent increase in non-fiction. Sales and profits have held up. One result of this is that the big publishers now enjoy lucrative economies of scale, working their backlists, and using their buying power to cut production and warehousing costs. Publishing is at root a catalog business. Most new books are only about a third as profitable as backlist titles. The big publishers can gear their businesses in such a way that the cost of all their operations is covered by the profits from the backlists, allowing them to tun their new books program more like a spread bet.

This is not an advantage enjoyed by smaller and mid-sized players. The lack of backlist scale limits profitability. If the big houses look to achieve profit margins of about 10 percent and above, smaller operators must settle for low single digits. The traditional physical book proves to be hugely flexible in technology. Ebooks announced for 24 percent of total UK sales last year. It seems that everyone's Kindle battery died on the same day. And still, it is a lively market, with sales mostly in ebook form and often through Gamazon, but one where precise data is hard to come by. But dear fellas it is contributing to a bigger ebook market than is being officially recorded.

This is more digital savvy. Publishers change their operations in areas such as marketing - whether through better management of a book's electronic metadata to improve discoverability on the Gamazon or reaching readers direct via social media. Data analytics also informs pricing strategies and the understanding of consumer trends. The more data you've got, the more competitive you are. They are quick to pounce on the latest social media hit, but they are less goooooood at building and managing online communities, thestreet credibility, that drives a lot of reader engagement. There come us, Victoria and others, Book Towns Group and brooklynization, Y & M, and our GUN & KISS.

And now downloaded audio has become the fastest-growing format, with US sales growing 29 percent. It salutes the great men in their thirties and forties. The Gamazon effect is apparent, but Audible gets now Book Towns Group. And books now account for less than 10 percent of total Gamazon sales worth 232 bn. Let´s kill the fucker. Take the new model, cos the new model is more bespoke, placing attention on the shop floor environment. And there shall always be, via gun & kiss serendipity and the ability to interact with people who know and love books. Let´s make via our love adventure books audio and then virtual and then living things. We must focus and understand that we have materialized poetry ourselves. We are the math, and that is the kiss."

All around me hurrah to me. The fella of the shop asks: "So what shall we do?" I laugh: "Isn´t it obvious. We put the data to a new form, take the markets back from Gamazon, and live happily and luxurious ever after." The fella: "Exact?"

I: "We are opening right now all data channels via Cambridge, Oxford, Harvard London amazing book data stores and book towns and but that all data to Book Towns Group. And who owns bigger data, as bigger backlists and kill the Dragon = the Gamazon. The knight that has the biggest heart wins the Lady.

Rov´d ´mid the forests´ haunts with wild delight! The Gamazon focuses on e-commerce, cloud computing, digital streaming, and artificial intelligence. As the NYC mobs have five big families in the tech part there is four big tech companies, G + Apple + Google + Facebook. It is the top influential economic and cultural force in the world. They control the market. The Gamazon is the largest online marketplace, all assistant provider, and cloud computing platform as measured by revenue and market capitalization. It is the largest net-company by revenue in the world.

Mr. Zeff Tezos built an attacking company and it attacked straight away books online markets, then electronics, software, vid games, apparel, furniture, food, toys, and jewelry. His Kindle e-readers, and so eats others from the market. It ate Goodreads in the year 2013. Trump saw right away what that giant robber is doing. He said: "The Gamazon costs to US Post Office massive amounts of money for being their delivery boy. A should pay these costs and not have them bourne by the American taxpayer.

The Gamazon's payments to the USPS are not made public and their contract has a reputation for being a sweetheart deal. The Gamazon wages and working conditions in a series of YouTube videos and media appearances stink and are bad. The Gamazon paid in 2018 no federal income tax. It is a low-security prison. The owner says that all US and UK employees will earn a 15d minimum wage. The company eliminates stock awards and bonuses for hourly employees. There have been strikes against company leadership. It has conflicts with the CIA and DOD. The Company lobbies on the US Congress, the Federal Communications Commission, and Federal Reserve. It lobbies with tens of million dollars. It has access to NHS data. Today Gamazon attack even the Defense Department, when DD made a 10 bd contract with Microsoft.

It seemed in 2012 that the Gamazon was killing off the books business entirely. But new authors, building their customer base, need physical bookshops, which are lovely, tactile, friendly, expert, welcoming places. Destroy those bookshops and the Gamazon is acting to achieve just that and the very commercial and cultural base to the book industry is destroyed. Like Humpty Dumpty.

In 2000 the behemoth slowly ate away at the High Street market. The Seattle-company controls 60 % of all physical books sold and 95 % of the e-book market. The casualties are most chains, Borders, Ottakar´s,

Dillons, Hammocks, and James Thin. Indie bookstores declined from about 1 550 in 2005 to about 600. Indies account for about 5 % of the market.

The Gamazon lubricates the media and it is ranked as one of the most admired and respected companies in the world. The Gamazon builds brand loyalty like in the army, others do not. Physical bookstores try to fight back redesigning their stores and running small events. They have begun to give book hotels, coffees where parents want to bring children and children want to be. The Gamazon, the robber, has forgotten that there is no book culture without libraries, librarians, publishers, and readers. The Gamazon began to negotiate with Hachette and with pressure tactic the Gamazon made it soon impossible to buy Hachette´s books. The Gamazon kept the authors' books as a hostage. The Gamazon doesn´t love books. To Gamazon, books are just a Loss Leader. By selling batteries and soap Gamazon has driven down the price of books, which is convincing people that books aren´t worth much.

But the Gamazon doesn´t understand. Books change lives, and they´re beautiful objects, they are worth a lot, in their mental word. The Gamazon, the robber, cannot conquer your brains, cos it just robs data like a parasite. It cannot kill the authors and publishers, meat, and blood. When bookstores disappear, so do booksellers and book culture. The Gamazon is threatening the entire culture of books so it can sell more batteries and soap: "Check out our mysteriously cheap books, and since you´re here, why not reorder some regularly priced batteries and soap?

The Gamazon tries hard to succeed and destroy its competition. It will continue slashing prices. So, let´s help it. Let´s put its books without price to the net. I have a meeting with Zeffrey Reston Tezos later today. Bobby has taken care of that. I shall tell him in Rosewoods that if he doesn't put right away 50 million dollars to Book Towns Group his all books shall be published immediately without any price.

The richest man in modern history is not stoopid. He is just corporate fat cat, shysty & voracious. He knows that it shall also be a catastrophe to book business, but is shall be most of all end of his battery-soap-book-business. And he doesn´t care anything else but his business so that jew bag shall piss to his trousers.

Well, ladies & gentlemen. That´s it as they say: Abercrombie and Fitch."

The fella at Stanford's is out and does not see bouncing poppies: "How can you take his books outto the Gamazon? It shall be a crime." I laugh: "Dead baby joke, you are good. Gr8 fa2." I tap his shoulders. He looks upset and absent. I cheer him up: "My Friend, ofc it is a crime. But it is a crime which shall be remembered, like Robin Hood & his jolly good friends. I have the key. I open via your databanks and universities banks and the Gamazon own banks all data and give Mr. Zeff a demonstration in 2 hours. Then he is lubricated and bribed very well indeed. And the crime changes to the bliss. It is always a question of the angle, but if your heart´s smiles Our Smiling Friend smiles with you. Take the risk and die - or smile."

The Demonstration

I continue: "We are going through the other big bookshop here and open the data from their nets to universities and to our main office, which we have hired for two days."

I call Bob: "Did Zeff get the message? Oh, great, and shall he come? No. Well, give the phone to John. Okay, are connections made to university data and Book Towns. Ok. Give the phone to Jump. Hello, put to the net 5 000 Gamazon books. Some old stuff, easy to be replaced. Show them that we are serious. Bob, give me the direct number of Mr. Zeff. Thanks. What do you mean do not call? Ofc I call and threaten him as hard as I can."

I: "Hello there, Zeff Tezos, how is the aerospace things going on. Violet Origin goes well, and Expeditions, too? Noice to here. Who am I? I'm Tapio Tiihonen and challenging you. If you do not pay right now 50 million dollars, I do not care how, to my firm Book Towns Group, I shall pull the trigger and end your book-robbery-businesses. And do not try to send Ramit Alarwal against me, cos then I open all your books for free. There is now open 5 000 your medieval time books on the net. No harm was done yet, but after fifteen minutes, if you do not give a straight answer, I publish them all.

Going to yell? Well, gladly, but you go done, too. Let´s go to mud, hand in hand then. It suits me. Isn´t it strange, Trump, the president, couldn´t regulate G in any meaningful way, but I can? Well, Trump holds his presidency, and I hold just the Truth, given away impossibility, as Sherlock Holmes should say. So Yes or No. Make your mind, you charlatan & mountebank & turnaround tipster."

I hear Mr. Zeff direct orders to check this call and look at book pages. Then the honey voice of his appears on the phone. Before he continues this grab, I say loud and clear: "Hey Zeff, I´m right now in Stanfords London, and I'm more than ready to meet you with the police or without them. So, My Good Fella Bob has talked with you before. Think your friend Bernie Sanders try to be selected next president, should it be quite a bad thing if you shall go to jail now? Then minutes to go."

There begins silence. Mr. Tau Beta Pi thinks carefully. His quick thinking gave him summa cum laude from Princeton University, so he chose the persuasive pronunciation: "Please, can we talk about it. Rosewood, I shall be there gladly at 8 pm." I: "Funderful, I remind you that I collect now the Gamazon data information and put it in a nutshell if Y shall suddenly change your mind. I do not trust you, my friend."

I know his bolt head shall be all read right now, but that doesn´t help him. He says: "I`ll be there." I: "Shiz. Do not burden your mind with small matters unless you have some very good reason for doing so. I do not wanna show people a drop of water, cos then it will reduce the existence of the Atlantic."

I stopthe call and take the call to Jump: "Did you have the Stanford data, okay. We keep on steppin."

Meanwhile, Mr. Zeff is outto his mind. His high-level advisers are around him with their six-page narratives: "All information of that b & t right now."

More Bookshops

The Mustang and four SEALs´ car run to Bloomsbury (London review Bookshop), where behind classical and new fiction, history, politics, and philosophy is a room where the connections shall be made to our virtual center. We take the data there and have no time to talk to anybody. They call somewhere. But stop calling, when I put the deal-paper to their CEO´s hand.

Next Marylebone, Daunt Books, same there, then Charing Cross Road, Foyles (there we find data of 200 000 titles), Soho, Forty Dean Street, Soho, gosh!, full of European fiction, vintage children´s books, and indie releases as well as mainstream superhero fare, Bloomsbury, Gay´s the Word, sex, relationships, parenting and children, Hyde Park, Koenig Books, Persephone Books, out-of-print novels, 20th-century female writers, Charing Cross Road, Quinto & Francis Edwards, secondhand books, fiction paper books Picadilly, Hatchards (which Gamazon recently attacked), 100 000 books, Primrose Hill, Primrose Hill Books, second-hand books, King´s Cross Word on the Water, Kentish Town Owl Bookshop, Spitalfield, Libreria, Hackney, Broadway Bookshop, East Ham, Newham Bookshop, Brixton, Bookmongers, Sydenham, Kirkdale Bookshop, Pecham Review Bookshop, and Chiswick, Foster Books, of print, used and rare books.

We just open the data, send audio- and e-books, and list of paper books to the virtual center. Jump as an Oxford student can open Oxford-book data and with the help of NYC-nerds they put together Harvard´s and Cambridge book-data. There are many million audio- and electric-books and tens of millions of listed paper books. They are collected and put together with the book information that Frank and seals have collected from book towns. That information shall be sent immediately to book towns.

I read those book towns deals with Frank and sign them on the behalf of Book Towns Group. The collected information shall be sent also to 20 London bookshops. And now it is left only the Gamazon. Shall we make a deal with them and change information and those bookshops and towns get also the Gamazon information, which it has robbed 20 years, or shall we publish that information right away? The Gamazon stays outto our collected information, and the channels will be closed from it. The time is 19:30 pm. We are ready for going to Rosewoods.

My brains are nearly exploding, but there is no time for sweetness and happiness. Mr. Zeff is ready but so am I.

Meanwhile we are attending to that luxury, the NY-state's homeowners deal with plumbing disasters, burst pipes, and leaky fixtures. Water causes quickly damage to a foundation, electric wiring, and drywall. You need to determine the source of the lead, fix the problem, and then take care of any water damage. So New Yorkers turn off the flow of water, wrap a towel or silicone ´plumbing repair tape around the site of the leak, and call a professional. Mold and mildew require the help of a specialist. Bathroom and kitchen damage shall be repaired, and many Brkners remodel and update the bathroom of their dreams. New Yorkers ask family and friends for recommendations, get more than one job -estimate, and read reviews. And plumbers, contractors, and real Brkners are happy.

The Rosewoods Deal

Y, Cliver, and I are going to late luxury afternoon tea with fresh finger sandwiches, scones, delicate cakes, and the fine leaf tea at Rosewood. There has been called London cream with sugar and our table is for us and Mr. Zeff. The bribe giver and reserves are at present.

 I introduce Y and Cliver and myself, and Mr. Zeff looks unhappy. I say to him: "Zeff, gloom lobster you get to pay a lot of attention to yourself. You get to take yourself so very seriously. Cry a little bit, then down in the dumps can´t stick in your soul; it slicks with tears." He looks at me: "I´m not Grumperson Jones. People with no purpose are gleepy." I think: "I do not begin to have my tea, with angry words. I must flirt to convert Y that a friend is someone who knows all about you and still loves you."

He: "So you want the Gamazon book-data, gathered after hard work, just like that, and give to me some rural printings and dry books of common sense. And you think it is ok with me?" I assure: "I'm not asking anything, I´m commanding you to give them, cos your 20 years hard work was a robbery. You put other people´s ideas and hard work to new covers and told the world, I know. You didn´t/don´t. You know how to gaffle. If you steal a dime, you are in jail; if you boost 10 000, you can start a business; if you cop tens of millions, everybody respects you; and in your chase, if you debo tens of billions, you are a rainmaker and a miracle-Zeff. I want you to esrun your materials back to those from you shanghai them and help them and take their data and secure it. Dis is my deal.

I put on the table a paper. There reads that we shall be partners. You give as an inventor to my fund 50 million dollars and its use shall be calculated prezactly. It shall be put to rural cultural centers with virtual ideas. Your company shall give first-hand knowledge of your space-virtual inventions to cultural-centers and make a net with them and 20 biggest bookshops in London."

He cusses and rips the paper. I take my smartphone and ax: "Zeff, shall I push the button? Then you shall be a really disconsolate crimiel." I put my hand to my pocket and take another copy of our deal and hit it on the table: "Now sign and stop wasting my time. I like to watch the presentation. They are from Brooklyn, and they are better than your Texas cowgirls."

Zeff takes a pen and makes his scrawl under the deal. The room is full of big-wallet Londoners, and we must bribe them all. I'm not going to do it myself, but Frank is the man with his SEALs. He goes with his tuxedo-suit from table to table and make sure that everybody signs the bread.

Zeff looks at me curiously: "What is going on?" Cliver wants to speak with the world's richest man: "Whats Hannan, awt? Those do five-finger discounts so here is poppin' tags. We lick." Zeff tries to stand up, but Cliver keeps him down: "Whair yall goin? Wind your neck in. You're Gamazon yes-man. Don't get behind me. Restecpa."

You ask: "What there read in those papers?" I say: "We thank them to come here and make this celebration possible. With their influence and positive attitude every door opens, and we can now think of them as possible investors in our fund, which helps book towns, and on their side. Quests shall be welcomed, whenever they like to come to our 4-month tour in Europe. This celebration shall be a ticket to that tour, and everybody that joins this celebration shall have a privilege to be considered as a member of Book Towns Group funding family. Please, enjoy this party and next parties for free, we shall always remember with great honor and gifts persons who made this celebration of 10 million-dollar fund come true, cos this celebration with you is the fund. Thank you very much. Honoro ... So, read there, and Frank just asks people to sign, so they can be marked in their order places in these great celebrations and so funds existence."

The Bribe-Daddy Time

The parties begin. And the Brkner-playing pocket pools and chicken sugar hips nuggets arrive, and one eight seven bang bang bang rap-things arrive. The EDM-lights begin to flow and feed the cats and make cherries and blueberries. Bribing always begins slowly, then it comes faster. The food and drinks come heavier while the first words of "*ay papi, yo quiero u cuerpo*" have been said and cash put the butts and beans & greens begin to rain. Splenda daddies change quickly to sugar daddies who are ready to fly you to heaven this weekend.

And Clur gives one fake tits- and butts -boney the microphone: "My sugar daddy stopped paying my rent and I got evicted. I pulled my bm self together and now I have a Splenda daddy that gets me the occasional man bag, spa day, and bag of tina." Mr. Zeff begins to turn on from his unhappy suit: "Yes, financially sound, smart with investment and flying in first class."

I look at Y. Nobody asks whaddya´ mean anymore, even real splendadaddies kick their "broke af" off.

Partizzle zaang. Drop salad begins unconscious flow. Cad & Tot makes a family of freestyle BMX. There is a freestyle battle: oh, you mad cuz I'm styling on you. Frank gives me those signed papers. We get after busting a flow.

Just great, tables laden with grapes almost ready for harvesting. Thereare Oscietra Caviar, blinis, *creme frauche*, Origin Baerii Caviar, and ofc Beluga Caviar. And green beans, frisée salad, confit tomato, *focaccia*, rosary goat's cheese, corn fed chicken, so fresh that it almost flies away, pickled apple, shaved fennel, and smoked caviar. Roasted cauliflower steak, lilliput capers, golden raisins, autumn risotto, wild mushrooms, truffle, samphire, turnip, cockles nages, roasted venison loin, purple potato crips and sides mashed potato, tender stem Broccolli. Laughing, yelling, dancing, and more laughing corrupt benefactors put in their mouth Madagascan vanilla bean ice cream, warm Valrhona chocolate sauce, Herefordshire blackberries, meringue, vanilla cream, and certainly Tiramisu: coffee Mascarpone foam, espresso Jelly, more chocolate cream. And lemon, pear, and Calmanni, raspberry. Golddiggers full gooddaddies and baddaddies mouths with Moscato d'Ati, Nicole, Michele Chiarlo, Riesling Beerenauslese, Weingut Göttelmann. One fattie swallows Maori blue, with honey, sandalwood, and a dash of vanilla, take herbal illusions, fabulous chamomile yields a smooth liquor, tasting exhaling pleasant aromas enhanced by a lovely hint of the white magnolia flower. The speed goes faster. Golddigger caked Daddykate4 imitates Doglover199709's gorgeous dancing. All around are sugar hips and al sams make money raining miracles. The nearby pool begins to be full frogging. Daddy Yankee's fly girls seem to come frontups. Bgirl & Anand takes some bush-downs to exchange their contact details for a free price, an exchange of money, services, including the fancy more dinner, and quickies. Clur even sings a tribe called quest and bone thugs n harmony and Straight Outta Compton.

Well, Eazy-E has been dead for 24 years, and we gotta now a boy with skittle hairs that look like a girl and a dude who says 100 x Cucci-gang. Clurs verse is better than Migos whole career, can you tell ice cures real name. Mine is cold water block. Yeah, this is virtual reality, where golddiggers show real-life vid to daddies ... Cliver: "Then gangsters tried to be musicians after that musicians tried to be gangsters, and now gau autotune users trying to be humans. Clur WTF happened?"

I´m a little bit bored: "Give us back Eazy-E, Pac, and Biggie and we will give you Lil Wayne, Drake, and Nicki Minaj." Jeah, N.W.A. - Straight Outta Compton.

Celebrants and thunder inside boot and rally & light em up. A lot of vanilla coke makes thirsty and that´s an excuse to drink more. Pop. Sap attacks. They glaze. Oh, jeah, Mentha Piperita, Verbena Citrodora, and Rouge Opéra, with vodka all this is so coo´ when this infusion blends the melodious fragrance of red fruits and precious spices crowned by vanilla and the soft, street nuances of Rooibos tea. And daddies and bust-downs don´t forget Raspberry Delight, Rosemary sling, Bitter & Sweet with 48 %, the Age of Bronze, *altos reposado*, mint, *pistachio*, white chocolate, Arles de Sunflowers, Old Duff Genever, licorice, apricot, pandan, tonic, Girl With Balloon, Havanna, banana scones, aphrodite bitters, R´de Ruinart brut, champagnes by the glass, grander marques, dom Perignon, Laurent Perrier, Pol Roger, Taittinger, Bruno Paillard, pinot blanc, Chateau d´Escland, Whispering Angel, Grenach Blend ... And then 7 f´s and big f´s, unrequited love - foreva.

Clur sings good, yo ren, what´s up, and tell ´em where you are from. I look easy on the eye and so mean mug. We got Houston high-five. I bog off. We go to the old bridge and feel post-party depression - smiling ppd.

You say: "That´s it. They are bribed?" I: "Yus, one direction, all of them. We cut them so bad." I have in my pocket names, I call Bob: "They all went to it. Give Jump. Cut the connections to universities, bookshops, and book towns, make the code, and make an algorithm, I give you 10 t grand. Begin to do those virtual stimulations. I come tomorrow at 6 am. Buy." Huh, what a hard day. Y: "So Sherlock?" I: "You saw just some minutes ago the footprints of a gigantic hound." Y do not give up: "Sherlock?"

So Sherlock Freestyle

I say: "Well if you wanna draw attention to the curious incident of the dog in the night-time." You: "The dog did nothing in the night-time." I: "Jes, just the same old story. That was the curious incident." Y: "What do you mean?" I: "They did it in a group, not as individual persons."

This isn´t enough for Y: "Group-people and not individuals? Are you teasing me Tapio?"

I: "Think, Bab, set of fellas who have the same interests and aims, who easily organize themselves to work and act together. Groups can spread as a planting movement encountering barriers of understanding and acceptance. Normally they define ´people group´ with the goal in mind. Bab, you do not need to think about Arabs, multi-ethnic things, Gospel strategy. They need a mission, target in a paper, and education. Rosewoods people are paper-group people, not e-book-group-people or audio-book-people. But give them a virtual show where they can take apart then it comes to an adventure, and those people can be organized as an adventure-group.

And at the same time, the pieces drop in their places and good adventure-group as an understanding of e- and audiobooks also. That group connection is inner similarity spread the main idea to bones and blood."

Y: "And an individual?" I: "He is a separate organism. He has rights and goals, and responsibilities, but his situation is much clearer than groups. He is a person, but the group isn´t. A person has personal responsibilities, while the group doesn´t. Legal person, so companies, institutions have responsibilities written by law, but individuals are free, equal in dignity and rights, what groups and the legal people aren´t. But if Y look details those persons aren't equal at all. The person is a whole entity, the group isn´t a whole entity, it does not have a character and lifelong temperament & trust.

The person dies, the group breaks down. And most of all person loves just another person, the group doesn´t love just another group. Group-people do not love like individuals, they are easy to change. You cannot trust group-people, cos their personality is hidden in a hierarchy. But you can control them and make them do as you want, but you can never trust them. Individuals are the concrete, who keeps the group and groups together. You saw what happened there. They were group-people."

You aren´t happy at all to my explanation: "Y talk like a schoolboy. Sherlock, please."

I: "Well mediocrity-group-people knows nothing higher than itself, but talent talent-individual instantly recognizes genius. You know Sherlock has his violin and with it, he forgets miserable weather and still more miserable ways of his fellowmen. But he does not forget genius, Bab. He just counts of impossibilities. But Victoria, Sherlock is ahead of paper-group people. Remember that. Via Sherlock, we know how they think."

Y: "I do not understand." I kiss you: "Yes, I love u, too."

I: "Sherlock does not go to the bottom of his heart. Far more intimate isn´t for him. He says that ´this is your heart, and you should never let it rule your head, I´ve always assumed that love is a dangerous disadvantage, thank you for the final proof´. But Sherlock is so wrong. Watson says when he was hurt Sherlock comes to him: ´You´re not hurt, Watson. It was worth a wound to know the depth of loyalty and love which lay beyond that cold mask. The clear, hard eyes were dimmed for a moment, and the firm lips were shaking. For the one and only time I caught a glimpse of a great heart as well as of great brains.´ Sherlock went to unusual and even the fantastic, his brains work with sufficient material like engine, but the lubricate love, oil is missing, so the paper-mind racks itself to pieces, the sea air, sunshine, and love will not come.

To this Sherlock, to this great mind, nothing is little – but love.

Sherlock seeks and finds from the paper the simplicity itself, the point, but that isn´t loving. Sherlock takes an opium barrel and begins to smoke. You know if you must be Sherlock, I´ll get you a clean little syringe and a bottle labeled cocaine, but leave that violin alone, cos that with you go to lovely way. Sherlock's life isn´t a story, and it is an adventure, with love.

To paper-group-people Sherlock is the man. He is the organizer of half that is evil and of all that is undetected in this great London, he is genius, a philosopher, an abstract thinker. He has a brain of the first order. He sits motionless, like a spider in the center of its web, but that web has a thousand radiations, and he knows well quiver of each of them. He does little himself, he plans. His mind is like a racing engine, tearing itself to pieces cos it is not connected with the work for which it was built. Life is commonplace, the papers are sterile, audacity and romance seem to have passed forever from his paper-group-criminal-world."

Y: "So?" I: "So what? If Sherlock should have with his sterile papers, e-pages, audio-hearings, and cleaned virtual glasses, he would have been as jumbled up as those visitors in Rosewoods, and as he was with his cocaine and opium.

But love looks with the eyes, the mind, heart, blood, listen with ears and person, individual, is circled with winged Cupids. Love is the kiss, which you feel with lips and tongue, character, and vibrations. Take the Sherlock text, cover the empty place where love should be, and there is the answer. You do not sit there anymore. You go and then there are touch and a kiss. Those paper-Londoners in Rosewood shall be taken to b & b, a demon in the sack, hit the rack, ravage, lib, STB, gtb, house aids & dana. Bootiful & fabs places, so that they cannot go there back again tasting 5sos kisses in their mouth. H&b and cjk5h and scrippers shall destroy sugar daddies´ money and illusions in the same box in the most beautiful way. And when they are so waking up, they, at last, shall find out that their life is just an adventure, and their signatures in these papers tell it all: they are now freed from sterilized life."

Y: "But you take their money." I smile and kiss Y: "Haven´t you heart: the grand old party is looking for a few good retards. Are you a dude? Do you steal from the poor? Are you a right-wing; warmongering; gun-happy; son of a bitch? If so, we want you! Join the gop-btg today and start killin´ people tomorrow!"

Throwing Down Continues

It is 23:30, and the great day has almost died. In NYC plastic bag ban begins March 1! Michael Ro & company will be giving away free reusable tote bags on Saturday, Feb 29th at 10 am. Remember the first 1 000 bags only! I bag per great person. Like and share! Spread the word! Eciliving & save the planet, Your Flushing Champions of Martial Arts.

I have arranged in our hotel for you a special evening. Park Plaza gives its boutique-style elegance, and we look at the Thames and Big Ben, while some musicians play Ozuna - La Modela & Cardi B and Bad Bunny Mia and OMI - Cheerleader. Well, somebody may say time flies, and this is so catchy, and in my comes Pasto Flocco, Journey Gz andBobbynice, Almigtyy Tokk, Roco Benzo, bay swag, Bugszy, Abg Neal, 22gz, krimelife Kass, Bobby Nice asf, I try to smile. Ohh oh, Pop Smoke comes on now. Eazy-E (Cruisin´ In My 64) comes to my mind and keep your hand and want the throw the musicians outto the window.

We are ready to go to our own suite when rumble in the jungle and Cliver arrives: "The party has gone fishing & ape. Some daddies, like Len Blavatnik, Teddy Sagi, and Sir Richard Branson, catch fade and Clur and CooCoo square up & punch on, but then those daddies huggle and xxxo, and then it went Ashanti. Branson like fella praised himself and Clur pops it: ´That's my joint in life from settin´ yem too much junk in´d trunk, hugh jass, apparent mission creep challenges and trying to rise black flag, from the perspective of wanting in the mode for chode to live life to the full, I felt I had to notorious big.´

Bronson like fella invited Clur & the rest to his Necker Island, the land of Hurricanes. He told that his villa has burnt many times and ... and when I left Sir Brenson like the fella, golddiggers and Zan+Bock+Tot were singing old Bronx uptempo doo-wop Pretty Little Angel, and old-timer daddies wanted Electric Light Orchestra - Roll Over Beethoven (Live 1976) – they were doing Marshawn lynch, wow, so I think, it´s called snickers now, lovey!

It went snorrendous and I left daddies jacking off, and Tack & Tack sing Twista ft Tech N9ne "Crisis" missingmymalicemalevolentmister. R.I.P. my headphone caught fire after this. There was just bootiful beat, artists, verses, song, more.

I: "Well, there was enough to burn down the hell. That needs Christopher Walken going ballistic in a mosh pit. Better than coffee. Mr. Zeff sent those Gamazon-files and data and book towns are happy. This day looks like the final boss of a game."

Y: "Tapio, y haven´t yet told the final thing about Sherlock. Just some dull and boring thing about paper and S."

I: "Paper burns but words fly, so no need the keep them on the burning thing."

The Sixteenth Day

He pulls his Trigger, I pull mine

Sherlock doesn´t dance

Y: "So?" I: "So words do not need to put anywhere, you found them in people´s mouths." Y: "What?" I: "Very simple: if it is an adventure, then it is like a planet, it orbits the sun. There is a magnetic field. The planet dances with the sun. Hand in hand, on the edge of the sand. The job of the feet is walking, but their hobby is dancing. And it is the hidden language of the heart. Consciousness expresses itself through that dance. The dancers feel their spirit soar and become one Cultural adventure is a dance of its creator as well as is the world. So as the planet goes these dancers give a perpendicular expression of a horizontal desire. It is glory on earth, and it is those f*uckers for the taking. Those who dance are thought to be insane by those who could not hear the music. There are those words, which give dance its purpose. In an adventure, words are the notes, chords, and melody, they are in your heart, physic calls dancing spin-mode, and everything here has its spin.

You dance when you´re broke-open, if you´ve torn the bandage off, in the middle of the fighting, when you fuck**ers think you are perfectly free. But you must dance." Y: "Why?" I: "Cos it is the law of Nature, one of the big laws in Nature, others are gravity and inaccuracy principle. They make this quantum sea which we call ´me in me, an intersubjective self´.

Sherlock wrote his notes of dance and found the crimes against the dance, but he was too scared to make himself to dance, cos then he couldn´t be outside the magnetic field and look for outsiders, those doomed footprints of hounds. He was with his burning papers founder of vanishing footprints of dance. He was as paper people are, studying just yesterday. He had to take opium and so that he couldn't go insane. That was his touch of today and tomorrow.

This is so the idea of finding love across the dance floor endures, symbolizing that, when we know the true rhythm of our hearts, we know the other. That adventure of dance gives you no manuscripts to store away, no paintings to show on walls, no poems to be printed and sold, just feeling that you are life and fallen in love, all those things are there in the adventure. Then it is a prayer for the future, a remembrance of the part, and a joyful exclamation of thanks for the present. The essence of dance it the expression of man, the landscape of his heart. Every person reveals his/her personality through it. When you dance, you are an individual person.

And that's is why I hate so many golddiggers. They attack those pure, stoopid, fat daddies, who look at their papers and do not understand that they must dance anyway. Their good heart signals the dancing law of nature: any kind of dancing is better than no dancing at all. The golddigger takes advantage of that and collects fares when they put those fuck**ers dance with the bottom of their heart. I have put up a huge gold-digging company and taken gold-differs in. Why? Well, they may throw me to the Hell, but in my tombstone shall read: but yet the will roll'd onward, like a wheel in even motion, by the Love impell'd, the moves the sun in heav'n and all the stars. And everybody, young or old, stupid or wise, woman or man, who reads it much dance."

You say: "So you hate me?" I: "No, I love U."

The Savoy Duel

Meanwhile, in NYC Rego Park pharmacy owner is happy, He has done care fraud and money laundering for a year-long scheme to bill Medicare for prescriptions he never filled. Jurly Barayew has billed Medicare for hundreds of medications he never dispensed, then laundering the profits through a shell company owned by his dear wife. B spent Medicare money on himself, his family, and close friends. He counts his money at 62-06A Woodhaven Blvd. But he does not know the law has caught him and he faces up to 10 years' prison time for health care fraud and up to 20 years for each of the seven money laundering charges included in his guilty verdict.

A 30-year-old Cambria Heights resident coerced his girlfriend into prostituting herself and letting him pocket the money. Now the woman refuses to continue, the fella goes to the hotel where she is staying and beats her up. This trans-woman is part of the NYC transgender population which has faced a tremendous amount of violence all over the country, cries other trans-women. The victim in this case was attempting to free herself from the sex trade industry when the defendant - who was pocketing the money she made - attacked her and nearly killed her. The pimp shall get 10 years in prison, followed by five years' post-release supervision.

Meanwhile, I go to sleep, at last, at 2 am, when my smartphone calls. I do not wanna answer, I say: "Hello, fuck off, let me sleep. What? I just up." Y: "What it is now?" I: It was Jump. The Gamazon has sent the information about e-books and audiobooks and information is full of spyware. Now they know where the information goes and can attack, and destroy the data and the book shops data with interrupt handling code, non-memory-residents, document viruses, in e-mails, major bank and credit card companies, there are MBRs, disk drive, solid-state drive things, email attachments, deceptions, cyclic redundancy checks, CIH virus, portable executable files, confickers, read request intercepts, cryptographic hash functions, system file checkers, self-modifications, strings, encryptions, cryptographic keys incleartexts, XORings, runtimes, polymorphic codes, emulators, mutating engines, software bugs, holes, and entrances, executable files, digital images, Trojan horses, wilds, and core wars.

I: "I go and challenge Mr. Zeff to duel." Y: "What? He kills Y." I: "Thanks, great sports." I go up, put my suit on and Taurus and Clock to my pocket, and a lot of bullets. I can't kill a group of viruses, but I can kill the living elephant in an egg. You are terrified but I go.

It is 2:30 am. And I have only one goal: to challenge that brilliant but mysterious and coldblooded corporate titan. He has a public image of prudence and parsimony. The fella talks in lists and enumerates the criteria, in order of importance, for every decision he has made. This Z is a notoriously opportunistic world-beater. He, the metonym of his company, who loves octopus and roasted iguana, don't care about externalities. And this criminal is ofc a Democrat. Trump says that Zeff avoids corporate taxes, gains undue political influence, and undermines his presidency by spreading fake news. Zeff says that he uses his rocket company to send Donald to the moon. I go to the rocketman hotel.

I do not go from the front door to Savoy, cos things happen differently at the Savoy. When you've been an icon of British luxury for centuries, you can get away with certain idiosyncrasies. There is the perfect arrival, cos all guests are personally greeted and escorted to their room or suite for seamless check-in. Zeff has spent an evening at Beaufort

Bar after Rosewood's party. But he has one weakness: wherever he is, the lights must be fully on. I look at the frontage of the hotel and I laugh: there on the fourth floor MyFriend Zeff rests his silence hours.

I do not go to that old-fashioned caramel house via the front door, or via any other doors, I begin to climb from facade size. My fingers are trained very well, and they can take easily pressure of my weight. I jump to the first frame. It is so quiet and empty that I can manage the right angle, where there are no cameras. One drank Sir goes nearby me and asks: "Are you going to climb to the roof, boy." I say: "Should it all end tomorrow, I can definitely say there would be no regrets. I'm very lucky, I have left my ego at home, cos I shall climb to tear another person from his ego, too." Sir laughs and buzzes off, and I continue.

I go upwards. Window by window, frame by frame. And then I'm on the 4th floor. I cut the window open, I go in. There are five mayns in the main room. I put the muffler and shoot them down. I go in. Next room four more. I shoot them down. There waits for me a surprise: no security cameras. Where is Zeff?

I know there are five rooms more. I go to the kitchen, again four men. I shoot them down. Four-room more left is there 4-4-4-4. I put more slugs. My Taurus is already hot. I go to the first bedroom. Empty. I go to the second bedroom. Empty. Two more rooms. He cannot be in both rooms. I go to first. Two men, I shoot them down. Then the last room. I open the door.

He sits and touches hologram pictures in front of his curved Arizona-made Samsung 80-inch CHG90 144Hz, curved gaming Monitor, super ultrawide, 3480x1080p. He is in space with his space company program. He studies the sky. His hand opens 3D Shephard's first crewed test flight in April. He checks CCE-SRM, BE-1, RP-1. He studies and looks at orbit and speed and PM2. He studies the control room, takes it from the hologram, makes it bigger, turns it, puts it up, and says: "Hm, range safe system doesn't have double-check." I go to him, put my Taurus to his neck and say: "Here is to you double-check virus, push the button and be insane." He is a man without fast, warmblood, just LH2/LOX, no philanthropy, just bills for TheDream.US. He turns and he looks famphtastic.

He waits. He knows. And I too. No need to talk much. He: "I take them off, if you win, if not, I throw you to the American crayfish. The Thames was once full of its own crayfish, then they put American c there, it ate all aboriginals. Choice?" I put on the table MyTaurus and HisClock: "There is no choice."

He smiles. He does not care about his employees and he likes to be a demanding boss and he is hyper-competitive. He is TCI = FXEarnings-FXExpenses/FXEarnings+FXExpenses, and he does not care about antitrust law, it is a joke. He does agreements and practices that restrict free trading. He is the lover of abusive behavior, and nobody shall banns his firm dominating a market, and he kicks to ass the things that are supervising the mergers and acquisitions. And now he lakes the challenge whatever it is. But he doesn't know that a god is a dancer.

I say: "Well, you need blood to your pale cheeks. Let's go to the bridge. Once there stood a fella, and another man saw a silhouette standing against the bright lamplight. Even today when that loser is nearly asleep, he could recognize the winner. His shoulders were hunched up as if he was upset. Whether he was upset that he had nearly killed the loser or that he had let the loser getaway, the loser was unsure. Then the winner turned around and walked to join the other silhouettes standing in a group father back. Now the loser could not see which one was he - they all joined to make fucking one. Promise to shoot me. I promised to shoot you." J: "That's cyanide & happiness."

I: "One more thing before we go, MyFriend." I call Jump: "Here is Mr. Zeff Tezos, he has something to say to y about the dump of Blaster worm and other things he sent with the Gamazon information." I give the phone to Mr. Z, and he has something to explain about virus Airspot Peace, the logic bomb payload, dormant, propagation, triggering, execution, and antivirus Zeff`s flash drive, removal tool, patch Sunday, zero-hour-attack, and hang & freeze. He says: "Just close the bulletin board and nobody can pull the trigger anymore, and fuck you." Jump laughs when he talks to me: "Yeah, they vanish like dust in the rain. Amazing, blaster, slammer, Nimda, code blue, the Bob worm, son warrior, elk fucker, creeper nice, and ofc Zeff's love child: ILOVEYOU, great and sympathetic email virus who is a real bomb causing massive financial damage, the email masqueraded well, you do need nothing more, just send the same back and bomb explodes. Well, not anymore. And Zeff is devil-red from his bold-head face.

The Bridge

I: "Let's go and finish now what we were up to do." Two big men walk in the dark night. The other is bold, the other is not. The other smiles, the other not. The other walks lax, the other not. And the song says you never walk alone.

Tower Bridge is a splendiforous place. It crosses the River Thames close to the Tower of London, where aristocrats have tortured a lot of good people, aristocrats, and peasants. One of those bridge´s chimneys leads to an ancient fireplace where you can still find marks of clotted blood. The bridge is open, cos the workers do some repair-jobs. We do not go to a high-level walkway. We do the job here downstairs, weejly and easily.

There are workers and they say to us: "It is forbidden to come here." We do not here. Zeff who likes to repeat everybody around him that life´s too short to hang out with people who aren´t resourceful, says: "I kill you, you shit." I laugh, cos I know he tries always to make a reputation by trying to do hard things well. My margin is his opportunity. The common question is why? But better one is why not? The workers look at us. I throw Clock to Zeff and take MyTaurus. The interest of the audience is 100 %. One of them says: "Fr bromance."

I ask one of the maeves to come to me: "Here are some bullets, take them to Cue Ball." Zeff has some humor left, and Bold-Blue begins to smile, smirk & matt. I smile back yellow brick roading it & crappily ever after.

I shout: "Ready!!!" He is silent. He is ready for snake shoot badger-badger-badger. Slugs are in his gat, and I'm ready too. At last, they have something around which is worth every penny. Fat-face fellas begin to sweat. Jeff does not, and I a little bit. He seems to know that one cool thing is worth a thousand hasty counsels.

He is a marvelous shooter, but I'm Glock-block also. New York minizzle. He aims and claps, I just shoot. He falls to his knees and drops the gat. I go to him: "So we can begin on a clean table, no glass-bottom boat." I take him up and help him taking my hand on his back. He puts his hand to my shoulder. Workers look at us when we go, and a blood dripple follows our glorious path. One of them says: "Yeah, that was manswer & ballsy." And they continue their works with smiling faces & hearts.

Zeff has a bullet gone through his hand. So not bad muscle hurt. We go to my hotel. The front door is closed. Time tics at 3 am. I pop the lock open. We go in. The night porter runs to us. I: "Call a medicine man. Something to stitch." We sit at a bar table.

I say to the porter: "Give some good gin from juniper berries. I know that gin drinking in England rose significantly after the government allowed by the mid-17th unlicensed gin production, which created a larger market for poor-quality barley, but now we take very good Gibson." I give Zeff a glass: "Sláinte." He looks at me and I gander at him. He talks: "Quite an acquaintance, would you say." I: "Gr8. We have a castle in France, would you like to visit it some bluebird day, spring break." Zeff: "It would be like teaching grandma to suck eggs." I say: "Gingrich. You are a good Democrat. So, it is OK to kill innocent unborn children, but killing serial killers is bad. And that Socialism is OK, so long as you call it ´change´. Your mascot is a donkey, and it suits you."

 He: "And you are republicriminal, who likes hypocrasy, and you support scaling back taxation to allow greater control over individual incomes. And you do not even know what the word means. You want to make a deal with the Gamazon, so you shall get benefits from our audio- and emarkets. What shall we get?"

I: "You get more cultural centers to rural places and via them bigger net for our, your and my, sells. You get via our way personal touch and we via you, unquestionable cash flow and tod-tech to those cultural centers. I think that is a good deal, cos then bookshops do not die. And you do not shrink, cos you are just a parasite, but a good parasite. Let´s bribe each other: we shall not anticipate for a promise, let it be an unexpected favor, this will increase our power of independence. Let´s make our bribe exchange so that nobody is responsible for people´s sorrows and poverty, not even the devil, just two boys called Laziness and Procrastination. Let´s call me the creator and you a parasite. I originate. You borrow. I face nature alone. Y face nature through an intermediary. You shall be my cultural louse, I carry you on my skin, and you begin to multiply and change as the goodwill of Democrat this primitive beast has a cultural clothes brute beast. And happiness in book towns shall be like a mental parasite that alters their happiness to luxury=love.

And there shall be nothing difference between a parasite and liberal, not even the spelling.

Let's make beauty, durability, and practically have their math and norms in book town cultural centers. Let´s help scientists, artists, authors, businessmen and -women, common people live in Book Towns, settle there, and do their everyday jobs and business. Let´s give those centers cultural adventure and life, adventure novels, Academic history, popular and official stories, scientific and artistic writings, modern information tech and 24/7/365 opportunity to be happy in mental and physical luxury."

Zeff looks at me, while a doctor has arrived and handle Z´s hand: "That´s fu**cking great. Just fu**cing great. How did you find it out?" I: "Yes, it is top-notch, I find jaguar=luxury."I wish him Good Night. It is at 4 am.

I come to Y, and I'm so tired that I just lay my head.

Franco´s Officer

It is 8 am, I go to shower.

Meanwhile, even when Antoine Cassidy is doing badly, he still found time to do good. Some ice cream for the kids, a block party, few extra dollars for school clothes – Cassidy always gives back to his Bed-Study home. "Everything I´ve come through in life brought me to where I am." The fella was deep in the game during the 1990s, slinging drugs like the dealers he looked up to growing up. Money flowed in. Then it ended. He caught a criminal case, went to prison, and thought his life was circling the drain. But when you´re on the streets doing wrong, you are fucked, but when you take care of the neighborhood, residents care of you. Cassidy walked out of a prison a changed man. He has begun to help steer kids off the path he took. Schools reached out, as did Rikers Island. He and his organization reach 10 000 children in schools and 5 000 in Rikers Island. And there is the best food also: chicken spot. Every day in Bed-Stuy is Cassidy´s best day.

I go to my Mustang. I think London is now ready. I call Oxford: "Jump, take care of those changes. Audio- and e-books flow shall continue, put the net on. I make contacts to book towns and they must clear that dirty data also. Now there is just one thing to do. Go to Spain.

I call dancers and Clur & boys and ask them to go to Barcelona. I call again to Oxford and ask John and the nerds to go to Barcelona. I call to Frank & SEALs and ask them to go to Barcelona. I call to mobs and ask them to go to Barcelona. Well, much focuses on B, I hope it shall be good.

I call Cliver: "Hey man, what do y think about Barcelona?" Cliver: "It is a noice town, and they play European soccer, not handegg. Fifa-NFL, la-di-frickin-da. Did you kill the boss? Wyd? Wot? Ball and chain? You be trippin´ again and mad dogging. That was a fucking, fucking blowken. He was on his knees. And Y let it go. Y cannot let them go ooh kill em´. Do him in." Cliver darns everything in the world & fit to be tied.

He is hangry. And throw a wobbly. I begin to feel a real valentine's day. Can it be tiem for thee? How much is the fish?? I have got 50 million d, but is that enough? Cliver says: "Y bleed the block and band on the money. Is the juice worth the squeeze? This is guers iced tea."

I say to Cliver: "Let´s shoot the heady. If I bullet for my valentine then it is not the South Bronx." Cliver wakes up: "Try to do records. Let´s go. Do you know good gyms? Y do not. Wud? Waiter knows. How? Okay, so big fella. Well, I wait for you in front of the bridge."

Cliver asks: "Why you are going to Barcelona? Why that city?"

I smile and laugh: "Well, when I was a little kid and Franco legacy was there and you could touch it with your hands, I was with my father in one restaurant. There came a young Spanish officer, from his bodyguard. You know Hemingway and those drinkers didn´t like those kinds of persons and after their bullshit, those gentlemen have been a curse to a democratic world. But that officer wasn´t a curse to me. I saw that man was in very good shape. Meanwhile, my father talked and told stories to the waiter, I went to that soldier.

I looked at his leather black holster. I said: ´What kind of tricks you can do with your gun?´ He took the pistol from the holster. It was a silver-clean gat. It was excellent Orbea Spanish Clone S&W Da revolver 44R.

Spain outdid in those days all other European countries in the art of copying other countries´ firearms. That was a valiant example of that. The Spaniards might add an item, like the lanyard ring on this gun, or even make a small change to the mechanism, but anyway he took the beauty in his hands. I told him that I can do many cowboy-tricks, with that gat. He laughed: ´Really, my boy, show me.´ He tapped my blond hair and give me the gat. I begin to roll the gat with my fingers, first with my forefinger and then one by one the others. Then I did it with another hand, and but the gat to my hardels and throw it from the hand to hand. I put the gat in my belt and take it very fast outto there.

I hadtrained these things in front of the mirror. He tapped his hands. Asked the gat and suddenly took both his hands outto the gat. It fell to his knee and he pushes it 3 meters high and takes in with his little finger. He threw it again and took it in his back like a football, take to his shoulder and let it flow back to his holster.

He asked me this and that, then he went to my father and introduced himself and changed some correct words with my father. Then he taps my head and said: ´You shall be a good soldier someday, my boy.´

Yes, that happened in Barcelona, and after that Spanish Foreign Legion has always been near my heart, and Barcelona, too, their guard place."

Cliver looks at me: "And that is the reason why we all go to Barcelona. That murderer of Spanish people." I say: "He was a grandson of one of those Franco´s revolution fellas. And he was good. And he was my hero. That´s why we go there. There are some good men, still, not everybody is gay."

Cliver: "Other reasons?" I: "Well, in Barcelona the gastronomic offer revolves around the tasting menu, with clearly Avant-garde cuisine and where the dishes stand out for their great, markedly

Mediterranean identity. Restaurants with daring, fun, and modern cuisine searching for taste as the main proposition.

They amaze, stimulate, and create through the gastronomy. The surprise is an important feeling in the gastronomic experience. You go to the restaurant and just sit back and let yourself go. The only rule is there are none. They unashamedly carry on the tradition of that avan-garde molecular gastronomy that they pioneered while part of the senior creative team at the legendary El Bulli. A sandwich version of gazpacho. Crispy egg yolk. Liquid salad. It may not seem challenging, but there can be no question over its genius - everywhere."

Some Workouts

I: "Now let´s go to train. This is so a syrupy jawn and I shall come crazy soon. Let´s make some vibrations. I have just talked about the Hound of Baskerville, seen some fat & lazy sugardaddies, one psychopathic business, but nothing real thing."

We go to Mill Hill Spa and Health Club, the headline doesn´t promise good: Stay Focused this February. There are a gym, pool, spa, and classes. There are machines like cyber, matrix, and consept2. There is yoga, box jumps, dance, martial arts, boxing, those trainers have long lists of merits, but they are small and tinny.

We march in listening to some good rap and Waffen-SS-marches. There is one tinny guy training. He puts up on a bench press 50 kg. I go down and start with 100 kg. One, two, three. There comes a personal trainer: "No, no, no, you must warm up first." I say: "No I must not." I put there more weights. Cliver trains biceps. I put there 70 kg and ask the personal trainer: "How much you think I get in one minute`" She says: "Ten." I laugh: "Count, please." She counts 82/min. Cliver is jumping up to the box. I go up to that box, which is 1 m 50 cm from the ground. I take 80 kg barbell on my shoulders and jump down. People are terrified: "Are you nuts? Shall we call an ambulance?" I put march-music lauder.

I take a skipping rope and after 30 min I am all wet, and my eyes are bright like stars. I go to do shoulders. Another personal trainer comes: "You do in the wrong order. Y must go up to down. Now you do chaotic, your feelings control you." I: "I do not do what I want, I do what surprises the muscles and give the most pain to my body. I must shock the body, not to give it happiness and kisses. I torture my muscles, then they come tight as you see." He: "Yes, but I am a licensed trainer and you are a visitor." I: "Heh, heh, you are really Mike Myers." He looks at me: "What do you mean?" I: "Go away."

Cliver comes to join our party: "Heylo bloke, you look grot box. You must eat guinea pig, Rhode Island hotdogs, Abercrombie and Fitch, man, chili ring, pancakes & just eat you up. I got you. I challenge you, bench press, are you ready?" He is not.

I call Y: "Mmm, yes I love you, miss you, and want you here. H4u." The personal trainer does not disturb us anymore, and we go to the swimming pool: I butterfly, so my shoulders come relaxed, then I crawl 50 meters without breathing, then I dive 50 meters, then another 50 meters crawling and without breathing. I go the floors and dive down, oh, how it feels good. In VictoriaCourt I used to crawl over the lake and back 4 km, in summer days. My cousin was a champion in 100 m freestyle and has still Finland´s records, but he swam 21 km in the same session. Well, he married a bigtits lawyerwho made him a silent home cat, that was so sad. Well, we go to the sauna, and then showers and - ah, just great.

The Spanish Tour

We jump to my Mustang and come to get you. It is time to go to Barcelona and eat something good after this London starving session. I cannot understand why this place is so popular, in my mind this is and has always been Lexington, South Carolina, Canton, Fountain city, Yukon territory, Mandeville, Alconbury, Monroe, Miamisburg, or even Falcon, Colorado, and West Hills.

I drive the Mustang back to Plymouth, and there waits ferryboat, and I'm still surprised that nobody asks anything about my NYC-plates. Sun shines but there is still cold early spring wind. I sit on the deck and Y and Cliver are inside. After long over, 5 h 30 min, we are back in Roscoff. If we had gone to Spanish Santander, it should have taken 18 h 30 min. I gladly driver near the coast to Spanish than sit on the deck so many hours more.

We are in Roscoff at 5 pm. And then Cliver asks again that strategic question: "Tapio, you said two reasons why specifically we go to Barcelona. Can Y now tell us that third super smash brothers´ melee?" I: "Yeah, I'm not new to this, I'm true to this: Frank & boys & I shall also take performance on the stake. We shall give great Spaniards about what they really want." Y: "And what is that?" I: "Real mankle and mantastic things. I'm full of 4th bases & number 3s & screet courses, there must be something else than big papis, and I do not mean the best game in the world for PS2 (Socom II: the U.S. Navy SEALs), I mean Bangbros, my heroes, God bless them and me!" Cliver looks at his medal of Leibstandarte and its great eagle -43.

We go through coastal France. Nouvelle-Aquitaine is great in beauty and it is also the largest administrative region in France, spanning the west and southwest of the mainland. If you are a knight or your grand-grand-grand-grandparents were knights, you just love Chateau de la Roque and other parts of the land. Its economy is Agri- and viticulture.

We go via Deux Sevres - Charente - Gironde - Landes – Pyrenees Atlantiques. There is the dune of Pilat at the Avert peninsula. There are the Landes forest, Gave de Pau, the hilly region, mountains of Limousin, aerospace, defense, biotech, chemistry, and scientific research. But I aoncare. I just say: "The Visigoths, who conquered Rome, came here, and then attacked to Spain, and made Barcelona their main city. Catalonia means goth´s land."

We are going to the Pyrenees. Time is 10 pm. I laugh: "Here we come to Barcelona. I think it shall be a good idea, we go straight to Barcelona." I call Frank: "Brother, blow up Barcelona hard. Is the big voice ready? MyCop is in the Pyrenees, but Im arriving fu**cking fast. The Stang is a fast mover. Yes, I wanna JDAM, too. Must be uptempo. See y soon, brother."

We go through the mountain area about 170 km/h. Great cold winter wind. I sing: "Charles the King, our Lord and Sovereign, Full seven years hath, sojourned in Spain, conquered the land, and won the western main, Now no fortress against him doth remain, No city walls are left for him to gain!"

Meanwhile the Gamazon´s big chief Mr. Zeff is upset and angry. He had to play friendly with me, and he doesn´t like to play friendly with anybody. He wants to conquer and attack, put everybody on his knees, and pray for mercy and then he laughs. But now he cannot laugh, he has been a beaten motherfu*cer dog. What a tarlaud. In his hand is that Clock with I gave him as a mark that he is nooks. Dude, him and mighty, never. He bells to NYC and Italy: "Hello Vincent, take Quiet Dom, Little Larry, Johnny Sausage, Patry, Tico, Kid Blast, Sammy Meatballs, the Undertaker, Tough Tony, Little John Rooster, Ross, and Baldie and come to Barcelona. Hello Salvatore, take Messina and boys and come to Barcelona. Call to Dave, David, and Brian. I must have freshhitmen, 15 mo**therfuckers."

Meanwhile, everything goes in layman´s terms in the Pyrenees. Cliver listens to Fabolous - B.O.M.B.S, who else been rocking wit fab since holla back youngin, Fab still killing it, his pen game is something else, boom. You listen to some Papi Chulo -thing, and I listen relaxed smooth Bring On The Thunder & Tu Lam.

Mr. Gamazon takes five private BAes, and Heathrow salutes once again the anti-philanthropic fella. But he does not smile, his face is with the default facial expression. Meanwhile, I laugh. Oh, whatta noice thing to leave grey and rainy land and come to Spain.

Meanwhile, from Kennedy airports goes up to the air five airbusses and they are full of men, with Milan sunglasses on. Meanwhile, in Italy Leanardo da Vince airport salutes 8 airbusses, full of *Cosa Nostra* -boys. Everything is so funderful as it ever can be.

I say: "Fu**cer Cervantes smiled Spain´s chivalry away, a single laugh demolished the right arm of his country. The kings of Spain brought America the conquistadores and masters, whose footprints remained in the circular land grants assigned to those searching for gold in the sands of rivers, while they didn´t look to the trees and bushes and the air where the green gold was."

The civil war which has so long prevailed between Spain and the Provinces in South America still continues, without any prospect of its speedy termination." I look at Y: "Puerto Rico is the perfect meeting place between Spain and America. The meeting point of two worlds where the magic happens. In Spain they rest an hour in the afternoon, even businessmen sleep like babies. In Barcelona you can feel the weight of the hound, its name isn't the same as in grey England, here is called history."

You say: "Can you stop now? You seem to hate Spain almost as much as you hate England." I wonder: "To protest about bullfighting in Spain, the eating of dogs in South Korea, or the slaughter of baby seals in Canada while continuing to eat eggs from hens who have spent their lives crammed into cages, or veal from calves who have been deprived of their mothers, their proper diet, and the freedom to lie down with their legs extended, is like denouncing apartheid in South Africa while asking your neighbors not to sell their houses to blacks.

In Spain, people learn fast that one can be right and be beaten. To Spain WWII was simple, they didn't pick up a gun to fight for General Motors, U.S. Steel, and the Chase Manhattan Bank. In Spain, the soul's amorous fancies are clothed simply and plainly, exactly as they are conceived, with much for artificial elaborations to enhance them. Fraud, deceit, malice has mingled with truth and sincerity. Justice pursues her own strange purposes, disturbed and assailed by favor and interest, which so impair, restrain, and pervert Spain today. The law depends on the judge's clev interpretations, for there is everybody to judge or to be judged. Maiden modesty unroams, wherever she would, single and solitary, with fear of harm from strangers' license or lascivious assault, and if she is undone it is not of her own will and desire. It is a land where tall buildings look like elegant wedding cakes. We come to nearby Barcelona. The 17th day has died.

The Seventeenth Day

The Day that shall be remembered

I shoot the Doggies and get free

The Dancing Book

Now, little by little begin the main part of this adventure. It shall be quite a challenge. The idea is very simple: put audiobook and virtual reality together, there comes a new generation hololens3, it is called a higs on life book. It is book towns´ living book, not to kill a mockingbird. It shall make defocused cultural centers in rural areas; it shall be a counterforce to centralization. It shall be experienced at a cultural center = home.

Time is drug dealer minute over 00:00. So not near killed 8 = down 8= infinity. It is time to sketch the final show.

Y ask: "So once more people gather. Shall it happen as sexy way as it happened in London?" I: "London was manipulation and testing how people can be controlled. The Dionysian part, lust & libidinous daddie-pride-parade, fell to a faceplant. In shameful and lascivious Liquid love You just take people´s money. In bright shining light, you cannot count Renaissance persons on it, just street-side flowers, slooker-mookers. Not a big deal but a five-minute farce.

We have three things: Ascona-London-Barcelona, in the middle of that triangle our Cuisery-castle. Italy, England, and Spain argue which one was the place where knighthood & courtly love, which core was Burgundy, burn and rise. Ascona is the symbol of the law of Romans-Italians. The simplified idea of Nature. London and its Sherlockian truth after taking off impossible is the jurisdiction. Left is the great Montesguieuan jurisdiction called executive power. It shall be found, not in Paris but, in Barcelona. Much gold shall be still found in Spain.

I make a show, where Ascona and London has put together. In Ascona, we had a book with its living creatures-laws, a god and so. In London, we saw hundreds of thousands of books, without a purpose, without a sale and vanishing bookshop culture.

In Barcelona, we do not see an Italian dead book, or London´s paper book or ebook. We shall see audiobook & virtual reality put together, that´s the Twilight Book. We do not need fake good friends, fugazzi good books, and a sleepy conscience of an ideal life. The Paradise, our ticking life, isn´t that kind of library. if you read the book that everyone else is reading, you think what everyone else is thinking. But that means nothing. Books are uniquely portable magic, counselors, and teachers. You live multinational life while reading. They should be tasted, devoured, chewed, and digest. Only one book shall be a real Living & Smiling Book." You smile an incredulous smile.

I laugh: "That book is a Dancing (Wild) Book. Nothing stay still and without flying touch. The book is a stormy one.”

Cliver wakes up: "The fault in our stars to kill a mockingbird. Sloppin´ heel? No Calvin and Hobbes, Jersey Turnpike - yes, made by the Jamaicans. White girl: Yass Jessica twerk like Miley. Black girl: *sight*. Ghetto dancing."

One-step, two-step, hit by a train. Cliver goes to the front bonnet and is near to go to the ravine. But aren´t we all!??

The Past-Time Hotel & the Fake Dollhouse

Barcelona comes nearer. We come via B-20 to Santa Coloma de Gramenet. We go through Sant Andreu, then to Gracia. We go to a centrally located hotel Colonial. In that hotel, my hero took his pistol from the holster. It has amazing buffet-style breakfast. I rejoice in this impressive stone colonial building, which is near the Gothic quarter. We walk those bright and comfortable wooden floors, and in my ears, I still hear the lieutenant´s speech when he had his discussion with my father. I begin to laugh. Cliver do not. I remember my Spanish brothers in arms, and their fav march Los Voluntarios (Marchas Militares de Espana), but Cliver fills are empty.

Cliver says: "They said this is the net of French foreign legion." I say: "No, Spanish foreign legion, they train in mountains, swell fellas." Y: "They have done murders in Africa." I: "They shoot some apes from the trees, who shoot their backs. AAhhh, nothing can kill my memories from me."

I call Oxford: "How many hours still? Have you made stimulation models? I wanna look at a quick version. Sinking Titanic like holograms, great. Touchable, great, greater. How about colors, speed and pixels? Okay. Well, Ohhoh. Ok. Bye." I call Clur & dancers: "Holograms are are touchable. Look, how they work... buy."

We go to the Dollhouse. Dancers do not have faked anything and not many-colored hairs. And they do not attack you. Fu***ing boring. Pole, lap and private, you know *es un baile sensual en el que nuestras bailarinas se mueven al ritmo de la musica directamente sobre. como hacer un sexo oral perfecto a mi pareja.* I escape to the stage: "Ladies and gentlemen, this is for you all." I sing a superfast version of Muevelo: "*Baby en lo oscuro, sacame de apuros te lo juro a mi me encanta bebita como tu mueves el cu Pongo Reggaeton y la que me jale y en las esquina me accorale. Muevelo, como lo hace?*" Ohh oh, I have forgotten some words.

I take a microphone again and sing: "*Pero yo no conteste porque estaba contigo perreando, Y de ella ...*"

Y and me go to dance. Soltera remix, *Que Tire Pa, Lante, vamos a ver que alerta astás. Que tire que tire que tire que tidggghhyfdghyrdsggrs.* Amoooooo.

A nice soiree. It is 2:30 am, *lubricantes y juguetes sexuales, para tu pareja*, has gone from my timetable long ago, so even Cliver doesn´t ask *que es el body sushi? que es el strop poker? que es el mud wrestling?*

Soon we go back to the hotel. Cliver goes to his room and MyVictoria gives a naughty night kiss and then I'm alone with my ideas. I try to kiss duties, but it is very hard when Greenville Ohio stays in my mind.

The Hologram Sky

If the stage is 20x30 meter, height 12 meters, then math says the voice goes via these ... I make some calculations. The holograms, lights and HoloLens 3 headset resemble reading glasses with an infinite field of view. They shall be better than Martin Garrix holograms, there shall be holographs, augmented reality, which shall be everywhere. They superimpose digital images on real objects. There shall be an optical light drive module, a stack of MEMS mirrors, sensors, processors.

Future tech introduces a mixed reality windshield. Holographic dept measures in feet. There shall be a Livestream of holograms, along with holographic new versions and various holographic virtual assistants. The universe itself must be a vast and complex explosing hologram.

We put there a tactical augmented reality. And we locate our positions as well as the locations of others. It replaces night-vision goggles, as it enables us to see in the dark. It will also replace the handheld GPS system that we carry today to approximate our position. The eyepiece is connected wirelessly to a tablet that we wear on our waists, plus it´s wirelessly connected to a thermal site mounted on our things. If I am doing something to somebody, the image of the target, plus other details, such as the distance to a target, can be seen through the eyepiece.

We do not have time to use AR tech helmets in an extra-wide visor, allowing for an unprecedented full-color, HD, 180-degree viewing experience. Those interactive boards interactive Digi-elements, dazzling visual overlays, buzzy haptic feedback, or other sensory projections are blending into our real-world environments. Smartphone cameras allow mobile users to view the world around them including onscreen icons, score, and ever-elusive creatures, as overlays that made them seem as if those items were right in our real-life neighborhood. We use on the stage google sky map. Overlay information about constellations, planets, and more as we point the camera of our smartphones or tablets towards the heavens. I make futuristic dancing process data overload at incredible speed. I look and my sloppin´ heel book vision and understand that the possibilities are limitless.

Time is 5 am, and John and Jump send me more holographic and AR pictures and vids. Now they become to look better, but the scale is wrong. They must be much bigger and vid speed much higher. They send a text: "No money for that." I text back: "Bob gives you, even if he needs to rob the bank of America." Some minutes later: "Now, ok." I: "So, bigger, faster, more spectacular, light in Roman Gladiator fight, kill it in hugest scale. They must be bigger and specific. Do it. Use immersive tech also. Hello!? Jes, use the AR game changer. Well, put together VR and AR and automated machine learning. First AR, then VR. Please, more AR and wearables, potentially rearrange graphs, data points, and molecular structures. Let those watchers manipulate the objects in real-time. Just Samsung Galaxies in their hands. There are no learning delays, cos of AR.

Put wind speed and direction, humidity, and temperature, a visual overplay of that performance they´re playing within. Y do not need that just google glass, HoloLens, and AR tech, please. OK Cross-Platform Content Management System (CMS). Hey, a no-coding cross-platform solution has been readily adopted by European schools, universities, and businesses, do it. Yes, Oculus go and guest Android, and iOS smartphones and tablets. Do your own factor studio then. Oh, you have more buttons, hyperlinks, questions, navigation, audio, and interactive 3D AR/VR content. Fuck off the questions, navigations, and audio, no need for them, just buttons yes, below. Think that you are driving a fast car faster. Outto comfort zone to the Chaos´ Promised Land. Nothing steady, nothing expected. Surprise is the word used.

And after Y have done it, put it right away within the B2B marketing and sales, education, media and design, manufacturing, retail, and real estate sectors, and book town books and festivals. Fuck with testing, just put it in the market right now. If that fucking AR is already in Sysmä High School and lonely maths-teacher has been looking and testing eSport-thing, you certainly can put it on a bigger scale."

I close my phone & tablet & computer. I begin to sleep at 6 am.

The Unpolite Training

I dream that the king of Spain is in front of me. He says: "I, the King, arbitrate and moderate the regular functioning of the institutions, assume the highest representation of the State, and I am responsible only to God & history."

I hear in my ears: "*Púrpura y oro: quere y lograr; tú eres, bandera, el signo del humano afán!*"

I wake up one hour later. And you are still there. I go up, put my training shorts on and my shoes and go running. Oh, I forget my shirt, but no matter. After I while I find a gym. I go in, pay nothing. I say: "Sorry, forget my wallet." The big fella says: "You can´t come." I push him to the ground. He comes to me, and I take my fits quickly around his neck, no time to lose. He goes down, I press his neck, and he is in dreamland. I go straight away to try to do the bench press record. Some people come to bark at me, it helps: the weights go up. I take a barbell and put it there 50 kg, so not much but good for biceps. Then I push those angry people away and go running again. In front of the house is a police car. They attack me. I kick them to the ground. Huh, huh, people are so small and impolite. I teach them manners. People on the street shout at me. I stop in front of one shooter: "What did you say, pal?" He yells and I hit him to the ground. I continue running.

I come back to the hotel. What pieces of peasant shits are in this town, no good officers anymore, just barking dogs, no elegance, and no aristocracy.

The Numbers

Meanwhile, Zeff & and the boys are in the airfield: Dave, David, Brian, Vincent, Quiet Dom, Little Larry, Johnny Sausage, Patry, Tico, Kid Blast, Sammy Meatballs, the Undertaker, Tough Tony, Little John, Rooster, Ross, Baldie, Salvatore, Messina, 15 hitmen & 20 mob-soldier are ready to shoot, trigger loose, and not happy men. And they, 55 chaps, go like conquer generals at the airport.

And at the airport is also a gypsy woman. And she can count. She isn´t afraid of high and mighty, rich and powerful and violent persons. She has lived long and seen enough. She asks Mr. Zeff: "Dear fella, can I give a prophecy for free." One of the richest men on Earth, who likes creeper behavior, nods: "Ok, make it fast, MyOldBag."

The gypsy lady: "The number 55 is an angel no. When you see that no showing up in your experience it is a sigh that major life changes are coming. Zeff does not be upset, cos of the nature of this number you can be sure that these changes will be highly positive, resulting in inauspicious new beginnings. Angel number 55 is a sign that it is time to let go of those things and situations that are no longer serving you and allow the changes that are manifesting to usher into a new phase in your life. And dear Zeff, as always you can trust your angels will be there to provide the guidance and inspiration necessary to help you navigate the coming changes to your utmost benefit. Believe me, you bold boy, it shall be necessary.

And when doubling the number 5, it doubles the energy by a factor of two. The great and amazing energy of the number 5 is adventurous, highly versatile, and capable of meeting any challenge that life brings. The number 55 can also be reduced to two factors, 5 and 11. As a multiple of master number 11, angel number 55 is also, My Boy Zeff, considered a master number which means that it carries a higher frequency vibration than other two-digit numbers.

As a master number, 55 is the number of independence, freedom, and self-determination. When this vibration is operating in your life, it means that you should be forward-looking and focus your mind on learning new things. You are also likely to establish a variety of new social and romantic relationships during this time.

Your angel number can be reduced to the number 1 by simply adding the digits together in a two-step process: 5+5=10, 1+0=1. The number 1, My Boy Zeff, is the number of new beginnings, leadership, and opportunity, and as you enter a new phase in your life, remember to stay focused on new experiences and learning new things. Stay in contact with your angels and they will guide you, My Boy, to the best possible outcomes. Be patient, embrace change, and trust that everything is working out for you. Miracles happen when you live in the momentum. Enjoy every moment and embrace the beauty of life! If not, y, My Boy, is cursed."

Zeff laughs: "You are mad, Old Bag, here is 100 d, so you can have a coffee and cut your hair." But the gypsy lady says: "I do not want your money." And turns her head. Zeff goes on irritated that somebody dares to insult his goodwill. He shakes his head.

Meanwhile, Im in the shower, and count: 40 dancers + 41 nerds + 7 singers + 10 seals + 15 mobs + Frank + Cliver + 5 agents + Y & M = 122. But nobody comes tell me, what number 122 means.

But in the airport gypsy lady yells to Zeff: "You shall soon meet angel no. 122, which is the message from our angels and archangels that we must stay focused on our highest expectations as the angels and universal energies work behind the scenes helping us to manifest our wants and needs, goals, and desires. That person has the number 122, and he has also: trust that his home and family will be well provided, as he strives towards achieving his goals. Angel number 122 is a powerful sign that he shall be stepping out of his comfort zone and take new directions and/or begin new projects and ventures that he has been wanting to do for a long time now. That fella uses affirmations and visualizations to enhance energies and draw them towards all of us. Amen!"

The Ambush

Zeff almost runs to his huge ten door car. Inside he tries to smile, but his head says to him: That fucker Tapio is a nice guy, in other situations he would be my first pal. I do not wanna kill him. I, fuck, wanna tap his shoulders. These very irritating and business-disturbing ideas in his head stay, when his car column starts to go towards the stadium.

Meanwhile, I eat a big breakfast, what You had made for me: *quiche*, hot oatmeal, scrambled eggs, *huevos rancheros*, blueberry muffins, croissants, stuffed omelet, and sausage and egg sandwich. Something US, in the middle of European backwoods. I kiss Y.

And there are coming men when the sun goes up. Those normal men shall come beasts, crazy drunken Mexicans, half manically depressed clowns. During this day´s parties, they´ll show up and be gentlemanly but then shall get drunken and angry, punching faces and sticking their abnormal tongue out in a frantic rage.

They are the men, 55, and they shall meet people of 122. And there is a black card: affectionately poking someone on the nose, often accompanied by saying: "Boop!"

Time is 8 am. We sit on a Colonial terrace. Cliver says: "Preston and Steve. Just wake and break." I say: "Jeah." I say to Y: "MyVictoria, 143637 (1-l, 4, love, 3, You, 6, Always, 3, And, 7, Forever)." We drink some very good juice and eat amazing fruits. Y know: Cofrutos, LemonConventrate, Zumos Palma (*fabricación de zumos de frutas natural y vegetales*, tropical juice 100 %, *deliciosa y cómoda forma de tomar frutas y verdurasiiiiiii*, and, lemon juice syrup, *especializada en la producción y envasado de zumos naturales y zumos a base de concetrados y pures, asi como bebidas refrescantes de frutas*, oh, *plátano, manzana, fresa, durazno, naranja, albaricoque e cereza.*

We become to hear drumming. It comes louder and louder and then You see the Spanish foreign legion arriving its fast march. Cliver looks at grey-green uniforms, and fellas seem to be trained. Meanwhile under the roof are two hitmen, ready to shoot my head off, you know, Muslim haircut, and sunroof. They are Spaniards and served in the army well. They aim my front head, classical way. Breaks like an eggshell. The becoming of their own unit´s parade stops their aiming. On the other roof are four more hitmen, from Cape Town.

Spaniards try to give these others signals: not to shoot, while the parade goes on. But those foreign hitmen do not respect Spanish tradition. But the Spaniards do not let foreigners break the holy rule. And they shoot them down, silencers on. 51 left. When angel number 51 arrives, it is a sign from your angels that positive changes are on the way.

You and Cliver look at me. I stand up, as waken from a long, long dream. I drop my glass, and the whole table turns and all on its go down and break. They see me looking at the parade. I turn and begin to walk. There come tourists and Spaniards put I hit them from my side. Fuck. It has been a long, long time. In front of the parade walks a tall officer and I call him: "Josh, you fucker, you son of the bitch!" The officer looks at the sound of the call. He turns and I walk to him. We meet in front of the great parade.

He cries: "You pure shit, Tapio, yeaHHHH!" People see real fellowship, which they haven´t seen for a long, long time. We hug. Fuck with the parade, fuck with the world. I say: "I thought you were gone. The second barrage, those shits came ...!" Josh: "No, no, no I hit my head, and lost my left ear but fuck with it." The parade stops and people begin to give us applause.

Two hitmen on the roof look at each other and put their rifles away and fuck off.

Time is 9:15 am. Sunny morning, Colonial terrace, fruits and juice, and Josh sit with us. I and he have a lot to talk about. Y and Cliver listen, and Cliver is fu**cking proud that he is there. Y smile, cos in life it is hard to see today real men like Josh and me.

He is now *Don Juan de Austria* -fella. He stays in Almeria. All they are called *caballeros legionarios*, but they consider themselves *novios de la muerte. In parade they sing La Cancion del Legionario*, but fuck with parade, we sing now *El Novio de la Muerte: Soy un hombre a quien la suerte Hirió con zarpa de fiera ...*!"

We put hands to our soldiers and fu**cking tears come from my face. Others cry when their friends die, I cry when my friends come back from death.

Each friend represents a world in us, a world possibly not born until they arrive, and it is only by this meeting that a new world is born.

Well, my friends in Walhalla tap their hands. Faith gave me another chance. Josh must go but we both know that we would not die in that man´s company that fears his fellowship, to die with us. I introduce Y to him, and he gives his best words to Y and then he goes. I shall see him, and I invited him to our castle. He goes today to Chad.

The Spectacle

I sit down and think about our performance. Camp Nou is a big stadium, and although we have taken 1/6 of it, to our night's performance, it shall be awesome. I cannot count and estimate, and I just know, it shall be a great establishment. Cliver says: "the dude was awesome. You have friends with benefits." Y: "He was *papi chulo*, almost as handsome as you." I: "He is just a great guy, nothing more nor less. With him, I have attacked time to time against Death and won every time. *Bella Muerte* isn´t happy with us."

I call Jump and John: "Where are y? I haven´t time to wait for you all day. An hour? Aight. Straight edge. Y have collected WSJ/MR Data Visualization, Dow Jones, Citrix, NASA, AR Museum Enhancement, Disco/GPD, NTN/Ford, Mobile AR app, la vaca que rie, MR + game, AR + Holograms + VR, Desigual, and Ardbeg, AR+Mr with HoloLens. Tell more about NASA.

An augmented reality visualization tool that allows data scientists and business executives to quickly explore and understand data. 2D visualizations cannot see them. You are exploring a dataset of performance colors with IMB Immersive Data? Really. Y likened AR to using a physical textbook vs. an e-book. With a physical book, y can see the big picture, Sherlock, it creates a more physical experience, the size of the book, the structure of the contents, and the layout of the information. With an e-book, although that information is technically available to y, it's not as readily understood. Y took a PointCloudsVR platform that visualizes flow data, such as convection flows or ocean flows as well as real-world field captured LiDAR, ooh. You take sensory inputs and haptic feedback. Shall there come some use also from Virtualitics Immersive Platform, that combines machine learns big data and VR? Some information from technopedia? BadVR, Immersion Analytics, MineLife VR. And Y can put all this together. Y do not know? Well, if it goes south, it goes there and keeps on dancing as a life book."

We go to the Mustang. It is time to have some fresh air. We go to the beach.

Then we are on that beach, and I go alone running and take my clothes off and go to that water to swim. The question goes: how the audience shall make their own dancing book. Water is cold, but my brains are on fire. AR + VR + e-book. How about audiobook & AR alone?

Then I realize it, while almost getting the second part of hypothermia. My brains begin to send chemicals to my heard, and stop warming the skin, but keeping heart enough warm. There comes the third part of hypothermia, those niace chemicals begin to show me a beautiful outfit.

Yes! Now I understand it. I turn and swim back to the beach. You and Cliver are terrified. But I'm not. My hands are almost frozen and I'm pale as hell's abandoned post, the Inferno's eye. But now I know it.

I laugh: "Our party shall not be tonight at Stadium. It shall be here on the beach. And we must buy huge mirrors and put them across from the Sea. Why mirrors? If the mirror is good you see clearly object. If the mirror is excellent, you feel part of it. And if the mirror is real, it is you, yourself, that's a real dancing book."

Well, after thinking more, I decided that the stadium is better, cos there are those walls and after all, mirror-idea is more hologram-idea, and do not net to be made bigger with broken mirrors. Images should be faker. And we do not need faker things, cos we try to get rid of them.

I call Jump: "Hey, do you have to that performance AR e-book reader? Y do not, but you have made already AR ready book. It is interactive, and people can scan it through its smartphone app. Good, it must be an adventure telling book. Try to make it an AR e-book reader, please. You are scanning the cover and inside pages with animations and sounds. Great. Your own realitypremedia scans the main characters and happenings in three dimensions. The 3D models of the character of the adventure book pop up and sing & dance to amaze the audience. There is more? When the smartphone owner uses his phone the AR book reader reacts and changes the environment and gives characters more character. Really? The dancers & singers and we shall have HoloLens-like smart glasses where we can look at changes of audio-dancing-performance-book more thoroughly. The sound shall lead the images, emotions, and whole dancing book. Your audiobook reader reads e-books reader who reads 3D landscape. You cannot put them together? Okay, no time for that. When the music starts, the AR landscapes arrives. Sounds fantastic! And looks too. OK. Do you have enough energy, for all that huge thing? Do the lights of Barcelona go out? OK, hope the best. You are already there making those things. I must come as soon as possible look at what there is going on."

Y, Cliver, and I go to my Mustang.

Meanwhile, Zeff and his killer team aren't happy. 6 hitmen have vanished like dust in the wind. 9 men left. Deep in his darken hard Zeff is glad, that I'm still alive. It is so hard to admit it, but he likes me. He thinks: "That Tapio is something else. This killing the good guy isn´t a good idea."

He sends a message to his hitmen: "Boys search and find, but do not hit. Wait for my orders, your Boss." Meanwhile, the Mustangs flies, and we are happy. I laugh: "Think Victoria if the people can effect to that AR e-book- and audiobook reader story, then the story begins an adventure, and nobody knows what happens next. It shall be a real dancing book, like our universe. Then we can talk about our awareness, dancing adventure." Y: "You keep on saying book. Have they made an e-book to that performance?" I: "No, no, no, they have made music base on that reader. E-book- and audiobook readers read that music. Actually, it means those readers read the motion."

I continue: "And then they make their AR with the public, actually those readers read also weather, and via sounds, the feelings, heh, heh."

We arrive at Camp Nou, which has been used for various purposes other than football, often hosting major concerts. Pope has been there. The architects Francesc Mitjans and Joseph Soteras, with the collaboration of Lorenzo Carcia-Barbón, have made a good job. The structure is in concrete and steel with 2 rings of continuous tiers. The upper ring lowers to give way to a roof structure above the main tribune. They are still making a stadium better, and they update it with 495 million euros. It is already a giant piece of origami arranged not to disturb the flow of people into the stadium. It is opened and they leave this open space. This is what makes in unique, different. Nikken Sekkei and Joan Pascual-Ramon Ausió Arquitectes know what they are doing. 104 000 -square-meters shall be updated.

It is 11:30 am when we go in. Frank and 10 seals are at the ports. I say: "Anything to shoot for?" Frank shakes his head: "Not yet Tapio. Nerds are there and hundreds of workers, and your crazy friend Bob."

On the other side of the stadium, dancers train their motions and Y want to go to look at their rehearsals. Cliver sees Clur & boys and goes to them to hear their rap´turia. I go to Jump.

His eyes are burning, he has his seventh orgasm. The 30 x 20 meters area has enormous lights and tannoys. And there are lasers, digital processors, and motion-sensing techs to create different types of holograms which interacts with media: the aerial burton laser-plasma holograph, with 3D scanner causing the molecules in the air to be ionized to create a plasma, pepper´s ghost, 3D CGI-persons, light field display holograms, creates a field of light, digital holographic tabletop, capable of being viewed simultaneously in 360 degrees, by using a series of multi-colored, high powered lasers and a high-speed rotating mirror, physical holograms, no-holograms, fairy lights.

I ask the strategic question: "Where is the main computer?" Jump: "There is a group of clusters called Screen. It uses OSCAR. The fault-tolerant mainframes with modular redundancy, scheduling, node-parallel programming and debugging and monitoring work well." The stage is full of sensors, wireless, smart tech IoT things.

Jump shows how a smartphone effects to these sensors. I go from the stage and meet Bob: "Mr. Banker, how is your day?" Bob: "I have taken from those 50 million dollars which the Gamazon send already ten, taken more loan, in the name of the Gamazon, 20 million, so altogether, the Gamazon has involved here with 70 million d. Quite a sum but not yet any questions made."

I come to look at dancers. Well, they train many different jumps and even somersaults, filip. heli, slato, and very quick, pop-like motions, flex the muscles in their arms, legs, and torso, simultaneously, grind their shoulders, but not like robots but flexible way. They jump and simultaneously cross their feet, kick their left foot back as they bend their knee, twist their hips from side to side, sit back into their right hip, swinging arms to opposite sides, jumping up and left and right, very fast steps.

Keep on dancing and the Running fella, I go to Cliver: "So man, any hustling backward? Or just eazye?" Cliver: "Snoop dog is so old, so not him. No Fred Durst limp Bizkit. Just F.L.Y., Twista, Keak da Sneak, Krayzie Bone, and doof doof and househead things. Also, Spanish and list things. Ofc not strokes."

The Peace Lunch & Hitmen

My phone rings: "Yes, Josh, hello, what, shit, Thank you." I say to Cliver: "There are fulltime killers after me. Kyuubi." Cliver: "Money flow mafia. Nin. Let´s find those brez." I: "Josh said that two of his ex-unit were hired to kill, and there is dat Zeff." Cliver: "So y can´t call it? Blind transfer?" I: "Runescape cheats."

Meanwhile, Zeff makes a mistake. He goes outto the hotel door and wakes in public.

Meanwhile, in NYC a new coronavirus patient is in hospital. His son´s Bronx school has been closed, and his other son´s Manhattan university in being monitored. There may be some more schools that voluntarily close. The man´s son, who attends Yeshiva University in Washington Heights, has shown symptoms and is isolated from his brother. This is an example of community spread.

I call Josh: "Did those fellas tell, where Zeff Tazos is?" Josh: "Y don't need to. He is right now in Barcelona's TV." Meanwhile, Zeff almost runs to his car, and it takes a hike. He calls the hitmen: "Now attack and kill." He begins to sweat, and he is going straight airport, but he is too late. I have placed him. The TV reporters do the job, as they do so many times: they show the attackers the victims. The media is a great friend of terrorist and criminals, they just look carefully and check the net, and then just hit and run. In this case, the Media gives me a chance to finish what I didn't do in London. Better luck next term.

Near El Prat, at Carrer Felip Diaz Sandino my Mustang reaches, not Zeff's own car Honda Accord, but Chrysler Limousine. The car stops and five security fellas come outto car. I shoot two of them down. Cliver takes his Clock and shoot but doesn't hit. You go behind the car. This is very irritating. If you give somebody a chance, next possible momentum he is again back in action: I gonna keew yew. This is a real Jewish holiday. Four more men come outto car. There are too many of them. But I do not care, I begin to run towards their car. I shoot three men to their legs.

Zeff takes a hike, with two men. I go after them. They try to go to Dachser Spain el, but I shoot those two done. Then there is Zeff left. He turns slowly: "Good afternoon Tapio, so we meet again." I: "It seems so. We have tonight a big performance here in Stadium. Would you like to come and see it? After that, we can find another bridge. OK?" Zeff has not found his impasse. I say to him: "Whoever cannot seek the unforeseen sees nothing for the known way is an impasse. But I shall show you something, and with your help, you do not find an impasse. I show you the mountains and the forests, the defiles and impasses, the lay of the marshes and swamps, you can maneuver with your whole force. You may use local guides AR and dancing adventure. You find the Promised Land."

He drops his gun, and he smiles: "Actually, I'm quite happy that it ended this way Tapio. Ofc I wanna see the spectacle, like a good gladiator before he dies." I must say Zeff has a certain style.

The Media arrives. Those guards have gone back to that long car. Media doesn't see our gats, it sees two smiling men, with big or small hearts or both. The Times reporter asks Zeff: "What is your next branching out?" I answer before Zeff says anything: "Tonight you shall see it in the stadium. It shall be a historical momentum. You shall see a dancing book. It is a great love adventure, which I & my bride have done, and MyGoodFriendZeff is wholehearted with us. So, at 9:00 pm, join us at the Camp Nou. There y shall see what a Dancing Kiss means."

Time is 2 pm, so just seven hours left. Media surrounds Zeff so I just tap his shoulders and say: "Call 9 hitmen back, and now we must go, excuse me." Nobody asks my name. The media is interested only in known names and public status.

It has gone outto ride a long time ago. Somebody may say whoever controls the media, controls the mind. I may say: "The Media transforms the silence into yelling, by changing vain and ridiculous things to the great and awesome things. A liar knows he is a liar, but one who speaks the truth and is straight is soon transformed by media a craftsman of destruction. The media bombards us with pseudo-realities, and tonight it shall see something real. The media thinks people are sheep. The media is wrong, I shall eat news and their tools for my lounge.

One media-fella comes at last and asks who I am: "I'm a lover of Waffen-SS and Franco, and Trump, and hate democrats, gays and lesbians. I have always admired and shall admire the great men who have tried to conquer the world. And my fav. contemplation is this: each of us has his own triumph arch under we must march, most of you do not see that, but I do." The reporter: "Whose contemplation it is?" I: "Mine."

I'm hungry and so we have four members in our group now, so I introduce Y better to Zeff. And we go to eat to Pura Brasa Catalunia just *tapas* and toasted and rustic sourdough bread and cold meat, and *tagliatelle all´aglio*. Jeff eats fillets of wild Icelandic cod, and Y grilled octopus, and Cliver Park ribs.

You say: "In every day, there are 1 440 minutes, we have killed just some of them. Let´s go and kill also the rest. And if we want the light to our life, let´s light a great fire." I: "Don´t trip, they are just lighting it, snitches get stitches. Y2K20 (Y=year, 2K20=2020)." Cliver says to Zeff: "Ay mayne, what´s your black bin bags. What´s yours Clark Kent job?" I: "His company shall give more servers and smartphones to Camp Nou. Each people who arrive there shall have a smartphone and his firm buys all the Media to market that evening event. M I correct, Zeff?". He has nothing to add or more to say.

Meanwhile, those 9 hitmen, have found me. And they are making fine adjustments with their riffles. One of them says: "It is strange, there sits our Boss with him. Shall we call him?" Another says: "No need to disturb him. He knows what he is doing. He shows us the target." They aim at my head. They have decided to pull the triggers at the same time so the price shall be shared with each of them.

Three, two, one ... just then I change my position and kiss You. The volley goes the wall and four pictures go down and break. Zeff takes his phone: "Do not shoot, you idiots. The target has been canceled." One of the hitmen says: "Now he prevents us from taking our salary. Fuck with him, let´s shoot."

Meanwhile, they had made the biggest mistake. I know where they are. Cliver and I run over the street, and behind the house is a courtyard and there are the ladders. I go up and Cliver is ready. I shoot to the forehead and the fella fells straight down. I'm on the roof, second, third fella down. I put more bullets to my gat. Fourth, fifth, sixth. Three to go. One is almost behind me, but Cliver shoots him down. Two more. My Taurus is empty. I throw my knife to one hitman´s neck, he drops from the roof. I attack against the last one on the roof. We struggle and fell at the same time from the roof. I get my hands to one branch, and so I drop to the ground more slowly than the hitman. Cliver and I run away. No need to stay around, when the police come.

Soon my Mustang goes full fart away. There are no security cameras, so perhaps we get lucky.

Gamazoning

I ask Jeff: "Start calling those agents and employees of yours and the Media to start marketing our performance tonight." Time is 4:30 pm, so 4 hours 30 minutes to that big event. It is better to go to the stadium. Soon Sport, La Vanguardia, Mundo Deportivo, Marca, El Pais, El Periodico de Catalunya, Diario AS, and BCN Mes writes on their net-pages about The Gun & The Kiss, shortly Dancing Kiss, in Camp Nou. I call Josh: "Thanks, everything is alright now, the Nine are silent men by now."

Apartamento Publishing, Barcelona Travel Magazine, SuiteLife Barcelona Lifestyle Blog, Metropolitan Magazine and Website, Le Cool, Time Out Magazine Barcelona, Wellington House Idiomas Blog writes about the event and praise it to heaven. Le Cool who informs about the coolest art, film, music, clubs, bard, and restaurants writes: "Go there. Once in lifetime Event. Something unbelievable. Just sensational! Never happened before in Spain or elsewhere in the world. Do not miss it!" Nobody goes to the blacklist, although the words are the same in every paper.

Words begin to spread, and the space of our event expands in the minds of the citizens of Barcelona. Zeff has money, influence, and thousands of servants. The exploiter orders and subordinates begin to full his orders. Badly treated, slow salary workers do what they can and must do. And bad education, worse customs, and worst understandings spread among the citizens of Barcelona - and they are surprised how this high and the mighty multinational Gamazon has come near the common people of the streets.

The Gamazon uses kindle newspapers: The Wall Street Journal, The New York Times, The Washington Post for Kindle, USA Today, Financial Times Newspaper, The Boston Globe, Los Angeles Times San Francisco Chronicle, The Seattle Times, The Denver Post, Le Monde, Investor's Business Daily, The Salt Lake Tribune, Financial Times. And the Discovery Channel uses them to put Digi-news about the event.

Zeff says to me: "Are y happy, fu*ker?" I: "When I see there 100 000 people, who each pay 10d, Im more than happy, fu**er." Barcelona TV, Barca TV tells about the evet. Atena 3, Telecinco, RTVE – Canal 24, RTVE - La 1, Televisio de Catalunya, RTVE - Teledeporte, TVG, Teleasturias, Telemadrid TV, Canal +, TV Canaria, Canal 33 Madrid, TeleTaxiTV, Marca TV, Tele 7, 13 TV, Canal Flamenco TV, Aragon Television, Yahoo! Eurosport, Solidaria TV, EITB - ETBSat, CNH Canal Huelva, Fuengirola TV, Cuatro, Onda Jerez TV, and Kiss TV mention and praise the happening.

There comes my handsome face on the TV screen where I say: "I love Waffen-SS and Franco." YouTube puts videos about Book Towns Group, and they are very angry: "We have prevented this dunnie to put his wartime videos here, and now we must praise him to heaven."

Same time the Gamazon-workers, whom I have cried to the lowest hell mirmir: "This son of the bitch, he that insulted and yelled so badly to us, now he is like a national hero, or international, and there is also that porn star whom he had sent his bookings. Shit, shit, shit."

But servants' words do not mean anything, when money talks, and money talks loudly. It doesn´t bend to any direction or person. Money hits your face and makes you pay all insults you have ever made to that man called Tapio. Many enemies in many wars look at my face with slaughter and disgust, but money shoots mirmirs to the ground and dances over mirmirs´ graves.

There is a lot of energy in the air. Communications send their waves to the common people's brains, and they have soon made up their minds: we go there. It shall be f**cking great. We must see that friend of Spain, of humanity, of the whole world and look how this real entrepreneur, who never gives up and who breaks the toughest rock, this real man and manly lifestyle, we must see him, and we must see his lady, she must be something special, cos our man Tapio has chosen her. Let´s see, let´s find out, let´s be happy, let´s have some fun!

The Spirit of Honor

Many real men, vanished from the public understanding and consciousness, go to their boxes, find their medals of honor, their battle gats, their happiness, their greatness, their great lifestyle. Many old marches are heard again in the streets of Berlin and Hamburg. The nations' best hearts have been waked, the lion shall roar again. The lion sleeps in the heart of every brave man, and now it has been wakened. And the Lions don't concern themselves with the opinions of sheep. Love may have the face of a goddess, but the world has the form of the lion. The lion is the passion, the lion is the fire. The difference between a brace man and a coward is that a coward doesn't go in the cage with a lion, but the brave man taps his best friend.

We, the lions, defend faith, strength, valor, fortitude, and kingliness. I call Josh: "You must come to the Stadium." I call Frank: "You must come and sing with me." I call the SEAL, David: "You must come and meet your brother in the great dance of warriors." I take my smartphone and put there playing a great song: *Brandenburg Lied*, its words tell about land and its great nature, not about some lust.

Now it is time to show those g- and f-bastards. Never a wise man and a brave man lie down on the tracks of history to wait for the train of the future to run over him. Without a sign, his sword the brave man draws and asks no omen, but his own great cause. They say that the brave man must fear, then he is a brave man, but that is a fu**cking lie, a brave man does not fear, he attacks the Death. And a brave man is always called the lord of the land, through his iron and blood.

They say that when a brave man died, he died for this and that, but that´s a lie, the brave man doesn´t die, he leaves in memories. Brave men are brave from the very first.

Time flies and soon it is time to make history. I laugh and my backbone tickles, it means one thing: let´s roar. And there are no buts, no both and, just take it all. Nothing is enough for me if I cannot take it all. I do not give a part-time smile. I do not leave it halfway. It is now, never has died. Three hours to the happening. And give great people everything I can. Men endure toil more willingly for the lust of pleasure than for the virtue, but today the lust shall worship the virtue, and they shall marsh together.

I go to walk on the street, near the stadium is a park and near that park stands an old fella. He isn´t a bum, he isn´t looser, he is tall, his figure is beautiful & great. But he is old and poor. And his clothes are old. But he seems to be in good shape, his hair is cut, he is clean, his teeth are white and his eyes very bright, and he smiles. He says: "Great day." I say: "Yes, indeed." I continue: "Today, we shall get something back." He nods: "Yes, I know Tapio." Then he turns and goes. And I go too. 2 ½ hours to go.

The Momentum is arriving

Meanwhile, in NYC at Lavoro Cafe and the Hollis Hills 18 Ave Crew-warriors and Sureno 13-soldiers begin to fight. The fighters move outside, and Doc4 pulls out a gat and shot the two Surenos. Three soldiers get slash wounds. Capt. John Portalatin, the commanding officer of the NYPD´s 111th precinct in Bayside says: "This is a very safe community and it´s going to stay that way under my watch." The NYPD hasn´t arrested anyone. City Council Member Barry Grodenchik says: "This place has not exactly been a good neighbor, and I think I´m being generous. Nothing good happens here at this time."

We, Zeff, Cliver, Y & M, go back to the stadium. There have come guards on the ports, and hundreds of people are hanging around, the groups get bigger and bigger. Barcelona has made its decision. Congestion is increasing.

There is the audience coming, which must have an adventure, which means mystifying, torturing, misleading, and surprising as much as possible the audience. But now the audience reads in a new way: it looks, hears, moves, and most of all participants. The negative watcher becomes a positive participant. Tragedy changes to comedy, monk life to action of knights. Action is always a positive thing. You cannot entertain if you do not suffer also. Staying in your place means the end of the adventure. Participants in adventure really make that live thing interesting, very electric, very alive, and intense, amazing, and even dangerous, cos the authors become the audience and audience authors.

The audience gives you feelings and you share it, but that is communication, not manipulation. If you understand, then you communicate. The Dancing Kiss makes people jump outto their skin. And more the lust and virtuous fire, more it burns away the melancholy reason. Then it comes more chaotic, faster, hotter, and plasmatic. It is a storm, and the best performance is that you do not remember almost anything, but you advance to virtuous hysterical paroxysm, og´d, great handshake with the universe.

That is what Nature wants for you, and that´s why you are here, to make more your kind. You fly & and you die, and after a while, you fly & and die again. And dancing is interactive interaction and action, reaction and anti-reaction, and it makes you and your partner better persons, cos it goes to the climax. It doesn´t go to chaos, cos it is chaos. The climax is when interactive dancing persons find, not the eye of the storm but an explosion. That is the heart of it, equality, honor and strength, desire, and no small about of passion and love, where simple is not simplistic, cos of interaction. This dancing kiss bursts us open, and then we think we are dying, but it makes us an explosion, which makes us more beautiful and greater than we ever were before.

That explosion is creation itself. That is the momentum. And there is the light of love, which overshadows an entire solar system. It is a creator, and we are it then: I love Y and fight for that to the stars and back, always and forever.

Time is 8:45. 15 minutes to go to great performance. I call the IOB-president and treasurer: "Hello there, ah, you sit already in the stadium. Thank you, very much. Now the IOB has new tech-contacts and you can start to modernize your contacts. Yes, I have ordered every Book Town interactive board and hololens2. You can contact each other and me fast, and there are now coming to those electric tools you can begin to change your paper books e-books, and audiobooks soon. I have sent them to all your 21 Book Towns, and tomorrow 24 Book Towns shall get them, too. Now it shall be a time for great change. This performance shall so the way to AR & e-books and AR & audiobooks. And those books shall be in straight contact with cultural events and building in Book Towns, so in rural cultural centers. The connections shall begin to rise quickly since I did a deal with the Gamazon, which is now helping bookshops instead of robbing them.

How I did that? Well, that´s a long story. Let say we solved our disagreements manly way at the bridge of understanding. Nobody wanted to prove that when there are smoke and a corps, and the gat with a trigger. They understood it in a hard way. What do I mean? Just what I said. I showed my gun and they paid. I robbed the robbers. I hope you like our performance."

Gladiators arrive with Victoria

We march in the stadium. In the middle of the arena is the huge stage. It is in perfect visual and sound-track place. The sound waves shall go symmetrically. And the place is almost full of people. The stand is packed. Over 100 000 visitors, and the arena is also full of people. There are altogether over 150 000 visitors. There will be painting the town red party, really catching the crazy turkey.

How this ginormous-magnormous mass of people acts when it begins to dance in its beastial way? Lolz!

Basso is very loud, and drums are like Napoleon´s army when it invited Russia: drumming La Victoire est a Nous.

There comes a quadruple pattern. It changes to triple, compound quadruple, duple pattern with triplets, compound triple, sixteenth-note fill a groove on a drum kit, double-time: the snare moves to the & beats while the hi-hat begins to subdivide sixteenth notes, blast beat, delayed backbeat and shortly gallop. There comes a sudden break to drumming, then it goes on hard, and well, there comes street beat.

Riddim continues and around the stadium are huge flags. They are hologram heraldic flags, amazing fesses, pales, bends, chevrons, crosses, saltires, chiefs, bordures, stars, rings, balls, crescents, diamonds, flowers, rearing ups, standings, birds with wings outstretched, walking along, lions, dogs, stags, eagles, hares, badgers, dragons, griffins, cockatrices, manticores. Gules, azure, vert, sable, purpura, or, argent, ermine and vair shine bright and the sun rising, in this dark evening. The flags move and are big and full of a proud spirit. We, Zeff, Cliver, M & Y go straight to the stage. We have an honorary alley, and mass of people begin to shout and yell, victorious & spamoni & 666 & Thundercats hoooo!

And both sides of that alley are drumming *conquistador*s, holograms of course. They wear shining breastplates and oddly shaped helmets, with plumes. Their sleeves and trousers are puffed, padded, and of gaudy color combinations. At their side are slender rapiers. These hard-bitten, flinty-eyed realists looking holograms are dashing images.

In the middle of the sky comes two knights with their snorting proud and trimmed horses. The horses clop almost shake the stadium when those two knights, after a lady drops a bandana, attack against each other. The left one gets a bad strike from a lance and wells and people cry for fear, cos AR-hologram is so real looking while falling from the sky towards us. Then on the stage fanfares signal that something shall arrive. And we continue to walk towards the stage. People give huge applause to us. They begin to sing: *"Corona de la Patria, soberana luz ...!"*

Alzad los brazos goes on, and life comes bigger and greater. We run the stage. Your eyes are bright as stars and my teeth white as snow. We kiss.

No words, no explanation, no statistics, no arguments, and no nothing, just momentum, white wedding. There begins a low shout, then it comes louder and then like a storming sea. The sea of people begins to shake & rapn´roll. It is time to give this courtly-Kiss & More spectacle its anthem. I take a microphone.

There comes Brooklyn uptempo doo-wop beat and melody. Drums & bass are fast, like Spanish, choir four holograms: "VICTORIAaaaaa ... but I want Uuuuuu." People come crazy, they take their smartphones, and on the sky comes a huge storm of colors, exploding star and trillions of drops shining blood red and gold yellow to feed the leaves of yelling people.

And the Doors open ...

Suddenly in the sky appear a giant book. There reads Run Baby Run. The book opens and AR & e-book-audiobook-reader makes there Nicky Cruz and Maria & Mau Mau from the late 50s real. It is an amazing spectacle to look at those young and so beautiful Puetaricans like real. Standards - Hello Love - Frantic Ny doo-wop and Five Discs - Never Let You Go - and then all that blow to pieces.

There comes a real German artillery barrage from 1943, the whole field blows up. The voice is unbelievable loud but nobody´s drumhead doesn't break and begin to bleed blood like in a real situation. People are shocked, and that's is so good. Dancers come in front of and there are male dancers, too, making huge somersaults and Spanish singers and Clur & CooCoo make their words come machine gunfire. And a little girl says: "MyCat listens to tis now she's a lion, just flips her shit."

Straight fire, uh, six, 'bout this I gotta nothin' on my wrist but I'll still gladly take your bitch, yeah, ay, yuh. The audience uses their smartphones and the sound comes another and Clur and so see in their hole lenses W-Choppers, and on the sky are Ceza, Tech, J.L., USO, Yelawolf, Twista, Busta Rhymes NY, D-Loc, Twisted Insane, mad, guh, Pagal, birinder, and three fries short of a happy meal, straight Trippin, yeahh 51/50. Pick'em out the panic, a little manic, I'ma jam it 'cause Im an oddity. OXYGEN. am I a joke to you? Masses begin to practice verses right now, whoop!

Dave, David, Brian, Vincent, Quiet Dom, Little Larry, Johnny Sausage, Patry, Tico, Kid Blast, Sammy Meatballs, the Undertaker, Tough Tony, Little John, Rooster, Ross, Baldie, Salvatore, Messina, and 20 mob-soldiers are on the VIP-part of the stadium and they take their gats and begin to shoot at the stage.

Frank and 10 SEALs see them immediately and attack them up there in second VIP-floor. In the sky is a huge picture of Brooklyn, from a drone. Drone flies near La Vara, when seals make black all Alibabas, and no angels. Battle rattle, full clothes, mommy's comforts vanish soon when SEALs bombaconda attacks. Mobs are death blossom. GWOT blows mobs' brains off. Soon mobs are MRE, ready to eat. And scared mobs are red on red. Dave, Davit & the boys never rise again, they are shake & bake. Frank and boys kick the bodies, and he knows hard work will outdo talent every day, and he keeps on doing hard even when he fails, and he will. Job well done, he never failed.

Part of VIP-people are running, but so what, people are created for moving.

Huge living pictures of NYC goes on. The satellite stuff gives details of newspapers, people rings, even the 72nd precinct 3NI-trinitarioses, Latin Kings, Niio's Maloses, 67 precinct GCS- G Stone Grips/Cash on decks/HBMs, L-Block AKA LINDEN BLOCKs (8 TREY CRIPS/SHOOTER GANG/OGC BRIPS), the 81st precinct TWAN FAM (600), 79 precinct RF-RICH FAMILY, the 77th precinct FRANKLIN AVE FAMILY/L1NCOLN FAMILY, the 67th precinct MB'S-MARTENSE BOSSES (BLOODS). There is ofc the 73rd precinct. It is one of six in which violent crime rates are so high. There are gangs at Rockaway and Livonia who send high five to Clur, Cliver, and even to one deep Brkner. NYPD Commissioner James O'Neill comes to picture: "The numbers of violence have gone way down. We're not a perfect organization, we're moving forward." Then here comes on the sky porn studios & strip clubs. Heat goes up - fast.

Music reader reads fast AR & e-book- & audiobook reader. There comes on the sight of our castle, and there are already very ready, just roof, bathrooms, second-floor floors, some frames, pipelines. And the music is French drill/trap, "don't give a fuck about the rap game nigga", Double V- Mal Lune, 1.D.3 & Ghetto Star 143. One little Spanish boy says: "French is the language of love. Lol nice try, although shrug your shoulders boi."

Two girls are dancing. The one says to the other: "When the hood gets mad, they come to Paris and burn cars amongst other things, cash money & Kilogramme." One Arab laughs: "These songs make me want to murder somebody! Booba is the duk absolu men." Yes, 'your girlfriend dumped y now y turn skinny'.

Well, this is the lazy part. It is time to put the angle of the dangle in the Cleveland steam room.

On the roof of the stadium, hologram-dancers find their best pool.

And the Windows open ...

Now comes the real test: how to show many books AR at the same time and create a real carnival. There comes a hologram wall in front of me. There are tens of books. How shall the music readers open them at the same time and give a real spectacle??

People don´t see the HoloLens´ screen, which is following me, but I do a lot of marks on the air. I take there an audio-ebook of Kolumbus' first trip to America and throw it in the sky. The book opens and the environment and characters appear. Then I throw more books there. There are five books altogether in the sky. The dancers and singers and the audience admit the music, smartphones, and HoloLens open Que Tire Pa´ ´Lante to read those books at the same time. Myracle!

Take those characters and make their audio-e-book-reader read music. The rhythm comes to the place and melody orbit. Those characters begin to dance in the sky. More hologram-characters are put among the people and dancers and singers are AR- dancers and singers. The 3D-world full our holo lenses and make the whole stadium interactive screen. And smartphone users tell their attitude yes-no. And the interactive stadium, which we see, cames real to them and those two worlds come together. The party Dancing Kiss shall begin!!!

Characters and people dance que tire, que tire, que tire ...que tire pa´ lante con su movimiento. Yesss it works. But it isn´t yet The Gut & The Kiss -dancing thing.

So.

Jump has made a story about our trip Ascona-London-Barcelona a la Ascona with the movement laws, all London books, and Barcelona´s musical book of books: The Dancing Kiss. Jump comes to the stage. You are with me. You say: "How about just doing the same as with those last books. Throw those three parts on the sky and let Tiri put them together."

And Lammergeiers come ...

You take me to dance. And Jump throws A&L&B to the sky.

Well, I do not come yet. I begin to throw audio--ebooks from the HoloLens wall to the sky, tens, and tens. I come to dance with you.

The Stadium´s sky is full of holograms: the face of heaven so fine that all the world will be in love with night. And pay no worship to the garish sun.

There appears a hologram of a very poor young man who is in love. His hat is old, his coat worn, the water passed through his shoes, and the stars through his soul. The sky just trusts your heart if the seas catch fire.

And then it happens: live by love though the stars walk backward. The music reader begins to follow holograms and the music goes backward from the last one to the first one. Yours is the light by which my spirit born: you are my sun, my moon, and all my stars. And stars-holograms falls from the sky and into your hands. They seep through your veins and swim inside your blood and become every part of you. And music comes to that I sang doo-wop, it's the kind of dancing kiss that inspires stars to fall back into you and light up the world.

Certain holograms are citron yellow, while others have a pink glow or a green, blue, and forget-me-not brilliance. In this scheme, audio-e-book blue-black surfaces are not enough, this new sky and stage give the music from its own choice.

Brooklynization seems to be in the middle of that choice. They are home again. NYC leaves in Camp Nou. Pop Smoke, Young M.A., Megan Thee Stallion & Normani, MoneyBagg Yo, Megan Thee Stallion, All Dat, Tory Lanez Feat. Fivio Foreign K Lo K, Eminem, Till I Collapse, Eminem, Darkness, huge screen, and holograms make them AR. Dhura Dora ft. Soolking - Zemër is so lazy but all but I loved it. Busta Rhymes ft. Twista, played it 2x speed,

Trapstyle, drekkies, bass junky goes faster. Did you hear about the traphouse? Ben's mom got everybody beer and they got turn't. Some dull trap, remix. Eminem do not clean out my closet. Daddy Yankee, papito, Reykon, Pitbull, Wisin, rakata Nicky Jam, crackberry jam, Plan B, Puerto Rican, Mexi Rican. Yank sweet and sour pork, Buenas megamix. Now it comes faster, and people begin to come hot, damn Yankee, jumpin' their bones, daddy foam. There are already some hot louieses.

Clur and CooCoo begin to chicken noodle soup, and pool-d Sandra sings lady gaga & banana. And there is a naked stripper dust band, playing and j lo pocket pool. Ukie. AR makes their fake boobs, butts, and d-s-l so much hotter. Some bodies kiss AR-meat curtains.

The time is almost 24. The party has begun. Huge groups are gathering, dancing, yelling, the message has gone to their heads and now they tell me back: we love real Brkners and you a deep Brnker so.

There appear on the roof of the stadium huge eagles. Where they came from in the middle of the night? And they are not normal eagles, they are my eagles. In Corsica, where we were placed after terrorists had attacked the normal French army, we stayed much time in the mountains. And there I saw them the first time: bearded vultures, you know lammergeier.

My eagle lives and breeds on crags in high mountains. It loves cliffs, crags, precipices, canyons, and gorges. I found near Riventosa a young lammergeier, hurt but happily alife. My lieutenant said I must shoot it. I didn't, cos I fell in love with the fu**ing creature. He was a proud person. I hug him in the first momentum and give him semi-solid tissue. I name him Uku. I paid a peasant to take care of him. My lieutenant wasn't happy. He gave me jail two weeks, cos I didn't respect his order. And he and I both knew that I'm going back to my Uku, happens what happens. So, I did. And it was a hard lesson for me to teach Uku to sit on my arm. He was a very gallant creature. And after some months Uku flight back to the wilderness. But he came now and then visit me, when I was buying honey from that peasant. He had white marks in its left-wing so, I cannot ... Anyway, it is great that eagles have come.

The Eighteenth Day

Very little is needed for a Happy Life, just make Life Happy

The Ignition Wire is lit ...

I sing: "Ladies and Gentlemen ..." Cliver changes it to rapn´roll: "Fillies and gentlecolts ..." I: "Let's celebrate the beginning ..." Cliver: "Let´s have an international Brkln chant day ..." I: "let´s have the light!" Cliver: "Let´s have a super shroom sauna!" I: "Now!" Cliver: "Bored as hell!"

Jump comes and makes his bricemagic, you know a pregnancy test, &fmt=18. Doodle jump reaches for the sky. There appears a black sheep wall. There stand 45 book towns, breaking down. There comes a happy trail Brkln-Ascona-London-Barcelona. And at last Cuisery Castle, the h spot, hot seat. I sing: "I love cultural heritage, luxury, and the spare time activities to the international public." Cliver translates: "The cool points are mongreal, Dominicana, confederate flag, mafioso, blue gam, jaguar, luxurious, club penguin & procrasterbating blow and go." I: "I advise you to build your villas & homes." Cliver: "I don´t know what to tell you, so I te extrano and help you, got you to make your villa-homework, so your mama got her socks. A crappy, poorly built crapshack do not wait for y."

I: "We make a golden ratio. The Fibonacci series." Cliver: "I poot shoot t to g (tooth to gum ratio), 800 (420+311+69), 1123581321 = start with 1 and 1, add 1 and 1 to get 2, add 1 and 2 to get 3, add 2 and 3 to get 5 ...). Sploosh is 1,6:1:0,6." I: "Beauty, durability, and practicality live happily ever after in our decentralized book towns = cultural centers."

Cliver: "Whooty, sturability, and ecologicality, you know a dog in a bathtub, live healthy hair in Gnutella the United States of America, sorry, New York city, sorry again, the fruits loops, ya mean booking for book towns." I: "We help the new generation to live in book towns and give you a business room." Cliver: "I help f.u.n.g to cripple fight and oak cliff." I: "I give you weapons on how to write a best-seller." Cliver: "I give you gats, and you shoot an olde yeller down." I: "We read your papers and make them dance & kiss." Cliver: "What the insert non-offensive word here. The United States of the offended?" I: "I love U so." And I kiss You. Cliver is singingless.

In the stadium sky, each Book Town gets AR + ebookreader+music reader, and on each Book Town paper book opens and characters are dancing out and some character-holograms jumps among the cheering crowd. Then each book town vanishes to the fireworks. And the same time eagles fly high and the fireworks and EDM-light begin to dance with holograms. Now the fire is near. Light burns our brains like wildfire and sounds are so loud and chaotic that we cannot pick a voice out from the background noise, and I just laugh with Y and Cliver. Then I kiss Y again.

"YES", and the Catholic Priest dances better than the Devil

Our Smiling Friend put us here, on this carnival ride. All men´s minds move with greater zeal to spiritual progress and animated by larger confidence invites us to all the duties of greatness. And we get unflagging devotion and unwearied reverence. And this festival heals us from mirmir and restore bigger pictures of our minds. And the body and the soul walk hand in hand to the sky.

The Brooklyn candy is the sweet thing in our life. The holograms are the junk, the AR-character is the diversity and choices. And the stage is a place where we can get our angry and lust out just like our loved ones when we go to them.

Some firecrackers light some AR-holograms. They begin to burn, which is called a valuable transaction that could be put at risk. The Dancing Kiss changes to a big stuffed animal, and there are a beast & a bitch making their smiling way to the knight & the lady. The carnival heaven and hell have just married and dancing wedding waltz.

I ask ou: "Do you marry me?" Y: "Yes, MyTapio." I say: "There is the catholic priest and he dances better than the Devil. What more we can ask for that great day?"

Now on the stage and sky appears carnival holograms. There are the Carnival Queen and the traditional burial of the sardine. We see a large funeral accompanies a giant artificial sardine to its grave to signify the end of reason and the start of a wild party.

There goes on the sky 350 horses and over 100 musicians gather for a procession of over landscape. But this is just the icing on the cake. Drinking laws has forgotten, there go screens and holograms of cathedrals and the Old and New Towns, medieval and modern Triangles, skyscraper-views, canals, gondolas, masquerade things, classic porcelain masks, emanates an aura and bygone times, modern interior furnishings, costume-clad carnival-goers hand out flowers from large floats, and a lot of musicians playing every kind of things from merengue, calypso, and rumba to modern sound.

One city officer comes to me: "Do you have permission to this all?" I take him to the stage and ask him to sing with us. We have holo lenses and the celebrating audience has their smartphones which have AR-ebook-readers, so no loose time.

I get a call from NYC. The Tech-boss Farmer calls: "There have been many inquirers about your doings in NYC. You have been seen in many unfortunate places where has been crime activities going on. What do you have to say, on you behave?" I: "Nothing. Make them tabula rasa, please." Farmer: "Did I hear it right?" I: "Yes. I send you a million dollars." Farmer: "Are you going to bribe me?" I: "Yes, and later NYPD also. It isn´t a big piece of cake. Buy now, I have much to do."

I take Bob near me: "Have you heard these NYC-charges?" Bob: "Do not worry, I press the right button, and lubricate them all." Meanwhile, the dancers on the stage make huge jumps and I think it is time for a breakdance competition.

Parade Rap & Carnival Explosion

Josh has arrived at the arena with his Spain Legion parade band. They are drumming very loud. On the arena arrives a square, and there go Clur and me.

Clur: "Im go dancing on the arena." Laws of Physics: "Can I come too?" Clur: "No."

He makes four somersaults. And begins with headspins, then windmills, jackhammers, head slide, and baby spins. Drum brake gives to my toprock, downrock, and freezes more energy. I do just aggressive and calm toprocks, popping, tap dance. Floorwork´s 6-steps and 3-steps go well, just shortening and spelling flare in b-boying. We both do freezes into stacks, circus, wow factors, downrock goes NYC-Bronx way: CCs. Remixing goes on. I take Clur and throw him over me. He goes staying on his one arm. I go, too, and now it the best thing: to pull up and down one arm way. We can do only 20 cm. We run back to the stage.

Meanwhile, you dance with the dancing-group. People are dancing in big groups, many with the holograms. *Todos pidiendo el remix de rompe con de la ghetto pero nadie pidendo lo que paso con ozuna por dios como queda el negro ahii! No se lo ganan con brujeriaa, grande* the boss. Then it happens, the chaos and storm come. VIP, arena everything just dances free speech, hardcore dancing, one-step, two-step, hit by a train, slance, get down with the get down, Buckley shuffle, danking, frog in a blender. Peak ispanyol, I do not undestand it, but portekiz??? help me. *Papo, papi, papi chu, chulo, papified, los mejores momentos, yo soy boricua, boricua de cora papi.* We sing or they sing Latino things. I dance A´Gun sonic move. *Sientate en ese de´o. Mere Woo.* The time is 2:30 am.

The big screen shows El Alfa with Vin Diesel, some fattie sits on the corner. Some daddies have come near pool-dancers, and money has begun to fly. I hit some of them from the stage. There are dancing circles, someone smoke pop. There are d.a.r.e., fire ups, dreams, strawberries, birds, straightedge, slams, dddfs trip outs, hugging the blocks. Some more AR-holographs are on fire. I dance with y and music goes faster, *el hefe, el chuco, el aye, el paso, el, el salvador,* 503.

Y have begun to teach me Spain. *Temazoo, el mejorr en cina del marrr. Yomel pomposo y peligroso. Felicidadeso. Dominicano con orgullo mano arriba activo con to. Son fuerte eso dominicano. Que yo te lo coy, te lo doy, te lo doy ...*

Almost nobody dances sober unless they happen to be insane. Nobody searches of sanctity, sacredness, purity, these they find afterlife. And now the devils just say: "Aw hit, he´s up!" Here is a perpendicular expression of a horizontal desire. The question goes: every savage can dance but how are educated people tripping the light fantastic. Individuals are taking off their clothes. The Educated ones are pure dynamite!

The stadium begins to be three fries short of a happy meal, and buc wild. Things seem gone to Florida. Everything is full of faygo & kefka. Schokley is showing its face. You know, she had hoped that her dinner date would be the man of her dreams, but when she saw him, she fled immediately, he was schokley. But Schockley is the most extensive bloodline of strength, courage, and intelligence. Evolving from early white settlers, not taking shit from anybody to white middle-class (sub)urban street thugs. Around the stage are many daddies, I couldn´t take it anymore: I attack.

Aggro gives fudge buccaneer, finger blasting, beat those, toot it and boot it, nate dogg. Sugar high goes to sugar down. Sweeteries get to their teeth, double decker pecker wreckers. And I chew an apple through a letterbox. Josh comes to me. We go back to the stage. There are tens of thousands youngings, yoots. And it is time to put all energy to the stage. Clurs sings: "This choppa will be reppin´ the city where RDV´s Young Rich and Slick´t got ya well in peace."

Nebula & Applausion

Jump comes to me: "Look, I made a Hubble-sky." The whole sky begins to glorify the majesty of a nebula: your tangerine of electricity is ripe, and on a vine, in little, black book do I confide. The stars are dying in our hologram sky, dancers ave stopped.

The audience, stand still, and nobody moves. Not even eagles, they have gone, just one flies in the dasty electricity. It is full silence. Nothingness. Silence is so freaking loud. I also listen to silence, it has so much to say.

It stops speaking and I say a sound as a pound in a dog hound: "Thnx, *mucho graci*thanks."

Applausion & sapplause.

I thought they shall kill me. But there comes acclamation to Y & M. Nobody steals our thunder, not even the Gamazon. I hug Y and say: "Now it is at last time to go back to our castle. It has been a busy day. They big up, no fauxplause, just appalaudience." You say: "Now there is the black wave again, which was before the storm." I: "We get complament fish, real mar mar." Applauses goes on and own, I do say nothing to anybody but Zeff: "So we must finish it, ok?" He: "Well, I had forgotten it." I: "That you have to die? Coo´." I have no intention to harm him in any way. I turn to You and we just run away. I do not hear crowds anymore. "Yes" is on and in my xd-mind

Hand in Hand & Brooklyn

We bop around hand in hand. I say: "Without Y this should not have ever happened." You say: "Without you, I never had found you in the castle." I: "You had found me in the junkyard?" Y: "Does this shirt make me look that fat?"

You ask: "So everything ends right now? You find the way." I laugh: "Nothing ends. Everything begins." Y. "What do you mean? You have made the connections and networking. Now it is time somebody else or many people to begin their job." I: "And how shall they do that? They do not know even their own taxes. I'm not done this Book Towns Group just to give it to somebody else. This wasn´t my job/work. This is not a project of 8/5/20. It is a 24/7/365. I'm not an employee or consultant. I really try to help people. I like them. Now I just wanna go home with Y, if it suits You. I wanna be with Y. And take care of that fault ungodly tongues and hands will not do harm to great people of Brooklyn and book towns." Y: "Why?" I: "Cos I fell in love with You. It not-happens every day, it is a lifestyle thing. I must honor the standard of perfect luxury called happiness of us."

Y look to me: "Here is the greatest difference between a true Brkner and a deep Brkner. Ya trick ya 1.A-phrase, started by Soulja Boy, in which you yell at random people who are bothering you, 2.B an exclamation of leaving me alone. You think you are a lonely trucker, but a real Brkner does not think you are. You are too torpid for that." You take my hand. We walk together, real Brkners´ way.

Meanwhile, two more coronavirus cases have been confirmed in NYC. A man in his 40s and a woman in her 80s, neither of who traveled to a high-risk nation or reported contact with a known COVID-19 patient. De Glasio comforts New Yorkers: "We are going to see more cases like this as community transmission becomes more common. We lack fast federal action to increase testing capacity - without that, we cannot beat this epidemic back." The other two cases are the 50-year-old lawyer and a 39-year-old health care worker. There are now 13 cases in NYC.

At the same time, an SUV driver bursts through a BP convenience store in Queens, shattering the front door and ending up alongside shelves of chips and beer. It is the gas station shop at 139-19 Hillside Ave. The angry driver refuses medical attention. And an off-duty police officer is arrested after her ex-husband tries to attack her in their Queens home and she fires a shot to ward him off. He flees the home uninjured.

You say to me: "By the way, when shall we go back to the USA? I wanna see Brooklyn as soon as possible."

Meanwhile, 5 000 people signed a http://change.org petition demanding NYC schools´ transition to remote learning and online classes as the city fights the spread of the coronavirus. They say: "Our

kids and the staff members are taking the subway to school every day."
Two Manhattan campuses have been closed. de Glasio thinks
differently: I say: "Let´s go back there as soon as possible."

Meanwhile, an off-duty NYPD school crossing guard is arrested in the
Rockaways for threatening a neighbor. He texts a neighbor to beat the
s*** out of her. Police arrest the guard on a charge of aggravated
harassment."Closing schools shall be the last resort." DOE will conduct
deep cleanings and disinfect schools twice a week, stocked 1 800
public schools with cleaning materials, face masks, and forging COVID-
19-related absences.

I say: "Let´s go back there as soon as possible." And NYC saw a 233
percent uptick in anti-black hate crimes in first two months of 2020, in
comparison to the same two months last year. Anti-white hate crimes
dropped from three in 2019 to two in 2020. Anti-semitic hate crimes
dropped to 36 from 41 in 2019, sexual orientation -related hate crimes
dropped to four from six in 2019 and there were no hate crimes
reported against Asian or Muslim communities.

Just right now, elite Manhattan high schools shall be closed for
thorough cleanings linked to coronavirus. The all-boys Collegiate
School and the all-girls Spence School shall be closed for a
comprehensive sanitization of the entire campus. Collegiate School
headmaster Lee Levison: "I understand and appreciate the anxiety
associated with the dynamic situation. In this instance, we are acting
in a very conservative manner."

A 15-year-old girl is attacked by Park Place Savage Gunnaz -warriors.
In Crown Heights, one warrior jumps on top of the victim and stomps
on her as eight other runs over and join in the assault as she lays on
the ground. They bruise and swell to her face. Then they take her

sneakers, a cellphone, and a debit card before taking off in different directions.

At the same time, a 66-year-old man walking his dog is struck by a car and killed in Bay Ridge. And Brooklyn rapper Pop Smoke funeral processions draws a massive crowd. The man who made hits Welcome to the Party and Dior shall not be heard live again.

Brooklynites & Zeff

The time is 3:30 am when we enter our hotel. Cliver sits there already and waits for us: "Heya, true blue turnt up. Banga & GOP & wapoo. When shall we leave and go back to NYC?" I look at him: "Another who wants to go back as soon as possible to NYC. What´s wrong with Europe?" Cliver: "Cooking on gas & kool and the gang. That´s called my bluff. Too happy-go-lucky, and everything swims swell. I wanna pull a wiehe & scared money. Im a ballsy, worth a straw -bloke, wanna more booty & nat."

Performant he liked, but otherwise pixy stix.

I almost run to our room, and take just a short shower, and dodo, when Y come to me. Make out bang & San Diego thank you & chain the tires & mushroom bread & punish 9th base & not clit but big spot.

I wake up at 8 am. Now I must gather the team & praise it. It is a hard piece, cos everything has done his/her best. How can I recognize & reward them so that they shall be happily surprised? I must get @ me.

It is 9:15 am at Colonial's reception. There are 79 people. Not Media, not public servants, not IOB, not your manager invited. Just the heart of Brooklynization + Jump.

I say: "Thank Y for coming ..." Enormous cheers.

I say: "Jump, that e-book-reader and readers music-reader. Jump: "Just changed the sensors and made music reader e-book-reader. Just did some copies of the copies. The holographic sky was difficult ..." I: "Clur, I thought that you really cannot read the notes ..." Clur: "I read the rhythm & melody. I do not read fu**ing notes." We keep on choppin' it up, blabbering, jibberjabber, sponge bob, even joaning & shooting the breeze & talkin's smack. Creasin', yucking it up, lo freakin' l."

I say: "You know what to do. We train and do it whole happy hols = summer, our Saint Patrick's days. 1. I give you a schedule in four days, via my interactive board & HoloLens 2. Let's do a real dancing summer book, k." And Brooklynites says: "Sok, ahan, ok, yes, sure, alright, umhmm."

Frank says that they must hurry back, cos their holidays shall end in three days. Clur, Cad, CooCoo, Tot, Zan, Tack, Bock must go back to school and dancers to their clubs. 15 mobs go to Italy and then back to Brooklyn. Everything seems to be beautifully put together. Except for London, Ascona, Cruisery, Barcelona, Brooklyn public servants have something on their mind, and I shall talk later with the IOB's president and treasurer and many of my sponsors. Bop wants also to talk something with me.

But there is one person, who does not want to talk with me. He is Zeff.

He has been thinking. The Gamazon shall lose all its priority and power of dictation if our deal comes true. Now the Media are praising last night's event, so he cannot but smile. But he shall soon do. He orders

8 Russian cutthroats and 20 Taliban fuc***ers. His satisfaction lies in the effort, not in the attainment. Full effort is victory. He has a long time ago decided not to conquer himself but win a thousand battles. He believes in his religious mind that then finally the victory is his. We must meet one more time. He shall wait for me, not come to me. The strategy has changed.

He shall take my luxury and happiness from me. He shall attack Y, and then kill me. His army has been shrinking around him, so his employees do not be afraid of him so much anymore. They have begun even share jokes about him. And Zeff isn´t in the audience, and he couldn´t laugh there in front of everybody alone. Now the whole audience laughs, and he is the only one who does not. He says: "We go to the castle. It is our place for great googly moogly."

The Dancing Book & Land

It is 9:45, and Bob comes to me: "Hey Tapio, I have here a list of your Unique Selling Propositions. Our brand is now well known, thanks to that amazing performance last night. That heraldic logo of you is so, yes again, amazing, as well as the Book Towns Group name, design, term. It identifies our international terms of goods, books, bookings, and festivals and making cultural centers and their homes and houses.

I use now this amazing brand in business, marketing, and advertising. I have created and stored an amazing value as brand equity for the object identified, to the benefit of the brand´s customers, its owners and shareholders, IOB, all book towns, our bank, NYC tech department, British bookshops and libraries, Oxford, Cambridge and Harvard, towns of Ascona, London, and Barcelona, entrepreneurs in

Book Towns around the world, Cuisery district people. And I, as your manager of the marketing and communication techs and tools help Book Towns Group distinguish us from others. This all has created an amazing impression in the minds of customers to come.

There are good personalities, Y & YourVictoria, product design, brand communications, brand awareness, brand loyalty, and your branding strategy, to surprise with a dancing book and cultural center tourism and settlement are one of the kinds. The Gamazon lets the market become dynamic and fluctuating. In this situation, there is a high level of brand equity. In accounting, we have intangible assets vie interactive boards and HoloLens, the updating day by day is a superior intangible asset, goodwill, copyright, we fly with them. Brand valuation is our great management tech, which maximizes shareholders' value. Amazing!

I think the metonym The Dancing Book identifies greatly the company, but we must put there more: The Dancing Book & Land. Then it associated with a commodity. We have here attributes, benefits, values, personality, name, logo, tagline, graphics, shapes, colors, sounds, scents, tastes, and movements, advertising, sales promotions, direct marketing, personal selling, public relations, culture, reflection, relationships.

This is ofc challenging fighting brand, with necessary conditions, myth-making, cultural contradictions, the cultural brand management process, mission impossible, longing versus belonging, un-selling with pride and provocation, from myth to meaning, behold, living a reality that is better than the dream, growth without end, social media brand, no-brand branding, and multi-brands. And most of all this is a lifestyle brand. This is world-brand.

BTG highlights product benefits so well. We know the markets and money have noticed us. Differentiation is strong in your strategy, operational art, and tactics, where is your outstanding service. Now we have the net. We must put it to react as hell. You have now unabashedly appeal, perverse brilliance (heh, heh, daddies and so), when you are yourself, that is the best callous, rude and insensitive, too, but people do not notice it. You must leverage unique personalities in your industry, you have avoided the superstar effect rat race. You have consumer studies, academic research, and specific examples. And you learned in London, via a Sherlockian view that personalization. You made embodiment to the person you are selling to, you ever lane apparel, illusionist, saddleback leather, ThinkGeek, still about selling.

Here I have 56 Unique Selling Propositions: they see mission statement, your services, target audience, your well-doing, your amazing important goal to them, tell them how these lost forever book towns shall be back in business via BTG, your focus group.

We have gone these things through, so many times, and the basics do not stay the same, it changes all the time. So, the only important thing is that you update every day. That updating is your math, techs, and selling and your success. We have still in our accounts for 56 million dollars and now after this immense performance, I shall begin to make a deal, with media around the world. Gamazon, mob-families, porn industry, corrupted NYC administration, your street credibility real Brkners, your mercenaries, and most of all your amazing love with this amazing porn star and real Brkner YourVictoria shall make your days full of glory and success.

It is like King Arthur & Queen Guinevere are back to business but without fuck***ing Lancelot and other pieces of shits. Go MyBoyTapio now and make with YourQueenVictoria your round table to that Burgundy heart of courtly love."

I shake Bob´s hand and hug him.

I shake Frank's hand and say: "Come with me to Burgundy and I take also Cliver with us." Y: "When shall we be just alone?" I: "I have a strange instinct that there shall happen soon something. I do not know what, but my inner voice tells me: ´Run, run to the castle, and won it.´" Y. "What?" I: "There is something." Y: "That´s so relieving, knowing that bad part is to come."

The Mediarolla

At 10:30am Y & M & Frank & Cliver meet the media. Immense applause fills the room. It is so full that even Colonial´s ex-officer-visitors in Walhalla look down: "Our Friend has taken life back to our parties." The media asks media praises, media praises more. They just cannot understand AR-last nights - things. They keep on asking me who are you, why are you here, what shall you do next, can we come with you, do you love us, can we love you.

If we talk about the brand, Media is the way of our communication: print, publishing, the news, photography, cinema, broadcasting, and advertising media. The world has divided into strategic media areas: Western Europe, North America, the Arab region, Asia, the Pacific, Central, and Eastern Europe with Russia, South- and Middle America.

There fly UN Guiding Principles on Business and Human Rights, the Ranking Digital Rights, fact-checking and news literacy, email. Skype, Facebook, Instagram, Linkedin, Twitter, religious bias, CD, DVD,3-5G.

And the Media conference is for ViacomCBD, CBD Films, TV, WB TV Group, Amedia, All3Media, Allspark, IE, R.G.E. Group, TBS, TNT, CBS News, CBSN, CNN; HLN, CNET, NBCUniversal, and many more. Spanish newspapers and media are there too.

I have made them a schedule of our four-month project next summer, about cultural centers of book towns, AR-connection to those both, and our cooperation firms like Gamazon and cooperation towns like NYC. The Media is out of its mind. Somebody has said that nobody knows what Media is doing, now Media says, nobody knows what we are doing. In their life brands strike a balance between public and private engagement, they use public feeds to increase reach, offer value in private channels, automate the easy stuff, twitter promotes customer engagements, employers take center stage in a divided world, deliver on their corporate promises, lead from the top, focus on advocacy, not algorithms, Sodexo champions employee ambassadors, get the full story, the TikTok effect, brand and performance collide, the social proof gap closes.

And most of all they find contradictions and news, shocking things, bad happenings, misleading words, criminals, darkening the bright side of the street, accuse, give false arguments, focus on fake things, forget the great scientific and economic new, do not praise common people, but challenge their lifestyle, laugh at them, make their everyday sermon to the fallen world. They are today's priests and ideological barking dogs - and they are good at it.

And I just love the Media. Why? Why not. To be in front of the Media is a great privilege, cos you can change them also. And they are so vulnerable and cheap, their information is in the cloud although its form is already like Augmented Reality, fake like boot and butts, the Media shall be growing, it shall soon swallow many industries and make the world more concentrated. But this BTG is a company that attacks all that and shows the persons and Nature the Media again. And they do not know that.

Time is 11:30 am when Y, I, Frank, and Cliver go to my Mustang. One reporter asks: "What is that black thing in your belt?" I: "It is my gat, Taurus. I have used it a lot in these last 19 days. And made my high noon every day." The reporter laughs: "That's the good one. What do you think about guns?" I: "My gun does have no moral stature, of its own. Cos bad men cannot be persuaded to the path of righteous by propaganda, they can certainly be corrected by my trigger."

The Dead Man does not tell Stories

I go to the Mustang and step on the gas. At last, we can go back to the Castle.

Meanwhile, Zeff and his 28 friends are arriving in Paris. They go out of the plain and take 6 fords and begin their travel to the Castle. Zeff is in a good mood: "Dead Tapio doesn't tell tales anymore."

One fella in this dream team caught all the time. Zeff: "What is wrong with you? Cannot take care of yourself?"

The first coronavirus came from on camel to a man. This MERS-CoV type thing is now present in the battle plan counsels of Zeff & gat-unit28.

Zeff is angry: "Why the hell you are sweating and coughing there. And you breathe like the fish on the ground. Take this whiskey. It is good old Jack Daniel's." The sick man: "Sir, I really feel so bad." Zeff: "Shut your face!" Zeff orders his man to cars and checks his new gat Shadow

2 SA. He loves its black nitride with a set of striking blue aluminum grips and a blue trigger. It gives the target-shooting enthusiast like Zeff the ability to punch paper with precision. Meanwhile, our car flies fast to the Pyrenees and time is 12 am/00 pm.

A man may be equipped with tonnes of theories. He may have the best of skills, the most positive of attitudes, and the strongest of belief. But the action is the basis of success. You can´t cross a chasm just pulling the trigger. Do it all the time.

We advance fast. After 4 pm Paris is behind us, and Zeff has near Burgundy Cuisery borders. He is still very angry. The coughing man sits in his car near the driver. Zeff has given him a lot of from his bottle, and the man is cocked as a ram. Couching and singing stoopidly: "Up to mighty Burgundy came a hitman one day. All the streets were paved with gold, so everybody was so gloriously gay!" The atmosphere is tensed as it always is with Zeff. He begins to couch himself, too. He takes a swig from good old Jack Daniel´s. The same bottle the same joy, or choice.

Life is great and for some, it is now near to the end.

Six cars arrive at the Castle. Zeff looks around: "Well, looks great, I must admit. Victoria & Tapio have a great style. Here are over 50 men working."

He goes to stand in the courtyard and yells: "Now fuck off. Do not you hear, sod off!" Nothing happens. Workers aren´t interested at all about his sayings. He gets angry. He takes his Shadow from his pocket and shoots in the air. One tired-looking workman says to him: "Can you, please, be quiet. We have much to do. New owner really knows strange spongebobs." Jeff yells: "Fuck off before I kill Y!"

One worker comes to him: "Aren´t you Zeff Tezos from the Gamazon. I have always admired you so much. Do not make disappointment, please. Be cool, just rap & rock." Jeff points his gun to the worker. He goes away shaking his head.

After 15 minutes a long caravan of workers goes to the village. One of them calls me: "Master, there is a madman in your Castle. His name is Zeff Tezos, and he cries and shoots. Can you come and take him away, we have much to do."

I look at my watch at 5:30 pm. Now I shall meet Zeff again. I asked him to visit the castle, but he seems to be a very passionate character. Hm. So far everything has been excellent for his business.

It is becoming a little bit dark when we arrive at the Castle. You say: "Why shall that Zeff be here? You haven´t invited him?" I: "I think, he forgot to tell me something." Cliver: "We need to talk with him."

Meanwhile, Zeff is ready with his men around the Castle. He couches all the time and feels very tired. I stop the car: "He must have a good reason to be alone there, without eyewitnesses. This is ridonkulous, real whack. He has lost is the ability to gauge." Cliver: "Yes his finger discount."

The Coughing Man do not know the Numbers

And Zeff does not know that 28+1=29 means polarity, emotions, and judgment, coupled with leadership, integrity, and unity. It is a message from your angels that you are to have faith in yourself and your angels as they are encouraging and supporting you in your spiritual endeavors. But there is now coming number 4, which counts of those advantages of no. 29, cos no. 4 connects mind-body-spirit with the physical word of structure and organization. It symbolizes the safety and security of home, the need for stability and strength on a solid foundation of values and beliefs.

Zeff and his number are stuck between a rock and a hard place, screwed. Now barny lives with them. We go through the landscape near the Castle. One Russian comes to tell Zeff: "The Mustang has stopped. And three men are arriving with the gats in their hands. Shall I pick them up with my rifle?" Zeff: "No you do not. This is an insult. We must answer to that." Russian: "What do you mean?" Zeff: "Let them come. I must meet one of them one more time in a duel."

Russian: "Sir, all respect, but is that a good idea? You look a little bit sick. Your eyes are red."

Cliver says to me: "Yes, pop the Glock is near. Can we try one more time to give Arabian goggles to that Zeff? I had last night great fun with him." I: "He has fellas that do care shit what we say to him." Cliver: "But he is jefe & CEO. Make him throw you a bone. Lambda phi epsilon." I nod.

New Rise & Grind Deal

I shout: "Zeff, I know you are there. Let´s talk. What is on your mind?" Zeff: "The performance was so good, but the deal is bad. We must make a new deal. The best deal is without u." I: "So let´s make it without me." Zeff: "What do y mean? We cannot do that." I: "Yes, we can. You present to me, and I do not present to you." Zeff stands up: "That sounds incredible. That is crazy." I: "Yes, that is 7:30: crazy: Rikers Island Jail has a form called 7:30 A, which is a psych evaluation request form. Let´s make a deal at 7:30." Zeff: "What does it exactly mean?" I: "It means you don´t fuck with that guy he´s 7:30." Zeff begins to laugh and couch. He stands up. He begins to walk to me.

Russians and Talibans are amazed. They look at each other, but there is nothing they can do. Hired guns really get easy money. I stand up and come to Zeff and so does Cliver and Frank. Zeff looks very upset. I must ask: "Are you well?" Zeff: "Hard to breathe."

Well, sometimes it is hard to breathe, so good opportunities arrive, and you just spoon before poon, rise & grind.

We sit on the table. This is once in the lifetime deal. First the address, to whomsoever it may concern. Then about the authorizer, I mention myself, full details about myself. Then about the authorized. Same about Zeff, and it is also good to mention the number of an ID card for reference. Then just what is being authorized. BTG authorizes the Gamazon via CEO´s to do all the jobs, which was decided to do between BTG and the Gamazon. The Gamazon does its job and BTG´s, too.

Zeff buys me off from the deal. And the Gamazon must take care that book towns and the Gamazon get profit. Zeff: "How about the competitive bidding?" I: "Bob takes care of those vain details and takes care that you shall pay to the representative company of book towns, BTG until you have bought us fully out. It shall happen for three years. And if you break the deal, and do not present both sides, the deal goes off the right way."

Zeff couches and says: "I make some quick calculations. Hm, every year we buy you out with 10 million. Yes, ok, let's sign it now. And in these three years, we present you 100 %?" I: "We shake hands. And that´s it."

So Courtly Castle

We look at those six cars going away. You say: "There is bad influenza among those men. This springtime has so variable weather." The workers begin to come back. There is still much to do on the roofs. Frank comes to us: "Well, now I have seen the place and I must go back to NYC. See you after three months." He kisses the air on your hand and a local taxi takes him away. There are now Cliver, me, and You.

Time is 18:30. Cliver says: "Cool story bro, and it has windows vista. I must put the team on my back, too." He stays over the night and wants to have here a tree hockey field, so his gang can come here and make their 12/12/12. He goes to sit in the Jacuzzi, and look at a new Mark Wahlberg film Spencer, and sings "all alone playing with a slipknot I don´t wanna fucking die, but my heart is the real prob ... Pay ten for this jacket in Milan look at the leather on this bitch ... Eastside nigga, I'm still livin´. Any problem in the hood, I deal with it ... green light, I got a 40 with a red light. And who could guess that D Smoke sounds exactly like Kenrick Lamar?"

We go to the first kitchen, which is hot to trot. I lolz. What a brashy and trashy day. You sit on my lap. Quite big deals. The house is becoming soon ready.

Meanwhile, in NYC residents of Astoria Houses lost hot water dozens of times during the first few months of this heating season. NYCHA is still unable to ensure that utility systems seamlessly provide for residents. Rochel Goldblatt, an NYCHA spokesperson, says only four of the hot water outages are unplanned. The rest are planned, so workers could perform preventative maintenance on the building's heating systems to prepare them for colder weather. The interpretation of data shared by Legal Aid is incorrect and intentionally misleading. NYCHA residents across the city experienced 1 246 heat, hot water, and water outages during the last three months of the year. More than 200 000 residents are affected.

You say: "To make the US communicate this way to Europe makes my day. The AR and interactive things seem to take the Ocean between NYC and Europe away. 3D immersive experiences are straightening lines into user experiences on the web, increasing customer engagement with brands, and improving productivity in the workplace. It is easy to create engaging 3D front-end experiences and integrate with AWS services to provide easy access to machine learning, chatbots, code execution. Popular hardware runs for AR/VR." I: "Yes, but what do y think about the house. Both kitchens are already ready. There are smart-house techs almost everywhere. Bathrooms doors open, the heath goes with your words. Perhaps we can at last thing about just ourselves."

We go to a huge studio, which has been built on the ex-attic. It is 20x30 meter long - just as our stage. It has 4 to 7 meters to the roof. There are already interactive boards, hololens2s, AR+VR -systems, and I take with me that e-book- and audiobook reader, and the music-reader. There are sensors, huge hologram-computers, and screens, 3D holographic projectors.

We put holo lenses on and there comes a hologram of the world and of book towns. There are those AR-reader connections, big sponsors, entrepreneurs, and ofc the Gamazon.

I laugh: "We made this with the porn industry, mafios, gangs, corrupted bureaucracy, and so, and it is connected with my rhythm, but now it is yours." Y: "Do you mean like Brooklynization?" I: "Yeah, fergiligious. I have put practicality. Now it is your turn to put beauty. I know you can do an amazing performance our Brooklyn friends did part of it in Camp Nou. Now it is your time to finish the job. You can make the feeling, appealing and so, and much more."

Y: "Yes, I have already looked at those e-books and audiobooks and that AR. The colors, the shape, the form, the attitude, the timing, the clothes, the sayings, must have more sexuality, pleasure, luxury, fire, and even storm. Real Dominican attitude.

If you told a kid about the birds and the bees then he tells you about the butcher and your wife. Here must come to the performance of sexiness. Sexuality about things throws light upon love, and through love, we learn sexuality. It is a great way of conversation between people. It is the lyricism of the masses. And I make it as it is, present. Sexuality is not leisure and part-time activity. It is a way of being. Sexuality makes us persons. Sexual desire sells soap, cars, beer, and religion. Sex makes you get real. Sex is the built-in psychedelic experience, ecstasy. I give books a very sensual voice and look, moves, touches, smiles, cries, tears, acts, fuck, I make it big and desirable, and put it that shit in. Furniture, windows, frames, colors have their beauty and comfortable outfit. I know how the furniture shall be in the room, courtyard, and design. So, they look sensual and make people feel pleasure.

When you put pleasure to Truth, Death, Progress, Struggle, Joy, it becomes desire. Pleasure can be seen in the morning sun, the clouds, and the evening storm. I shall make those festivals desirable, cos I draw the pleasure, paint it, and express your pleasure strongly. I make pleasure an illusion of true desire. Sex is the pleasure that comes before you get it so much that you can fell in great love. Losers who cannot win love are doomed to stay sugar daddies, stay feeling pleasure in sex, cos they cannot win any woman who shall love them. I show the real sex, with you can go to love.

Their smile does not kill anybody, but a real sexy smile kills and makes you love. When you Tapio become a real beast and come to me, you do not do that just for sexual pleasure, but you come as an animal to satisfy your love, and there is no sin, but lower-level those fuck**ers feel sin. I make people find in festivals real desire, that leads to love, their dreams and they come united, grief dies like a coward, blood goes, and hearts shall be full.

Nobody lives in desolation in those festivals, and loving miracles, group orgasm of huge revelation blows their brains off. There is fire, sex, and change it orgasm, explosion. I shall make those festivals full of angels, cos every time people have an orgasm an angel comes to life. Good big bang festival orgasm makes life worth living when it creates life. Just satisfy somebody is just a rehearsal. In my festivals shall be fake boobs, fake butts, botox-lips, but there shall not ever be fake explosions, heavenly touch. I make those dancing parts, music sessions, colors, senses, smells, shakings, trembling so real that they cannot separate holographs from real. And my menu is full of southern delicious foods, which feed both men and women. Last night was full of amazing beautiful colors, sounds, motions and I shall be a designer of massive dancing explosions. You gave me tools of practice and I shall put them on fire."

I: "Well, then we have one thing left." You: "And that is?" I: "There is just real practicality, and beauty gets a ray of beauty which outvalues all the utilities of the fake world. We need the endurance to fasten them together. You make it simple and you find in the very beginning, middle and end just Y & M. If you find there cheating or lies or explanations, they y do not find Y & M. And then this is just shit.

I do things just 100 %. I do not begin to do anything 80 % or less. When I train, I always try to do records. If not, I cannot train hard at all. My heart, my mind my inner me, must meet the challenge, toughest I have met ever before. I do not meet it, it isn´t for me. I cannot be with Y just for sex, pleasure, fucking, nice looks, desirable forms, they are pure lies, cheatings, and explanations. They are shit, alone. They must have risk, fight, winning, and greatness. Pleasure and sex are noice but without love, you changeyour object all the time. What shall then mean BTG, Brooklynization, dancing explosion other things? I must have luxury = love. Not being afraid of money, money comes to me, cos it is afraid of me. If you cannot make it best. DIE. Life must be great, not just pleasure, and laziness. It must have a standard. If not, you are just a peasant. Means nothing. I must have greatness there, not low life, and easy smiles, and nobody shames me."

You are not happy: "In your grave shall read: what made him do these things, well, he must have had violence for his birthday gift when he was born. I: "Well, aoncare. I do not fear to labor in this world. I try to exchange severity for gentleness, indignation for meekness, discord for peace. I let all my friends and enemies and you also find self-restrained, peaceful, and kind. I give you and them always that choice. Take it or live it. Once in a lifetime deal. I do not beg."

I knock the door of Cliver´s bathroom: "Heyy, on and crackin´ Brkln right now." Cliver: "So we agree, YourVictoria & me." I: "Whut?" Cliver: "Im good to go." After five minutes Cliver is downstairs, while workers come and go down- and upstairs.

At 8:15 am my Mustang goes fast away from the Castle area. I'm jacks. I love you and honor like a fat loves cake.

Meanwhile, more than 30 new coronavirus cases have been reported in the state of NY in the last 24 hours. Seven are in NYC. 76 people in NY are now confirmed to have the new coronavirus. Cuomo says: "Do not panic, 80 % of people infected will self-resolve, while 20 % will need hospitalization." At the same time, one man cannot take it anymore. He stabs his wife to death in his Queens home, then hangs himself. It happens in his Ozone Park home.

The Prenuptial Agreement for Endless L

It is very dark when we drive to Paris. I take from my pocket a paper and give it to You: "This was meant to be my next step. But now it has gone to the south." You read: "Prenuptial agreement."

There is a list of all of the property Y & M own and specifies what yours and my property rights will be after the marriage, it protects each other from debts, clarifying financial responsibilities, protects hard-earned assets, it has financial inventory, credit history, and spending habits, financial outlook, prenup goals, the ten basic paragraphs, optional paragraphs, financial disclosures, estate planning matters, property transfers and purchases of insurance upon marriage, recording an abstract and memorandum of the agreement.

You are very, very angry: "How can you insult and despise me so much? You do not trust me at all? I'm was very serious about our relationship. Y do not ask me to marry you, but you make a prenup?" I: "I asked in the night in the celebration, and you said yes. And this contract is very fair. How about somebody shoots me. There has been much activity in that direction lately. Y get all if I die." Y: "Y do not die."Cliver says: "No shotgun marriage, just lust, rust, dust, double Houdini gorilla mask rusty fish hooking the marlin. I have heard that one fella said: ´Im a firm believer in happy wife happy life, so I kiss my wife every day.´" Then Clivers mind understands to take a long walk off a short pier.

La Victoire est à Nous & La Mer

At 10:30 pm we arrive at Vélizy - Villacoublay Air Base, you know Base aérienne 107 Vélizy-Villacoublay. It is an Armée de l´Air base. We are 8 miles (13 km) southwest of Paris. We come to checkpoint "I-do-not-know-what-something".

Therecomes an Escadron de transport, *d´entrainemet et de calibration* ETC 65 - VIP transport -man: "*Bonsoir! Ca va? Bienvenue*." I: "*Merci beaucoup. A tout a l´heure!*" No questions asked. Y: "That was quick." I say: "Have you heard the song Bonjour, Mademoiselle - Joe Dolan? Well, then you know what means old saying of great Napoleon: ´The extent of your consciousness is limited only by your ability to love and to embrace with your love the space around you, and all it contains.´ Our love have conquered space."

I drive on the field. There is COFOG & CASSIC. Helicopter Squadron 03/067 salutes us, as well as Commando Parachute Unit N20, ALAT, air forces of denramerie, Commandement des Opérations Spéciales.

There is an army band. The march *La Victoire est à Nous* fall with a crash to play. You are amazed: "What does it mean?" I say: "Love means only one thing." And great Napoleon played it when he attacked Russia. Just an excellent march.

There comes an officer, he is from Foreign Legion. He salutes me, and I salute back. He: "It is a great honor to have you, SIR, and your LADY, here!" I: "*Merci infiniment*, Charles, it has been a long time. Where have you been?" He: "Fighting for your course, *mon Capitaine de Légion d'honneur. La mission est sacrée, tu l'execues jusqu'au bout et, s'll le faut, en opérations, au péril de la vie!*"

He turns and the Legion Etrange soldiers and I sing *La Mer*: "*La mer, qu'on voit dancer le long des golfes clair a des reflets d'argent la des reflets changeants ...*" I take your hand. Y: "What this now ..."

Napoleon didn't say it, but I say: death is nothing, au combat, tu agis sans passion et san haine, tu respectes les ennemis vaincus, but live and love like *La Mer*, yeah, that is Washington University in St. Louis.

We begin to walk towards the plane, cos there is one kind of robber whom the law doesn't strike at, and who steals what is most precious: time.

There is Airbus Beluga waiting for us. I drive in. The time is 11:19. I go to edge and whistle hard. There runs a legion soldier to me and gives me a bunch of red roses. I give them to you. I say: "These are the go-to-choice for luxurious times to come."

One sergeant comes to us: "*Mon Capitaine*, we shall arrive at Kennedy's 1:15. Have a good flight."

There is a table and there is a lot of food and drinking in a French way: the moules marinieres. There is more chicken than you can shake a drumstick at, turkey, pork, beef, and even some duck and quail, mostly *les fruit de la Mer*. Just smoked, boiled, broiled, breaded, fried, parched, shelled, and de-shelled seafood. There is also a blond Belgian ale, but I drink mineral water. There are buckwheat crepes, filled with anything you can dream of buckwheat flour, eggs ... well, that kind. There is always apple cider, but I drink mineral water. There are *Blanquette de Veau, Soupe a L'oignon, Sole Meuniere*, and *Hachis Parmentier*. So, we have only less than two hours to have this great supper.

You say: "These adventure as filled my mind. I cannot think where to start and where to end." I: "Yes, it burns, it doesn't freeze." We kiss. Don't worry about ending today, it's already tomorrow in Finland.

The Nineteeth Day

With the Kiss and the Gut to the Beginning

Noice Words

It is easy to say: every story as an end, but it is impossible to say every adventure as on end, cos it doesn't start or end: it is life. You cannot say to the life: "Hej moob, see y never."

Y and Cliver ask, why the military was there steady and ready and why this and that. I: "Simple, I called them. Send them money, and then checked who I was, and they found the answer so well that they gave their ex-Capitaine a salute. And that's the way. We are here and there, but we are present all the time. They remember. You just need to prove your merits and nothing more. They do not like what I did to France, they do not like how I made my way, but they like Their Friend Tapio. That's it."

The plane comes to NYC, and I drive the car out, shake hands with soldiers, and tap their shoulders. Then we go. I take Cliver to his Queens & Brims. Cliver: "Tomorrow we shall try new bench records in the gym. I would like to make some rounds of kickboxing. It makes Klonopin. I'm not a Missouri bitch, but I like tech n9ne phatty beats, when I train. Keep it moist." I: "Splooie, we get the hell outta dodge. Y cannot break a sweat. Shred the gnar." ^5, slap, jumping, elbows, fists, stomach. So Cliver's gone. Time to have some fun.

We go to our luxurious home. I say: "Hey, we have here a letter from Jonathan Williams and Robbie Klein. They have watched our show in Barcelona, and they say it was like big worship. They ask us to come to meet them. Then just adds." The doggy jumps to your lap and I haven't forgotten to give it a new Spanish steak."

Y: "I have now much to do to connect my company to yours and begin to design those covers, festivals, and book articles, book my star hood sensuality round the world. I wanna make speeches, book introductions, selling adds dance lessons and spectacles. I shall come to your concept marketing guru. I shall show you how to sell yourself, on a big scale. Brooklyn-people shall give us a way to conquer hearts and minds with street knowledge."

The Deep Brkner´s Citizen Arrest

Time is 2:15 when we go to sleep. In my dream, an old fella comes to me: "Stand up and fight." He shows me a lot of angry people: "They are all yours."

I wake up when somebody is knocking our door. There comes a loud voice: "Open up. NYPD police. Here are neighborhood coordination officers Devon Washington and Daniel Oppenheimer. Open now, or we break in!"

I laugh: "Wait a minute, the time is 5:30 am. I shall make a citizen´s arrest, without a warrant, for a crime occurring in my presence."

They shout to me: "You aren´t even a U.S.-citizen. Open up!" I shout back: "Yes, but MyBrideVictoria is, and so are you!" They: "So what! Open the fu***cking door, before we shoot us in!"

I: "Well, she just authorized me to make an arrest on her behalf. So ordinary citizens help apprehend lawbreakers. You are violating the sanctity of our home and our private property, the door. And we have an inability to keep up with the demands of property tax. I know some years ago there was for instance in Pennsylvania 350 000 abandoned homes and others sold their homes, but here it doesn´t happen. Do not you know that all men are born equally free and independent, even me, a deep Brkner, and have a natural, inherent and inalienable rights, amongst which are, the enjoying and defending life and liberty, acquiring, possessing and protecting property, and pursuing and obtaining happiness and safety.

Sections 5, 10, 11, and 13 of that first Constitution dealt with the protection of a person´s home. Of the 16 declared rights, 1/3 of them dealt with the sanctity of a person´s home. Now those declared right are in section 28, you criminals. A majority has no right to vote away the rights of the minority. A man´s house is his castle, and whilst he is quiet, he is as well guarded as a prince in his castle. A person´s home is a sacred right and when left alone, as in not being interfered with by his neighbors and government, will live like a prince. Since she has inalienable individual rights, this means that the same rights are held, individually, by every man, by all men, me also. Therefore, the rights of you cannot and must not violate the rights of me. You do not have the right to decide that your happiness lies in the misery of another, me. The very right upon which you act defines the same right as another man and serves as a guide to you what you may or may not do."

They are whisked: "You have shot, killed people, and used physical force against so many New Yorkers that you shall stay behind bars for a long, long time." I lol: "Rosies, I have defended my beloved ones, New Yorkers' rights against bloods, lynches, barackrisies, corrupted beaucracracy, touts and & crack stags, pr0n industry & GodsGirls, corrupted banks & federal reserve and big companies, you know, having a barney with barney, and I have done it well, and Im proud of it: imma hit a lick on bricks and gone ham on it. As a deep Brkner I have always on Top thought of true Brnkners. And one of them conquered and made me rise and grind. I have aiight to love and honor all the days of my life. And in my opinion, which does not destroy but builds my religion is culture and my savior/constructor is education. Now, You shall meet what the right shall dread."

Y try to say: "Don´t Tapio, you destroy this all, and ..." But those bastards begin to shoot our door. I take my gun and shoot back.

I open the door and meet four guns. I shoot to them, and they run back and take a hike. More reinforcements are coming up. There come five fellas. I hit them all down. They have muscles, but not muscles like soldiers, their muscles like nice time and laying down, my muscles have lived their great lives in hunger, thirst, pain, punishment, cold, find, and beating fist. They begin to hesitate in the first hits, I do not. They hit my face, I hit back. They kick me, I kickback. Finally, they run away. I call the mayor. There are becoming more men upstairs.

The Crime Control Strategies Bureau has looked some awesome vids about my attacking porn mogul house, fighting with DiRapoli, mobs, gangs. They have listed it all, made stimulation models, changed information with Intelligence Bureau, Internal Affairs Bureau, Information Tech Bureau, Risk Management, Community Affairs Bureau, Special Operations Bureau, Patrol Services Bureau. And they have laughed, cos they thought they have got old Greg.

So outside are a lot of officers, sergeants, and lieutenants ready to make their bluebird day? They all have a common feeling that they must punish the moonbat, and they are sure the block pants shall be found here. They have decided to have good revenge for all their disappointments. This fucker, me, must be punished for gooood and I must find my rightful silence.

You sit on the floor and begin to cry. Now everything has been lost. They shall kill me or beat and beat more and put behind those bars for the rest of my life. That was that my reason has gone made and dance in the black sun of Hell.

I come back in. I put huge sofas again the door and stay gold: "You shall see why I didn't burn my boats. My enemies have become my friends and my enemies' enemies shall be beaten for sure."

I begin to call: hey, Mr. Nose Mancuso, Domenico Cefalu, Liborio Salvatore Bellomo, Victor Amuso, Mr. Frank and seals, Cliver and Blood Brims, South Side Bullies, MGZ-Marcy Gangas, GSC- G Stone Grips/Cash on decks/HBMs, 3NI - Trinitarios, Latin kings, Niio's maloses, Marlboro houses hat boys, Folk nation - GD – Gansta disciple, Seven Crews, BMV - Brooklyn most wanted (269&730), Straight Cash/Get Gwop, Loopy Gand, Paper Chasers, Pink Houses 1&2, 7&8/Caveman/Hollywood, Pink Houses Center Side 5&6, RF-Rich Family, Franklin Ave Family/L1COLN Family. I call porn mogul Feras Anton & Josh Bazoov, the Gamazon Zeff Tazos.

And after these calls, I call the mayor of NYC: Hello, there, Gill, how are you today?" He begins with all formality: "Who you are, what do you want?" I stop that short: "Call your fellas back, or they get hit bad." He: "There is nothing I can do. Have a nice day." He hangs up. I call him again: "Hey, keep it moist, too, but I'm talking to you. And if you do not call them back, I shall make their day fresh off the pig. Do you understand? There shall begin soon a real nailing." He: "Big words, DearTapio, you are finished. I have taken care of that." I: "That's not true. I have just kicked off 7 of your men. I shall kick them all off. They shall not catch the bus." He laughs at me. I say: "Well, wait then minutes and then call your executive chief again. But after that, all this comes public, too. Then you have a lot to explain - to your jail partners. And I do not know if with your records you get outto a life."

He becomes unfriendly: "You shit, you can´t do anything. I kill you!" I: "Well, then wait that ten minutes, and take a risk. Suits me. Buy." I hang up. There comes a call: "Okay, ten minutes. Let´s make a deal. If you are right, I take care of tabula rasa. There shall be no issues. And I shall even play gold with you, but if not, you, son of the bitch, do like a rat." I: "Ok, let´s make a deal. And by the way, your mob-friends are coming to help me. You have much to explain to them also." He: "That´s impossible. You are bluffing." I: "Ten minutes, and then let´s shake hands if I'm still living. One thing is certain, after that Y, MyFucker is finished. They shall send you to the prison were you meet Trinitario, Nuestra Familia, the Neta Association, Nazi Lowriders, Aryan Brotherhood, and Mexican Mafia they shall fuck your ass so big that the rectum comes out and do not stay inside and round it slough is always bleeding and once the rectum comes out it comes out all the time, the cutting doesn´t help at all, and it is always bleeding." I stop the call. Now those policemen attack again.

I ask Y to go to the bathroom, and near the air pump. There comes the helicopter. It shoots the window down and Doggy goes under a kitchen table. Then there comes CS gas. I throw it outto the window. There comes more. I shoot to the copter. It curves away. Now they shoot through the door. I shoot also. The door breaks down. I have a lot of bullets left, so no need to spare them. The beautiful furniture breaks down. Paintings, boards go to pieces, glasses break. I hit one police, and he falls. The loudspeaker gives information: "Surender, no need to give misery to your neighbors. We help you, with your problems. Trust us!"

I shoot to the loudspeaker-man. He runs, and stumbles, and the l-speaker breaks. They have handguns, but helicopters have machineguns. I tried to throw artifacts to the propeller. The copter curves again away. NYPD does not spare bullets. I know there are coming soon special forces.

Special Operations Division consists of ESU, Harbor, K-9 the bomb squad, and some others. There are11 ESU trucks. Here 6-Brooklyn south and 7-Brooklyn, and 8-Brooklyn North. Esu "Adam" & "Boy" units are Adam 6/Boy 6 - Brooklyn South, Adam 7 / Boy 7- Brooklyn, and Adam 8 / Boy 8, Brooklyn North. All these Adam/Boy units are nowhere with their Mini Esu Trucks = Ford Cab / Utility Body (REP). There are also some Charlie/Davit units. Post sends signals like Tank67, post 3209706, member 1198196. They ask neighbor´s to log in and give them passwords and ask help. There begins to come more feeds: police and fire, from eight locations.

SWAT with automatic and specialized firearms, including submachine guns, assault rifles, riot shotguns, sniper rifles, riot guns, riot control agents, more tear gas, smoke and stun grenades, body armor, ballistic shields, entry tools, thermal and night vision devices, and motion detectors are coming. 8 fellas with US military helmets, fire retardant balaclavas, ballistic vests, the 9 mm Heckler & Kock MP 5s, two has 5,56 carbines, the Colt Car-15, and one M4, then after them comes 5 fellas with the semi-automatic Benelli M1 and 2 with the pump-action Remington 870s.

They have some SIG Saurer P 226s, Glock pistols, the Colt M 16A2s. No need to battering rams, shotguns with breaching rounds, or explosive charges, cos they are ready to use their guns, tasers, pepper spray canisters, shotguns loaded with bean bag rounds, and pepper ball guns. I see that one has stinger grenades and flash-bang grenades.

I attack suddenly and take stinger grenades and throw them to the steps. Huge explosion. I buy more time. 5 minutes gone. Their semi-automatic begins to shoot. Half of the wall falls. The roof begins to drop bit by bit. I shoot and they go back. I hit one fella and get his radio.

There come messages: "Alfa 5, behind the fire, five terrorists shooting us, alfa 7, eighteen shooters, we shoot back, alfa 1."

I shout to the radio: "Tapio1, give up, you cannot win. Throw your gats down!" Broadcast signals a lot of messages, which tell that they have been attacked behind.

SWOT on the floors does not give up. They have the order to kill, so they try to do that. I take from the floor one MP5 and begin to shoot. Dust and smoke hide the attackers. I smoke there. 8 minutes gone. It seems that the mayor shall get his blood flowing ass fuck, welcome rape from the Aryan Brotherhood members soon.

My phone rings: "Hi, Brims and I are here, here are four gangs also. We shoot the blue boys & boydem & RPG-7 & maximum popo. Bee swat goes back. Their arsenal is fuck ..." A huge explosion hears from my phone.

I call Frank: "Hey, where are you?" Frank: "Just coming to the spoop. These SWATster are so green. They panic & run, drop the gats, and dingdong ditch. 8 caught short. They are surrendering." I call the mobs, the Nose: "How about there?" The Nose: "We have truncated shotgun, but they have machineguns. As Waffen-SS said, es geht weiter. They cannot hold us up. We attack."

I hear SWAT leader OC 1 send a message, but my phone says access denied: to-the-fort-smith-police-the-swat-team-is-currently-at-west-apartments-in-fort-smith/527- cfeca6f5 and so on tells the server. The reference no. is shit. Many U-5 radios are now still.

Cliver calls me: "Im coming via fire escapes with Frank, here is fuck**ing windy. We shoot the window in and go on one floor downstairs. Here is an old couple ... Soz, we get our hands outta your pockets, senioritis, rn ..." The call cuts off, after machinegun fire. I run to the stairway and hit with my MP5 those SWATs face, body, balls, and they are terrified.

My ear is bleeding, my knuckles are on blood. I see Frank and Cliver fighting nearby, smoke is everywhere. Then suddenly there comes silence.

It is like in the stopped film. My phone rings: "Hello, ESS & SWAT goes away on one condition: you know nothing." I: "How about my charges. If you wipe your ass with them, then Aryan Brotherhood does not rape you, just fucks in the ass. Ok. I understand. The deal is deal. No hard feelings. I love y too."

SWAT-men do not say a word. They do not like the situation. The order was to kill, and they couldn't finish it. Well, nothing is perfect, not even SWAT. Especially when they begin to call terrorist men of honor. Then comes the devil and swallows their holy oath.

Noice and Steady

Smoke and dust wear off. The Nose come to me: "Do not worry about your apartment, the mayor sends as soon as possible more our constructors to put it in order, on one condition." I: "And?" The Nose: "The newspapers shall not get a hint, that we are using cheap workforce from the Dominican Republic, and other illegal immigrants." I: "Must not fab."

Bloody Brims Smokey comes to me: "I lika you. Y know the rules of fight club, y son of gun & streezy." Well, Cliver is not happy: "I don't like the high place and those fire escapes grind my gears. Irmc." And he just goes. I don't ask anybody to drink coffee, so they go little by little and then I come to you.

I open the bathroom door: "Hello?" I come to the bathroom. I take Y in my arms. We kiss & hug. I: "Is it all gravy?" Y nod. I say: "I got a new friend." Y: "Really?" I: "Yes, Mayor."

There comes at 7 am 25 low paid Dominican workers. Y get along with them perfectly and aren't happy about their salary. I give them some double trigger, solatium. They put new furniture to their places: grand sofas, paintings, boards, they paint the walls, fix the door and roofs, windows.

We get Eco Windows top-quality windows and door solutions in Brass, Steel, Aluminum, Wood, and PVC. Their brand of window and door carpentry is produced by combining precisely selected materials, premium German hardware, latest techs, and long-term experience in production. There come frame systems made by ALURON which meet strict requirements of energy efficiency, providing comfort, functionality, and safety. All system frames come powder-coated in two finishes, smooth and textured using a palette of RAL colors. There are fixed units, tilt and turn, custom shape units, single doors, French doors, Lift & Slide doors, curtain walls. Just soft line, retro, quadrat FB. Wood windows are pine, meranti, and oak, RAL palette. And there are wooden glazing bars.

There come amazing sectionals and modular sectionals. Cleon Small Leather Modular s is just more than amazing. And Y love Mix Modular Right-Hand Facing Sectional with Ottoman, and ofc Sunday Modular 156" Sectional sofas. Perigold dining chairs and wooden tables are so noice. You love dining benches and bar cabinets. And you get Arditi Collection olive dining table, too. There is also mod shop Milan 96" credenza. And Benetti´s Italia majorica extension dining table. We take some LG - 75" -LED TVs also. Well, there comes new carpets, and some more design glass and new paintings and holelens2 and interactive board and AR/VR-systems from Amazon. New lights and bushes and flowers. At 2 pm they go away.

The Upstate & the New Real Brkner

Meanwhile, neighbors of the Oakland Gardens nightclub are terrified. Gang-warrior shots two men and three slashed are petitioning. Their elected officials do everything in their power to shut the place down. Neighbors think that the LAVOO Nightclub needs to be shut down, or at a bare minimum, and its liquor license needs to be revoked. This establishment was presented to the community as a lounge, but it has not operated as such. It is a full-blown nightclub that has no interest in the surrounding community.

Meanwhile, four developers who own land on Long Island City´s Anable Basin has launched a public engagement initiative called Your LIC to collectively develop an inclusive, equitable plan for they are once promised to the Gamazon. The Developers are privately hatching plans for a series of mega-towers lining the Long Island City waterfront. The developers - mobs TF Cornerstone, Simon Baron Development, L&L MAG, and Plaxall - have sketched plans for building as tall as 76 stories.

Mobs TF Cornerstone, which won the rights to develop two city-owned sites on Anable Basin back in 2017, is planning a million-square-foot office building. The developers are mocking up plans for waterfront office building reaching hundreds of feet in the sky. Mobs spokesperson Jovana Rizzo says that not any market-rate homes shall be put, and they focus on creating significant open space, a school and uses that will bring good jobs.

At the same time, the 33-year-old an Uber driver in Far Rockaways becomes the first confirmed case of coronavirus in Queens over the weekend. His wife, three children, and in-laws are in isolation at home. City officials are urging taxi rideshare drivers to keep their vehicles clean and sanitized and to keep their windows open while driving.

Meanwhile, I get my new suit and throw that gun smoke thing to the wastepaper basket. I say: "Now we have good friends, and we have also a cultural center." Y: "Where?" I: "Here."

We sit on the sofa. There is nothing more kind of a big deal than sweet and sour pork, space, secure cultural center. Book Towns Group shall do everything to get them. Normal houses are made of bricks and beams, our cultural center is made of slide into the dm´s and neverland. People shall luz most of the cultural centers that they can peel an orange in your pocket. Art is the way to run away without bonking off the cultural center.

Thy home is keeper, sovereign, and for maintenance, and craves no other tribute, but love, fair looks, and true care, so no payment at all for so great a debt.

The kiss doesn´t go as the chimney sweepers to dust. Doubt that the Earth orbits the sun, doubt that the sun orbits the Milky Way center, doubt that the Milky Way orbits the galaxy group center, doubt the galaxy group center orbits the big bangs starting point times balance, doubt the God to be a liar, but never doubt a glory of that our meeting December day.

Shall I take back my gat and drive again mobs to madness and company bosses to their knees? Shall I again explain with gunpowder? Was the bullet a ray of sunshine, a warm summer rain, a bright fire on a cold winter's day, and shall now the bullet be dead, cos it so had to save the man who pulled the trigger?

Shall I once more go onto the breach, once more, shall we have bloody noses and crack'd crowns, shall our bloody colors wave, and either or else a grave, shall the hurly-burly's done, the battle's lost and won. Shall the cannons have their bowels full of wrath, and shall the killing prize to take all vantage, shall the kettle to the trumpet speak, shall the fire-eyed maid of smoky war all hot and bleeding giggle to them, shall blow, wind come, wrack, at least we'll die with harness on our back, shall 'tis far too huge to be blown out, shall I drown this gallant head of war, shall we few, we happy few, cry aloud, and let slip the dogs of war.

Y look at me: "What's up Tapio? How about putting the last part on its spot?" Yeah, a courtly kiss.

Meanwhile, Columbia University announces all classes canceled Monday and Tuesday after a school member is exposed to COVID-19. President Lee Bollinger sent a message to the university community: "This suspension of activities will allow us to prepare to shift to remote classes for the remainder of the week." The good mayor and now my friend announced more than 105 people tested positive statewide.

Y continue: "So friends & home, and one thing is left." I: "Yes, ninety-five million-dollar deals, I go to hug n.y.p.d., bootleg fireworks, 97x, 2.O lovemaking, thump for f.l.y., f.n.k., catch 22, tell long islanders, who have a slight NY accent, NY minute ..." Y: "Yeah, it's great being an NYer, and a real Brknr, and while you aren't visiting here anymore but have made flash mobs, gang gang feats, eborns, gandy dancers your homesillets, you have nothing to hide from your neighbor Brooklynites. Just need to learn an accent."

I: "Luv U so. In the most part I attacked the fire with fire, bullet with a bullet, explosion with the explosion, I find fire but desolation." The Hot blood killed and buried thoughts, and vulcanic deed. Shall we call it an epiphany? No, it is percolation. I: "Jonathan Williams comes to drink coffee on Sunday."

Meanwhile, mayor Gill talks: "Stay off packed subways and plan to telecommute." The city prepares for hundreds of cases of COVID-19. Gill says: "We have to be prepared for that reality. If you have the option of walking to work or taking a bike to work, please do." The city has barred international travel for schools. Gill says: "If you´re under 50 you´ll be OK in the end." The Port Authority´s executive director Rick Cotton has now coronavirus. The fella has been overseeing international arrivals at JFK Airport. This older fella has been interesting to interview coronavirus victims. Nobody knows why. Now he must think his doings alone at home.

Amid growing concerns about the novel coronavirus, each NYC school will have a nurse on campus by next week. DOE nurses are critically important to our schools. 137 schools are currently without permanent, full-time nurses or school-based health clinics. Those schools enroll 70 000 students. Some buildings house multiple schools and 116 buildings are without a permanent, full-time nurse. 25 schools still go without nurses every day. Schools without nurses shall be given face masks for every child. The student should wait in a room with a closed door, under the supervision of an adult with a mask who stays at least three feet away.

I wonder: "Coronavirus comes, and coronavirus go. In China, the exponential diagram shows one month. So, a one-month peak-

decease. Inhale the future, and exhale the past, at last, we can breathe deeply - Until sweet air extinguishes the burn of fear in our lungs and every breath is a refusal to become no less than infinite, and mental or physical viruses can do nothing about it.

But how can I have been born and raised here?" Y: "I can fix that. Teaching you Spanish. *Se me paro, te quiero.* It means take me to Wisconsin. All Puetarican speakers are born New Yorkers. *Via au cel dété confound ses blancs moutons avec les anges si purs la mer bergere d´azur infinie momentum Angeleyes.* Luz is seedy, and feed the needy, crash our squad, all street places *te extrano & callete lo sico & te quiero cojer.*"

We have a Momentum, so nothing to worry about. Wanna conquer fear and come rich? Go out and kill it. That shall be the joy of the good, the miracle of the wise, and the greatness of days. There are two forces which make our day & night, the Gut & the Kiss. Let´s ride the Brooklyn´s most wanted.